PATENT
TO **KILL**

ALSO BY APRIL CHRISTOFFERSON

After the Dance
Clinical Trial
Edgewater
The Protocol

PATENT TO **KILL**

APRIL
CHRISTOFFERSON

FORGE®

A TOM DOHERTY ASSOCIATES BOOK
NEW YORK

PATENT TO KILL

Copyright © 2003 by April Christofferson

All rights reserved, including the right to reproduce this book, or portions thereof, in any form.

This book is printed on acid-free paper.

A Forge Book
Published by Tom Doherty Associates, LLC
175 Fifth Avenue
New York, NY 10010

www.tor.com

Forge® is a registered trademark of Tom Doherty Associates, LLC.

Library of Congress Cataloging-in-Publication Data

Christofferson, April.
    Patent to kill / April Christofferson.—1st ed.
        p.   cm.
    ISBN 0-312-86898-7
    1. Indigenous peoples—Crimes against—Fiction.   2. Pharmaceutical industry—Fiction.
3. Traditional medicine—Fiction.   4. Physicians—Fiction.   I. Title.

PS3553.H749P37   2003
813'.54—dc21
                                                                                2002045458

First Edition: August 2003

Printed in the United States of America

0   9   8   7   6   5   4   3   2   1

For my dear father, DuWayne,
Always with me

And in loving memory of
Sweetness, Tex, Libby, and Austin

ACKNOWLEDGMENTS

I want to thank Steve, Ashley, Mike, and Crystal for their daily inspiration, amazingly generous spirits, and a life that is never dull.

A huge thank-you to my editor, Natalia Aponte, a person of extraordinary heart, talent, and vision. Everyone at Tor/Forge is a delight to work with. I particularly want to thank Tom Doherty, Linda Quinton, Paul Stevens, and Jodi Rosoff.

Special thanks to my terrific agent, Ken Atchity; also to Chi-Li Wong, Erin Reel, and Brenna Lui of AEI, as well as to Danny Barror.

Twelve years ago I attended a writer's conference in Jackson Hole, Wyoming, where lawyer/author Gerry Spence delivered a speech that made me rethink how I look at the world and what I wanted to accomplish with my writing. I've been grateful to him ever since.

I love having this opportunity to thank Steve Linville, Charlie Peterson, Monte Ahlemeyer, and Mike Montana for their longstanding support. A better group of guys cannot be found.

Others whose support I greatly appreciate include Suzy Lysen, Ruth Scharetg, Judy and Joe Peterson, Simone Kincaid, Mary Ann West, Sally Teeters, Laurie Christomos, and Tommy Thompson.

And to my mother, Isabel, my undying appreciation for the dreams, and the fight, you instilled in me.

Let good science, flavored with compassion, light our way.
—David Brower

PATENT TO **KILL**

CHAPTER **ONE**

DAY FOUR.

As the Mexican sunlight inched its way across the floor's red tiles, Jake Skully reached for his wife, Ana. Even half-asleep, the thought of making love to Ana before they got up for work had him fully aroused.

They would have to be quiet, and quick. The boys had begun waking before the alarm.

But the cool, unruffled sheet that greeted Jake's groping hand cruelly shattered his sleep-induced amnesia.

Jake bolted upright and swung his legs over the side of the bed, sweat beading on his face. As the now familiar black dread once again encompassed him, he dropped his head into his hands and moaned like a wounded animal.

Ana was gone.

Reaching for the clock that sat on the bedside table, Jake turned the alarm off and threw back the single cotton sheet covering him. He went to the bedroom door and peered across the still darkened hallway into the room in which his two sons slept. The older of the two, Michael, lay facing Jake, his back pressed to the wall to accommodate his little brother, Antony, who had crawled in bed with him sometime after Jake tucked them both in the night before.

Reassured by the sight of his boys, Jake pushed the door shut silently, grabbed the terry cloth robe hanging on the back of it and headed for the cordless telephone on the bedside table. Slipping into the robe and knotting it loosely around his trim waist, he picked up the phone and punched in the number he'd memorized.

"Policia," a female voice answered.

"Sergeant de Santos," Jake said impatiently.

Jake paced frantically while he waited. It took almost ten minutes for a familiar voice to come on the line.

"Sargento de Santos."

"It's about time," Jake said impatiently. "This is Jake Skully. What news do you have?"

The pause was short but noticeable.

"*Buenos dias,* Dr. Skully. No, we have no news on your wife. At least, nothing that would be news to *you.*"

Jake stopped in his tracks.

"What do you mean?"

De Santos ignored the question.

"As I've told you many times, you will be notified the moment my investigators turn up something."

"What are your investigators doing?" Jake's grip on the phone tightened. "How can a well-known physician just disappear? Someone had to have seen something. It was the middle of the day when she left to meet her friends. Your men are bungling this. How many of them do you have on my wife's case?"

De Santos cleared his throat.

"More than I should. Your wife is not the only missing person in the city of Nogales, Doctor."

"What about those names I gave you? The list of her patients? Have you checked them out? My wife had just treated someone from the Guerrero drug cartel. He'd come in with a gunshot wound and told her not to report it."

"And did she?" de Santos asked. "Did she report it to the authorities?"

"Of course not. Ana knew better than to cross the cartel. She's treated them before. But maybe this time they decided not to take any chances." He ran his free hand through his disheveled hair as his pacing quickened. "They had something to do with her disappearance. I'm certain of it."

"Perhaps you should look a little closer to home."

Jake stopped dead in his tracks.

"What the hell does that mean?"

"Maybe your wife *chose* to disappear."

"Are you out of your mind?" Jake's raised voice carried across the hall, to the room in which his sons slept. "Ana would never just leave, vanish without a word. She would never deliberately put me through this. You're just making excuses for your own incompetence. I tell you, de Santos, something happened to my wife. And I'll hold you responsible if the bastards who took Ana aren't found and brought to justice."

"Dr. Skully, contrary to what you would like to think, my people have indeed been investigating your wife's disappearance." The sergeant's voice held a note of amusement.

"And what have they found?"

"You told me, Dr. Skully, that all was well between you and your wife."

"It was," Jake answered quickly.

"This is not what I hear." A new sense of dread rose in Jake, knotting his stomach into a giant fist. "My investigators tell me that you were having an affair."

Ambushed, Jake fell silent for several seconds.

"Who gave you permission to snoop into my private life?"

"Did your wife know about your lover?"

Jake did not respond.

What de Santos was implying could not be. They'd worked it out. He'd promised Ana he would end it. De Santos was just desperate to deflect the heat off his own investigators for their failure to find the culprits who'd taken Ana. Ana had not left him over the affair. He was certain of it.

"Dr. Skully, I repeat. Did your wife know about your affair?"

"Yes," Jake said hesitantly. "She did. But my affair had nothing to do with Ana's disappearance."

Memories of the days before her disappearance—the days after Ana discovered that Jake had become involved with one of the hospital nurses—slipped, uninvited, into Jake's mind. Memories of Ana, stone-faced, welcoming patients into her office. Or reading to the boys before bed, her voice void of its usual theatrics.

Of Ana turning away when Jake reached for her during the night. Even after he'd told Francesca it was over.

"You still have not explained the envelope found in the wastebasket in your bathroom."

Jake's jaw tightened.

"I told you, I know nothing about that envelope."

"But it was addressed to you. And you yourself identified the handwriting as belonging to your wife. What did you do with the letter, Doctor?"

"Stop it, will you? How many times have I told you? Ana was leaving with friends for the weekend. Maybe she started a note to me, to say good-bye."

"Then where is the note?"

"I don't know. Don't you think I'd give my right arm to have it now? To read what it said? But maybe she never even wrote it. Maybe she ran out of time."

"Yes, ran out of time . . ." de Santos mimicked cruelly.

"Dammit, de Santos, you've got to stop focusing on me and that note. You're wasting precious time."

"Perhaps your wife will return to you," de Santos said lightly. "Sometimes they come back. Good-bye, Dr. Skully."

A creak from behind him suddenly caused Jake to turn. Antony stood in the half-opened door. Still, Jake did not loosen his grip on the phone.

"Don't hang up, you bastard. You can't stop looking, do you hear?"

Antony's huge dark eyes widened in horror at the sight of his father, usually the definition of cool control, screaming into the telephone.

"Papa?"

Jake placed a palm over the phone's receiver.

"Just a minute, Tonio," he said impatiently.

He lifted the phone to his ear again.

"De Santos? Are you there?"

A dial tone.

Sergeant de Santos had hung up on him.

"Papa?"

Jake placed the phone back on the table and crossed the floor to where Antonio stood. He wanted to hold him, to comfort him, but his shame was so great, his guilt so visibly painted across his face, that he could not bear to meet Antony's eyes.

Instead, he simply said, "Go back to bed, Antonio. Everything's fine."

"Will he find Mama?"

Slowly, Jake raised his eyes to Antony's. What he saw in them— the fear and uncertainty—stabbed at Jake's heart.

He dropped to his knees and placed his hands on Antony's narrow shoulders. Antony had always been on the chubby side, but just four days without an appetite had already taken their toll. His huge brown eyes searched Jake's for comfort.

Jake could not refuse.

"If he doesn't find her," Jake promised his son, "then *I* will. One way or another, we *will* find your mother."

DAY FIVE. THE FIRST MORNING since Ana's disappearance that Jake did not call de Santos.

Rosa arrived as the boys were finishing the oatmeal and toast Jake managed to burn for them.

"I'm late," she huffed, still breathing heavily from her walk up two flights of stairs. She circled the table and planted a wet kiss on each of the boys' foreheads, jabbering all the while. "Lo siento, Señor Skully. I did not sleep all night. Next thing I know I am waking to the birds." She raised a flattened nose and sniffed the lingering smell of carbon, then eyed the oatmeal disapprovingly. "You had to fix breakfast for the boys. Lo siento. It's all my fault."

A good Catholic, Rosa loved to beat herself up for her sins.

"That's not a problem, Rosa. I'm glad you got some sleep."

She turned and trained huge almond-shaped eyes, already filling with tears, on Jake.

"Have you heard anything?" she asked hopefully.

Rosa had worked for Ana's family ever since Ana was an infant. When Ana became pregnant shortly after she and Jake completed their residencies in Tijuana and moved to Nogales to open a clinic in the heart of the city, Rosa moved in with them to take care of the next generation of Zedillo children. Jake, who was raised an only child, did not like having a live-in. He bought Rosa an apartment two floors below their spacious eighth-floor home, which enabled Rosa to be there to fix breakfast and, on the nights Jake and Ana dined out, tuck the boys into bed.

Jake shook his head.

"No, no word."

"Dios mio," Rosa sighed. Licking two fingers, she pressed them against the cowlick at the back of the thick black hair Antony had inherited from his mother.

"Is Mama coming home today?" the child asked, eyes fixed on Rosa.

"Dios mio," she repeated, wrapping her arms around him and pressing his round cheeks to her swollen bosom. Releasing Antony, she went to Michael and enveloped him.

"Mi pobre hijo," she cooed, stroking his brow.

Michael wiggled his way out of her bear hug and turned to confront Jake.

"You told Antony you'd find her."

"I'm trying, Michael."

"Not hard enough. I don't think you even *want* to find her."

"Miguel," Rosa scolded, "how could you say such a thing to your father?"

"He wanted her gone," Michael replied, staring blankly toward Jake. "So that he could have his affair."

Rosa's gasp filled the tiny kitchen as, with a sickening wrench, Jake realized that it hadn't just been Antony at the door yesterday morning during his conversation with de Santos. Michael must have been there, too, on the other side, listening.

"You're too young to understand, Michael," Jake said.

He reached for Michael's hand, but upon feeling Jake's touch, Michael jerked violently away.

"You're the reason Mama was so unhappy. *You're* the reason she ran away."

Antony began sobbing uncontrollably. Rosa, one hand pressed against her heart, clutched at the child with the other, but her own shock was so great that she could not find words to comfort him.

"That's enough, Michael," Jake said sternly. "You're upsetting everyone."

"*I'm* upsetting them?" Michael screamed, jumping up from the table. As he backed out of the kitchen, still glaring at Jake, he stumbled over the chair he'd upended. "You're full of shit. You know that? You're worthless. You made her leave, and now you can't even find her. *Nobody can.*"

With Antony's wails filling his ears, Jake grabbed the keys to the clinic from the hook near the back door and stormed out of the kitchen.

Taking the steps two and three at a time, he descended eight flights of stairs, then stepped outside, into the early morning heat.

Could Michael be right? Did Ana leave because of Jake's affair? The discovery had shaken her to the core, Jake knew—at a time when, because of what had happened to Michael, she was already fighting to hold on. But even if Ana would leave Jake, he knew with absolute certainty that she would never, even in her darkest hour, leave Michael and Antony.

Still, he had to have an answer, for Michael and Antony as well as himself. The uncertainty had become too much for all of them to bear, and it was pretty clear that the police had all but given up now that they believed Ana had left because of Jake's affair.

Ignoring the blast of a horn from a yellow cab, Jake stepped off the curb and jaywalked across one of Nogales's busiest streets.

There had to be a clue to Ana's whereabouts somewhere. He'd start at the clinic. He'd given the police access to all the files, but they'd come up with nothing. It was time for Jake to take matters into his own hands.

He'd turn the clinic upside down if he had to.

He would find Guerrero's man, the one whom Ana had treated, and beat a confession out of the bastard.

Today the five-minute walk took less than three.

Approaching the clinic's front door, Jake stepped over an inert form covered by a piece of cardboard with the words *Whirlpool refrigerator* emblazoned across its center. Brown legs, thickly coated with coarse dark hair and ending in laceless imitation Nikes, extended from underneath the makeshift blanket.

Jake plunged a fist into his pocket, fishing for his keys. As he opened a door that read:

Ana Zedillo de Skully, M.D., emergency medicine
Jake Skully, M.D., family practice

the cardboard stirred. An arm reached out, palm turned up to reveal a pincushion of needle marks on the inside of the elbow.

"Dinero? Tienes pesos?"

Jake ignored the plea and passed through the door, flipping on the light switch. A blast of cold air greeted his arms left bare by his short-sleeved shirt. Ana always turned the air conditioner down each evening before they left. Jake had been operating in such a haze these past few days that little details like that had fallen by the wayside. He went to the thermostat, pushed the setting higher; then, remembering last night's prediction of temperatures over one hundred, he pushed it randomly back down again.

That simple act—the confusion and disorientation it represented—set something off in him. Clenching his right fist, he pulled back, then slammed it full force into the wall. Not satisfied with the hot flash of pain that shot up his forearm into his elbow, he punched the wall again, this time breaking through the plaster.

It wasn't until he stood back to stare blindly at the damage he'd done to the wall that Jake realized he was not alone.

He swirled to find himself face-to-face with two uniformed officers. *Policia, Cuidad de Nogales*, the patches on their brown shirtfronts read.

"Dr. Skully?" the taller, more heavyset, of the two men said.

A sick dread instantly seeped through Jake's veins.

"Yes?"

"We'd like you to come with us."

Jake was startled to see the smaller officer, a swarthy balding man in his mid- to late forties, glaring at him with undisguised hatred. He looked vaguely familiar, but in his agitated state, Jake could not even think straight, much less place him.

"*Where?*" he said.

"The city morgue."

Jake's world began to spin. He reached for the back of a chair, clutching at it.

"We've found your wife's body," the officer continued. He might as well have been reporting the weather, for all the emotion his voice held. "We need you to identify her."

"My God," Jake cried. "They murdered Ana?"

The shorter officer's voice was not so dispassionate. It came out in a deep snarl. "The cartel didn't kill her. *You* did."

Jake suddenly recognized him. One of Ana's patients. And also, he quickly concluded, the investigator who'd discovered Jake's affair.

Growling low, Jake lunged at the man, grabbing him by the collar of his uniform.

"It's your fault," Jake screamed. He shook him, literally lifting him off the ground to eye level.

He wanted to kill him, to make him suffer the same fate that Ana had suffered. But before Jake could get a blow off, the man's partner grabbed hold of Jake's shoulder and swung him around.

Forty pounds heavier than Jake and combat-trained, he wrestled Jake's arms behind his back. Jake felt as though his right arm might break in the hold, but the pain did not stop him from spewing his anger.

"You wasted valuable time investigating me and let the bastards get away. I told you, I knew all along, Ana didn't disappear of her own free will. If you'd listened, you might have found her in time."

Jake could feel the grief rising in him like a tide. His Ana, dead. Murdered by the cartel.

Fighting against the breakdown that he knew would come, he finally quieted, saying (almost to himself), "I knew Ana wouldn't leave us. She'd *never* leave."

"Ah, but, Doctor," the man said from behind, "you don't really believe that."

The shorter man, Ana's patient, stepped up to Jake, his nose just inches from Jake's.

"If I had my way," he said, "I'd arrest you for criminal interference with this investigation. But Sergeant de Santos, he refuses. He says you are *too important* a man." He said it mockingly, thrusting an accusing finger into Jake's chest. "You've put on a good show for us,

Dr. Skully, but now we know what you've always known. What your wife told you in that letter you destroyed."

"What?" Jake cried, struggling to get free. "What do you know?"

"We know that because of her husband's affair, Ana de Zedillo committed suicide."

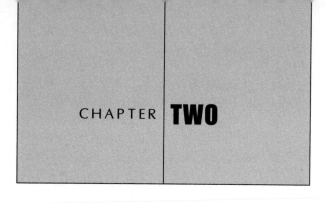

CHAPTER TWO

ASAHEL SULLIVAN'S MOOD matched the Seattle sky. Somber, gray. Turbulent, whipped up by an ungodly late spring wind. Only Asahel's late spring wind had been another dream about Angie.

They were coming more and more regularly now. Asahel's therapist, Dr. Patzwald, said the dreams would pass. That they were a form of post-traumatic stress syndrome.

Patzwald always had a name for everything that Asahel felt or did. Maybe he thought the labels made Asahel feel better—that if there were enough people who went through the same things she did so that it actually warranted a name, maybe Asahel wasn't so screwed up after all. But labels didn't help.

Sometimes Asahel didn't think anything would. Not the therapy. Not the pills. Not the new life she'd adopted.

Certainly not the prospect of another day on the job at Mercy Pharmaceuticals. Especially when she was late. And especially when her day started with the worst possible news.

"Your father's been looking for you."

Tammy Nguyen, Asahel's paralegal, looked up from her computer screen and eyed Asahel as she opened the door to the legal department.

"Great," Asahel replied, shrugging out of her trench coat.

"He wants to see you right away. He's been down here looking for you twice now."

Before Asahel had finished hanging her coat on the coat tree in the corner of the reception area, Nguyen's intercom issued a harsh buzz. Then a voice came over it.

"Has Asahel arrived yet?" Parker Ramsey, Philip Esser's administrative assistant.

Asahel waved to get Nguyen's attention, then shook her head back and forth violently, mouthing a silent, *No.*

"Not yet," Nguyen answered. "I'm sure she'll be in soon."

"Let's hope so. He's fit to be tied."

When the static signaled that Ramsey had gone, Nguyen and Asahel exchanged glances.

"Can I bum a cigarette?" Asahel said.

"You quit."

"I know."

Nguyen reached into her purse and produced a pack of Camel Lights. Asahel withdrew one, then went into her office and smoked it beneath the NO SMOKING sign that adorned every office at Mercy.

She knew what this was about. She'd known the reaction her letter would get from her father, Philip Esser, founder and CEO of Mercy Pharmaceuticals.

Dr. Patzwald had advised her to either quit or climb on board at Mercy, make peace with her father. But she hadn't told Patzwald everything. There were some things she just couldn't talk about, even to her therapist.

The cigarette made Asahel feel ill. Crushing it out, she headed down the hallway to the executive offices.

Parker Ramsey sniffed the air and raised her eyebrows when Asahel stepped inside, but she said nothing about the faint odor of tobacco that wafted in with Asahel.

She nodded toward the door marked: *Philip Esser, M.D., CEO.*

"He's been waiting for you."

When Asahel opened the door, Philip Esser raised his eyes from that morning's issue of *Bioworld.* They were small, close-set eyes. Hawkish and cold. Otherwise quite handsome, with a thick head of hair and an air of arrogance, Philip Esser exuded the confidence and power that went along with ruling lives.

Now, with the look of a madman, he reached for a sheet of paper on his desk.

"What the hell's this?" he said before Asahel even had a chance to sit down. He shook the paper in the air.

Asahel stopped short of the empty chair and decided to remain standing, knowing her father would perceive it as insolent.

"I assume you mean my response to the threatened lawsuit."

"Of course that's what I mean. What the hell were you thinking?"

"I was thinking it's a good thing you have a good lawyer."

"Don't play games with me. You know damn well what I mean. And sit down."

"I'm in a hurry, *Father.*" She said the word with such disdain that even Esser flinched. "Let's get this over with as quickly as possible. For both our sakes."

"You offered to settle," Esser railed. "Without even discussing it with me first. You sent the letter out, then copied me after the fact."

Asahel did not avert her eyes from his hateful glare.

"As Mercy's attorney, I'd decided it was in our best interest."

"To pay some hypochondriac half a million dollars? Are you out of your fucking mind?"

"The woman is not a hypochondriac. Two months after beginning Bioleve, she developed MS. She had no family history, no genetic predisposition. Those facts are incontrovertible."

"It wasn't because of our product."

"You'd have a hard time proving that at trial."

"No harder than she'd have proving that it was."

"Are you forgetting that two percent of the participants in Phase Three complained of neurological problems? That the FDA's approval stipulated we keep a close eye on Bioleve for that very reason? Do you know what the publicity from a trial would do to your precious product?"

Esser's eyes widened in rage. He strained toward Asahel, looking as if he wanted to reach over his desk and grab her by the neck.

"That's it," he cried, "isn't it? That's the reason you caved in, settled this thing. You see it as a victory against me, don't you? I ought to fire you, turn you in to the bar. You can't make an offer of settlement without your client's go-ahead and you know it."

Asahel's lips turned up in a half smile. She couldn't help it.

When she saw the effect this had on Esser, her smile instinctively widened.

"Another threat, huh?" she said. "You're good at that."

Esser held his voice steady, but everything else about the man looked as though he'd stuck a finger in an electric socket.

"They're not idle threats, Asahel," he said. "Remember that."

He studied her, looking for the terror that he knew his words would stir in her.

"Remember what it was like. What happened to you there. And remember, I'm the only one protecting you from that. Never forget it."

Asahel felt her knees weakening. Refusing to allow Esser to see it, she leaned against his desk, bracing herself with her hands.

They were as close to eye-to-eye as they'd come in the year she'd worked there.

"Any attorney worth her salt would insist that you settle this case," she said. "We had one day to respond, one day before they filed suit and went to the media. You were out of the office all last week. Out of the country and, apparently, out of touch, because I tried half a dozen times to call you."

Esser knew she was right. She could see it in those eyes, those eyes that had always, for some reason, held contempt for his oldest daughter. Even when she was a child she'd seen it. She'd seen the way Philip Esser looked at his beloved Angie, then the way he looked at Asahel.

She straightened up, willing her legs to be strong, just long enough to get her out of Esser's company.

"Now, are we done?"

Esser tossed the sheet of paper down on his desk.

"No," he said, "we're not. I want you to pull all the contracts on HydraDerm. Manufacturing, distribution, everything."

HydraDerm was Mercy Pharmaceutical's skin therapy that worked miracles with burn patients.

"Why?"

"We're terminating them. All of them. We're pulling the plug on HydraDerm."

"What?"

Asahel dropped into the chair. A look of triumph flitted across Esser's face.

"Why would we do that?" she asked. "It's a successful product."

Now it was Philip Esser's turn to smile.

"Successful? Are you kidding? We've lost a quarter of a million dollars on it in the six months it's been on the market."

"But it's still new. It takes time to build a new product."

"Angiogen's new skin replacement therapy gets better results. Our most recent market analysis shows that sixty percent of patients are already choosing it over HydraDerm."

"But what about the other forty? A lot of them can't afford the skin replacement. Or they aren't even candidates for it."

Esser had already gone back to scanning *Bioworld*.

"We'll never make money on it," he said lightly. "We're pulling the plug. Review those contracts and find the cheapest way out. Then report back to me."

"What about Betty Rimmel? Alonzo Lowe? People like them."

During HydraDerm's launch, Mercy had run a very successful TV campaign featuring two patients who, very movingly, testified that HydraDerm had given them back their lives, allowed them to go out in public again without feeling that the world was gawking at them.

Because of other health complications, neither would be candidates for Angiogen's skin replacement therapy.

"What *about* them?" Esser asked, looking at Asahel over the rims of his bifocals, one eyebrow raised.

"Will you give up the patent? Let someone else produce it? You know Graham Pharmaceuticals has been interested for years. It's the perfect complement to their other products."

"Are you kidding?" Esser replied. "If bioterrorists ever unleash smallpox, there'll be a huge demand for it. It may be the only product that eliminates the scars survivors end up with. We'll gear back up if that happens. That patent could be worth something someday."

"It's worth something *now*, don't you see?" Asahel found herself practically shouting. "This isn't why I came to work for Mercy, to help you make money, regardless of whom it hurts. Regardless of what's best for the patients who need our products."

"*Our products?*" Esser laughed. "Now it's *our* products?" Then he grew deadly serious. "We both know why you came to work here. And that hasn't changed, has it?"

Esser reached for the phone. He looked immensely pleased with himself, victorious.

"Now, if you'll excuse me," he said curtly, "I've got business to take care of."

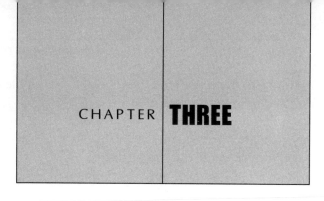

CHAPTER **THREE**

DIEGO CAVALLERO HAD grudgingly come to the conclusion that having the American join his Lost Tribes Project was a good thing.

For the time being, it was in the project's best interests for Cavallero to focus on lobbying politicians for continued support, which meant he needed all the help he could get. He'd just have to live with the American.

For the time being.

But that didn't stop the son of a bitch from getting under Cavallero's skin. It was time to set things straight.

Now, as he sat in his stuffy, cramped office in one of Manaus's shabbiest buildings, Cavallero looked forward to doing just that.

A knock on the door drew his attention up from the press release he'd been editing.

A tall sandy-haired man stood in his doorway. Obviously American, he was dressed in blue jeans, a white linen long-sleeved shirt and top-of-the-line hiking boots. While he was not good-looking, he still looked as though he'd just stepped out of a Crocodile Dundee movie.

"You sent for me?" he said.

"Why are you here? In Manaus?" Cavallero asked. "I didn't schedule this for you."

"What? You got spies following me around or something? How'd you even know I was here?"

"You think someone like you shows up in town and I'm not gonna hear about it? Why are you here?" Cavallero demanded.

"Just stocking up on some supplies."

"I left you all the supplies you need. Up in Acre. If you needed something else, Iquitos is a helluva lot closer to where you're working than Manaus. Why didn't you stock up there?"

" 'Cause Manaus is the only town I know, that's why. What's the problem?"

"The problem is you're supposed to be out in the jungle. And you didn't even inform me that you were here. *That's* the problem. I have to hear it from some fucking street cop."

"So shoot me. You know, this is just a job. It's not my life. I'm entitled to my free time."

Nothing could have set Cavallero off faster.

"Do you know what's at stake here?" he screamed, gesturing wildly in the air, his trademark Marlboro dangling from between two fingers, one of which had been broken three times. "Do you?

"I've spent my whole life working with Brazil's Indians. Lost one wife 'cause she thought I was crazy and another to the malaria my work exposed her to. I've lived in the same crummy two-room apartment for almost twenty years. I drive a beat-up Volkswagen Golf. I've been held hostage twice now, and last year I buried my best friend, who was killed by the people we're trying to protect. And you expect me to worry about your fucking *free time?*"

Clearly unfazed by this tirade, the American lifted a booted foot up and plopped it down on the corner of Cavallero's desk. "Take it easy, *compadre*. So what do you want with me?"

Cavallero slapped the boot off. He tossed the cigarette to the floor and immediately lit another.

"Since you're in town now," he said, "I thought we might as well do that training session we had scheduled for later in the month."

Cavallero didn't mention that he had deliberately sent the American out into the highly dangerous Amazon without adequate training, wanting him to fail—to fall flat on his face so that Cavallero's boss, Orlando Vasquez, would see how foolish this whole plan was and call it quits.

The American looked at his watch.

"How long's this gonna take?"

"You got something else going on?"

"Yeah," he replied. "A hot date. I need to get laid. Any rules against that?"

Sighing in frustration, Cavallero motioned toward the empty chair, though he remained standing.

Diego Cavallero was a man who could not bear to sit still. Wiry, with a cloud of receding hair, he clutched his cigarette in one hand, reached for a wooden pointer with the other and began his customary pacing.

"Sit down." He motioned with the stick.

The American dropped into the wooden chair.

"Tell me about your plane."

"It's a Beechcraft. T-34."

"Lotta plane," Cavallero observed. "I saw from your file that you've only had your instrument rating two years. You know what kind of conditions you're going to come up against during the rainy season here? It's just a few months away."

"Don't worry about me. I can handle weather."

Cavallero had dealt with his share of overly confident assholes before. This guy, he was right up there on the list. But it was time to put that aside.

"The Amazon rain forest is the world's last refuge for indigenous tribes that have had no contact with the outside world," he began, his cigarette dangling from the side of his mouth. "Without the Lost Tribes Project, their days are numbered. In 1988, the government promised to set aside nearly two hundred million acres, which is roughly eleven percent of Brazil, for its remaining Indians. Our job is to find and identify tribes, document their existence, which, in turn, documents their entitlement to a share of these lands."

"Government charity, huh?"

"No," Cavallero answered emphatically. "The government isn't giving the Indians anything they aren't already entitled to. All it's doing is recognizing their rights. It's not a matter of charity. It's *not* a matter of being nice. We have a historical and moral duty to protect these lands for them."

Cavallero's allegiance to Brazil's Indians grew out of an unconventional but happy childhood—a childhood spent living with one deep-forest tribe after another. His father worked for the government, as a teacher to half a dozen tribes. Though his parents were Spanish, for all practical purposes Cavallero grew up Indian, hunting and fishing with the native children, moving through the forest like one of its panthers.

As Cavallero spoke, he noticed the American surveying his office. His cool eyes had come to rest on some of Cavallero's most prized possessions—thirty-two tall feathered spears that adorned one wall. But despite his curiosity, the American had apparently been listening.

"So once I locate a tribe," he said, "what do we do? Send in doctors and missionaries?"

"We leave them alone."

"What?"

"We leave them alone. We never even make contact. That's rule number one. No contact. And we protect them."

"Protect them how?"

"By stationing armed guards to close off river traffic to the region. We don't allow white settlers in."

"Can you do that? Close off the river?"

"Right now we can. But if some of our opposition get their way, we may not be able to in the future."

"Tell me about the opposition."

"The opposition is headed by a right-wing political asshole by the name of Marco da Luz. He's built his campaign for reelection on the idea that Brazil doesn't owe the Indians anything. Before 1988, our government's policy was to assimilate the tribes into Brazil's social and economic mainstream. The result is that remote tribes not only lost their culture; they ended up exploited for cheap labor or, worse, dead. From white man's diseases they'd never been exposed to. Whole tribes were wiped out. Cultures lost."

"And that's what Brazilians want? They want the Indians wiped out?"

"What they want now is the Indians' land. It's rich farmland, loaded with minerals, timber, wildlife. The 1988 constitution protects it for the Indians. That means that three hundred thousand Indians own eleven percent of Brazil. Not everyone likes that math. Especially da Luz, and he's making sure everyone's arithmetic skills are sharpened."

"Sounds like you might have some enemies," the American said. "But you must be a popular man with the Indians."

Crushing a butt burned all the way to his orange-tinged fingers in the paper plate that served as his ashtray, Cavallero finally let out a laugh.

"Don't make the mistake of thinking the natives see us as some kind of heroes. They don't. They've killed hundreds of FUNAI agents over the years. Most recently, my friend. When I put up a cross in his honor, they knocked it down and came after me with their arrows."

Deriving some satisfaction from the reaction these words seemed to invoke in the American, Cavallero continued.

"Just last month, I had to fly by army helicopter to the state of Acre to rescue twenty-one FUNAI employees who'd been surrounded by one of the tribes we'd just located."

"What were they going to do to them?"

The American was trying to keep his expression neutral, but Cavallero thought he saw a flicker of alarm in those cocky eyes. He couldn't help himself.

"Most likely, eat them," Cavallero said, deadpan.

The American had fallen silent.

"So why do you continue to do it?"

"Because there are thirty-four areas of the Amazon that we haven't explored yet."

"And it's worth getting killed for?"

Cavallero paused from his pacing to draw another Marlboro from the pack in his shirt pocket.

"People don't understand what isolated Indians are like," he replied. "They're persecuted, harassed, always on the run. They have a lot more reason to distrust us than we have to be distrustful of them."

When the American failed to respond, Cavallero said, "Mind telling me why you came down here? I mean, you don't seem to know a whole hell of a lot about this project, which means you probably don't give a rat's ass about it."

The American shrugged.

"I work for a guy who's interested. He's really loaded, always trying to help, does a lot of stuff with our Indians back home. You know the kind. I'm a pilot; I like adventure—he asked me if I wanted to come over here." Realizing how indifferent, even mercenary, he probably sounded, he then added, "But who's to say I don't care? I just didn't know much about it. I'm not without a conscience, ya know."

Eyeing a yellow legal pad in the middle of the chaotic pile on his desk, Cavallero grabbed it and tore off the top page, which had scribbling on it, tossing it into the wastebasket.

"Here," he said, shoving the pad the American's way. "Take notes."

Cavallero walked to the only bare wall in his office. He reached for a cord dangling from a long metal cylinder bolted at the juncture of the ceiling and wall and pulled down a large colorful map of Brazil. The north and northwest states of Pará, Roraima, Amazonas, Acre and Rondônia were splattered with round red and turquoise adhesive dots.

"Each of these blue dots," Cavallero said, using the pointer to jab at the screen, "represents a known tribe. About two hundred of them."

The American had appeared sleepy when he first walked into Cavallero's office, but Cavallero was pleased to see that he now studied the map alertly.

"These," Cavallero pointed to several red dots in succession, "they're the tribes the Department of Isolated Indians has found. Tribes that either we never knew existed, we thought had become extinct, or whose existence we only suspected. There are twenty-seven so far."

"That include the one I found?"

"Yes," Cavallero answered. "You can ignore the blue dots." A half inch of ash fell to the floor from Cavallero's cigarette as he waved it toward the map. "They're FUNAI's business. But the red dots, they're ours. We're here to see that they're protected. And we're also here to find more red dots. You got that?"

The American nodded.

"We know there are plenty more tribes. We've had reports of up to thirty-four that are definitely out there but have had no peaceful contact with outsiders. Your and my job is to find them."

Cavallero reached for a file he'd compiled for the American and tossed it across the desk at him.

"Here, study this. *Know* it. It's a list of all the known tribes in the territories you'll be covering. You speak Portuguese?"

"No. Some Spanish."

"Spanish'll help."

"I thought I wasn't supposed to come into contact with them."

"You're not. But you'll be running into settlers along the rivers. It'll help to be able to communicate with them. They can give you valuable information."

"What kind of settlers?" the American asked.

"What do you mean, what kind?" Cavallero replied.

"White? Black?"

"White. We call them deep-forest settlers. They live off the land. Many are on the run from the law. Most of them are friendly. They like company. Some speak English, but most speak only Portuguese. Now, open that file. I want to go over some of these tribes with you.

"You'll be doing almost all your work in these two states," Cavallero said, tapping a knuckle on the two westernmost states. "Amazonas and Acre. Acre's ninety-two thousand square miles. Ninety-four percent of that is jungle. The tribes in Acre belong mainly to two linguistic groups: the Pano and the Aruaque. You can read all this in that file. But there are a few tribes I want you to make note of."

He stabbed at the map.

"The Arara," he said. "In 1986 there were ninety-two of them. Haven't been seen or heard from since. They're hunter-gatherers. Fishermen. Have their own language."

Moving even farther west, he pointed to a river near Rio Branco.

"The Jabuti. Last seen in 1990, and at that time, far as we could tell, there were only five still living. It's our job to find out if they're extinct now."

Cavallero's cigarette swung north, to the state of Amazonas.

"Nineteen forty. Three hundred Juma were documented as living along the Rio Acua. A tributary of the Mucuim. They were an especially isolated tribe. Called themselves Kagwahiva. Haven't had a documented sighting in the last two decades. If they're still there, I want you to find them. Same with the Monde. In 1995 we counted thirty along the Apidia River. If they're still there, find them."

"What about this one?" the American said, his eyes glued to a map he'd extracted from his file and now held in front of him.

"Which one?"

"The Arua," he struggled with the pronunciation. "Or Arawa."

"Extinct. You can cross that one off your list. No one's seen an Arauan for half a century. Maybe even longer. Same with the Guana."

"That's what that *e* after a tribe's name means?"

Cavallero nodded.

"That list contains at least half a dozen tribes that probably don't exist anymore," Cavallero explained. "And my bet is that there are at least that many, maybe more, out there that aren't on that list because no one—not a goddamned soul—has ever seen them or come in contact with them. Which reminds me, never forget rule number one, which is—"

The American's hand shot up, cutting Cavallero off.

"Never make contact," he said. "I'm not as dumb as you seem to think I am. And I can hear just fine. Rule number one is *never make contact.*"

He looked at his watch.

"I gotta go."

"It's still early."

"I told you," the American said. He'd lost his patience. "I've got plans."

"A date?"

"Yeah, a date."

"Then what?"

"Then I'll head back into the wilds. Find you some tribes. So maybe you'll get off my ass."

With little more than a nod Cavallero's way, he rose and strode confidently out the door.

Cavallero watched him stride down the hallway.

"Keep in touch," he yelled just before the American reached the exit, but did not look back.

There goes one cocky son of a bitch.

Something told Cavallero that it would be a very good idea to keep a close eye on him.

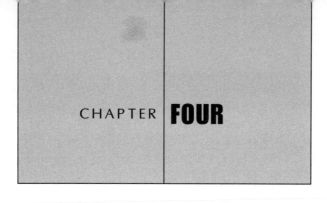

CHAPTER **FOUR**

I WANT YOU to know how sorry I was to hear about your wife."

Jake Skully met the dark gaze of Torrell Hughes head-on.

Surely this wasn't the same Hughes he'd talked to from Nogales on several occasions. That Hughes had been cold, arrogant. A real SOB The first time they'd talked, he'd even lost his temper and called Jake a fool when Jake explained that Ana did not want him to take the job Hughes offered him with his Seattle-based biotech company, Gen-Chrom. Ana thought Michael had enough to adjust to without moving to a new country. Instead, she'd talked Jake into starting their own research project, designed to find a cure for their son.

Hughes had grown dead silent at this announcement and then angry.

At one time, that alone would have been enough to make Jake write the bastard off—along with the prospect of working with him—once and for all. But all that had changed now.

This Hughes, well, he'd actually arrived for their meeting with a playful young dog in tow. And expressing sympathy for what had happened.

Maybe it wasn't safe to judge someone solely on the basis of a couple of phone calls. Before today, Jake had been convinced he'd dislike this man whom he expected to become his employer.

"Thank you," Jake replied, choosing not to elaborate. "I'm glad you still want me on your research team."

"Want you? Hell, of course I want you," Hughes replied. "But I want to be up front with you. This job involves travel. Lots of it. And these aren't boondoggle, company-financed vacations I'm talking about. They're hell. Pure hell. GenChrom is heavily involved in bio-prospecting in the Amazon. The most inhuman, inhospitable place you'll ever have the misfortune to visit. You sure you know what you're getting yourself into?"

Tanned and trim in his green golf shirt and khakis, the gray at his temples offering the only hint of his age (which Jake would put at midfifties), Hughes stroked the dog's head absentmindedly.

"That's where you think you'll find it?" Jake asked. "G32?"

"Yes," Hughes replied. "We have reason to believe that a tribe known to exist in the remote Amazon basin forests at the turn of last century carries G32. If that tribe still exists, my team plans to find it."

"Count me in," Jake said.

"What about your boys? You're comfortable with leaving them here? I understand you're raising them alone now."

"I'd hoped to get their nanny to move up here with us," Jake continued, "but she has a large family of her own down in Nogales. I'll just have to find a good situation for Michael and Antony before I start to travel."

"We'll see what we can do to help you out with that," Hughes replied.

The brown leather of his chair groaned softly as Hughes leaned his long, lean frame forward and pressed a button on his desk.

"Yes?" a female voice responded over the intercom.

"Bring that employment contract in, will you?"

In less than a minute, the door opened and Marilyn, the pleasant, heavily made up receptionist who'd shown Jake into Hughes's office, entered. She carried a stapled document.

"Here's the contract," she said, flashing a smile Jake's way. "Hey, Zeus," she said then, bending down to pat the dog's head. "How's the big boy doing today?"

This seemed to irritate Hughes. Jake's view was obstructed by Hughes's desk, but if he didn't know better he'd have sworn that Hughes actually reached over and pushed his receptionist's hand off the dog.

"That's not Zeus," Hughes said sharply. "It's Lottie."

Marilyn rolled her eyes, clearly for Jake's benefit, as she left the room.

Hughes pushed the contract she'd given him across the desk.

"Here, why don't you look this over now and we can get the formalities over with."

"You mean here?"

"Sure," Hughes answered. "Why not?"

"I just hadn't expected to sign anything today."

"I don't believe in wasting time. I wouldn't think you'd want to, either."

That suggestion struck a chord in Jake.

"You're right," he said decisively.

He grabbed the stapled document and began reading. It all appeared standard for an employment agreement. The confidentiality section and intellectual property provisions didn't surprise Jake—he fully appreciated the fact that a biotech company's success, its viability, depended on the protection of its trade secrets. Finding it all in order, Jake skimmed through the legalese quickly, pen poised to sign.

But then a sentence at the end of the IP section jumped out at him:

> Employee grants to GenChrom an irrevocable and exclusive license to use all patents granted by the United States Patent and Trademark Office in said employee's name.

"What's this?" Jake asked, turning the document around so that Hughes could read it.

Hughes grabbed it.

"Let's see. I never even read these goddamn things anymore."

He grew silent as he read the section Jake had pointed out.

Then he reached for the phone and punched in four digits.

"Put Gina on," he said. Looking up at Jake, he mouthed, *Company attorney.*

When a new voice came on the other line, Hughes said, "Gina, what's this provision in the employment agreement you just did for Jake Skully? The one that grants GenChrom a license to anything he's patented."

Jake watched as Hughes listened to the attorney's answer, his expression vascillating between boredom and annoyance.

"She says that's in all our contracts," he explained to Jake as he cradled the phone on his shoulder. "It's standard in the industry."

"That's fine for anything I invent while working for you," Jake said, trying to strike a diplomatic tone. "But why would GenChrom be entitled to any patents I held before I went to work for you?"

"Good point," Hughes said to Jake. Then, into the phone, he asked, "Did you hear him? Why the hell would he give us a license for a patent he already holds?"

Hughes let the attorney go on for a while, then cut her off, saying, "Well, I agree with Jake. Makes no sense to me. What do you want me to do with that clause? Let's get rid of it."

After another brief exchange, Hughes hung up the phone.

"She says to strike it out, then initial it." He chuckled then. "Damn attorneys. They'll suck every last drop of blood out of you if you let them."

All in all, Jake considered that this initial meeting with Hughes had gone well. But even if it hadn't, he knew nothing would deter him from going to work for GenChrom. Not now.

Jake had made a promise to Ana. This certainly wasn't what he'd had in mind when he made that promise. What he'd had in mind was he and Ana, together, leaving no stone unturned, applying all their expertise, all their training, channeling all their love into finding a cure for their son. But when Ana disappeared—he could not bear to think of it in any other terms—everything had changed.

Jake reached for the contract and drew a line through the offending sentence. Then he initialed his change, signed the last page and handed it back to Hughes.

Hughes took the document, flipped immediately to the last page and scrawled his own signature. A look of satisfaction momentarily warmed his eyes.

"Now that that's settled," Jake said, "can I ask you something?"

"Of course."

"Why is it you changed courses?"

Hughes's expression darkened instantly.

"Pardon me?"

"I mean your work on environmental mutagens. You'd spent decades studying them, the damage they're capable of inflicting on human DNA. Your name's at the top of the list of experts in the field. So why this new direction these past few years? What got you interested in G32?"

For a moment, Hughes studied Jake without speaking. Then, his eyes shielded, expressionless, he answered.

"I guess I just like new challenges."

HE'D LEFT THE BOYS waiting in his locked car in the GenChrom parking lot. They'd arrived just the day before and had spent the night at the downtown Hilton. When it came time for Jake to leave for his interview, Michael had declared that he planned to wait for Jake at the hotel. Jake and Ana had, after all, allowed him to baby-sit Antony during the day many times in the past.

But Jake would not allow it.

Of the three of them, Michael had taken Ana's death the hardest.

He'd already been undergoing treatment for depression before Ana died. Jake had not been able to bring himself to tell the boys that authorities had ruled Ana's death a suicide, had not dared to. Getting Michael and Antony out of Mexico and away from the rumors about Jake and Ana that had quickly made the rounds had been one of the biggest benefits of Jake's decision to move to Seattle.

The fifth day after her disappearance, Ana's car had been found at the bottom of a steep ravine. Her neck had apparently snapped in the 200-foot fall, like a dry twig, killing her instantly. She had not been wearing a seat belt. According to the Nogales police, a witness had seen Ana accelerate her Volvo and deliberately veer off the side of the mountain road.

Jake accused both the witness and the police of lying. Ana would not have done anything that cowardly, nor would she have left them without first making certain that every detail of the boys' lives was planned to perfection.

But of course there was the matter of the empty envelope.

An envelope upon which Ana had scrawled Jake's name.

What had it contained? The police had no doubt about what the letter was, right from the start, but especially after they found her body and heard the witness's account. Ana had committed suicide. Jake had driven her to it.

What was it you planned to tell me, Ana?

At any moment of the day or night, Jake could close his eyes and vividly see his name scrawled in Ana's flowery script. Surely she would not have written his name in such a manner—the large, fluid letters, the curlicue at the end of the last letter *e*—if the letter intended for the envelope was a letter of death. A letter that would cause the pure and complete destruction not only of Jake's heart but of Michael's and Antony's as well.

Jake refused to believe it. Despite his affair, despite Ana's shock at its discovery, despite the witness's account. His Ana would not do it.

But the letter. The letter is what troubled him. The letter is what drove Jake mad.

For, despite his denials, a part of him wondered whether Ana had, indeed, written it to say good-bye and then lost her courage, tossing the envelope in the wastebasket.

What else could have been so awful that, in the end, she could not bring herself to actually deliver it?

No, it couldn't have been a suicide note.

Both because he refused to believe the police ruling and because of the devastating impact Ana's committing suicide would have on them, Jake had told the boys their mother's death was an accident. Still, something told Jake that Michael knew, and as a medical doctor, Jake had heard plenty of stories of one suicide prompting another. He was not taking any chances leaving Michael and Antony alone in their fourteenth-floor room while Jake interviewed with Torrell Hughes.

Enduring the obscenities that Michael uttered (in Spanish) under his breath, Jake stood firm with his insistence that Michael and Antony accompany him and wait in the car.

Now, as he walked across the open-air parking lot, hip-hop music came at Jake in loud waves from his Ford Expedition. That—the shared love that Mexican and American teens had for music by performers such as Destiny's Child and Eminem—might at least prove to be one constant in Michael and Antony's recent tumultuous life.

Neither boy noticed his approach. Jake knocked on the window of the driver's side. From the backseat, Antony leaned forward and pulled up the knob locking the driver's door. Jake climbed in, eager to tell the boys his news.

"I got it," he said, turning to Michael, who sat in the passenger seat. But Michael did not respond. His eyes hidden by dark glasses, Jake's handsome brown-skinned son kept beat to the music with his head, which bobbed forward with each thrum of the acoustic guitar.

The music was deafening. Maybe Michael had not heard him.

"I said, I got the job," Jake repeated, loudly this time.

Michael continued to stare straight ahead, never missing a beat.

"That's good, Papa, isn't it?" Antony yelled from behind him.

"Yes, it is," Jake shouted back, over the music.

It was Michael whom he'd most hoped to please with this news, but as he'd been doing ever since Ana's death, Michael ignored Jake.

"Turn that down, will you?" Jake finally shouted over lyrics that made him cringe. Ana had refused to allow the boys to listen to hip-hop, but Jake had enough problems to overcome with Michael and Antony without adding that battle to the list.

Antony, always the peacemaker, leaned over Jake's shoulder and reached for the radio.

"I'll turn it down," he said cheerfully.

Jake grabbed his younger son's chubby arm.

"No. I asked Michael to."

Antony's eyes grew wide with anticipation.

Michael's therapist had told Jake he should stand up to Michael when he was being unreasonable. That advice had resulted in some terrible showdowns, which no doubt accounted for the fear in Antony's eyes right now.

However, this time, instead of a showdown, Michael decided to cooperate.

He leaned toward the center of the car and reached for the dashboard, running his hand along the top for several inches, then down, adeptly feeling for the volume knob on the radio. When his fingers came to rest on the dial knob instead, Jake had to fight the impulse to shout out, *Not that one, the one on the left.*

Despite the therapist's warnings about being overly protective, Jake wanted, with every fiber of his being, to shield Michael from the mistakes, the embarrassments, the dangers that went along with what had happened to him.

With a sigh of relief, he watched as Michael's fingers continued on to the correct knob and, finally, turned the headache-inducing volume down.

"Thank you," Jake said, finally able to speak in a normal voice.

Michael had turned to face him. The afternoon sun sat high in the sky and, with Michael's head turned, its light shone through the space behind his sunglasses, illuminating his brown eyes. Eyes that no longer jumped with mischief or joy or even anger. But for a fleeting moment, Jake swore he saw a flicker of life cross them.

"You got the job?" Michael asked.

The note of hope in his son's voice caused a wave of anger and fear to rise in Jake's throat. He swallowed against it.

"Yes. I start next week."

"Can we start looking for an apartment now?" Antony asked excitedly from the backseat.

"Yes," Jake said. "Right away."

Michael appeared to be pondering Jake's news.

"So how long will it take?" he asked.

Now Jake recognized Michael's tone and realized he'd been wrong. It wasn't hope he'd detected in Michael's voice. It was mockery.

Another chunk of Jake's soul died. But he obliged Michael and played along.

"Will *what* take?"

"How long will it take for you to fix *this*?"

Michael reached up and removed the sunglasses, aiming dull eyes his father's way. The pupils did not constrict at the bright sunlight.

Michael might not be able to see, but he knew, every bit as well as if he could, the effect this had on his father.

Jake's hands knotted into tight fists.

"I don't know, Michael," he said. "But I promised your mother you would see again, and I intend to keep that promise."

He'd set himself up; Jake knew it the moment the words left his mouth.

"You promised Mom that?" Michael asked, the malice in his voice palpable. When you and Mom got married, didn't you make another promise to her? Didn't you promise her you'd be faithful?"

Jake reached out and grabbed his son by the wrist. When Michael attempted to jerk his hand away, Jake clamped down on it fiercely.

"Michael," he said. "I may have broken that promise, but I won't break this one. Believe me."

At last, a smile played across Michael's lips.

"Sure, Dad," he said. "Just like I believe in Santa Claus."

CHAPTER **FIVE**

THE SHRILL RING of the phone awakened Asahel. She'd just dozed off, hadn't she? She looked at the clock on her bedside table and cursed.

Six-thirty. Her wake-up call.

Asahel crushed the pillow down over her head, which felt like someone had clubbed her during the night. The insomnia had become so bad that over the winter she'd developed a nasty wine habit. At first one glass would put her to sleep, but recently it took two, sometimes three. More often than not, several hours later she'd end up wide awake, and sometimes when she felt really desperate, like last night, she'd pad into the kitchen barefoot to guzzle a few more gulps from the bottle that she left on the counter. Anything to numb her, put her to sleep.

Her pillow still pressed to her ears to blot out the whine of the shower running in the unit below, after a few minutes Asahel lifted one corner and squinted outside to check the weather. She rarely drew the blinds on the French door that led from her kitchen to the balcony of her small attic apartment, which was located on the top floor of one of Capitol Hill's grand old houses. She'd moved her bed so that she could see all the way through the kitchen and outside, to the bird's-eye view of the city of Seattle, the south end of Lake Union, and, in the distance, the Olympic Mountains. That—the sight of the mountains, so distant yet still so remarkably forceful and dominating—somehow soothed her; reminded her that, in the whole scheme of things, her problems were pretty inconsequential.

On this morning, only a seasoned Seattleite could recognize the fact that the day had indeed dawned, so thick and foreboding were the clouds. So gray that at first Asahel didn't even notice the pile of dark clothing huddled outside against her door.

But when the pile moved, Asahel let out a gasp.

She reached for the phone to call 911, but suddenly, out of the heap of fabric, a head rose. That of a young brown-skinned woman.

It was her hair that stopped Asahel short. It had been chopped off by crude handmade instruments. Asahel knew that because she'd seen hair just like it before. On a trip, a trip made in her former life. And it was that—the realization of where she'd seen it—that caused Asahel's heart to race wildly and, as she slipped out of bed, her already fair skin to turn a shade paler.

No, it can't be.

Trembling, Asahel tiptoed toward the door wearing nothing but the T-shirt and panties she'd slept in.

The woman had not noticed her yet. Her back still pressed against the door's glass, she rubbed her eyes, then reached with quick, darting hands for a small bundle she'd been using as a pillow.

When Asahel's linoleum floor creaked under her feet, the woman froze. Slowly, she turned.

Huge eyes locked with Asahel's. Eyes filled with even more fear than Asahel's held.

Clutching her small bundle to her chest, the woman drew back.

The long sheet of brown fabric she wore tied under her equally brown arms engulfed her emaciated frame. She was little more than a skeleton.

One thing struck Asahel immediately, despite the circumstances, despite the half-light: the woman had the bluest eyes Asahel had ever seen.

But they held only terror as the woman began scooting backward on her rump, away from Asahel, propelling herself with her sandal-clad feet.

The balcony was small, less than ten feet wide, with a short rail. Each blind push backward brought the woman closer to its edge and a four-story drop to the cement sidewalk below.

Afraid a sudden move could send the woman toppling into space, Asahel watched, frozen in fear and disbelief.

Then it came to her. Another memory of a day three and a half years earlier. One of those memories Asahel fought so hard to keep buried, banned from her conscious mind, as she did every memory from that time in her life.

Asahel lifted her cupped right hand, then pulled it forcefully to her chest.

Thump, thump, thump.

She repeated the movement three times.

The woman's cornered-animal eyes never left Asahel's face; however, upon her seeing this gesture, a wave of relief washed over them.

She stopped her retreat and eagerly lifted her own right hand, mimicking Asahel.

Thump, thump, thump.

Three beats to the chest, *the heart.*

An Amazonian sign Asahel had learned in the rain forest, during her days as an activist for IPAF—the Indigenous Peoples Advancement Foundation. Back in the days that Asahel felt she could change the world, make a real difference.

Back in the days before she got her own sister killed and became her father's prisoner.

The irony of the sign did not escape Asahel, even now, under the dire circumstances.

For the sign the two women exchanged meant *"I come in peace."*

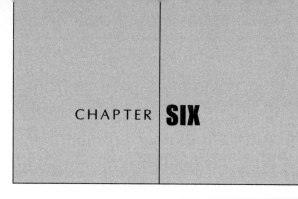

CHAPTER **SIX**

SO TELL ME about the work you've been doing these past few weeks."

Torrell Hughes, dressed on this unusually warm day in a blue linen shirt and khaki shorts that revealed long, well-muscled legs, pushed back in his chair and studied Jake.

Jake had grown accustomed to seeing Hughes's dog at his boss's feet. Usually it gnawed noisily away on a bone or some kind of a toy, but today the canine seemed more subdued.

"I've been doing single-cell gel microelectrophoresis assays, trying to assess DNA damage," Jake answered.

"And what have you found?"

"I'm trying to determine what type of mutation I'm dealing with. Flow cytometry indicates a point mutation."

"What caused it?"

Jake shook his head.

"That's the sixty-four-thousand-dollar question. Something caused genetic damage to these cells, something external."

"What cells are you working with?" Hughes asked.

Jake froze. He knew this moment would come, but he hadn't expected it this soon. He'd hoped to have already proved his value to Hughes before he divulged the truth.

"They're eye cells," Jake finally said, meeting Hughes's gaze head-on. "From my son. He went blind almost a year ago."

Hughes's face registered no emotion at this announcement as he studied Jake silently.

"Now I understand why you changed your mind. Why you came to work for me."

"Michael was fine the first time you contacted me. And then, several months later, it happened. He lost his sight."

The intensity of Hughes's gaze made Jake uncomfortable; still, he would not apologize for his actions. Jake's priorities—honesty and squeaky clean ethics used to rank right there at the top—had undergone some reordering recently.

"You've had some rotten luck," Hughes said.

"You could call it that."

"Tell me about Michael's condition. You obviously think it's the result of genetic damage, or you wouldn't be interested in my research."

"Yes. I think Michael's developed an environmentally caused version of retinitis pigmentosa. Similar to Leber Congenital Amaurosis. The gene that makes the pigment necessary to perceive light has been destroyed. In naturally occurring Leber's disease, they're born without the gene. In Michael's case, something external destroyed it."

"Such as? Environmental pollution? Trauma?"

Jake shook his head. How many times had he asked himself those same questions?

"There was no trauma. At least none that any of us were aware of, which pretty much rules that out. An environmental mutagen's my guess, but I haven't come up with anything other than the fact that Michael's school was downwind from an American nuclear waste disposal facility. But in that case, you'd expect other incidents, and there were no other reports of vision impairment in other students or faculty."

"What about your son's general health? Family history?"

"Other than asthma, Michael's always been in excellent health. No familial history of any kind of eye problems." Jake shook his head in frustration. "This thing's a total mystery to me. Yet something did it. Something destroyed a gene that's key to Michael's sight."

"G31," Hughes murmured quietly, almost to himself. Then he bored his eyes into Jake. They could be cold eyes, piercing. "The gene Leber patients are missing. Researchers have tried to reinsert G31 from healthy eyes in Leber patients, but it hasn't restored their sight. But about a year ago, in dogs, they found what they believe to be a mutated version of G31. They call it G32."

Jake knew the canine research well.

During the months after Michael lost his sight, Jake and Ana had made a decision. They would do everything in their power to find a cure for Michael—everything *except* move to Seattle to work for Torrell Hughes. That, Ana believed, could push a depressed and fragile Michael over the edge. Ana had picked up most of Jake's medical practice so that Jake could focus on research.

But one name came up repeatedly in Jake's study of the literature about G32—Torrell Hughes. When Ana died and the rumors of her suicide (and her and Jake's troubled marriage) began flying, Jake had made a soul-tormenting decision. He knew that Ana's first priority—the most important thing in the world to her—was Michael's sight. He just hoped the therapist's assessment that Michael was strong enough for the move—that he might even benefit emotionally from it—was right. He'd called and asked Hughes if the offer of employment was still good.

"The canine version of G32 restored sight to two dogs at the NIH labs," Jake pitched in. "And there's no reason why a human version of G32 wouldn't do the same in humans. G32 displays a heightened sensitivity to light. If a similar gene exists in humans, we should be able to duplicate the success the NIH had with those two dogs."

"That's why you want in on my research."

Jake's jaw jutted forward determinedly.

"That's right."

In the prolonged silence that followed, a doom settled over Jake. Hughes knew the truth now. What would he do about it?

"Under any other circumstances, I'd fire you on the spot for not getting my clearance before conducting research on the DNA of one of your family members. Maybe I still should, but I respect what you're doing."

"The fact that this is personal to me," Jake replied without a hint of apology in his voice, "is your guarantee that I'll give this research my all."

"Oh, believe me," Hughes said, a strange glint in his eye, "I understand being personally motivated to find a cure."

Curious, Jake waited for Hughes to offer more, but instead Hughes went on, "But no one's ever been able to reverse genetically caused blindness in humans. Experiments have indicated that the delivery mechanism that worked in those two dogs won't be effective in humans. So even if we find the gene—a big *if*—we're a long way from curing your son's blindness. We still have to find a way to deliver the gene to the eye. It's never been done."

"Then I'll be the first. I'm not stupid, Torrell. I know why you wanted me to join your team. It wasn't hard to figure out. I'm hardly the cream of the crop for what you need. Before my son went blind, it had been years since I'd done any serious research. You wanted me on your team because I hold the patent on Tech System 47—which you tried to get me to hand over with that employment contract."

Hughes's eyes widened briefly.

"That's quite an accusation," he replied defensively, but the glint in his eye seemed to say he found humor in the situation. This was a game for Hughes.

"You really expected me to believe that charade about your not knowing that provision was in the contract?"

Hughes stared at Jake. Blatantly avoiding answering, he said, "I was a big fan of your father's. I followed his research."

"Then you know how he felt about patents."

"No, tell me."

Jake did not believe Hughes's feigned ignorance of Samuel Skully's views on patents. If he'd followed the elder Skully's research, he would know. Everyone who knew Samuel Skully knew he loathed patents.

"My father abhorred the expanded interpretation of the patent code," Jake said. "The USPTO's granting patents left and right on human materials—DNA, blood, cells, organs, embryos. My father fought it tooth and nail. He found it reprehensible that the system allows pharmaceutical companies to own rights to treatments that should be made available to everyone who needs them. Pharmaceutical researchers run around scarfing up human material like some indiscriminate vacuum, tying up all the rights and making sure that if there's a drug discovered in the process, they control who has access to it. Those who need it most, desperately ill patients, have only one option and that's to pay through the nose for it. That means the poor, or in many cases simply the uninsured, suffer, sometimes even die, when a perfectly effective treatment is available."

"How ironic, then, that your father chose to patent TS 47."

"My father knew how important TS 47 would be. It delivers genetic material from one human's cells to another, targeting with a specificity that other technology can't even touch. Coupled with the right genetic material, like G32, it has the potential to do miraculous things. My father patented it specifically to avoid its falling into the hands of pharmaceutical companies that would limit its use to patients able to pay sky-high fees. He wanted to be sure that anyone who needed the technology—especially the poor—would have it available. That was my father."

"And now that he's dead, that's your goal, too."

"My first goal is to make sure my son sees again. That takes priority over everything else. Even my father's wishes."

"I take it you don't think your father would approve of your coming to work for GenChrom?"

Jake did not answer right away. Ana's refusal to uproot the boys had kept him from accepting Hughes's first offers of employment; his father's distrust of companies like Mercy helped make Jake comfortable with that decision.

"If we can find G32," he finally replied slowly, thoughtfully, "I believe TS 47 will allow me to save Michael's sight—or at the very least, prevent him from passing his blindness on to his children. I would hope my father would approve of that."

Hughes's gaze zeroed in on Jake.

"If we find G32," he said, "GenChrom will acquire the patent to it. Just like you hold the patent to TS 47."

His message was clear. They each had something the other wanted. Jake could not cure Michael's blindness without G32. And in exchange, Hughes expected a piece of the patent on TS 47.

The door suddenly squeaked behind Jake. Hughes's dog jumped up, bumped clumsily into the corner of Hughes's desk and started toward Marilyn, who stood in the door's opening. With lightning quick reflexes Hughes jumped up and grabbed the dog by the collar.

"I told you not to interrupt us," Hughes snapped.

"It's Nelson Zimwe," Marilyn said. "He said it's important."

"We're just finishing up," Hughes said. "Tell him to wait a minute." He guided the dog back to its bed, next to his feet. When the dog settled back down, Hughes turned back to Jake.

"So," he said, his gaze more intense than ever. "It seems we've got all the cards on the table now, doesn't it?"

"Yes," Jake replied as he rose to leave. "I believe we do."

NELSON ZIMWE, ANOTHER RECENTLY HIRED RESEARCHER at GenChrom, nodded at Jake as he slipped past him, into Hughes's office. He carried a two-page document: a printout of an E-mail attachment he'd just received.

"What is it?" Hughes asked impatiently. "What's so important?"

He did not offer Nelson a seat.

Nelson hailed from Zaire. Like others from his country determined to make a better life, he'd come to the United States to receive a college education. Also like many of his countrymen, he'd left behind a family—a young wife and a baby girl—hoping that one day they would follow. Grants had enabled him to get an advanced degree, which led to a position on an NIH research team whose focus was the development of cancer drugs from plants found in the lush forests of third world countries. Then, when GenChrom took note of Nelson's promising research and offered him a job, again he stayed on, hoping that his wife, Samri, would soon join him. But after the World Trade Center tragedy, Samri refused to come to America. Nelson often spoke of his plan to return home someday—after he'd gained more valuable experience with medical botanicals—to provide for his family and help his people.

But now he announced that the plan had changed.

"I have come to tell you I must leave," he said to Hughes. "I am going home, to my wife and daughter. To my homeland."

He had Hughes's undivided attention now.

"Please, sit," Hughes said. "You can't mean this." Hughes had been counting on Nelson's expertise gained at the NIH. "What's this all about?"

Nelson's frail arm reached forward, offering the sheets of paper in his hand to Hughes.

"It's an article," he said. "From my wife. Her brother lives in Houston. He works for an oil company. This appeared in one of his newsletters and he sent it to Samri."

Hughes took the article and began to read:

Oil Exec Walks out of Jungle after Plane Crash

A plane bearing Alton Oil executives crashed on an exploratory trip to Brazil, killing the pilot and one of four Alton executives. CEO Arnold Browning survived the initial crash, along with two other, as yet unidentified, Alton employees; however, it took Browning almost two weeks to emerge from the dense, dangerous rain forest. With a broken leg, Browning finally managed to make his way to a settler's cabin, where help was radioed. The other Alton employees were not so fortunate. Browning told a tale of one man being crushed to death by a thirty-foot boa constrictor while Browning repeatedly battered the snake with a broken branch. The third employee died when the three were attacked by natives as they slept.

Along the way, Browning reported discovering the debris from another recent plane crash, a not uncommon occurrence in the dense forest.

Once his companions had both died, the only other person Browning came across during the entire two-week trip was a primitive lone native woman, who, surprisingly, had blue eyes.

This horrendous tale illustrates the dangers that our industry's personnel encounter on a regular basis in trying to locate oil to meet the world's energy needs.

"Samri," Nelson said in a thick, smooth accent, "she became hysterical when her brother sent her this. She insist now that I return home. Right away."

"But we need you for our next trip to the Amazon. That's why we hired you, to help us locate plants."

Nelson shook his head, his mind clearly made up.

"No, I cannot go. I had a dream. It told me to go home, to my family. They need me. My people, we listen to our dreams. I have been away too long. It is time for me to go home."

"You can't just do this to me," Hughes said angrily. "You have an employment contract."

Nelson stood erect, his gaze never faltering.

"No, I do not. In my country, we do not need to put our word on paper. You gave me the document, but I did not sign it."

Nelson rose.

"I am very sorry, Dr. Hughes. But this is the right thing for me to do."

His face screwed tight in puzzlement as he looked at Hughes.

"Dr. Hughes?"

Hughes's gaze had dropped back to the article. Were his eyes betraying him, or did Nelson detect a hint of a smile on his soon-to-be-ex boss's face?

When Hughes looked up, he almost seemed surprised to see Nelson still standing there.

With a waving motion, Hughes dismissed him, saying, "Do what you have to do."

Relieved, Nelson hurried out of the office, marveling at how well Hughes had taken the news of his departure.

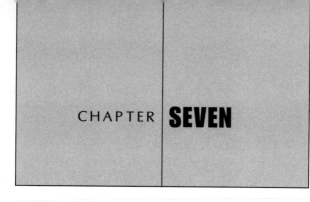

CHAPTER **SEVEN**

"I'M NOT COMING in today," Asahel said, mouth pressed to the phone while her eyes remained glued to the surreal sight on her kitchen floor.

"Are you sick?" Tammy Nguyen asked.

"Let's just say I'm having a bad day."

"What about the meeting with QA?"

Asahel grimaced.

"That was today?"

"Eleven o'clock."

She sighed.

"You'll have to call it off," Asahel said. "Reschedule it for tomorrow."

"What should I tell your father if he asks about you? Parker called and said he's planning to be at that meeting."

"Why would he want to be in on a meeting with Quality Affairs?"

"Got me."

"Well," Asahel said tersely, "tell him I'm sick. Tell him I'm dying." A short pause. "No, I'm just kidding. Just tell him I didn't feel well, but it's nothing serious. Whatever you do, don't alarm him. Understand?"

"What is it, Asahel? You sound really stressed."

"I'm fine, just fine. I just need a little time to myself, that's all."

Time to herself. Hardly. A half-starved, terrified woman sat huddled on her kitchen floor.

Asahel hung up the phone and for several seconds simply stared at her visitor, who had burrowed into the comforter Asahel had ripped off her bed when she saw her surprise visitor's arms and legs shaking. After Asahel wrapped it around her frail shoulders, the woman proceeded to disappear inside the blanket. At first Asahel saw only those amazing eyes—two buttons of blue sky—staring back at her, but now they, too, had retreated inside the cocoon.

The Amazonian greeting had gone only so far. Once Asahel got her visitor inside the kitchen, she had dropped to the floor and cowered next to the door—clearly her planned escape route—refusing Asahel's efforts to move her into the living room.

The hiss of boiling water drew Asahel's attention to the stove. She opened the cupboard and found what she was looking for. Tearing the two packets of hot chocolate open, she emptied the powder into mugs and poured the steaming water over it.

Suddenly Asahel flashed back to a morning three and one-half years earlier. Asahel sat by a fire, watching steam rise from a makeshift pan—a five-pound can of corn left by missionaries—as a Zubiyu Indian brewed Asahel *chaca*. Shaken by the memory, Asahel sidestepped to the next cupboard. An assortment of vitamins, minerals, and other supplements greeted her when she opened it. Asahel reached for a small tinted vial and withdrew a pretty blue capsule.

Today would not be a good day to skip her antidepressant.

The sweatpants she'd grabbed when she darted into her bedroom for a blanket for her visitor lay in a heap on the floor. Asahel eased her long limbs into them, her eyes back on her visitor, who had not moved.

Outside, the wind howled, blowing rain sideways across the deck. Asahel shuddered. At least she'd gotten her visitor out of the rain.

When the hot chocolate had cooled enough to drink, Asahel took both mugs and walked softly to the kitchen door. Lowering herself to the floor, she placed one mug on the linoleum, then reached out, offering the other.

"Here," she said quietly.

The eyes, dazzlingly blue, slowly appeared, peering over the fabric. They stared at Asahel's face, then shifted to the mug, its steam still rising, and stayed there.

"Drink it," Asahel said. "It will warm you."

Warily, a hand emerged from the folds. Asahel placed the mug in it. Then she picked up the other cup and slowly, deliberately, sipped from it.

"Now you."

Watching Asahel drink broke down the barriers. With shaky hands, the woman lifted the mug to her lips and drew the creamy liquid into her mouth. First tiny, cautious sips; then, as it cooled, long, greedy ones.

Asahel watched, her disbelief keeping stride with the growing sense of dread that had encompassed her since awaking to the extraordinary sight.

"Do you speak English?" Asahel asked, knowing, even before the words left her mouth, the stupidity of the question.

The woman stopped, midsip. Her eyes darting up to Asahel, she remained silent.

"Portuguese?" Asahel pressed.

Still no response.

"Wait right here," Asahel said, pointing to the floor for emphasis.

She sprinted into her bedroom, wondering, *Why am I running? Because I'm afraid she'll leave? Wouldn't that be the best thing that could possibly happen?* Still, as Asahel's eyes swept the books on her bedroom shelf, she hurried.

Where is it?

There. Asahel reached for a thin red volume and hurried back to the kitchen. Seated back on the floor, she opened the book, *English to Portuguese Dictionary*, and flipped to the *n*s.

Name. *Nome.*

"What is your *nome?*" she asked. Then, remembering some of the Spanish she'd learned in high school, she improvised, "Que es tu nome?"

The woman simply stared.

"I am Asahel," Asahel said, poking her index finger at her own chest. She repeated, *"Asahel,"* then pointed at the woman. "Ques es tu nome?"

Nothing.

Flipping from page to page, she went on, determined to get some response.

"How did you get here? Como tu viajar here?

"Que tu queira?"

But none of her butchered questions—part English, part Spanish, part Portuguese—evoked any reaction other than a wary stare.

Asahel's voice began to rise with her frustration.

"What do you want?" she pleaded. "Why are you here?"

The blankness of the woman's stare caused Asahel to suddenly snap.

She reached out and grabbed her by her shoulders.

"Talk to me, dammit. *Talk to me.* Do you realize how dangerous this is?"

A look of absolute terror in the woman's eyes brought Asahel to her senses.

"God, I'm sorry," she moaned, letting go of the frail frame. "I'm so sorry. How could you possibly know?"

The comforter had fallen open. Suddenly Asahel spotted something inside its cocoon.

"What's this?"

She reached for the small dark bundle she'd seen the woman clutching.

The woman shrank back against the door, shook her head no and tightened her grasp.

"I'll give it back," Asahel said, her eyes meeting the woman's, prevailing upon her to trust Asahel. When she did not relinquish her grip, Asahel jerked the bundle from the bony hand.

The woman drew a breath in sharply.

"I'll give it back," Asahel repeated.

It was a pouch, made of some kind of animal hide, tough and crude and drawn together at the top with a string, also fashioned, Asahel knew, of something once living. She could feel several hard chunks of something inside but little else.

Asahel pried it open by inserting two fingers inside, turned it upside down, then gasped when its contents fell into her open palm.

Diamonds.

Three large, dazzling stones.

"Where did you get these? They're worth a fortune."

The woman looked on in fear as Asahel rolled them in her hand, fingering them. She held them up to the light. Hard, rough-edged. Like something just hacked from the earth. Where had they come from?

And why would this frail woman be carrying them around in a pouch?

One thing was clear. Asahel wasn't getting any answers out of her.

She knew what she should do. Call the police. Legally, Asahel had an obligation to.

That's right; that's just what she would do. This wasn't her problem; it was an immigration thing.

Resolved to make the call, Asahel began dropping the stones back in the pouch, one by one. But on the third, she noticed something inside the pouch, stuck up against its wall.

A square of paper, old and weathered, its corners frayed by time and handling.

Asahel reached inside and pulled it out. The feeling of dread, the premonition of doom, hit her even before she could read the worn-out print on its surface.

Actually, she didn't really even need to read it. She knew what it said. Her first glimpse of it had already brought back a flood of memories, so vivid and painful that Asahel let out a small moan.

A business card.

She stared at it, then mechanically put the card back in the pouch, along with the nuggets, and handed it back to the woman.

She could not call the police.

Deep down, she'd known that all along.

"THIS IS COMING SOONER than I'd expected," Jake said.

Torrell Hughes had summoned him to his office before lunch. Jake assumed that Hughes wanted to go over Jake's protocol for using gene-sequencing analysis to detect the point mutation he believed responsible for Michael's blindness. Jake had succeeded in isolating the mutation and had been anxious to share his findings with Hughes. He was anxious, as well, to get Hughes's input.

But Hughes quickly announced another agenda.

"I told you this job would mean travel to the Amazon," Hughes said. He'd brought his dog into the office with him again. The pup seemed even more subdued than the last time Jake saw it. "We leave next week. With any luck, we'll be having one of the nation's leading experts on the genetic makeup of Amazonian tribes join us. Terrance du Pont."

Jake could hear only one thing. That Hughes expected him to leave his two sons.

"But I haven't had time to make provisions for Michael and Antony."

"I knew that would be a concern for you, so I took the liberty . . ."

As if on cue, the door behind Jake opened and a low, sexy voice said, "Looks like the World Summit's taking place in here."

Jake turned to see who'd joined them.

"Here she is now," Hughes said. "She's finally returned after a month in Rio, which tells me I must be paying her too much. Leah Clay, meet Jake Skully."

"Nice to meet you," Leah said, extending a hand. To Hughes she said, quite pleasantly, "You pay me exactly what I'm worth, no more, no less."

Clay's appearance epitomized the classic Seattle businesswoman, which, to Jake's mind, was not necessarily a desirable thing. He'd loved Ana's voluptuousness, which was typical of Mexican women. Leah Clay looked anorexic. She had no noticeable breasts. Dark, severely styled hair, cut blunt at the chin, framed a face devoid of makeup. She wore closely fitted black pants and a white camisole covered with a see-through white linen blouse, which she'd tied at the waist. Jake wondered when she'd had her last good meal. Or a beer.

But she did sport a nice tan, no doubt from Rio, and an inviting smile.

"Nice to meet you, too," Jake answered.

"Leah," Hughes said, "I called you in because Jake has boys about the same age as that nephew of yours. I thought maybe you could help him find a sitter for our trip to the Amazon."

"Really?" Clay said, turning to study Jake. "How old are your boys?"

"Thirteen and seven."

"Do they play soccer?"

The question stabbed Jake in the heart. Michael had been the star of his sixth-grade team.

"Antony, my youngest, does."

"My nephew lives and breathes it. He's eleven. We'll have to get them together and see if they hit it off. In fact . . ." She turned to Hughes. "When are you leaving?"

"The tenth."

"You're kidding. Jason's mom's in the army reserve. She's been called up for a week's duty, starting the eleventh. Jason's staying with me. It would be great to have your boys, too, to keep him entertained."

"I couldn't do that," Jake said.

"Why on earth not?"

"I just couldn't," Jake replied. "You see, my oldest, Michael, is blind."

Leah exchanged glances with Hughes.

"I heard. I'm sorry. But I don't see what that has to do with it. Surely he goes to school?"

"Yes, of course. But he's already going through so much. It would be unfair for me to leave him now, not only to Michael, but to you, too."

At this, Hughes broke in.

"You're not saying you can't go along on this trip?"

Jake felt the beads of perspiration on his brow and top lip. The boys had just begun feeling settled in the new apartment, used to their new routine. Michael had even softened a bit with him these past few days. To leave them now . . .

"I don't see how I can," Jake answered.

Hughes stiffened in his chair.

"Well then, let me put it this way," he said. "You signed on as part of this team. The team's going to Brazil."

Jake stood his ground.

"I may not be able to go, Torrell."

"In that case, hand in your resignation."

Stunned, Jake sat opposite Hughes, his head and heart spinning out of control. He had not only promised Ana that he would make Michael see again; he'd now promised Michael. But the cost to do so . . . leaving his two sons now, so soon after Ana's death, and in a new city.

"You can't mean that," Jake said, unable to hide the anguish in his voice.

"I'm afraid I do."

A bitter hatred of Torrell Hughes was born in Jake at that instant. The man was a monster. It was clear from his expression that he knew the soul-wrenching dilemma he had put Jake in. And equally clear that he did not care.

Suddenly Jake felt a tug at the sleeve of his shirt. He turned to look at Leah.

"Please," she said softly. "Reconsider. Your boys will do fine with me. I'll take great care of them. I love kids."

Jake trained angry eyes on Hughes.

"How long will we be gone?"

"Until we find what we're looking for. And if it's any comfort to you, we'll have a satellite phone with us. You can call your kids whenever you want to check on them."

Greatly appeased by that notion—the news that he would be able to talk to Michael and Antony from Brazil—Jake turned back to Leah.

"Are you available for dinner tonight? I'd like to have you meet the boys. Then we can go from there."

"Yes," Leah replied. "I'm available. And I think that's a very good idea."

JAKE USUALLY ATE LUNCH at the office, but after his meeting with Hughes, he went directly to his car.

He headed up Queen Anne, not knowing where he was going, just knowing he could not stay in that building a moment longer.

At the top of the hill, he turned west, slowly negotiating the narrow road lined on either side with parked cars. He did not notice the homes with million-dollar price tags due to their spectacular views of the city and Elliott Bay. ,

At the end of the street, the road dead-ended at a park.

He got out and walked to an empty bench.

Staring out at this city, this place, that was so unlike the world he had known with Ana, an ache, an emptiness, gripped him.

What do I do now, Ana?

A dog ran up to the bench, sniffed at Jake, then, nose to the ground, continued pursuing its trail. Birds sang; a distant horn signaled the approach of a ferry below.

Jake had never felt so miserable, or so alone.

What would Ana want him to do? How could he leave Michael and Antony alone in this new city?

How could he not?

Why did you leave me, Ana?

He groaned, and dropped his head into his hands.

Wait. What was that? Despite his denials, despite his telling himself time and time again that Ana had been murdered, deep down did he believe she'd done just what the police said? That Ana had chosen to leave him, leave the boys? That she'd committed suicide?

Jake lifted his head. A woman walking a small dog nearby had been looking at him, but now she looked away.

No. He did not believe that. He could not. Ana would never have done such a thing. No matter how angry and hurt she was, she would never leave Jake to make such soul-wrenching decisions alone about Michael and Antony. She just wouldn't.

But there was that envelope.

The envelope haunted him.

She'd made his name large, and beautiful—Ana's way with everything. What was she feeling when she wrote it? Had she already finished the letter meant to be inside? If so, had she destroyed it?

Or had she started with the envelope?

What did you write, my dear Ana?

What did you plan to tell me?

"MORE BLOOD?"

Gina Castle's expression made it perfectly clear what answer she hoped for, but that's not what she got.

Torrell Hughes replied with a nod of his head.

"Yep. Here's some preliminary information for you. To save you time once I get back."

He tossed a thin manila file onto her crowded desk.

"Damn, Torrell," Castle muttered, pulling self-consciously at the hem of her skirt. "I haven't finished the filings on the blood from your last time down there. After that trip, you said you thought you'd find what you were looking for in the samples you brought back."

"Well, we didn't," Hughes replied sharply. "And something new has come up. We leave in a few days. I'd suggest you get those other filings in order, because I want to move on the samples I bring back from this trip the minute I return."

"How can we file before we have an indication?"

"Read the file. I've set out the indications."

"Before you've even gotten your hands on the blood? You act like you're trying to beat someone to filing."

Exactly, thought Hughes. How many others had heard accounts of a blue-eyed native in rain forests of the state of Acre? Had his nemesis? If so, every single day counted. But Gina Castle did not need to know that.

"That's ridiculous," he said. "I just don't want to take chances."

"You're not being straight with me, Torrell. Do you actually think I don't know you well enough by now to know that?"

"Back off, will you? I don't need the third-degree treatment from *my attorney*." He said the words with disdain. "And keep this trip to yourself. We're telling everyone we're going back east, to the NIH."

"Oh, that's great," Castle said, her round cheeks flushing with indignation. "That's all I am? Your attorney? It just so happens that I'm the one putting my neck on the line here, and you don't even show me the respect of giving me a straight answer. That's just perfect."

"They've granted the other patents, haven't they?" Hughes replied. "You're getting uptight about nothing."

"But what about informed consents?"

"I told you. I've got a stack of them. Brought back two dozen the last trip to Peru."

"I don't even want to know how you got those," Castle said. "If they ever decide to investigate, to match up our consents with the blood we're patenting, I could lose my license. Or worse."

"How many times do I have to tell you?" Hughes asked, slamming a flattened palm against the side of Castle's desk, which sent cold coffee flying from the Styrofoam cup on its surface.

He loved to intimidate Castle. Simply couldn't resist it, in fact. And he was convinced that in her own perverted way, Castle actually liked it.

Before deciding to become a patent lawyer, Gina Castle had attended a seminary in Charleston, South Carolina. She wanted to become a minister, help save mankind. But somewhere along the way, the heavyset, plain daughter of antiabortion activists had a change of heart. Desperate for male attention, she'd also ended up having two abortions in the decade since she passed the Washington State bar exam. It was this trait—her desperation to be loved—that Torrell Hughes had picked up on during Castle's employment interview. In this business, what would come in more handy than an attorney just begging to be exploited? Gina would do just about anything for Hughes. Including enduring his abuse.

Castle's small brown eyes suddenly filled with tears.

"Don't get angry with me. Please. I just want you to confide in me, tell me the truth. You said we were partners in this. This whole thing frightens me, Torrell."

Hughes sensed that he'd gone a bit too far. He couldn't risk alienating Castle, not when he desperately needed her cooperation.

He took a deep breath and forced a smile.

"I've told you, many times. Nobody's paying any attention to us. Nobody gives a damn what a small, privately held company like GenChrom is doing. At least not yet. And that's just how we want it."

Castle sniffled and said, "I hope you're right."

She patted the file that Hughes had dropped on her desk.

"I'll start in on this right away," she promised. Then she turned saucer eyes on him. "Do you have time to run to Tully's for a latte?"

Hughes stood and looked at his watch. It was the last thing he wanted to do. In fact, if someone had given him the choice of time alone with Gina Castle or a root canal, he'd be in the dentist's chair in a heartbeat, but maybe half an hour now would buy him a reprieve from the night together Castle had been pushing for. Six months had passed since their last tryst. He was shooting for a year.

"Sure," he said.

Castle's grin carved a dimple in the middle of each puffy cheek.

Jumping up, she tugged at her skirt one more time, then grabbed her black-and-white cowhide purse from the top right drawer of her desk and followed Hughes eagerly out the door, her conscience and professional worries temporarily assuaged.

CHAPTER **EIGHT**

YOU'VE GOT TO help me, Toby. I can't get involved with this kind of thing."

A lock of Asahel's copper-colored hair trailed across the foam topping her cappucino as she leaned across the small metal table.

Toby Fuentes, an old friend and former coworker, reached over and brushed her hair out of the cup. Lanky and lean and wearing his trademark jeans and leather jacket, the only thing that had changed about Fuentes was the gray now streaking his long brown hair, which he'd tied back in a ponytail.

"Take it easy, Ash," he said. "You know I'll do what I can." He studied her for a moment. "Do you know how good it is to see you stirred up about something again? How good it is to *see you*, period? You promised you'd stay in touch."

Ash looked away. She remembered making Toby that promise. A promise she knew she'd never keep.

"I couldn't. I'm sorry."

"That's okay," Fuentes said. "I suspected you wouldn't. I knew you needed to move on. That's why I didn't pester you. But I've missed the hell out of you."

"I've missed you, too," Asahel said.

They were on the top floor of the REI building in Seattle—an outdoors equipment store just down the block from the IPAF offices, where Toby worked. Asahel had suggested it as a meeting place because it was far enough away from the GenChrom offices that the chances of a coworker seeing her, especially this time of day, were almost nonexistent. They'd chosen a window table at the restaurant there, which, on a nice day, would have given them a fabulous view of the downtown skyline, but a light drizzle oozed from a dense cover of low clouds outside, obscuring all the building tops. The gray outside blended quite nicely with the cold starkness of the restaurant's cement floors and dark steel tables, most of which were empty.

Asahel waited for the apron-clad waitress striding toward them to deposit their orders before telling Toby her news.

With a plate of nachos between them on the table, she finally disclosed to Fuentes her reason for calling him.

"I have a visitor."

Fuentes looked only mildly interested.

"Who? From where?"

Asahel shook her head.

"I never saw her before yesterday morning. I woke up to find her on my deck. She doesn't speak English. She's from the Amazon, Toby. I'm sure of it. And something terrible has happened to her. I can see it in her eyes. And they're a brilliant blue. Do you remember that tribe I told you and Angie about, after I came home from my trip? The one with blue eyes? It was so striking. The only blue eyes I ever saw down there."

"I remember. We looked them up, but no one had seen them since the early nineteen-hundreds."

"That's right. Even the Lost Tribes Project classified them as probably extinct."

At the talk of their shared past, Toby's eyes brightened. He became the Toby Asahel once knew. He reached over and grabbed her by the hand.

"Do you remember those days, Ash? Do you remember the excitement? The passion?"

"Those were dangerous days, Toby."

He smiled, a sad, nostalgic smile.

"You never seemed to mind. In fact, as I seem to recall, you thrived on it. You said that it only drew more attention to the cause, that it only stood to gain sympathy and strengthen public support."

The admiration in Fuentes's voice was unmistakable. It cut through Asahel.

Had she actually been like that at one time? Someone that a person like Fuentes looked up to?

Suddenly the memories Asahel had fought so hard to suppress came rolling like windblown tumbleweed through her mind. She felt helpless to stop them, especially when Fuentes said, "Remember NIH?"

Asahel nodded.

"You could've died that day," Fuentes said.

"We both could have," Asahel replied.

•   •   •

As THE LINE of police pressed nearer—near enough for Asahel to see the anger in their eyes, through the thick plastic masks of their riot gear; near enough, thought Asahel, for their batons to do plenty of damage—she tightened her grasp on the hands on each side of her.

"No provocation," she said, keeping her voice low, her eyes never shrinking from the glares of those approaching, many of which were fixed on her. "Pass it along."

"No provocation," echoed down the line from her right.

"No provocation," from the left, rippling its way along the human chain encircling the research center of the National Institutes of Health. A chain one hundred strong, by Asahel's estimation, gathered to protest the meeting taking place inside. A meeting of scientists and pharmaceutical execs from corporations across the world. Asahel wondered briefly whether her father had slipped by—avoiding, as usual, any contact with the radical daughter to whom he had not spoken in almost a decade—and whether Philip Esser now sat inside, a renowned and esteemed figurehead in a world of corporate depravity and greed. The thought empowering her, she lifted her head higher, her fine-boned jaw jutting out defiantly.

"Looks like the bitch with the red hair's in charge," she heard one of the blue-uniformed policeman say.

Asahel's eyes swept slowly along the faces of those approaching, momentarily daring them to use their batons, though in truth, she had vowed to avoid violence. What she saw was a whole gamut of emotions on the faces—mostly young, in their twenties and thirties—staring her down. Contempt, confusion, amusement. Concern. She'd seen it all before. She let her gaze come to rest upon a black officer. Hair graying at the temples, a neat mustache. Kind eyes. He did not want to be there. Asahel could see that. He did not want anyone to be injured. As an older officer, he would most likely have more rank than the overzealous-looking recruits on either side of him. Asahel knew that if she made a connection with him, he might just be the one to stop the mace or, worse, the use of those batons.

"This is a peaceful protest," Asahel said, locking eyes with him.

He did not respond, but neither did he avert his eyes.

"The people inside this building are supposed to be saving lives, not endangering them," she said, trying again.

At that moment, a loud crackle emanated from two giant speakers that workers had been scrambling to set up. A voice followed, its volume over the loudspeakers deafening.

"This is Police Chief Daniel Grable. I am ordering you protesters to disband. The meeting inside is about to adjourn and participants are to be allowed to leave without any harassment or obstruction of their pathways. Any person who violates this order will be arrested. Is that clear? We will tolerate no harassment of the departing participants. No harassment whatsoever."

Asahel's eyes drifted beyond the police, to the sign flung over the roof of the neighboring white brick building. It flapped wildly in the wind that had kicked up only minutes earlier. As she'd stood in line for the past two hours, chanting, singing, being interviewed by Andrea Tinkham, the local anchorwoman—a beautifully dressed, gauntly thin woman with intelligent eyes—she'd watched the storm clouds rolling slowly in from the coast.

Pharmaceutical biopirates don't kill, they patent, read a huge banner that hung from the top of the building, thanks to the skills of several activists who also happened to be mountaineers. Asahel had helped string another one, a banner she painstakingly made back in Seattle, between the branches of two leafy oaks. This one read: *Mercy Pharmaceuticals: putting profit over human lives*

Most protests, like WTO the year before in Seattle, focused on blockading meeting participants from ever entering the forum. The decision to form the human chain to prevent the scientists and pharmaceutical execs inside from leaving *after* their meeting had been Asahel's. Pharmaceutical execs, she knew only too well, were downright paranoid about being associated with charges that their actions endangered the very public—the very market—they claimed to be dedicated to helping. Any sign of protest before the meeting would have sent them scurrying, like barn rats when the lights suddenly snap on. IPAF didn't want that. They wanted all America, all the TV cameras that day, to see the faces, the name tags bearing company logos, behind the corporations that put the lives and health of those who bought these same products, as well as innocent indigenous peoples from around the world, at risk.

She could still see Andrea Tinkham, several yards behind the police line. The newswoman's back was to the group as she spoke into a microphone, KVMI cameras rolling. Off to the right, Asahel could also see Anise, stationed a safe distance away, ready to catch any action on her video cam. Frail, dear Anise always wanted to be part of the action, but due to her health she was usually relegated to the role of videographer. Asahel had assured her that it was an important role. The media was selective about what it aired—especially if one of its corporate advertisers happened to be a pharmaceutical company, which these days was inevitable. IPAF couldn't trust KVMI's cameramen or news team to show, or even catch on video, the right excerpts of speeches or the sporadic police hostility and aggression while the demonstrators adhered to an oath of complete nonviolence. That was left to Anise and two other IPAF videographers.

As the main door to the NIH research facility opened behind her and the lead group of conference participants, surrounded by police guard, emerged, Asahel, who had placed herself dead center in the sidewalk leading from the building to the parking lot, had a vivid premonition that Anise and the others would get an eyeful today.

"You heard Chief Grable," the black officer said directly to Asahel. "Please, miss, step aside."

When Asahel and the protesters on either side of her—Toby Fuentes on her left and Arch Davis, from San Francisco, on her right—did not budge, a young blue-eyed officer directly in front of Asahel said, "Let's use pepper spray."

"Not until Grable gives the order," the black officer answered, staring straight ahead now, avoiding Asahel's green eyes.

"This is bullshit," the other shot back. "I'm breaking through."

Lifting his baton, holding it horizontally in front of him with outstretched arms, elbows locked, the officer stepped forward.

Asahel braced herself.

The baton appeared headed for her shoulders, but at the last second the officer lifted his hands and Asahel took all of its blunt force in her larynx. Reflexively, she let go her grasp of the hands on either side of her. Clutching at her throat, from which radiated a pain so thick and terrifying that it alone—the pain—rendered her nearly unconscious, she gasped for air. But it would not come.

"You sick fuck," she heard Toby shout. She could feel him beside her, lunging at the officer, but unable to breathe, she fell to the sidewalk.

"Stand aside," she heard someone say. The next instant, she heard the sickening crunch of wood meeting skull. Toby let out an animal-like moan before collapsing to the sidewalk next to her.

All hell had broken loose. Complete chaos.

As Asahel felt herself losing consciousness, she actually found herself wondering fleetingly whether Anise was getting all the action on tape.

She became aware of Arch, trying to lift her from the pavement. But a hand grabbed him by the shoulder, pushing him away.

"We've got to clear her air passage."

It was the black officer. Asahel recognized him as he dropped to his knees beside her.

His round, scowling, distressed face was all she saw at first. Her vision ebbed and flowed like afternoon waves on Alki Beach. But just before her world went completely blank, Asahel Esser thought she saw something else. Another face, looking over the officer's shoulder.

The face of her father. Philip Esser.

"EARTH TO ASH," Fuentes chided. "Where the hell did you just go?"

Asahel shook her head, trying to clear it of the past.

"I was just thinking about that day. The NIH protest."

"They're still happening, Ash. We still need you. We need your passion. Your courage."

Asahel looked him dead in the eye and said, "We both know courage is one thing I'm sadly lacking."

Fuentes's eyes drilled back into Asahel's.

"Then why don't you prove us both wrong?"

"We've been there before, Toby. Let's not go there again now. I need your help with this woman. I can't handle this, especially now."

Fuentes studied her, clearly weighing the situation.

"You're absolutely sure she's Amazonian?"

Asahel nodded, relieved.

"How do you suppose she found you?" Toby asked, leaning toward her, his focus now totally upon the story unfolding.

Asahel reached into the pocket of her tan fleece vest and pulled out what looked like a business card.

She handed it to Fuentes. It was weathered; its letters—superimposed over the image of two hands clasped together, one dark-skinned, the other pale—were faded, some barely readable. Fuentes took it and, squinting, read out loud: "*Asahel Sullivan, Fifth and Roy, Seattle, WA 98102.*"

His brow creased into a deep scowl.

"What's this?" he said.

"It's a card I had made for my trip to the Amazon five years ago."

"The trip you made for IPAF?"

"Yes." She nodded.

Fuentes nodded slowly, knowingly.

"Now I remember. IPAF's policy forbade us from giving out personal information. The brochure they wanted you to leave with the tribes you visited only listed the D.C. office address and phone number."

"That's right. I argued with them about it. Told them no matter what happened, no native would ever be able to work up the nerve to contact some big, faceless organization in Washington, D.C."

"But they wouldn't budge, so you had your own card made up. Something friendly," Fuentes said, eyeing the clasped hands. "Something you could leave there, in case anyone got in trouble and needed help."

"Exactly."

"And this woman's in trouble."

Asahel sighed.

"Big trouble. She's like a frightened animal. I can't even get near her without her flinching. She's seen something, Toby. Something awful."

"What do you suppose it was?"

"I don't know," Asahel replied.

She'd tried to find out. Tried to talk to her visitor, using sign language and drawings.

Asahel had drawn a stick figure to represent herself; then she'd poked her index finger at her own chest.

"Me," she'd declared. *"Asahel."*

She also drew her apartment, including its view of the Space Needle, which clearly fascinated the other woman.

Finally she'd pushed a blank sheet of paper and a pen in front of the other woman, pointing at her.

"Now *you*," she'd said with exaggerated enunciation. "Tell me about *your* life, *your* home."

She'd pointed then at the paper.

The woman understood.

Slowly, tentatively, she'd picked up the pen and placed its tip on the paper. But it did not move. Instead, in the next instant, the pen dropped from the woman's trembling hands.

She covered her eyes and began moaning. A sound so guttural, so full of grief and despair, that Asahel had instinctively turned her face to the wall, a pathetic attempt to give her visitor privacy.

Asahel had scrambled to the phone and called Toby.

"Are you still with Stan?" she asked him now. "Can he talk to her?"

Stan was Toby's partner. He was also a linguistics professor at the University of Washington. He'd volunteered his skills numerous times to help at IPAF.

"We're still together," Toby answered. He paused. "Now I see why you called me. Stan can probably communicate with her, find out what happened. What made her come all the way to Seattle to find you."

Asahel studied Fuentes closely.

"That's not the only reason I called, Toby. I need for you to take her. Take her in."

"Me?" Fuentes said, his eyebrows raised in amazement. "Let me get this straight. She comes to you for help, because—in violation of IPAF's rules—you gave her this card and basically *told* her to. But now you're just going to turn her over to me?"

"I didn't mean you; I mean IPAF," Asahel said, immediately on the defense. "You know I have no choice."

"And you obviously know we'd never turn her away," Fuentes replied. He was angry; Asahel could see it, hear it in his voice. "But you *do* have a choice, Ash. Don't kid yourself."

"You're wrong, Toby. I can't get involved. I won't let her stay with me. Not for long."

"You can't live like this, Ash," Fuentes said testily. "In constant fear of your father."

"Don't you tell me how I can or cannot live," Asahel snapped at him. "Who are you to judge me?"

Toby's only response was his silent stare.

"Are you going to help me or not?"

"I'll talk to Stan," Fuentes finally said. "But finding her someplace to stay may take time. Like it nor not, you might have to keep her for a while."

He eyed her disapprovingly.

"After all, you're the reason she's here, aren't you?"

CHAPTER **NINE**

YOU PROMISE IT'LL only be a couple of weeks?"

As he stared down into Antony's huge, wet eyes, Jake realized that he still had enough of his heart left for it to break.

"I can't promise you that," Jake said, kissing the shock of dark hair at Antony's forehead. "All I can promise you is that I'm going to work really, really hard so that I can come back home as soon as possible. And listen to this: I'll be able to talk to you. Dr. Hughes is bringing a satellite phone, which means I can call you whenever I want."

"Every day?" Antony wanted to know.

"Well, probably not every day, but I'll call often. I promise."

"Hey, butthead," Michael said to his little brother. "There's nothing to cry about. We're gonna have fun with Dad gone."

Jake glanced at Michael.

Michael had exhibited no reaction at all to the news Jake would be going to South America, nor to the announcement that he and Antony would stay with Leah Clay while Jake was gone.

Jake reached out to ruffle Michael's hair.

"You sure this is okay with you?"

It didn't matter that Michael could not see. He looked back at Jake with pure contempt.

"Why wouldn't it be?" Michael said. "We're okay without Mom. We can be okay without you."

"No," Antony cried. "This isn't like Mama." He looked up at Jake, his eyes full of fear. "Is it?"

Jake sat down on the bed and pulled Antony onto his lap.

"Of course it's not. I'll be back. Soon."

Jake glared right back at Michael. He wanted to both hug and spank him.

"Michael, I don't want to hear you say another word like that. Do you hear?"

Michael stood, rigid, in the doorway to Antony's bedroom.

"You're the reason Mom did it."

"Stop it, Michael."

"You're the reason she's dead. You know it, too."

Antony whimpered in Jake's lap, burying his head in his shoulder. *"That's enough."*

"That's what the police said she said in that letter. They say you took it. You didn't want them to read it. You don't want to admit it was your fault."

Jake gently lifted Antony off his lap, deposited him on the bed, and walked over to where Michael stood.

He grabbed Michael by the chin.

"One more word like that and . . ."

"And what?"

Suddenly, deflated, Jake dropped his hand. His shoulders drooping, he turned back toward Antony.

But Michael wasn't done.

"Maybe I won't be here when you come back."

A fear so basic and instinctive that it threatened his very survival struck Jake.

He whirled around and grabbed Michael by the shoulders.

"What do you mean?"

Michael's chin jutted defiantly.

"Maybe I'll do the same thing Mama did."

"Michael, stop this. It's killing me. And Antony."

"You don't care."

"Of course I care."

"If you cared you wouldn't do what you did."

"I care, Michael. I care more than anything in the world. You and Antony, you're everything to me. Everything."

Suddenly Jake saw tears form in Michael's eyes.

"Then why are you leaving?" Michael whimpered. "And why can't I see?"

When Jake crushed him to his chest, Michael did not fight him.

"I can't answer why you can't see," Jake replied.

If only he could. Jake had gone over those few weeks a thousand times. One morning Michael stumbled clumsily into a kitchen chair; two weeks later, he was totally blind. No one could explain it—not Jake, not Ana, not the specialists they took Michael to.

What Jake wouldn't give to be able to answer that one question for his son.

"But I can answer why I'm leaving," Jake continued. "I'm doing it for you, Michael. I'm doing it so that you can see again. So that you can have your life back . . . And I'm doing it for your mother."

Silent sobs shook Michael's shoulders.

"I loved your mother more than life itself," Jake said quietly. "I miss her so much I can hardly stand it."

He stroked Michael's back, kissed the hair on his head.

"Promise me, Michael. Promise me you'll be safe while I'm gone."

Michael nodded.

"Say it. I have to hear it."

"I promise."

Jake closed his eyes, fought back his own tears.

JAKE'S PLANE WAS LEAVING the next morning at 7:00 A.M., but since he needed as much time together with the boys as possible, he let them both stay up late.

The shocking words he'd spoken earlier seemed to have softened Michael, drained him of his fight.

After eating a pizza, Michael and Antony climbed into Jake's king-size bed. They'd rented *Dumb and Dumber* on the way home from the grocery store. Michael had already seen it, before he lost his sight. He laughed along with Jake and Antony, and for once, his frosty demeanor with Jake seemed to thaw. In fact, when Antony dozed off beside Michael he climbed over Antony, then Jake, and nestled in next to Jake, on the side opposite Antony. Finally, just past midnight, Michael, too, fell asleep.

Jake lay with one arm around each son all night long. Listening to their gentle breaths coming in and going out, studying their faces in the dim light that filtered through the window curtains, covering them back up when they kicked aside the blanket.

He did not allow himself to sleep. He did not want to miss a single moment with his sons.

Right now, in his sleep, Antony still looked like the little cherub he'd been before they left Nogales. But more and more lately, Jake had noticed changes. Antony had grown half an inch, and those chubby cheeks had hollowed out some. How Ana had loved to plant big, wet kisses on those cheeks.

And Michael. Michael had grown even more handsome. He'd always been the more somber of the two, even before all the tragedy. But now, in his sleep, he appeared at peace.

At just past four, Jake slid out from under the covers, out from between Michael and Antony.

It was the hardest thing he had ever done.

ASAHEL SCANNED THE MEETING room with relief. At the head of the long conference table sat Robert Darcey, Director of Quality Affairs. Hilde Oldham, an independent consultant hired to walk Mercy through FDA compliance, was seated at his left and Ilya Omani, one of Mercy's top scientists, on his right. Two lower-level employees, most likely interns or assistants, both of whom Asahel had seen in the hallways before, filled out the rest of the table. No sign of her father.

Asahel took the only available seat, at the end, opposite Darcey.

"Morning," Asahel said all around as she hoisted her briefcase to the table's surface and began rummaging for the itinerary she'd prepared. Darcey had gotten wind of a planned FDA "surprise" visit to Mercy's manufacturing facilities, which was to take place within the next month, and passed it along to Asahel. Darcey and Asahel had never gotten along particularly well, but when it came to matters of company loyalty or devotion, Asahel could count on Darcey to go the extra mile.

Mercy couldn't afford any negative findings by the FDA, especially the sort that could result in heavy fines or, worse, a disruption of manufacturing of any of their drugs. While everyone at the table already knew what had really prompted this meeting, all official communications—the meeting invitations, agenda, and minutes—would label it a routine "status update" meeting.

Asahel passed copies of the itinerary she'd had Tammy Nguyen prepare to everyone seated at the table.

"I apologize for any inconvenience it caused to reschedule yesterday's meeting," she said.

"No problem," Darcey said, pleasantly enough. And then, "Must've been one hell of a sale at REI."

Asahel felt the blood rise to her face.

"I'm sorry?" she said, as though she hadn't quite heard Darcey correctly.

"My wife said she saw you at REI yesterday, with some long-haired hippie guy. Must've been a good sale if it was worth missing a scheduled meeting for."

Asahel had always believed the old adage about one lie leading to a dangerous web of deceit, but recent events had her so jumpy she instinctively ignored it.

"Your wife must have been mistaken," she replied. "I was home sick yesterday."

She might have convinced Darcey had it not been for the shade of pink her cheeks had now turned. Her visible discomfort only served to egg Darcey on.

"That's really odd, 'cause Lauren met you at the company Christmas party and she just swore it was you. She said you two looked pretty cozy. New boyfriend?"

"I don't know what you're talking about, Robert. I never left the house yesterday."

Darcey's eyes danced with merriment at Asahel's obvious embarrassment, then shifted to the doorway, immediately behind Asahel, and remained fixed there, as did those of the others sitting at the table.

A sense of dread filled Asahel as she turned to see what the distraction was.

Philip Esser stood, somber-faced, his eyes on Asahel even before she'd fully turned to face him.

"Good morning," Asahel said, turning quickly back to the table, where she buried her face in her papers. Still, she had no doubt that her father had noticed her embarrassment. She could feel the heat still radiating from her skin. Esser had always teased her mercilessly about the ease with which she blushed, its telltale nature.

Esser declined the seat offered him by Darcey, choosing to stand against the wall during the first fifteen minutes of the meeting. He did not say a single word, but Asahel could feel his eyes on her. She didn't have to see him to know how piercing they were, how unrelenting. Thank God for the itinerary she'd prepared, for she was so distracted by Esser's presence that the meeting would have been a disaster without it.

She managed to conduct the meeting, orchestrate Mercy's plan for explicit FDA compliance, in spite of her preoccupation, in spite of the one thought that played itself over and over again in her mind, even long after Philip Esser slipped out of the room.

Just how long had her father been standing in the door before the start of the meeting? How much had he heard?

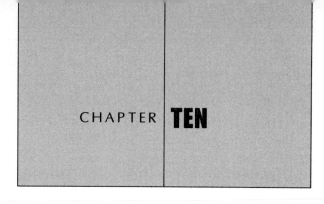

CHAPTER **TEN**

JAKE HAD NEVER been good at dozing on planes, but as he strode down Sea-Tac's international terminal, it was the one thing he looked forward to—boarding the plane and dropping off to sleep. For the way he saw it, sleep was his only hope of escaping—even if only temporarily—the mental torment of leaving his sons, the bitter anguish caused by Michael's veiled threat.

Jake considered the dilemma facing him nothing short of the work of the devil. Though he believed Michael's threat to be a frightened, angry boy's way of striking out at the father he blamed for his mother's death, Jake had to face the fact: there was at least *some* degree of risk in leaving Michael right now. But, in making his decision, Jake had to balance that short-term risk with the long-term—perhaps lifelong—risk of *not* leaving, of passing by the opportunity to find G32 and, possibly, a cure. Without a cure, might not Jake spend the rest of his life in abject and absolute terror that Michael would one day make good on his threat?

How had Jake's life come to be ruled, tormented, by a single word, a single fear? Suicide.

First Ana, now Michael.

Of course, Ana had *not* committed suicide.

Suddenly the sight of Hughes, up ahead, jerked Jake from his troubled thoughts. Half a head taller than most of the other passengers strolling toward the international departure gates, the GenChrom scientist was easy to pick out. Jake hung back. Hughes strolled purposefully, his laptop in one hand, a large duffel-style bag in the other, dressed in a tan canvas bushman jacket, faded, but neatly pressed, blue jeans, and white sneakers.

Jake only hoped that Marilyn hadn't booked his and Hughes's seats together. With his mind and heart so full of worry about Michael, the mere prospect of forcing conversation with Hughes for the next eight hours drained Jake. He'd be spending enough time with his boss over the next few weeks, and that thought gave him a decidedly unsettled feeling.

The steady stream of passengers thinned more at each gate until, finally, Jake felt compelled to catch up with Hughes.

"Morning," he said, falling in step alongside Hughes.

"There you are," Hughes responded. "Your boys settled in over at Leah's?"

"The nanny I hired to help Leah out will take them over there later today. She'd just arrived when I was leaving. The boys were still sleeping."

"Leaving can't be easy," Hughes said.

The see-through attempt at empathy only angered Jake.

"It's not."

They fell into silence for the rest of the walk to the gate, which was the last in Sea-Tac's international terminal. As they approached their gate, Jake was pleased to see they'd already started preboarding and even more pleased when Hughes stepped forward at the call for first-class passengers.

"That's me," he said, striding away from Jake.

Ten minutes later, Jake's row was called. Passing through the first-class compartment, Jaw saw a flight attendant fussing over Hughes, helping him store his duffel bag. Hughes did not look up.

At Jake's request, Marilyn had booked him an aisle seat. A well-coiffed, uptight-looking woman dressed in a business suit occupied the window seat. She did not look up from her thick tome. The middle seat, to Jake's pleasure, sat empty. Jake settled in, but as luck would have it, just before takeoff a giant of a man—at least six-five and bordering on obese—came rushing down the aisle. Stopping alongside Jake's seat, he excused himself to get to the middle seat.

Jake stood, moving into the aisle to let him by.

"Thanks, mate," the man said, huffing audibly from his dash to catch the plane.

He squeezed past Jake, and with no small amount of jostling and experimentation with different angles and body positions he finally settled into the seat, his knees pressing against the back of the seat in front of him. Its occupant turned, looking over his shoulder, no doubt imagining the joys of an eight-hour flight with two bony knees in his back. The woman at the window looked across the newcomer's bulk, toward the aisle, her expression panicked at the prospect of being trapped for the long flight.

Jake had remained standing in the aisle, observing.

"Why don't we trade seats?" he finally said, hiding his disappointment. Jake hated middle seats. Besides the confinement, they doubled the odds of having to force unwelcome conversation.

The man had been struggling, digging in the space between seats, to find the short side of his seat belt. At Jake's suggestion, his head—large, like the rest of him—swung round. A line of perspiration traced its way down his forehead.

"That's incredibly good of you, mate. Bloody travel agent knows I can't fit in the middle, but seems to put me 'ere every other flight. Sure you won't come to regret it?"

"There are some advantages to being five-ten," Jake answered.

Several minutes later, they had both settled in and the aircraft began its taxi down the runway. To Jake's relief, the woman on his left immediately buried her nose back in her book and, once they were airborne, the grateful giant pushed back in his seat and promptly fell asleep.

Jake quickly followed suit.

"I WANT YOU TO FIND OUT what she's up to."

Philip Esser pushed back in his lambsuede chair and trained his beady eyes on the mammoth ex-Marine turned private investigator seated across the oversize marble-inlaid desk from him. Impatiently tapping the tip of his handmade cigar on the matching marble ashtray, he waited as Marcus Cook cleared his throat to speak.

"It might help, sir," Cook said, "if you gave me some background on your daughter. Of course, anything you tell me will be held in the strictest confidence."

Esser pushed an eight-by-eleven manila envelope across his desk.

"Read this."

Cook picked the envelope up, unfastened the two-prong clamp, and peered inside.

"Later," Esser chided. "Those are the reports from the last investigator I hired."

Cook's eyebrows shot up.

"What happened to him?"

Esser took his time answering, staring at Cook as he lit the cigar.

"Fired him. He was ex-military, like you." Esser's hard eyes flickered briefly with emotion. "Son of a bitch should never have let things get out of hand, should never have let it happen."

"What happened?"

"Read the file. It's all in there. All the bullshit that girl's put me through."

"Your daughter?"

"Yes. Asahel. She made a career out of getting under my skin. Literally. She used to run the Seattle office of a group called IPAF. Have you heard of them?"

"No, sir."

"The Indigenous Peoples Advancement Foundation. They're a bunch of anti-American, capitalist-hating radicals. Fucking bleeding hearts. Most of them grew up privileged little brats, like Asahel. If they'd ever had to actually work a day to put food on their tables you can bet they'd sing a different tune." His fist came down on the desk's top with a thud. "I spent a lifetime building this company, building a reputation for myself in this industry. Asahel wanted nothing more than to destroy that."

Cook scribbled a few notes in a binder, then looked back up.

"You said she used to work for IPAF. What's she doing now?"

"She works here, at Mercy. She's the company attorney."

Cook's thick eyebrows shot back up.

"You must've been happy to have her do such an about-face."

"Happy?" Esser replied, snorting a short laugh. "Nothing Asahel does makes me happy. She robbed me of one of my only true joys in life." He paused, thinking back to that fateful day. It was all Asahel's fault. "And I'll never forgive her. But at least now I can keep an eye on her. At least I was confident she was staying out of trouble. Until now."

"Something's changed recently?"

Esser nodded.

"A day or two ago, the wife of one of my employees saw her at REI with a long-haired hippie type. I want you to find out who it was."

"You have someone specific in mind?"

"Yes, I do. I think it may be one of my daughter's former coworkers. An activist named Fuentes. I called the woman who saw them. It's been a while since I've seen Fuentes myself, but her description of the guy she saw my daughter with would fit."

"I take it you don't approve of her seeing him."

"The guy's a worthless piece of shit. But more than that, it's what it means if Asahel's seeing him again."

"And if it turns out to be this Fuentes?"

"Just find that out first. Then, if it is him, we'll figure out what to do about it."

OTHER THAN GIVING very precise orders to the flight attendants about her food (no dressing on the salad or mayo on the sandwich) and drink (chilled bottled water only), the woman seated by the window never uttered a word the entire plane ride, but when the giant awoke he struck up a conversation, which actually helped the time pass. He was employed at the Australian embassy in Brasilia.

"Sort of a liason between the local police and any of my fellow countrymen who run into trouble down there," he said. "And a mite few of them manage to. Which is why I'm stopping first in Manaus. To bail an Aussie out."

His colorful stories of the troubleshooting his job entailed occupied the last two hours of the flight. As the plane touched down, Jake strained to catch a glimpse of the city that served as the gateway to the Brazilian rain forest.

Jake had read about Manaus before leaving Seattle. On the shores of the Rio Negro, ten kilometers upstream from the Encontro das Aguas—the phenomenal confluence of the Solimoes and Negro Rivers, which joined to form the Amazon—Manaus was Brazil's waterway equivalent of a congested bus terminal crossed with Kmart. Nine hundred miles inland from the Atlantic coast, oceangoing vessels on their way to Iquitos (1,400 miles upriver) stopped at Manaus to unload their goods and allow bargain-hungry passengers to barter for goods. More than happy to accommodate them, hundreds of Amazonian natives flocked to Manaus each morning via canoes, cargo boats and rafts, all loaded beyond capacity with goods for sale—fruits, vegetables and colorful crafts.

Despite its hustle and bustle and a downright electric air about its commerce, the Manaus of today paled when compared to the Manaus of the late nineteenth century. Those had been true glory days, thanks to the rubber boom of the late 1800s and early 1900s. But with the advent of synthetic rubber and the development of rubber plantations in Southeast Asia a couple decades later, it had all ended.

In an effort to revive Manaus's flagging economy, in 1967 the government declared the city a duty-free zone. That, coupled with the fact that the Amazon and its tributaries represented the only means of transportation of goods in and out of the jungle, created the Manaus of today: a wild, vibrant, crime-infected city that looked to Jake from the airplane window like one endless flea market.

As they stood in the aisle waiting to deplane, Jake's newfound Australian friend handed him a business card. It read: *Randall Oates, Australian Embassy.*

"You run into trouble, mate, don't hesitate to call," he said good-naturedly.

A wall of intense heat greeted Jake as he stepped out of the plane. As he stood at the top of the jetway, waiting in the line to descend, Jake's eyes scanned the tarmac for Hughes. No sign of him.

Fifteen minutes later, minutes spent standing in the relentless late afternoon sun, Jake finally made it inside the terminal and began looking for Hughes. He spotted him at a pay phone, standing with his back to Jake.

Jake approached. Normally, he would make a point of letting Hughes know he was there; but for some reason, he did not. He approached casually, stopped several feet behind Hughes. With the terminal one flowing sea of bodies, Hughes did not notice him.

"That's right," Jake heard him say. "His name is Jake Skully. He's an M.D."

Then, after a brief response: "I don't see why it makes any difference to you."

When Hughes grew silent again, listening, he turned to rest his elbow on the shelf of the phone booth. That was when he caught sight of Jake.

"Meet me at the Tropical's lounge," he said into the phone. "In an hour. We can go over everything then."

Glaring at Jake for his failure to announce his presence, Hughes hung up.

"That was our guide," he said brusquely.

"We're meeting to go over the agenda?" Jake asked. He was anxious to get started and would not allow Hughes to intimidate him.

"You don't need to be there."

"Don't need to be there?" Jake answered. "Of course I should be. I should be in on the planning."

Jake would soon learn that Hughes's response was a portent of what was to come: a resistance to Jake being involved on any level other than that of performing specific services, which would be judiciously spelled out by Hughes.

"No," Hughes answered forcefully. "That's not necessary. This is just a preliminary meeting. I need to iron out the business arrangement with the guide. Go check the markets out, why don't you? Then make your way back to the Tropical. We board our expedition boat tomorrow morning at six A.M. I'll meet you in the lobby at five-thirty sharp."

With several hours of daylight left and obviously no choice about Hughes's meeting with the guide, Jake decided to take Hughes's advice. He followed him to the taxi stand outside the terminal, where they parted ways without speaking.

After a wild ride that had Jake bracing his arms against both of the backseat doors, he called, "Stop here."

He stepped out of the cab, in the heart of the city, and was immediately assaulted by a fog of exhaust fumes, screeching brakes and blasting horns. At the first respectable-looking hotel, he entered. A sharp-featured, pock-skinned man with long sideburns and a handlebar mustache sat behind the desk.

Jake looked around. Several well-dressed light-complected patrons relaxed in the ornately furnished lobby.

"Can I leave my bags here for a little while?" Jake asked in Spanish. It felt good using the language that had served as his primary tongue since he and Ana married and moved to Mexico.

The man nodded, extending his hand. Palm up.

Jake slapped five bucks in it.

"Five more when I get back," Jake said. Insurance.

The man grinned.

"Trabajo a las nueve." *I work until nine.*

Jake got the message. If he didn't return in time for the man to get the extra five, the deal was off. Jake could kiss his bags good-bye.

Jake nodded and left the hotel.

He strolled the crowded litter-strewn streets for forty minutes. Twice he was jostled, both times by young men who smiled and apologized profusely in Spanish. And both times during the encounter Jake felt a light touch, someone from behind, groping at his back pocket. He'd lived in Nogales long enough to recognize the teamwork, long enough to know to stash his wallet in the inside pocket of his blazer.

This was a far cry from the Manaus described in the glossy travel brochure Marilyn had provided him before the trip. Sloppy hand-painted signs in the shop windows advertised the sale of every type of imported goods imaginable: from cameras, to fans, to jewelry, to air conditioners. Many were in English.

Best prices in the world. Best quality. Almost gone. Hurry. Hurry.

Jake continued walking past the shopping district, until he found himself in a residential area that consisted mostly of decayed mansions that now housed tenements.

In the plane's in-flight magazine Jake had read about the Teatro Amazonas, a famous opera house constructed during the rubber boom. He stopped a teenage boy and asked in Spanish for directions, but the boy ignored him. Passing a grizzled old man who stood in an open doorway, his arms resting on a weathered wooden gate as he stared, forlorn, out onto the street, Jake repeated his request. The old man answered in Portuguese. Jake picked up a word here and there, but after thanking the man, he mostly based his new direction on the man's wild gestures and pointing.

The Teatro Amazonas proved worth the detour. Waves of mosaic tiles drew Jake toward the marble-colonnaded entrance of the Italian Renaissance–style theater, at one time a symbol of Manaus's having the richest per capital wealth in the Americas. But when the rubber boom went bust, the opera house closed its doors.

In an attempt to attract tourists, the theater had since been restored.

As Jake slowly walked through it, he could practically hear Ana gushing enthusiastically about the elaborately wrought balustrades on the balconies. Or the ornate chandeliers.

Ana loved old, beautiful things. She appreciated the passion that went into their creation.

They used to lie in bed and talk about the trips they would one day take, the churches and castles and ruins they would visit. When the kids were older. When they'd hired another doctor to help with the clinic. There was always something stopping them, but that was okay. They had plenty of time.

After a romantic dinner on their last anniversary, while they lay (giddy with champagne, and naked) on a deserted beach down from their Guaymas hotel, Jake had promised Ana a trip to Spain for their fifteenth anniversary.

The minute she got back to Nogales, Ana began research for the trip. She'd read about the little mountain town of Ronda, its ancient bridges. And even though their anniversary was still two years away, she'd already started collecting travel brochures.

Jake stared at the crystal twelve-tiered chandelier dangling from the forty-foot ceilings of the old theater. Then, dully, he turned away.

They thought they had all the time in the world.

•   •   •

He HEADED NEXT for the waterfront. At a floating market, Jake saw riverboats of every imaginable color (turquoise, orange, magenta, mud brown) and shape—from small, crude, handmade canoes to thirty-foot power cruisers—lashed haphazardly, one to another; as many as six or eight deep, creating a loosely formed island in the river. Vendors picked their way across the network with an agility that represented a lifetime spent on water, while shoppers paused often, wobbly-legged but doggedly determined to see it all, to find the best buy.

A young boy, naked save for a pair of cutoff blue jeans, scrambled across the armada, carrying a bag of limes and a loudly squawking, wildly flopping Muscovy duck.

Everywhere Jake looked, vendors peddled produce fresh from the jungle, which hemmed in the city on all sides.

Jake didn't trust his sea legs to venture far out into the floating market, but a canoe in the row of boats tied alongside the boardwalk (whose broken boards made looking up a decidedly risky proposition) caught his eye. Or actually, his nose.

The aroma of fresh bread drifting Jake's way brought him to a halt.

"Quantos pesos?" he asked the dark-skinned vendor, pointing to one of dozens of loaves of bread sticking out of two crates nestled between the bench seats, in the center of the boat.

All the men seemed to dress alike. Light-colored loose-fitting clothes—long-sleeved shirts and long pants—topped with a straw hat against the sun.

"Diez."

Jake paid his ten pesos, then selected a long, thin baguette.

"Gracias."

Suddenly ravenous, Jake broke off a big chunk and stuffed it into his mouth while he continued down the pier. When the toe of his boot suddenly caught on the edge of a broken board, he almost ended up in the water.

Deciding that it would be prudent to put solid ground back underneath his feet, Jake moved on to the open-air market.

Row after row of booths overflowed with their colorful, often bizarre goods. Bright red cotton cloths hung overhead, creating a tunnel between rows of tables. The offerings here were even more exotic than at the floating market.

An old, bent woman with parched skin so creased with sun and age that it looked like mud that had dried, then cracked into thousands of pieces, called to Jake in Spanish as he passed.

"Snakeskins? Dried toads? Alligator teeth?"

Jake shook his head no.

She gestured toward a row of small clay bottles on the table.

"Magic potion?"

Again, he shook his head, and continued on.

Thirty minutes later, the day's light finally fading, the tables started emptying as vendors closed down their booths. As Jake headed back toward the center of town to retrieve his bags, he saw the woman again, walking slowly, with the aid of a cane.

He passed her, but she did not look up. Seconds later, he heard a cry behind him, then shouts.

Jake pivoted to look back.

The old woman lay on the ground. Surrounding her, three youths pulled at the large canvas bag she'd had slung over her shoulder when Jake just saw her.

The woman held on to it fiercely, clucking at them with unintelligible words. At the same time, she managed to swing her cane at them as they laughed at her. One youth, luckily barefoot, kicked her in the ribs repeatedly.

Jake went for them with a vengeance.

"Off, off," he yelled, bringing the youth who still kicked at the old woman down with a tackle.

One of the other boys jumped on top of the two, grasping Jake's back like a monkey. The woman's cries meant the third boy continued the attack on her.

Both Jake's assailants were agile and wiry but too frail to offer any real contest. A hard elbow to the jaw freed Jake of the one on his back. Then a glancing blow to the other's face caused him to let go of his hold on Jake and roll to the side, both hands covering his nose, from which blood spurted freely. By the time Jake got back on his feet, the third boy had succeeded in ripping the bag from the woman's hands. He began to run, with Jake in pursuit. Throughout the entire episode, pedestrians had strolled by, paying little to no attention.

Jake hadn't run a sprint in twenty years, but he soon discovered the speed that had won him a scholarship in his youth hadn't deserted him entirely. He caught up with the boy, grabbing him by the shoulder and spinning him around.

Jake stood a head taller and outweighed the boy by sixty or seventy pounds. When he pulled back his fist, the youth dropped the bag and took off.

Jake returned to find the woman struggling to her feet, her other two attackers nowhere to be seen.

He helped her stand, retrieved her cane, which lay several yards away, against the wall of a stucco building.

"Are you all right?" he asked in Spanish.

"Sí, sí," the woman muttered, eagerly grabbing the bag he offered and pulling it tight to her body.

"You're sure?"

"Sí."

Scanning 360 degrees for the boys, who had disappeared, Jake smiled at the woman, then turned back in the direction of the hotel where he'd left his bags.

"Esperate," the old woman cried.

He turned.

She held up a knobby, bent finger, then began rummaging in her bag, finally withdrawing a small snakeskin bag. Dropping the hooked end of her cane over one arm, she held the bag reverently in both hands, closed her eyes and mumbled several phrases that Jake could not understand—clearly not in Spanish—over and over, three times in all.

"For you," she said, reverting to Spanish. She extended her hand with her offering. "To protect you. It will frighten off evil spirits. And bring you good fortune."

Her small eyes became mere slits as she studied him.

"Ooooh," she sighed. "You will need it."

Satisfied that her debt to Jake had been paid, she turned and hobbled away.

Jake stood watching her go; then he loosened the drawstring at the bag's top.

Inside he found a small clay pot, the size of a plum. He held it up and shook it, listening. Liquid.

He removed the cork and lifted it to his nose. A biting odor, reminiscent of diapers left wet too long, caused Jake to draw back sharply.

He'd seen other bottles just like it, at the woman's booth in the open-air market. They'd lined the table, under the snakeskins and necklaces of alligator teeth that hung like a beaded curtain from the booth's roof.

The old woman's words came back to him.

A magic potion?

Jake studied the jar, twirling it between his thumb and forefinger. His first instinct, once the woman was out of sight, was to set it on the stucco wall that lined the sidewalk and walk away.

But something stopped him.

Carefully, Jake slid the clay pot back into the bag. Then he opened his belt buckle and threaded the snakeskin pouch onto his leather belt, wondering just how powerful its contents might be.

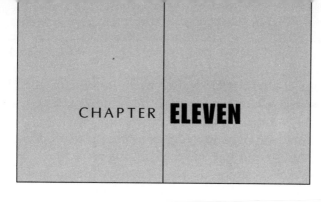

CHAPTER **ELEVEN**

STAN YASAVICH HAD always turned Asahel off. Asahel found Stan, fifteen years older than Toby and, with two doctorates, considerably more educated, stuffy and unpleasant, totally devoid of humor. True, he was good-looking, in an utterly plastic kind of way, but she'd never understood what Toby saw in him or why he put up with Stan's arrogance. But today, as the three of them sat at an outside café table, trying to carry on a conversation over the ruckus of a play yard full of toddlers, Yasavich's obvious concern redeemed him somewhat in Asahel's eyes.

Toby and Stan had gone by Asahel's apartment that morning to talk to her visitor. Asahel had had to leave. She didn't dare miss the meeting she'd had Tammy reschedule, even when she learned that this morning was the only free time Yasavich had to help. When Fuentes left a voice message on Asahel's office phone, telling her to meet them at University Village, Asahel's hopes for a speedy solution to her predicament soared. But one look at the expressions on Toby's and Stan's faces when she arrived at the upscale shopping center had sent those same hopes into a nosedive.

The sun had finally chased away the rain. With a cloudless sky and temperatures in the midseventies, the threesome had taken their *panino* sandwiches outside to one of a dozen tables in the courtyard. A small army of toddlers played in a fenced area nearby, while their Banana Republic– and Eddie Bauer–clad mothers watched over them, Starbucks cups in hand.

"You were able to communicate with her?" Asahel asked excitedly.

"It wasn't easy," Yasavich answered. "She speaks a primitive language particular to her tribe alone. It's similar to that spoken by the Kaxinawas, Yawanawas, Nukuinis and Araras, all of which belong to the Pano linguistic group of the Amazon Basin. I'm fluent in Portuguese, which helped, too. It took some piecing together, but I was able to get a great deal of information from her. To start with, her name is Caina."

"Caina," Asahel repeated.

"As you already suspected, she's from the state of Acre. Her tribesmen are the Naua," Yasavich said. "Or, I should say, *were*."

"What do you mean, 'were'?"

Yasavich and Fuentes exchanged somber glances. Yasavich leaned across the table toward her. He lowered his voice.

"They were slaughtered. All of them, women and children included. Caina witnessed it. By a group of white men."

Asahel gasped.

"Oh my god."

"She told a horrible story," Fuentes said, his voice and eyes visibly haunted by what he'd heard just hours earlier. "That poor girl's been through hell."

"Why?" Asahel asked. "Why were they murdered?"

Yasavich looked at Toby.

"Toby has a theory, which I'll let him tell you, but Caina doesn't have any explanations. She had been banished for several weeks and was returning home. It's a frequent form of punishment in some tribes. She'd gotten herself pregnant."

"What's wrong with that?" Asahel asked.

"Plenty, at least according to the Naua. The elders decide who'll have babies, and when. Caina wasn't on that list. The tribal shaman made her some kind of concoction that caused her to abort, and then they kicked her out."

"Barbaric," Asahel muttered as she began to realize the situation was, quite possibly, even worse than she feared.

"If you want barbaric, just wait," Stan continued. "The day Caina returned, she came upon her tribe being slaughtered. She hung back in the woods, watching. One Naua survived, by pretending to be dead. He only lived a day after the white men left, just long enough to tell Caina what had happened. When he died, she set out to find *you*. The region the Naua inhabit used to be rich in diamonds. The tribe had a stash of stones. Caina used them to buy her way here. It's a wonder she made it, but apparently some deep-forest settler took her under his wing and accompanied her all the way here. Of course she made it worth his while. She started out with over a dozen diamonds—probably half a million's worth. Pretty expensive passage, but at least the guy had the decency to get her to Seattle."

"Was it my card? Is that why she came here?"

Yasavich nodded.

"She was a young impressionable girl when you showed up in her village. You were the first white person the Naua had ever seen. Before you, the tribe always feared anyone light-skinned, but because you were so kind, because you offered your help, her elders came to the conclusion that the white man wasn't so bad, and you—you became almost a mystical figure to them. Caina believed that you had magical powers."

Fuentes had been observing Asahel's reaction closely.

"That's why she came all the way here," he announced. "For you to help her. She actually thinks you can bring her tribe back to life."

Asahel stared, dumbfounded.

"She can't really think that, can she? I mean, even the most primitive of cultures know it's impossible to bring someone back from the dead."

"That might have been true before the white men came," Fuentes answered. "But after what they taught the Naua, Caina had reason to be hopeful."

"What do you mean?"

Fuentes took over now.

"Before they killed them, the white men told the Naua they had the magic to make new human beings from their blood."

"You mean, clone them?"

"Yes. No doubt that's what they were saying. They were telling the Naua about cloning. Of course, with the language and cultural barriers, it has to have been a very crude discussion, but the Naua came away believing that the white men could grow new life—new Naua— from their blood. The Naua equated it with magic."

"They took blood? That means . . ."

Asahel's eyes locked with Toby's. They both knew exactly what that meant.

"Yes," Fuentes said, finishing her sentence. "It means the men who killed them were researchers, after DNA."

"IT CAN'T BE TRUE."

When Stan reluctantly excused himself for his next class, Asahel and Toby had moved into her car, where they could speak without fear of someone overhearing. The sun streamed through the car's windows, warming Asahel's bare arms.

"It is, Ash. Believe me. If you saw her, saw the terror in her eyes when she was telling Stan about what happened, you'd have no doubt."

Asahel thought back to her attempt to get Caina to draw a picture of where she came from.

"I've seen it," she said. "I just didn't want to believe it was something this serious. This awful."

She shook her head, momentarily squeezing her eyes shut.

"Has it really come to this, Toby?"

Toby nodded.

"We knew it would. Eventually."

"I agree. We saw it coming, after my trip down there. After we realized what a great job the Naua have done of isolating themselves. It made them the perfect population for sampling DNA."

Toby leaned Asahel's way and grabbed her hand.

"Their blood was so fucking pure. It's just what the pharmaceutical companies are after. Isolated populations." He paused, troubled. "But why kill them?"

Asahel's grip on Toby's hand tightened.

"Don't you see? So that no one else stands a chance of getting their hands on the blood. It's the patents. The only way a pharmaceutical company's going to get rich on a drug is to secure a patent that stops anyone else from competing with them. You and I both know that patents aren't even necessary to create new drugs. But it's the capitalist way of creating a monopoly. Hell, there's this hideous gold rush under way by genomic and pharmaceutical companies to patent gene sequences. DNA. The basic blueprint of life. *Blood*, for Christ's sake. They're patenting blood, human life. Collecting it like madmen, all over the globe, in the hope that somewhere in all of it they'll find the next miracle cure. They take a blood sample from some unknowing native somewhere who doesn't have a clue what they're telling him—*if* they're even telling him anything—then they commercialize it, make millions. The poor native loses control of his own genetic material once it's removed from his body and when the drug companies get rich, he doesn't make a penny."

"I bet the only reason they told the Naua so much is they knew they were going to kill them," Toby offered. "What better way to make sure no one else can beat them to the patent?"

"My god, Toby, we knew this day would come, but we never dreamed it would be this soon."

Fuentes's eyes softened momentarily.

"A lot's happened since you left, Ash. It's a new world. The stakes have never been higher." He studied her. "Do you see now why we need you so badly? Why it's so important that you come back?"

Asahel pulled her hand away abruptly.

"I'm not coming back," she said. "What gave you that idea? I told you, Toby, I can't get involved."

Fuentes looked disbelieving.

"Even after hearing this? How can you not?"

"Do you realize what you're asking of me? What's at stake? I'm working in the industry now, Toby. For my father's pharmaceutical company. There's no way I can mess with this stuff again."

He reached for her hand again, but Asahel held it tightly against her torso.

"Your father wouldn't have to know," Fuentes said. "No one would. You could be so valuable to us, Ash. You're an insider now; just think how much more information's available to someone like you."

Asahel glared at Fuentes.

"You mean go undercover?"

"It wouldn't have to be anything formal. If you want, we wouldn't even have to tell anyone at IPAF. It could just be between us. You helping me. Just some information here and there. You know, like E-mail addresses, research files, who's heavy into bioprospecting down there, in the Amazon. Whatever you can get your hands on."

"Are you out of your mind?"

"No. In fact, my mind has never been more sound."

"Let me get this straight. I call you to help me out with this native who arrives on my doorstep and next thing I know, you're expecting me to start spying on my father's company? No, not just his company, the industry in general?"

Fuentes's smirk held no amusement.

"Look who suddenly got religion? Is this the same person who risked her life in Mexico to protest the import of genetically contaminated crops? Who wrote an investigative piece about the millions of people dying of AIDS in developing countries because they couldn't afford the ten thousand dollars a year that American pharmaceutical companies were charging when generic drugs were available for a couple hundred bucks—but couldn't be used because of fucking patents?"

Asahel turned her face to the window.

"Stop it, Toby."

"An article that shamed the drug companies into offering discounts? An article that saved lives, Ash."

Asahel felt Toby's hand on her chin. He turned her to face him.

"You could do the same thing again. Write another investigative report. This time on biopiracy."

She pushed him away.

"I'm not doing it, Toby. Flat out. No. I can't get involved. And I want you to come get her." She could not bring herself to say her name. "I'm sorry for her, terribly sorry about what she went through, but I can't keep her. Do you understand?"

Fuentes reached to open the car door, but before he slid his long frame out he turned and said to Asahel, in a quiet, somber voice, "You know, your sister didn't just die that day. She took you with her."

He climbed out of the car, a rigidity replacing his normally fluid grace. Before closing the door, he stooped to eye Asahel one last time.

"I need you to keep *Caina*"—he deliberately emphasized her name when he said it—"a couple more days. I'll call you when I've got things set up for her."

Then he closed the door and walked away.

CHAPTER **TWELVE**

*T*HAT SON OF *a bitch has to go."*

Orland Vasquez, the hefty, soft-spoken head of FUNAI, Brazil's Department of Indian Affairs, looked up from his conference call to see Diego Cavallero standing at his desk.

Vasquez shook his head in frustration. He was accustomed to Cavallero's tirades, but as head of the Lost Tribes Project, Cavallero was so valuable to Vasquez and his agenda that he long ago decided to put up with them.

Motioning for Cavallero to take a seat while a voice from the speaker phone droned on about legislative reforms up for a vote in the coming election, Vasquez punched a button, taking the call off the speaker, and placed a hand over the phone's mouthpiece.

"Do you realize you're supposed to be on this call?" he asked Cavallero. "It's for all my department heads. That includes you."

"I told you a long time ago," Cavallero replied. "I don't waste my time on bullshit bureaucratic meetings. I need to talk to you. Now."

Vasquez issued a long sigh.

"Something's come up here," he announced into the phone. "I'm going to drop off this call now. The rest of you continue your discussion. Bellido, drop me an E-mail telling me what you decide."

Hanging up, Vasquez pushed back in his chair and studied Cavallero, who, contrary to his boss's order to sit, remained standing over Vasquez's desk.

As far as Vasquez was concerned, Diego Cavallero was a spring wound just a tad too tight. One of Cavallero's hands clutched one of the Marlboros he chain-smoked during his every waking moment, which no doubt contributed to his deeply lined face—though most of its furrows could be traced directly to Cavallero's first love. The Amazon rain forest, which he'd spent decades exploring and protecting. And which no doubt occasioned this morning's visit.

"Okay," Vasquez said. "*Who* has to go?"

Cavallero's wild eyebrows shot up.

"Who do you think? The *americano*."

"What's he done this time?"

"Several of my people have seen him around Manaus, in the bars."

Cavallero had "people" just about everywhere in Brazil. He frequently cited them to Vasquez as if they were sources equal in stature and credibility to the Reuters News Service.

"The man's entitled to do what he wants in his free time," Vasquez replied. "He doesn't get out of the jungle often. When he does, he must need some company."

"That's the problem. The company he keeps. He's hanging out with American scientists. Fucking *pharmaceutical* people."

A hint of surprise flickered across Vasquez's eyes. Cavallero saw it. But Vasquez kept his tone even.

"All the Americans hang out at the same bars. You can't blame a guy for wanting to spend time with people from his own country. I'm sure it's just a coincidence, the fact that he's been seen talking to some researchers."

"Coincidence?" Cavallero ranted. "You're willing to write it off as a coincidence? Well, I'm not. American pharmaceutical companies are the enemy. They're out to destroy the Amazon, and its people."

"That's not how our government sees it. American pharmaceutical companies pump money into Brazil's economy."

Cavallero uttered a string of obscenities—delivered in Portuguese.

"They've raped our forests," he said, his voice rising in pitch. "Stolen our native medicines, the plants our tribes have used for healing and cultural ceremonies for centuries. Now it's DNA. *Blood.* They're sweeping down on our people like giant corporate vampires."

Vasquez shook his head dismissively.

"As usual, you're overreacting. I don't like the pharmaceutical companies any more than you do, but we have to learn to live with them."

Cavallero leaned over Vasquez's desk, lowering himself face-to-face with his boss.

"You listen to me, Vasquez," he said, shaking his index finger. "You hear my words. These American biotech companies will stop at nothing. The fact that this gringo's been seen with them is enough for me. I'm going to fire the son of a bitch."

"You'll do no such thing."

Cavallero pushed himself up and away angrily, glaring at Vasquez.

"Why would you protect him?"

"It's not him I'm protecting. It's you. Your project. The Lost Tribes. We've gone over this before, Diego. We need the American right now.

Even if it's only temporary, which I assure you it is. Besides, with the kind of work he's doing, why would we get rid of him?" He reached for an eight-by-ten black-and-white photograph sitting on the corner of his desk and held it up, clearly pleased by the sight. "This is quite a find."

Cavallero barely glanced at the photograph: in a small clearing, surrounded by dense foliage, fifteen long, narrow straw-thatched huts.

"I would've discovered 'em in half the time," he said bitterly. "I'd had him flying over that area for weeks. Would've never taken me that long."

"How did you know they were even there?" Vasquez asked.

"The bodies of those three white settlers," Cavallero answered through a cloud of cigarette smoke. "I told you about them. They were found last month near the Peruvian border. They'd been slain by arrows. That meant a tribe had to exist in that section. There was no other explanation. But that region is so dense and inaccessible, I'd begun to doubt whether he'd ever actually find them. It was killing me to let that fuckin' American look for them when that's what I'm supposed to be doing."

Vasquez gingerly laid the photo on his desk and removed his bifocals. Lifting the front flap of the wrinkled white cotton shirt that hung loose over his round belly, he pushed back in his chair and used the shirt's hem to wipe the smudges off his glasses. When he replaced them, he studied Cavallero tiredly.

"We've gone over this time and again. That's why I brought this guy onto the team, to free you up. Right now we need you to spend all your time lobbying to keep the project alive, not out there in that plane of yours."

Cavallero's dusty cowboy boot shot out and kicked at the dust on the floor.

"And I keep telling *you*, I'm not a fucking politician," he said. "I need to be out there, in the forest. Every day I spend in an office or kissing the butt of some political asshole is one more day wasted. A day I could make a find like *this*."

He slapped the photo on Vasquez's desk.

"Tell me this, amigo," Vasquez said, looking up at him from his chair. "What good's it gonna do to find more tribes if these political assholes you hate so much revoke the constitutional provision giving the land back to them? Or if they cut off funding for the Lost Tribes Project.

"Don't lose sight of what this is all about," Vasquez continued.

"Protecting Brazil's indigenous people, making sure they survive. That takes maintaining the existing constitution. And money. Lots of it. And these political assholes, as you like to call them, are the ones that control both. Without their support, all that finding more tribes does is expose them to the outside world, more and more of which wants them annihilated. It becomes a moot issue—no, worse than that. It actually puts them in danger. Can't you see?"

Wild-eyed, Cavallero lifted a tobacco-stained hand to his mouth and drew heavily on his cigarette.

Vasquez eyed him nervously. He held tremendous admiration for Cavallero. The man had single-handedly taken up the cause of Brazil's indigenous tribes, and in the few short years he'd headed the Lost Tribes Project he'd managed to locate and ensure the survival of dozens of tribes. In the process, despite the country's mixed feelings about the project itself, Cavallero had become a national hero.

A most unlikely, reluctant hero.

Cavallero simply loved his job, the sheer treachery of it, the days and weeks spent hacking his way through treacherous dense jungle, or crisscrossing low overhead in a Cessna that was on its last legs. He lived for the excitement that such daily perils promised. And then the incredible rush of actually finding a new tribe.

Getting Cavallero to accept Vasquez's hiring of the American had been no small task.

"Just tell me this. Why'd it have to be an American?" Cavallero said. "If you were gonna hire someone new, why a fucking gringo?"

Vasquez swatted at the cloud of Cavallero's exhaled smoke as if it were a swarm of bothersome flies.

"The publicity you got for winning the Bartolome Award brought us sizable donations," Vasquez said. In May, Cavallero had traveled to Spain, where the Prince of Asturias had awarded him that nation's prestigious Bartolome de Las Casas Award for his work. "Some European. Some American. One wealthy *americano* volunteered to provide both the pilot and the plane. How could I turn him down?"

"You could've. I don't trust him. Especially when I hear he's hanging around with American pharmaceutical companies."

"I told you," Vasquez said. "That's just a coincidence. And you might as well get used to it. Research scientists are a fact of life down in the Amazon now. We don't dare come down too heavy on the pharmaceutical companies. The money they've spent down here . . . hell, if we're too vocal about them, it'll just be one more nail in the project's coffin. Especially if Marco da Luz has his way."

"Da Luz." Cavallero practically hissed the name of the right-wing congressman from the state of Amazonas who'd decided to make the Lost Tribes Project the linchpin of his platform for reelection. "Da Luz is only concerned about all the goddamned money he's got invested in that mining company. The minerals on those protected native lands could make him rich, and he knows it. That's the real reason behind his opposition to the project."

"That's true, but Marco da Luz has touched a nerve with some of our people. Don't make the mistake of underestimating him," Vasquez warned.

Cavallero's eyes narrowed threateningly.

"Don't worry," he said, grinding his cigarette butt into the linoleum with the heel of a snakeskin boot that had been worn smooth with time. "The only way Marco da Luz is gonna get the constitution's protection for Indian lands overturned is over my dead body."

Vasquez studied him again, long and hard.

"That's precisely what worries me."

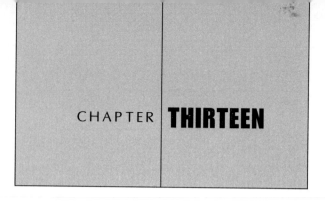

CHAPTER **THIRTEEN**

A HIGH-PITCHED shriek awakened Jake with a start. He padded barefoot to the window he'd left open the night before and peered out.

The hotel sat in the middle of a huge man-made clearing, but as the day's light began to break, Jake could make out a wall of huge trees—the start of the rain forest—less than an eighth of a mile away.

Once again, the cry—perhaps that of a jaguar—pierced the early morning stillness, sending chills down Jake's bare arms.

He turned off the alarm that he'd set for 4:00 A.M., stripped out of his boxer shorts and stepped into a shower stall so small he barely had elbow room to wash. He dressed in khakis, a T-shirt and the hiking boots Hughes had insisted he purchase from REI before departing Seattle; then double-checked all his bags. If he'd forgotten anything, today might well be his last chance to purchase supplies.

With a growing sense of anticipation, at five-fifteen he headed down the stairs.

Hughes was waiting.

They did not speak in the cab on their way into the city, which suited Jake just fine since it was only 2:00 A.M. Seattle time.

As they passed several of Manaus's piers along the Rio Negro, all of which were crowded with mostly crude, rickety-looking vessels, Hughes finally broke the silence.

"Not many of them look seaworthy."

Jake nodded. When it came to the boat that would take them up the river, his bigger concern centered around how close the quarters would force him to be to Hughes.

But when the taxi dropped them off at a pier on the far side of Manaus, a nearly new fifty-foot motor yacht, named the *Tapuya* (which Jake recognized as Portugese for "toucan"), awaited them.

Jake's spirits picked up immediately.

As he and Hughes strode down the pier, Jake could see three figures on the *Tapuya*. Two dark-skinned men hustled about, one on the top observation deck, another disappearing inside through a door off the middle deck. A tall, fair-skinned man leaned against an open door, watching their approach. As Jake and Hughes neared the gangplank to the *Tapuya*, the man finally pushed free of the doorjamb that had held him up and strolled casually across the plank to greet them.

Hughes simply nodded and handed the man the heavier of the two duffel bags he carried.

The man immediately proceeded to drop it to the pier as he eyed Jake.

"Morning," he said, without cracking a smile. "My name's Brent." He spoke with a strong midwestern accent.

Jake stopped short of the plank, dropped his three bags—his laptop, an oversize duffel bag and a backpack—and extended his hand.

"I'm Jake," he said, "Jake Skully."

Hughes had walked forward, but now he stood on the *Tapuya*'s deck, waiting for the other two.

"Give him Cabin Two," he called to Brent. "But drop my bag off in my cabin first."

Brent scowled at this, but he picked up Jake's bags without saying anything. Jake assumed Brent to be the guide that Hughes had telephoned from the airport.

"Wait here," Brent said to Jake.

Jake stood looking over the rail of the *Tapuya*, into the inky waters of the aptly named Rio Negro. The sun had risen, but it had not yet reached the water. A line of boats approached from the west. It wasn't until they drew even with the *Tapuya* that Jake realized they were chained, one to the other. Fourteen vessels in all—mostly canoes with single occupants. The lead boat was motorized. The chain passed the *Tapuya* on its way to the markets of Manaus, each boat laden with a cargo of produce or crafts.

After several minutes had passed, Jake walked forward, along the *Tapuya*'s lower deck, to a wide balcony that surrounded the entire front of the boat. What must it cost GenChrom to charter the *Tapuya*? No doubt a bundle.

As Jake stood on the forward balcony, one of the crew descended the stairs from the top deck. A short, compact man, he nodded at Jake and flashed a broad white-toothed smile but said nothing. He wore a Chicago White Sox T-shirt and cargo type shorts that revealed finely muscled but bowed legs. Jake smiled in return and greeted him in Spanish.

"Nice morning," he said.

The man nodded, still smiling, and padded quickly past Jake, along the *Tapuya*'s deck, toward the rear.

What was taking Brent so long?

Jake continued following the railing around to the aft side of the boat. About one-third of the way down, he picked up voices coming from one of the open windows.

"I told you, I need him along. I need him on this team."

Jake recognized this voice immediately. Hughes.

"Why would you have any objection to him going with us?"

Jake heard Brent offer a muffled response.

"Well, we'll deal with that if and when we have to," Hughes replied. "Until then, just keep an eye on him."

Suddenly the crewman Jake had just met reappeared from around the back of the boat. Jake turned and headed back to the balcony at the front of the boat, a maelstrom of alarm beginning to whirl in his head.

Brent obviously didn't trust him. And it appeared from Hughes's answer that there was no great foundation of trust there, either.

For the first time, Jake realized that the motors of the *Tapuya* vibrated quietly beneath his feet.

An impulse to bolt, flee the *Tapuya*, seized him. He was about to venture into dangerous territory with two men he'd just overheard discussing keeping "an eye on him."

The *Tapuya* would push off from the dock any minute now. Once they were river-bound, there was no turning back.

Brent's and Hughes's muffled voices continued to drift from the window, signaling to Jake that the coast was clear. There was still time to walk off the *Tapuya*. Return to his boys.

But that very thought triggered the image of Michael, on the night before Jake left, laughing bravely through a movie he could only hear and no longer see. And instantly Jake's resolve hardened.

He could feel success in his bones. G32 was out there.

Michael's only chance to see again.

Nothing would stop Jake now. Nothing.

WHEN HUGHES AND BRENT showed up, Jake startled at the sight of an AK-47 slung over Brent's shoulder.

"What the hell's that for?"

Brent held it up. The early morning sunlight glinted off the steel barrel.

"She's a beauty, isn't she?" he said. "I bought her off a coke smuggler in Manaus."

"Planning to go into the drug business?" Jake replied. "I thought we were looking for plants. And blood."

"We are," Brent answered, smirking. "But just the same, this baby'll come in handy."

"Brent put your bags in Cabin Two," Hughes said. "Might as well enjoy the luxury of the *Tapuya* while you can. Eventually we'll end up on a sixteen-foot skiff and in tents."

"How long before that happens?" Jake asked.

Hughes nodded toward Brent.

"Brent can answer questions like that. That's what guides are for."

Brent shrugged his shoulders.

"Depends on how everything goes. Maybe a week. Maybe ten days." He glanced Hughes's way and scowled. "That's assuming fucking du Pont shows up before long."

Brent turned and walked toward the back of the boat.

Hughes had stayed by Jake's side. Jake turned to him.

"Du Pont?"

Hughes nodded.

"I mentioned him earlier. He's Australian. An expert on the genetic makeup of remote Amazonian tribes. He signed on at the last minute—for a pretty penny, I might add. He was supposed to be here by now."

As if on cue, the squeal of brakes turned both men's attention toward the parking lot. A beat-up turquoise Impala with a TAXI sign bolted to its roof screeched to a halt.

"That must be him," Hughes said, resting both elbows on the railing of the *Tapuya* as he watched the action unfold on the other side of the dock.

A rangy curly-haired man emerged from the backseat of the cab, carrying a single large duffel bag. He waved cheerfully in Hughes and Jake's direction before bending his long form at the passenger window to pay the driver.

Tapping the roof of the car to dismiss the driver, he raised the dark glasses that hung from a cord around his neck and slipped them on his nose, then walked at a good clip down the dock toward the *Tapuya*.

"G'day, mates," he called ahead.

Jake had difficulty believing this could be the renowned researcher Hughes had just described. This guy looked more the part of a California surfer.

By now, Brent had noticed the commotion and returned to stand at Hughes's side, the AK-47 still slung over his shoulder. He glared at du Pont, but du Pont either did not notice or did not care.

"Terence du Pont," he said, extending his hand as he approached the group. "But they call me Doc."

Jake took the hand. Du Pont's grip surprised him.

"Nice to meet you," Jake said. "I'm Jake Skully."

Du Pont's smile was broad, and easy.

"Jake Skully, it's good to meet *you*."

Next, du Pont shook Hughes's hand, but when he turned to Brent, he froze, his eyes on the rifle.

"Bloody fine rifle," he said. "But mind tellin' me why you brought it along?"

Caught off-guard, Brent made a sneering face that Jake found quite comical, then turned and walked away.

"Nice chap," du Pont offered under his breath.

Jake smirked to himself, but du Pont caught it.

Hughes chose to ignore the rocky start.

"We're happy to have you with us, Terence. Doc. I was just telling Jake here about your credentials."

"Nothin' to write home about," du Pont replied. "What about you, mate?"

He turned to Jake.

Hughes broke in.

"Dr. Skully is a highly skilled practitioner and researcher. He brings a special interest in G32 to the team."

"Let's be honest, Torrell," Jake said. "What I bring to the team is TS 47."

Du Pont studied Jake but did not ask for an explanation. Jake sensed the questions would flow more freely when neither Hughes nor Brent was present.

"Glad to have you along," Jake said, quite sincerely, to du Pont.

Hughes gave Jake a reproachful look, then addressed du Pont.

"Let's get your bag stowed," he said crisply. "I'll show you your cabin."

The two men disappeared, leaving Jake alone.

AS THE *TAPUYA* DEPARTED Manaus, Jake felt a growing sense of excitement.

He peered down at the water. The *Tapuya* headed due east at a good clip. Just ten kilometers out of Manaus, they reached the Encontro das Aguas.

Jake had read about the stretch of water where the two rivers flowed side by side, as though separated by some invisible wall. Still, the turbulence of the muddy brown Amazon running alongside the inky waters of the Negro took him by surprise. Almost immediately, they turned west, up the Amazon and toward the heart of the rain forests.

After Hughes and du Pont departed, Jake went to look for Cabin Two. He found it on the aft side of the boat, just past the window where he'd heard Hughes's and Brent's voices. The accommodations were small but roomy enough for a queen-size bed. The walls' solid wood raised paneling shone with varnish. The window would give Jake a view of the forests from his bed.

Jake tested the window. It opened. A hot breeze caressed his face.

Jake's cabin included a private bathroom, with a shower, toilet and sink. He dropped his bags on the bed. Opening the duffel, he took out a picture.

Ana, Michael and Antony, all wearing swimsuits, grinned back at the camera, a stunningly blue ocean glittering behind them. Ana's long black hair hung wet over her shoulders, down over her full breasts. Her dark eyes shone with exuberance as she draped a thin brown arm over each boy's shoulders. Guaymas. Their last vacation together.

The sight stabbed at Jake with such violence that he almost replaced the picture in his bag. Instead, he lifted the pillow and placed it gently underneath. Then, quickly, he left the room.

He wandered up to the observation deck. An awning provided partial shade. Two hammocks beckoned, but Jake felt wired, on edge. He had to keep moving. He paced the deck, staring first out at the north shore of the river, which they hovered near, then crossing the deck to stare at the more distant south shores.

As the sun rose higher in the sky, Jake got a foretaste of the tropical heat to come. With the trees creating a high-walled canyon through which the river ran, the breeze created by the boat's movement offered the only relief from the temperature, which had already climbed into the nineties. Jake soon became drenched in sweat.

"Amazing specimens, aren't they?"

Jake turned to see that Doc du Pont stood behind him. He'd changed from linen shirt and pants to a T-shirt and khaki shorts. Du Pont nodded toward the wall of trees.

"Never seen anything like them," Jake replied.

Giant trees of every size and shape lined the riverbanks and reached heights of 150 to 200 feet. Their wide buttresses reminded Jake of the fins of a gigantic rocket ship. No two trees looked alike, and all had something growing on them—weeds, fungi, vines (the thickness of three of Jake's forearms) hung down, trailing into the water. Orchids and bromeliads added orange and red specks to a world largely brown and green.

"Look," du Pont said, nodding toward the canopy, high above.

Jake turned his eyes upward. Brightly colored parrots flitted from one side of the river to another. A monkey swung lazily by its tail, its shriek blending in with the screams of dozens of others hidden in the dense growth.

Du Pont had joined Jake at the rail.

"Hughes tells me you're an expert on the DNA of the Amazonian tribes."

"*Expert* seems a mite strong a word, but I've spent the better part of the last five years studying the gene pool here."

"What about G32? Do you agree it's here, in the Amazon?"

Du Pont turned to study Jake.

"Don't believe in wastin' time, do you, mate? But it's a fair question. Do I believe we'll find G32 down here?"

He stared out at the river traffic, mostly dugout canoes—tree trunks hollowed out with fire—while formulating his answer.

"I'd give us a fifty-fifty chance. If the rumors are true, I'd put it at seventy-five or eighty."

"Rumors? What rumors?"

Du Pont's brow furrowed.

"You don't know?"

"No. What rumors?"

"Odd that Hughes hasn't told you."

"Told me what, dammit?"

"Sorry, mate, but I really don't think it's my place."

"Hughes," Jake muttered, shaking his head. As soon as he got him alone, he would ask about these rumors.

Jake stared out, pretending to watch the sights they passed but seeing only images of his boys, left behind without him while he went on this trip that kept taking one strange turn after another.

Du Pont, seemingly oblivious to the concern he'd caused Jake, remained by his side, watching the shoreline with the relaxed expression of someone on a luxury cruise.

After they'd passed several small settlements, the *Tapuya* hardly drawing a glance, the smiling crewman Jake had first encountered on the front balcony appeared and, opening his mouth wide as a bass, mimicked spooning food into it.

Time to eat.

Jake and du Pont followed as the good-natured fellow led them inside, to a large salon lined with windows and the same beautifully maintained woodwork Jake had noticed in the cabin. Situated at the front of the boat, the windows lining three of the room's four walls afforded its occupants 180-degree views of water and forest. Hughes and Brent sat at a long table, iced drinks in hand. Jake spaced himself one chair away from Hughes, across from Brent. Du Pont settled opposite Hughes. The crewman instantly appeared with two drinks in hand.

"Brent and I have been going over our itinerary," Hughes announced.

Brent unrolled a map lying on the table.

"For the most part," he said, running his finger along a thick black line that snaked almost due west from its outlet at the Atlantic Ocean before dropping south toward its origin in the Peruvian Andes, "we'll stay on the Amazon for approximately two hundred miles, until we reach the Purus. That will take us south by southwest, eventually into Acre. We'll take the *Tapuya* as far in as the river permits; then we'll be traveling in the skiff and sleeping in tents. At this point," he jabbed at the map, "we have a decision to make. The most direct route into Acre—and let me qualify myself by saying the word *direct* has no place in this fucking country—would be to stay on the Purus at this fork, follow it till it meets the Yaco, then head into our target territory on the Yaco."

"If that's the most direct route, why do we have a decision to make?" Hughes asked.

"Because right here," Brent said, his forefinger striking a portion of the map just beyond the fork, "Zurito tells me that there's one hell of a waterfall. We'd have to portage around it. That means walk, carrying everything."

"How much time would it save us to go that route?"

"Maybe three, four days."

"We can't waste that much time," Hughes stated matter-of-factly. "We'll portage around it."

"There are only five of us," Brent responded. "Pedro will stay on board the *Tapuya*. Lotta work for five men to carry the boat and supplies."

"How far around the waterfall?"

"Distance?" Brent replied. "Hell, who knows? Nobody measures distance here. It's all in hours, days, weeks."

"How far in hours then?"

"I'll talk to Zurito. He's never actually seen it, but he knows other guides who have."

Jake was growing very curious about this Zurito. He'd decided he must be the other dark-skinned man that he'd seen just briefly upon boarding the *Tapuya*.

"Do that," Hughes said. "And if we need more men, we'll hire natives along the way."

"Where exactly are we headed?" Jake asked, relieved to finally be let in on the plans.

"We'll stop for samples at several villages along the way, but our ultimate destination is deep in the terra firma—the high country jungle—in the state of Acre."

"There's someone living there?" Jake asked. "A settlement?"

"We've heard interesting rumors coming out of that region," Hughes said.

"What kind of rumors?" Jake asked. He could feel du Pont's eyes on him.

Hughes's gaze locked with Jake's as he waited for Jake's reaction. Brent's expression was difficult to read.

"Rumors of natives with blue eyes," Hughes answered.

Jake's heart rate skyrocketed. Across from him du Pont smiled broadly.

G32 was known to have two characteristics: It was only found in the purest of populations, which is why researchers had zeroed in on remote, indigenous donors.

And it was believed to be linked to blue eyes.

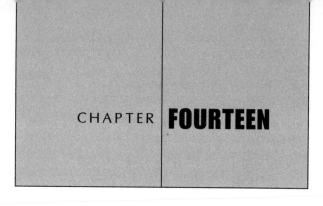

CHAPTER **FOURTEEN**

ASAHEL AND CAINA had fallen into a routine of sorts. Each morning before leaving for work, Asahel made a breakfast of oatmeal and fruit. Caina had developed a taste for melons—cantaloupe and honeydew. Asahel bought three and four at a time, along with the only other staples, besides brown rice, she'd been able to interest Caina in. Seattle Sourdough bread and Oreo Doublestuffs.

They had also developed their own language—mostly gestures and invisible drawings in the air, but they now shared a vocabulary of a dozen or so words, some English, others Caina's native tongue.

Asahel had given Caina strict instructions to keep the blinds down in the kitchen and never, ever answer the telephone or door, which did not present a problem, as Caina's experiences had so traumatized her that, for the most part, she wanted little more than to watch television, which had taken control of her days and, often, nights. After their first evening together, when Caina bolted upright at the sight of a commercial for an upcoming special on the destruction of the Amazonian rain forests, Asahel had ordered more channels on cable, including the National Geographic Channel. At all hours of the day and night, Caina channel-surfed for anything that even remotely reminded her of home. If she succeeded in finding something late at night or during the early morning hours, Asahel would often find Caina still sleeping when she left for work; but today, Caina wandered into the kitchen just as Asahel picked up her briefcase to leave.

"Maha."

Hand on the doorknob, Asahel turned.

"Maha," she said back. She smiled and pointed at the oatmeal she'd left on the stove. "For you."

Caina nodded, returning a shy smile. Dressed in Asahel's sweatpants and UW sweatshirt (she seemed unable to get warm, even now that Seattle's weather had finally turned), her hair standing haphazardly on end, she looked like any college coed just tumbling out of bed.

Asahel had surprised herself with her reaction the day before, when Toby called with good news.

"I've found someone to take Caina," he'd said. "I'll pick her up by the end of the week."

"Wait a minute. I can't just let her go with anyone. Who is it?"

"One of my coworkers. She's out of town right now, but she'll be back Friday."

"What's she like?"

"Asahel, in case you forgot, this is what you asked me to do. This is what you said you wanted."

Asahel hesitated.

"It is. I do. But I'd like to know more about her, that's all."

"Well, you know as well as I do that's not a good idea. Not now."

Toby was right. Within organizations like IPAF, it was understood that the lines could be tapped.

"You can tell me what kind of person she is," Asahel persisted. "Caina wouldn't be comfortable with someone loud, or pushy. And where does she live? How safe is her setup?"

"For someone who's desperate to get rid of her, you're being a little picky, aren't you?" Fuentes finally responded testily.

Asahel had ignored the comment. What did he expect of her? She might not be willing to keep Caina indefinitely, but she wasn't exactly heartless. More and more, Asahel had the feeling that her father was keeping an even closer eye on her than before. If that was true, it wasn't safe for either of them—Caina or Asahel—for Caina to stay with Asahel much longer.

"Remember," Asahel said now, before leaving. "Don't answer the door." She pointed to the door, shaking her head no.

Caina nodded acknowledgment.

"And the TV," Asahel said, shaping her hands in the form of a box. "Keep the volume low." She made a gesture with both hands, pushing toward the floor.

Caina gave Asahel a thumbs-up.

Asahel laughed out loud. She didn't remember teaching Caina that one. She must have picked it up from a TV show.

"Remember, I'll be home late tonight." She pointed at the 9 on the clock. She had already explained this to Caina the night before. "I have a meeting."

Caina nodded.

"Will you be okay?"

Again, the smile and a nod.

"Bye," Asahel said, glancing back at her guest one last time before stepping out onto the deck.

"Bye."

PARKER RAMSEY'S DOOR sat wide open, but as Asahel stepped inside Parker's office her father's assistant was nowhere to be found.

A voice—her father's—drew Asahel's eyes to the door connecting his office to Parker's. It, too, stood open, just a few inches, which meant that Parker must be inside. Not wanting to see her father, Asahel turned to leave. But as she did, her argument with Toby came back to her.

"You're an insider now; just think how much more information's available to someone like you."

"You mean go undercover?"

"It wouldn't have to be anything formal. If you want, we wouldn't even have to tell anyone at IPAF. It could just be between us. You helping me. Just some information here and there. You know, like E-mail addresses, research files, who's heavy into bioprospecting down there, in the Amazon. Whatever you can get your hands on."

Asahel eased her way closer to the door. Esser's agitated voice carried clearly to Parker's office.

"You mean they're down there?" he said. *"Right now?"*

Asahel inched even closer.

"Where? What part of the Amazon?"

As Esser listened to the other party's response, Asahel heard an angry thud—his fist slamming down on the desk.

"Acre! That can't be a coincidence. They must know something. That fucker. I ought to . . ."

"Excuse me?"

At the sound of a voice behind her, Asahel's stomach jumped into her throat. She swirled around and came face-to-face with Parker Ramsey.

"What are you doing?" Ramsey demanded.

Remembering how frazzled she'd allowed herself to become during the QA meeting, Asahel channeled all her energy into delivering a nonchalant response. She smiled graciously.

"Oh, there you are," she said. "When I saw the door open, I thought you were in with Father." She rarely used the word, but now she even managed to say it with affection. "I brought the compliance papers you asked me for."

She extended the hand that held the stapled documents.

Asahel's composure appeared to throw Parker off. She immediately drew back from her initial attack mode.

"Oh," she said, taking the papers. She eyed the open door, still wary. "Did you want to see Dr. Esser?"

"No," Asahel replied breezily. "That's not necessary. Have a great day, Parker."

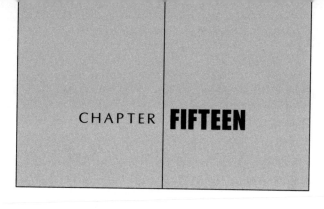

CHAPTER **FIFTEEN**

THE SPRING MEETING, hosted by the biotech division of the Washington State Bar, started out with dinner at the Roosevelt, a recently renovated turn-of-the-century hotel on Broadway—a selection that pleased Asahel because it happened to be just blocks from her apartment. She'd felt uneasy about leaving Caina alone so long and was eager to get home.

She'd thought about skipping the after-dinner meetings, but she'd received a notice warning her that she was short on Continuing Legal Education credits and just by signing in at one of the seminars she'd be able to claim two hours. She'd originally signed up for a contracts management session and had planned to slip out once they'd passed the roster, but then a poster in the lobby of the Roosevelt caught Asahel's eye. It was for the IP section.

The Patenting of Life. Room 310A.

Despite the fact that Asahel did not handle Mercy's patent work—it had long been outsourced to a prestigious D.C. law firm—she joined the throng of lawyers moving toward the third-floor conference room.

The session moderator, a slick *GQ* type wearing a crisp white shirt and purple suspenders, wasted no time in getting started.

"What a time it is," he said dramatically, "to be a patent attorney."

Heads nodded all around him.

"The challenges that face us are greater than ever. But," he smiled, "so are the rewards."

Yeah, thought Asahel, *in the form of outrageous salaries and overblown stock options.*

"I look around and in this room alone," the moderator continued, "I see faces associated with some of the most far-reaching, exciting patents ever issued. Joseph, you handled AEM's patent on that Andean bean, didn't you?"

An equally slick-looking attorney standing at the back of the room raised his hand.

"How many varieties does that patent cover?"

"Thirty-three," Joseph answered. "At last count. And if I have my way, we'll make it to fifty."

Laughter echoed around the room.

"Jennifer Leland helped the University of Wisconsin obtain its patent on supersweet genes extracted from the berries of the *brazzien* plant. Where's that plant from, Jennifer?"

A female voice called out, "West Africa."

The moderator raised a hand to pat the top of his hair.

"And I hear that L'Oreal's patented kava. To reduce hair loss."

Everyone but Asahel got a big kick out of this one. Kava had been used as a ceremonial beverage in many Pacific countries for centuries.

"What about De Code's patent on Iceland's population?" someone called out.

"That's right," the moderator cried, delighted at this reminder. "De Code Genetics has exclusive rights to the DNA of all of Iceland's inhabitants."

While all around her heads nodded in enthusiastic approval of the groundbreaking patents being granted right and left, Asahel experienced a sick, visceral reaction to what she was hearing. She'd routinely protested patents like these during her IPAF days, patents that commercialized sacred tribal medicinal and cultural plants and that all too often stripped the rights to use them anymore from those same tribes, without recognition or compensation. But her abhorrence of the patenting system alone did not explain the extremity of her reaction. So much that had happened recently triggered memories Asahel had thought she'd buried along with Angie, but nothing hit her harder than hearing this recital of the same greed and exploitation that had started Asahel down a path of activism—a path that ultimately ended in the death of the one person she loved most.

When the discussion of Moban's recent patent fiasco—the company had first opposed another company, Agrom, in their species-wide patent on all genetically engineered soybeans and then, after acquiring Agrom, turned around and resolutely defended the very same patent—ended and the floor was finally opened for the standard Q and A, Asahel breathed a sigh of relief. The session had accomplished nothing more than upsetting her. She couldn't wait to get home.

Immediately, a petite dark-haired pixie of a woman jumped to her feet. She looked barely out of law school. The effect wasn't helped by her heavy black lip liner.

"I'm with Cell Cyte," she said. "As you probably know, we're an upstart. And I'm not the most experienced patent attorney." This statement drew a couple of snide remarks from some of the older attorneys in the group. "So I'm hoping I can pick your brains tonight. My question is this: how many therapeutic applications are reasonable in a patent application for living matter? And how far along does the research have to be to be named in an application? Obviously, it'd be in our best interest to make our applications as broad as possible, as early as possible, but I don't want to start off on the wrong foot with the USPTO."

When no one in the room made any effort to respond, the moderator, who had been skimming the group—no doubt eyeing networking opportunities, for that was what these meetings were all about—directed his eyes toward the last row of the room.

"Gina Castle would be a good person to ask that question. From what I hear, GenChrom has had some productive bioprospecting trips to the Amazon. Gina? Mind giving us the benefit of your experience?"

Asahel turned to see a heavyset woman, dressed in a snug pink suit, rise reluctantly from her seat.

Castle cleared her throat.

"Actually," she said, "I've probably got less experience in this field than many of you. Most of the products we have in the pipeline are biochemical."

"But GenChrom is actively sampling in the rain forests, aren't they? Surely you've filed on some of that work. Of course, we're only interested in generalities, the patent process itself, nothing specific or confidential."

Castle's expression darkened.

"I don't know where you get your information, but it's actually been quite a while since GenChrom has been in the Amazon," she said, without offering more.

It was apparent that Castle had no intention of sharing what knowledge she did have.

The moderator thanked her stiffly.

She'd made him look foolish, and Asahel sensed that he was a man who'd eventually find a way to make Castle pay.

For her part, Asahel simply stared at Gina Castle, who'd dropped back into her seat and now tugged at the hem of her skirt.

Something about Castle's response, her entire reaction to being put on the spot, did not ring true. Suddenly Asahel thought back to the one-sided conversation she'd overheard earlier that day, outside her father's office. Reference to someone being down in Brazil—the state of Acre no less. The state where Caina's tribe lived. And the general region in which GenChrom was bioprospecting, according to the moderator. Could there be some connection?

THE MOMENT SHE STEPPED outside of the hotel, she heard the sirens.

Sirens on or near Broadway—the main strip and heart of Seattle's funky Capitol Hill district—were nothing new to Asahel, nothing to get stirred up about. Capitol Hill residents' propensity to exercise what they perceived as their civil liberties to the fullest extent possible made for plenty of excitement, day and night. But as she walked down Roy Street toward her house on Bellevue, the sirens grew progressively louder and Asahel instinctively picked up her pace.

She passed one of the new upscale high-rise condominiums that were springing up all over Capitol Hill and rounded the corner to a night suddenly bright with flashing lights. For the first time Asahel realized that the commotion—two police cars, an ambulance and fire truck—took place at her own building.

Running now, to the scene, she saw paramedics carrying a heavy stretcher toward the back of the ambulance, which stood, ready, with open doors.

As she raced across Roy and approached the sidewalk below her apartment, a beefy Seattle cop stepped in her path.

"Sorry, miss. You gotta stand back."

"I live here," Asahel said, her eyes darting to her top-floor apartment, which appeared completely dark. That, in and of itself, meant nothing. Caina had declared artificial light an insult to one of the many gods worshiped by the Naua. On the few occasions Asahel left her alone in the evening, she'd come home to an apartment lit only by the TV, the light from which couldn't be seen on this side of the house.

"Then the sergeant over there'll want to talk to you," the cop said. "But not before he's done with those guys."

In the flashing lights, Asahel made out two of her neighbors—a couple who had only recently moved into the first-floor apartment—huddled with another uniformed officer, who was taking notes.

"What happened?" she asked the cop. "Please. I have to know."

"Someone fell from one of the upper decks."

Asahel gasped. *Caina.*

"Please," she said, grabbing the officer by the arm. "I have to see. I live on the top floor. It may be a friend of mine."

The cop looked toward his superior officer, then back at the ambulance, into which the stretcher had already been loaded. Inside, he could see that the two paramedics had already begun treating the victim.

"Go on," he said suddenly, dropping his arms to allow her by.

Asahel sprinted for the ambulance. She reached it just as its driver approached to close its back doors. All Asahel could see of the victim was a hand resting on the chest.

A man's long, slender hand.

With a sigh of relief, Asahel began to turn away as the first door slammed shut. But then one of the paramedics, huddled over the patient, stretched to reach for a bag of fluids, and in that instant Asahel caught sight of a familiar face.

"God, no," Asahel sobbed.

As the driver began to close the second door, Asahel threw herself between it and the back of the ambulance, blocking it.

"Wait," she cried. "I have to go with him."

The driver drew back, startled, to check her out.

"Are you a relative?"

"Yes," Asahel answered instantly. "I'm his sister."

"Quick," the driver said, "hop in."

With a boost from the driver, Asahel jumped up, into the back of the ambulance. Her heart pounded mercilessly in her ears, blotting out the instructions being barked efficiently between the two paramedics, who were huddled over the frighteningly still form lying on the stretcher.

Asahel hovered near the back of the ambulance, which had begun racing toward Harborview, its sirens clearing the way.

Helpless to do anything but watch, she reached out and grasped the slender ankle—anything to connect with him. Anything to let him know she was there. That he wasn't alone.

It was the one weakness she'd always teased him about.

For Toby Fuentes had always hated to be alone.

SHE WAS STILL IN A STATE of profound shock. She'd been through this before. It had all come back to her. She knew what to expect now; and if she had any choice in the matter, she'd have chosen to remain in this state, this numbed state of shock. Because she knew that what came next—the grief—would be unbearable.

"So are you admitting you lied?"

Asahel lifted her head from her hands and looked up at the officer through blurry eyes.

Toby had never regained consciousness.

Asahel had been sitting in Harborview's ER for two hours when a doctor dressed in blue scrubs entered. He scanned the full room, then headed her way.

"Are you with Mr. Fuentes?"

Asahel jumped up.

"How is he?"

He'd taken her gently by the elbow, guiding her to a quiet room, just off the busy ER.

Then he'd turned to her.

"I'm afraid we couldn't save him."

"No," Asahel had cried.

"He died during surgery. We were trying to relieve intracranial pressure."

Suddenly Asahel noticed another man standing behind the doctor, in the doorway. A uniformed police officer. She recognized him as the sergeant she'd seen speaking to her neighbors.

Asahel had wanted to rush home to check on Caina, but the sergeant had insisted on interviewing her right there, in the hospital's waiting room.

"Yes," Asahel admitted now. "I lied."

"You're not really his sister?"

Asahel shook her head.

"I just said that to get them to let me ride to the hospital with him. I didn't want him to be alone."

"How long have you been friends?"

"I don't know," Asahel said, her mind numb like the rest of her. "Years. Maybe ten. We worked together." She swallowed a sob. "He was my best friend."

It was true. Toby had been her best friend. The years apart hadn't changed that. Nor had the tension over Caina. His death was incomprehensible.

"Were you expecting him at your apartment tonight?"

"No. He'd said he'd be over later in the week."

"For business?"

"No. We don't work together anymore. It was social," she lied.

"Are you aware of any health problems he might have? You know, something that might cause him to get dizzy, maybe pass out. Those stairs up to the top floor, they're pretty steep."

"No. Toby's been up them a hundred times."

"Did he drink?"

"An occasional glass of wine. Not enough to make him fall."

"*If* he fell," the sergeant said. He'd introduced himself to Asahel, but in her state of confusion she hadn't processed his name.

"What do you mean, *if?*"

"The two guys on the first floor, they thought they heard voices. Raised voices, maybe an argument or a scuffle."

"Coming from my deck?" Asahel asked.

"They couldn't be sure. They were watching TV. Had their window open. Could've been someone in the next house. I saw that they have a rooftop deck over there. I've got an officer over there now," he said. Then he asked, "Does anyone live with you?"

Asahel thought back to the chaotic minutes on the sidewalk, before she'd climbed in the ambulance. She hadn't seen any sign of Caina.

"No," Asahel lied again.

Asahel told the sergeant about Stan and gave him Stan's name and the address of his and Toby's apartment. During Toby's surgery, Asahel had called Stan a dozen times from the pay phone and had finally left a message urging him to come to the hospital.

Under any other circumstances, she would have asked to accompany the officer to notify Stan that his partner and beloved companion was dead. But a sick dread had risen inside Asahel. She had to get back to her apartment. Had to see if Caina was okay.

Her interview finished, Asahel headed back to the phone she'd used to call Stan. But as she approached, she saw a woman, crying, clutching a soggy handkerchief, already using it. She rushed down the hallway, looking for another phone, to call a cab, and literally ran into a paramedic.

"Sorry," Asahel said, hurrying on without recognizing him as one of the paramedics who'd treated Toby.

"Hey," a voice called from behind her.

She turned. Wasn't "sorry" good enough?

"Aren't you the lady we brought over here in the ambulance a couple hours ago?"

Now she recognized him. She stopped and waited as he approached her.

"Yes."

"I'm sorry about your brother," he said. "I wish we could have done more."

Asahel fought to hold on.

"Thank you. You tried. I could see that."

When he continued standing there, Asahel said, "I don't mean to be rude, but I need to get home right away."

"I didn't get your name."

"Asahel. Asahel Sullivan," she said. "I'm sorry, I really do have to go."

She turned her back to him again.

"Did he call you *Ash?*"

Asahel froze in her tracks.

She swirled back around.

"Did your brother call you Ash?"

"Yes." She reached out and clutched at his arm. "Why?"

"He had a message for you."

"A message?"

"He was conscious for a few seconds, when we first got to him. He was mumbling something. He said, 'Tell Ash it's called Greta,' or something like that."

"Greta?" Asahel cried. "That's my mother's name. Are you sure that's what he said?"

The paramedic shook his head, trying to remember Toby's exact words.

"You know, he was mumbling. I could've got it wrong. But I thought that's what he said. Poor guy lost consciousness right after that."

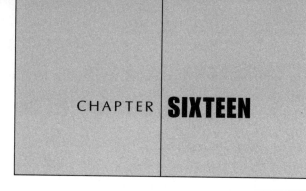

CHAPTER **SIXTEEN**

AS ASAHEL SAT waiting for the meeting she'd arranged with Michael Sullivan, she couldn't help but wonder just how much her ex had changed over the past few years.

She'd chosen a booth at the back of the *Spokane*—the ferry that shuttled commuters across the dark, heavily trafficked waters of Elliott Bay, between Seattle and Bainbridge Island—not just for privacy but also because it gave her the opportunity to check Sullivan out before he could do the same with her.

The ferry blasted its third and final warning, and when Asahel looked toward the line of passengers streaming in from the stairway to the car deck, her eyes were met with the familiar blue of Sullivan's. He froze for a moment, then, nudged by someone from behind, continued toward her.

And then his handsome face—fuller now, and even from this distance she could make out lines that had not been there before—broke into a grin.

Asahel stood as he approached, and they hugged. Asahel's long, heartfelt grasp surprised him.

"You okay?" he said, pulling back to eye her.

She nodded and said, "You look good, Sully," then pulled him into the booth alongside her.

"You look *fantastic*," he said, his eyes wide and admiring. "How long has it been?"

"Almost four years."

"Since just before you moved to Seattle to accept the job with IPAF. Bet you never thought I'd follow you."

"Yeah, right," Asahel replied sarcastically. "That's why you've been such a pest."

"No, really," Sullivan said, his expression making it clear he was being truthful. "I followed you. I asked for a transfer because I was determined to come out here and win you back."

This made no sense at all. In all this time, aside from a couple messages from Sullivan after Angie's death, Asahel had never heard from him.

"Guess you decided on the slow, watchful approach, huh?" she teased.

Sullivan suddenly looked sheepish.

"Not exactly. I was gonna give you a little time to sort through things, and during that time," he eyed her closely, "I fell in love. I'm married again, Ash."

Asahel's silence only lasted a few seconds.

"Wow. That's great, Sully. Congratulations."

"Thanks."

"You look happy. I take it she's not an activist."

Sullivan's laugh echoed down the row of booths. They'd had more than their share of differences, but Asahel always loved the way Sully laughed—unabashedly, pouring all his joy, all his appreciation, into that one moment.

They'd met at an Animal Liberation Coalition protest at Meade Pharmaceuticals' primate research center. It was Sullivan's third year in the FBI and he had gone undercover, presenting himself as a protester from San Francisco. Rumor was that the protest preceded an ALC plan to break into the center and kidnap the baboons held captive inside sometime in the near future. It was Sullivan's job that day to identify the leaders and real troublemakers. He'd pegged Asahel as one.

He'd followed her throughout the day, positioning himself near her. They'd made eye contact early on, and when the police tear-gassed the group and Sullivan helped a fallen protester to her feet, he'd earned a smile and a nod from Asahel. After that, they'd stuck together, running through the streets, both half-blind from the tear gas. When he fell and broke his nose, she'd taken him to her apartment, only blocks from the melee, and tended to him.

Later he told Asahel he'd already fallen in love with her by then. Truth be known, though it would take her a lot longer to admit it, even to herself, by that time she was pretty much a goner, too.

He hadn't confessed his real job to her until they'd been together for several months. Asahel had actually attacked him, physically pummeling his chest. He offered no resistance.

She threw him out of her apartment and her life. But two weeks later, she'd knocked on his door in the middle of the night and climbed in bed with him. They made a sometimes uneasy peace with the situation, and Sullivan requested to be removed from the ALC assignment. They married that year.

And divorced when Asahel was asked to run IPAF's Seattle offices.

"Trudy's a housewife, and mother," Sullivan answered. "I've got two stepsons now."

"How about you?" Asahel asked. "Are you still on the street?"

"I'm a Special Agent now. Pretty much a desk job, with better pay."

"I would think you'd miss that. The action."

Sullivan shook his head.

"Nah. Look how much trouble it got me into in Boston."

She studied his face to see if he was teasing her.

"You mean me? Us?"

"What else?"

"I can't see you behind a desk," Asahel said.

"It's safer. My wife likes that," Sullivan replied. "How've you been, Ash?"

She stared at him for a moment.

"Okay," she replied. "Actually, that's a lie. Things pretty much suck. I called you because I need help, Sully. Information."

"What about?"

"Let's get something straight first," Asahel said. "This is all hypothetical, okay?"

"You mean that game we used to play? The one where you test your radical plans by bouncing them off me first? I take it you're about to tell me something that as an FBI agent I'd have an obligation to act upon if it were really true. But you want me to promise not to do that."

"Something like that."

He hesitated, but only for a moment.

"Okay, shoot."

"What do you know about biopiracy? Specifically in the Amazon."

"The Bureau knows it's happening, but they haven't had much luck fighting it."

"Why's that?"

In a habit that had once amused Asahel, Sullivan held up an index finger and began counting his answers to her question on his fingers.

"One," he said. "Proof. If crimes are being committed, they're taking place in distant, hard-to-reach areas. The victims are generally dirt-poor and afraid of any kind of authority. Plus half the time they've been threatened about talking. In short, it's damn near impossible to prove that anything illegal's taking place, especially without willing witnesses."

The second finger shot up.

"Because of the aforementioned," he continued, falling into almost comical agentspeak, "it would take forever and cost a small fortune to do an exhaustive investigation."

He stopped then, too abruptly.

"And?" Asahel coaxed. "Three?"

"Three," he repeated, but he'd dropped his hand back to the Formica table, "you know this answer already. It's the pharmaceutical companies who commit ninety percent of the biopiracy. The rest is done by none other than our own government, and then a splattering of independent researchers. Ain't nobody more politically connected these days than the pharmaceutical industry. And needless to say, the Bureau's not anxious to dig into the affairs of other governmental agencies."

"So you're saying these crimes aren't vigorously pursued because of the toes that would be stepped on if they were."

"You know you'd never get me to say that," Sullivan said, sounding testy for the first time. "Draw your own conclusions."

"Do you know anything about a Seattle biotech company called GenChrom?" Asahel asked.

"Why?"

"Remember Toby Fuentes?"

Sullivan nodded his head. He had always resented how close Ash was to Fuentes.

"He's dead."

Sullivan's eyes widened in surprise. He reached for Asahel's hand.

"I'm sorry, Ash. How did it happen?"

"He fell from the deck of my apartment. Tuesday night."

"God, no."

"I think he was pushed, Sully."

Asahel could see the wheels spin into action inside Sullivan's brain, the pieces of the puzzle he was already gathering. The ones he would slowly piece together for that report he couldn't stop himself from writing, even if it was only in his head.

He pushed back, against the back of the booth, all business now. All ears.

"Why don't you start by telling me about Tuesday night?"

ASAHEL PAID THE CABBIE, slipped under the police tape blocking the sidewalk and took the stairs up to her apartment two at a time, her fear for Caina the only thing keeping her from breaking down about Toby.

She looked up. No lights, inside or out.

Drawing her keys from her briefcase as she ran up the last flight, Asahel reached for the door. With the light above the door out, she had to feel for the keyhole, but as soon as she touched the door's knob, the door creaked open.

Asahel stepped inside. In the dark, she sensed it immediately. Something was wrong.

"Caina?" she called.

Flipping on the hall light, Asahel ran from one room to another. A chair in the living room lay on its side. Other than that, and the fact that Caina was nowhere to be seen, nothing seemed out of place.

Then she saw it. The inside door, the one to the stairwell. Open, like the back door. Caina never failed to lock both doors every time she went in or out, even if she only left long enough to run down to the foyer to pick up the mail for Asahel.

Frantic, Asahel sprinted down the inside stairwell stairs; then, stepping outside, she cleared the three porch steps in one leap. She circled the house twice, dropping on her knees to peer under bushes and under cars parked in the carport. Jerking open the door to the laundry room, she startled one of the downstairs tenants—a blue-haired girl who had recently moved in—especially when, without explanation, she bent to check inside the giant dryer. The girl watched warily through the door as Asahel opened each in the line of half-full Dumpsters sitting in the alley and called inside one after another.

Asahel circled the block. Fighting to keep a clear head, she came up with a search plan. Widening her circle, she added a block at a time, running, stopping to look under porches, inside cars parked along the curbs.

This went on for hours, until Asahel's rubbery legs had taken her all the way to Broadway. Until she began to make out the faint outline of the Cascades in the eastern sky.

Maybe, while Asahel was searching, Caina had returned.

By the time Asahel ran up the series of hills on Roy, then climbed the last flight of steps to her apartment, fire burned both her lungs and thighs.

She found the apartment like she'd left it. Empty.

Asahel's fear was turning into a certainty that something, something horrible, had happened to Caina.

In her kitchen, Asahel reached for the phone and dialed Stan. Voice mail picked up. Toby's voice.

You know we're never home, but leave a message . . .

"Stan, it's Ash. I . . . I can't . . . I'm sorry, Stan. . . . I'm so sorry. . . ."

With Toby's lighthearted greeting still echoing in her ears, Asahel finally broke into uncontrollable sobs. Hanging up, she dropped to the floor, her head in her lap, cradled by her thin arms.

She let it come.

Suffocated by her grief, she fought for air, rocking, moaning. Her shoulders heaving. Crying first for Toby and then for Caina.

It was when she sobbed Caina's name that she felt it—a touch so light it might have been Toby's spirit, not yet ready to go.

But this was real. A hand on the top of her head.

Asahel lifted her tear-streaked face.

"Caina!"

Jumping to her feet, Asahel threw her arms around the other woman.

At first Caina's arms hung limp at her sides, but slowly Asahel felt them tighten around her, pulling Asahel close.

Comforting her.

"WHERE HAD SHE BEEN?" Sully asked.

He'd pulled out a paper and pen to take notes, but Asahel stopped him.

"Stan actually showed up at my apartment a little while after Caina returned. He'd been trying to reach me when I was out looking for her. He was devastated, barely holding it together, but he had to have some answers, more than the police had given him. He knew there was a chance I hadn't told them everything. A chance this had to do with Caina."

Asahel thought back to that black, ugly night.

"When he got there, he was able to talk to Caina," she continued. "Find out what happened."

"What did she tell him?"

"She said she'd been watching TV when she heard someone knocking frantically at the door. It scared her. She's sure that whoever killed her tribe will come after her one day, too. She slipped down the inside stairwell, then outside. She just ran, as fast and far as she could, without looking back."

"You think it was Toby at the door?"

"It had to have been. He'd told me he was going to pick Caina up later in the week, but he must have found out something. Right before he lost consciousness, Toby gave the EMT a message for me. I think that's why he came to my apartment Tuesday. To tell me something important."

"What was his message?"

"It doesn't really make sense," Asahel said, shaking her head slowly. "He said, *'Tell Ash it's called Greta.'*"

Sullivan's brow furrowed into three deep creases, creases Ash had once traced with her fingertips.

"Your mother?"

"I don't know. It must be. I mean, it can't just be a coincidence."

"Did Toby know your mother's name?"

"I don't know. I may have mentioned it, but I wasn't even on speaking terms with my parents the entire time I worked with Toby, so who knows?"

"It could be some kind of code."

"I hadn't thought of that."

Sullivan leaned closer, close enough for Asahel to reach out and trace those lines once more.

"So Toby shows up at your apartment, pounds on the door, scaring your visitor. Caina. She sneaks out. Then he either loses his balance and falls or . . ."

"Or he's pushed."

"Which would mean someone had followed him."

"Exactly," Asahel replied.

"Where was Caina all this time?"

"At first she was lost. When she finally found her way home, she saw the ambulances and police cars, and that really scared her. She hid in someone's garage until it got light. Then she finally decided to risk coming back to my apartment."

Sullivan fell silent.

"Why would anyone want your friend dead?"

"That's what I want to know. The police are investigating, but . . ."

"But you figure the kind of stuff you're suspecting isn't exactly their forte. That's why you came to me."

"I need information, Sully."

"Go on."

"Toby and I had just recently reconnected."

"He didn't work at IPAF anymore?"

"No," Asahel replied. "*I* don't."

Sullivan's scowl reflected his confusion.

"What group are you with now?"

"I'm working for Mercy Pharmaceuticals. As their attorney."

"Your dad's company? Come on, you're kidding. Right?"

"No," Asahel said, her eyes evading Sullivan's. "I'm not. It's not something I want to talk about. Okay?"

Sullivan grew silent.

"Does this have something to do with your sister's death?"

"Leave it alone, Sully."

"How'd he do it, Ash? How'd he force you to come to work for him?"

Abruptly, Asahel half stood, but she could not leave the booth. Sullivan blocked her way.

"Let me out," she demanded.

He grabbed her by the forearm.

"Sit down, Ash. Okay, I'll let it go. Just sit down. Please."

Warily Asahel settled back into the booth.

"But if you want my help, you'll have to confide in me."

"That's fair," Asahel said, nodding.

"Okay," Sullivan said. "Tell me more about your pal. Toby."

"He'd been trying to help me. I'm in a bad situation, Sully. Two weeks ago, Caina just showed up on my doorstep."

"You mean you never saw her before?"

"Yes," Asahel answered. "Well, no, not exactly. I guess I did see her before, but I didn't realize it at first. Caina's from the Amazon. I visited her tribe three and a half years ago."

"Her showing up had to do with that visit?"

"Caina witnessed her tribe being slaughtered. Wiped out by Americans. She came to me for help. I turned to Toby, and somehow I think it got him killed."

"He knew who did it?"

"I thought it was just a theory."

"Who? Who did he think killed them?"

"Researchers. From the pharmaceutical industry."

"Christ almighty, Ash. You just can't leave that activism shit alone, can you?"

Asahel shot him a withering look.

"Is it possible that people are being murdered down there?"

Sullivan shook his head wearily.

"There's a special task force for this kind of thing. I can ask a few questions. But tell me this. Exactly how did this poor native woman from the depths of the Amazon rain forest manage to get here?" Sullivan said, his voice making clear his doubts about this wild tale. "To America? To your apartment no less?"

"She's illegal. Her tribe's from a region that used to be rich in diamonds. Apparently they've had a stash of stones hidden away for decades, as sort of an insurance policy if anything really terrible ever happened to them. Well, it did. Caina took some of the diamonds. She used them to buy her way up to North America and over the border."

Sullivan's eyes scanned the ferry's passengers before returning to lock once more with Asahel's.

"Assuming that part of the story is true," he said, "the part about her finding you—which I don't buy, by the way, not by a long shot— just what made your pal Fuentes think a pharmaceutical company killed her tribe? What evidence did he have?"

Asahel knew that with Sully it would come down to this. Evidence.

"None that I was aware of. But maybe he'd found something and that's why he came to my apartment Tuesday night. No one knows these things better than Toby. He had an eerie sixth sense about them."

Noting a hint of triumph entering Sully's eyes, she grabbed his wrist.

"Listen to me, Michael. People like to think that activists like Toby are irrational, just plain crazy, but that's because no one wants to believe the truth. Even with Enron and Worldcom and all that's happened to open eyes recently, no one really *wants* to believe, or to even *know*, what's happening in places like the Amazon. Enron, now that got everyone riled up. People lost their life savings; it wreaked havoc with the stock market. That affects people. Scares the hell out of them. But admit that the same corporate mentality is taking advantage of tribes down in the rain forest—doing far worse things to them than deflating the value of stocks . . . ? Hell, we're still clinging to the idea that we Americans are saints, the world's saviors. Especially now, with the war against terrorism. It'd be downright unpatriotic to even think it's happening.

"But people like Toby make it their business, their *life,* to learn the truth, to monitor what corporate America is doing to these indigenous people."

Sullivan's eyes took on a familiar combative glint.

"I'm sorry about your friend, Ash, but please, spare me your activist rhetoric. It just doesn't work on me. I'm an FBI agent. I operate on facts. Cold, hard facts. Not suspicions based on some dead guy's sixth sense."

Asahel flinched. She squeezed down on Sullivan's wrist.

"I want you to find out about a Seattle biotech company named GenChrom. I think they've been down there, bioprospecting for new drugs."

"That doesn't make them murderers."

"I know that. But it's at least a starting point. Can you check them out?"

"Your friend's death is one thing. If the police determine he was pushed, and there's evidence it was related to his work at IPAF, the Bureau would definitely get involved. But that's a big if. And I can pretty much tell you that the Bureau's not gonna do *anything* based on the testimony of this one woman. An illegal immigrant at that. You want my honest opinion? It's some kind of scam. She's feeding you a pack of lies. You better watch her. Find out what she's really after. Better yet, let us. Bring her in for us to talk to. We know how to find out if what she's saying is true."

"You mean a lie detector test?"

"That'd be one way. But we can find out just by asking her the right questions, observing her reactions. I know you're no big fan of the Bureau, but you have to admit, we've got a little more experience in questioning people than you activists do."

Sullivan had blamed all their problems on her activism. It was clear that bias hadn't changed since they'd broken up.

"And what if it turns out to be true?" Asahel replied. "What happens to her then?"

"Either way, she goes back to Brazil. And a lot of people there aren't particularly fond of the Indians, on account of all the land the government's awarded them. People may not like this kind of story being spread. The pharmaceutical companies come in and pump big tourist dollars into Brazil's depressed economy. She could end up in trouble there. That's a dangerous part of the world these days. Not unusual for folks down there to take justice—as they see it—into their own hands."

"So you're saying she'd be deported, sent back to a country where her life could be in danger, and that even if they believed her, the FBI's not about to act on it. Well, let's see. This is a tough decision to make."

Asahel held both hands palms up to the ceiling, balancing back and forth as though they were the arms of a scale.

"To bring her in or not to bring her in . . ."

Sullivan reached for her hand.

"Don't do it, Ash. Don't get involved with this. You've apparently come to some kind of a truce with your dad, and that's probably a good thing. I always worried about what he might do to you one day. He's not a man to cross, Ash, and sounds to me like this is something you should stay out of."

"I'm already involved, Sully. Can't you see? Caina's here, in my apartment. And if there's a connection between this and Toby's death, I have to make sure it's uncovered. That's why I came to you, Sully. No one's better at this stuff than you."

It wasn't a ploy. She meant it.

"Will you help me?"

Sullivan let out a sigh.

"Okay," he said. "I'll see what I can find out. But in the meantime, you keep your nose outta this. You hear?"

CHAPTER **SEVENTEEN**

JAKE HAD NEVER used steroids, but he imagined this was what they felt like—a sense of impatience and frustration, an anxiety so deep that he felt he was about to jump out of his skin.

He'd taken to wandering around the *Tapuya* restlessly at all hours of the day and night.

As the sun crept higher in the late morning sky, promising another day of relentless heat, he came across Zurito on the lower deck. Grease-stained rag in hand, the native was hunched over the motor of an aluminum boat.

"That the skiff we'll be using once we leave the *Tapuya*?" Jake asked.

Zurito, whose back had been to Jake, sprang to his feet and swirled to face Jake, fierce eyes boring into him.

A strikingly handsome man, aquiline-featured and possessing a magnificent physique, there was a wildness about Zurito, a warriorlike sense that—despite the blue jeans and thin white ribbed T-shirt—he belonged to another place and time.

"Sorry," Jake said, stepping back. "I didn't mean to startle you."

Zurito stared at him but did not respond.

"Motor problems?" Jake asked.

"What you want?" Zurito asked.

"I didn't want anything," Jake answered. "I was just saying hello."

Zurito gave him a look of disdain, then dropped back down next to the boat and resumed work.

Jake stood watching him for several seconds, wondering what the source of Zurito's distrust—no, it was more than that; it was an animosity, a loathing—might be, and how it would affect their mission.

Then he turned and walked away.

• • •

IT ONLY TOOK TWO DAYS for Sullivan to get back to Asahel. They'd met at Myrtle Edwards Park and settled on a wood bench facing Elliott Bay.

"Well," Sullivan started, turning to face Asahel. "Nobody's reported anything like what your friend described. I don't think it happened, Ash. She's a scam artist. Get rid of her."

A cool breeze off the water blew Asahel's hair in her face. She brushed it away from her eyes angrily.

"I see you're still the world's greatest skeptic," she said, "at least when it comes to those without power, the ones who need your help most. Just because the FBI hasn't received some kind of official report on the slaughter doesn't mean it didn't happen. You and I both know there are regions of the Amazon that no white man ever lays eyes on. It's not at all far-fetched to think this could have happened and that no one's discovered it yet. Caina's no scam artist, Sully. She's no liar. If it weren't for her surviving, her tribe's slaughter could go undiscovered forever."

Sullivan shook his head in frustration.

"Why can't you talk about this stuff without overreacting? When are you gonna see I'm on your side, Asahel? I promised I'd look into it and I did."

It occurred to Asahel that maybe she shouldn't alienate him before finding out what he'd come up with.

"Okay, so what did you find out about GenChrom?" she said.

"The Bureau's been keeping an eye on them. Your information was right. They've been all over the globe, to half a dozen third world countries, including Peru and Brazil."

"Does the FBI have anything on them? Any proof that they've committed biopiracy?"

"No. Nothing. There's nothing in the file to connect GenChrom with this woman you're harboring." His blue eyes drilled into her. "You have to turn her in, Ash. You know that, don't you?"

Asahel ignored him.

"When was the last time GenChrom went to Brazil?"

"They've been down there at least three times this past year."

"So it could be them," Asahel said. "They could be the men Caina saw murder her tribe. Maybe Toby found something out. Something to connect GenChrom with what happened."

Sullivan held up a hand in protest.

"Listen, Ash, even if what your visitor says really happened, you're still a long ways from connecting GenChrom to it."

"But it's a start."

"Pretty circumstantial, wouldn't you say?"

"Maybe."

"No maybes about it. Can your friend tell you the exact date this slaughter supposedly took place?"

Asahel had been waiting for this one.

"No," she replied, her chin rising defiantly. "The Naua don't keep track of time like we do. After talking to her, Toby's partner said he thinks it took place at least a month ago, but he couldn't get her to be more specific than that."

The expression on Sullivan's face was far too smug for Asahel's taste.

"When was the last time GenChrom was down there?" she asked testily.

"Two months ago."

"Well, this could have happened two months ago," Asahel said. "I told you, the Naua don't have an obsession with calendars like we do."

"I suggest you get this woman's facts straight before you start making accusations," Sullivan chastised.

"Apparently it's pointless to make accusations the FBI doesn't want to hear," Asahel shot back.

"So now this is official Bureau business, is it?" Sullivan replied. "I thought this was all hypothetical, like the good old days."

Sullivan could see that the sarcasm with which he said that—*the good old days*—stung Asahel.

"I thought you might like to know that GenChrom is actually down there now," he said then. It was a peace offering.

"*In Brazil?*"

"Yes. They left on the tenth."

Asahel's eyes grew wide at this announcement. That meant it could have been GenChrom she'd heard her father talking about. He'd been furious to hear someone was down in Acre.

She grabbed Sullivan by the forearm.

"What are you going to do about it? Follow them down there?"

"They have the right to go wherever they please, including the Amazon. And you've asked me to keep this thing on the Q.T., so I can hardly traipse off after them. Hell, the truth be known, even if I told my super what you've told me, there's not enough to warrant the Bureau getting involved. But just for your sake, I've called an agent based in Ecuador. He'll keep his eyes and ears open."

Asahel tightened her grip on Sullivan's arm.

"That's not enough. Someone has to follow them. We have to find out what they're up to."

"I told you, Ash. There's no connection between GenChrom and the story told by this new pal of yours. You're barking up the wrong tree. Fuentes's fall was an accident. A sad accident."

The wind had plastered several loose curls against Asahel's face, momentarily obscuring the determination in her eyes.

"Someone has to expose them, Sully," she said. "Someone has to find out what's really happening."

Sullivan pushed her hair back and looked into her eyes.

"What the hell are you thinking about doing?"

Avoiding his gaze, Asahel turned to stare at the waters of Elliott Bay.

"YOU'RE *WHAT?*"

The expression on Stan Yasavich's face caused Asahel momentary doubt about the decision she'd just announced to him. Had all that had happened recently caused her to go crazy? Lose her ability to think rationally?

"I'm going to Brazil," she repeated. "I'm going to find out what happened to Caina's tribe. And if there's any connection between that and Toby I'll find that, too."

Yasavich looked awful. His tan had faded. Every time Asahel had seen him since Toby's death, his eyes had been rimmed with red. He brushed a hand lightly over them now.

"I don't know, Asahel. Toby wouldn't have wanted you to put yourself in danger. He never meant for that to happen. He just believed that you'd never be happy if you let your father hold you hostage for the rest of your life. But I'm not sure he would approve of this."

"Don't worry about me, Stan. I think Toby would approve of my plan. He's the one who gave me the idea. I'm going to write about it. All of it. An investigative piece that will open the world's eyes to what's happening. Toby would have approved."

Yasavich looked dubious.

"What about your job?"

"I'll find another."

Yasavich reached for Asahel's hand, grasping it as though it connected him somehow with Fuentes.

"What exactly do you think you'll find?"

"Biopiracy. Pharmaceutical companies that destroy Amazonian cultures, break international laws and endanger natives' lives. That's the very least I expect to find. There's a company named GenChrom; they're from Seattle. I asked my ex to check into them. He's an FBI agent. They've been down in the Amazon River Basin three times recently. And they're back there again now. Maybe they're the ones who killed the Naua. I'm going to follow them and try to find out. At the very least, I'll find out what they do down there and write about it."

"Damn right," Yasavich said, suddenly convinced.

"It's a way to open eyes, like Toby spent his life trying to do. To let people know what these companies are doing, how they're raping the natives and their forests. And if my hunch is right, maybe even prove who killed Caina's tribe."

Yasavich's voice was barely a whisper.

"And Toby."

"Yes," Asahel said. "And Toby."

Yasavich took a deep breath. A healing breath. Asahel had just given him a way to channel his grief.

"Okay," he said. "What can I do to help?"

CHAPTER **EIGHTEEN**

ASAHEL GLANCED AT the phone, then at the clock on the stove.
Nine A.M. Her plane left at 11:30. She'd heard the international
lines at Sea-Tac were a nightmare. There really wasn't time to call Stan.

She headed for the door, then impulsively dropped her suitcase on
the floor. A couple minutes couldn't hurt.

Stan picked up on the first ring.

"Hi, it's me," Asahel said.

"I thought you'd be gone by now."

"I'm about to walk out the door. Just thought I'd see how you are
today."

"I'm okay, Asahel. You?"

"Nervous."

"That's understandable."

"You're sure this is okay with you? Staying here with Caina?"

Asahel had been around Stan enough now to know that the pause
meant he was trying to compose himself.

"I meant it when I said it was a godsend," he replied. "Something
Toby would want me to do. And, to be honest, I need to get out of
the house for a while. The memories . . ."

"Oh god, Stan, what have I done?"

"Don't do that to yourself. You didn't do anything. But now you
will. You go find who did this—to Caina's people and to Toby. And
then come back safely."

When she hung up, Asahel couldn't help herself. She tiptoed into
the living room, where Caina slept under the window, on the floor.

Caina's features took on a completely different look when she was
sleeping—relaxed; lacking the fear and memories that haunted her
waking hours, she looked younger, even more beautiful. Asahel pulled
the sheet up around Caina's shoulders. Then, quietly, she tested the
doorknob on the door to the stairwell.

On her way back through the kitchen, she picked up her suitcase.

Outside, she'd just inserted the key in the dead bolt when the phone rang.

Stan. He must have forgotten to tell her something.

Dropping her suitcase again, she opened the door and crossed the kitchen to the phone.

She recognized the voice right away.

"Asahel?"

"Dr. Patzwald."

"I tried you at the office," Patzwald announced, "but they said you hadn't come in yet. I was concerned about you. You missed yesterday afternoon's appointment. And last week's."

Asahel tapped her foot impatiently. She didn't need this now.

"I'm sorry, Dr. Patzwald. Things have just been kind of crazy. I'm afraid I forgot my appointments. I should have called to cancel."

"Crazy in what way?"

"You know, work. We just have a lot going on down there."

"How are things with your father?"

"Great," Asahel lied, wanting only to get off the phone and head to the airport.

It was the wrong thing to say. The line went silent, and Asahel knew she was in trouble. Patzwald had an uncanny ability to see through bullshit. She knew. She'd tried to deceive him before. It never worked.

"So what's really going on, Asahel?" he finally replied, in that voice that cut through all nonsense. "Do you want to talk about it?"

"What do you mean? I just told you."

"And you think I buy it?" Again, a long pause. "I'm concerned about you. I think it'd be a good idea for you to come in this afternoon."

"Well, that'd be pretty close to impossible."

"And why is that?"

"Because in about two hours I'll be on a plane to Brazil."

"What are you doing, Asahel? Talk to me."

Asahel hesitated just a few seconds. What, indeed, was she doing?

"I really don't have time to explain. I'm afraid I have to go. Good-bye, Dr. Patzwald."

His voice became urgent.

"Asahel, please. Tell me what's going on. Don't I deserve at least that much?"

Asahel actually issued an abrupt laugh.

"Dr. Patzwald. I'm shocked. Since when is my therapy about you?"

"If you think I don't care about my patients, about you in particular, you're wrong. I'm human, Asahel. All too human."

"I'm sorry. Of course you do," Asahel replied. "This is just something I have to do. And in some way, you've probably made it possible because you've helped me, Dr. Patzwald. You've made me stronger, and I thank you for that."

"Asahel, listen to me. This sounds crazy. Maybe even dangerous. You know I support your taking back control of your life, but I'm not sure you're ready for whatever you have planned. You're still fragile."

"We'll see about that, won't we?" Asahel replied. The clock on the stove caught her eye. Time to go.

"Good-bye, Dr. Patzwald."

"Don't do it," Patzwald warned.

The faintest trace of a smile played at the corners of Asahel's lips. Without another word, she hung up the phone and strode out the door.

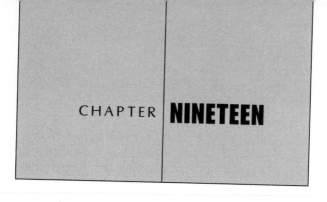

CHAPTER **NINETEEN**

TO CALL THE scattering of thatched huts a village was a little like calling the town of Rock Springs, Wyoming, a metropolis.

Hughes, Zurito, Brent and Jake had boarded the sixteen-foot skiff, leaving behind Pedro on the *Tapuya*, to embark upon what Hughes called a "little sampling side trip."

As they drifted down the tributary, Brent suddenly pointed toward shore. A young boy who had been fishing along the banks scrambled up its slope and disappeared along a narrow path into the trees.

Minutes later, six men stepped out of the forest to stand side by side on the shoreline, expressionless, as they watched the skiff approach. They were dressed in long cinnamon-colored wraps made of tightly woven crude fiber.

Brent waved to them, but none responded.

"Let's get to work," Hughes said, his voice rising in excitement. "Who are they?"

"Most likely the Ucayali," Brent answered.

"Zurito," Hughes asked, "are they friendly?"

Eyes fixed straight ahead, Zurito nodded.

When the boat reached the bank, Zurito maneuvered it expertly up against the bank and jumped out.

"You stay," he ordered. "I do the talk."

He tied the boat's line to a thick vine and, with the other three men waiting behind, approached the group of six.

From the corner of his eye, Jake saw Brent's right hand reach under the bench upon which he and Jake were seated. Glancing down, Jake saw the butt of the AK-47.

"Are you crazy?" Jake asked. "They're not armed."

"I think I recognize this tribe," du Pont offered. "They're friendly."

"Shut the fuck up," Brent answered. "I'm not gonna use this unless I have to."

In front of them, on the skiff's front bench, Hughes turned and shot them a withering look.

"*All* of you shut up."

All fell into silence, eyes pinned to the summit taking place on the shore. Jake could hear the voices plainly, especially that of Zurito, but they spoke in a language unknown to him.

"They're negotiating," du Pont observed quietly. "So many researchers come down this way now, it's become a bloody cottage industry for the natives."

Finally, as if on cue, five of the six men turned and disappeared back into the forest, leaving behind a young man who Jake would guess to be in his late teens or early twenties. He stood, alert, watching as Zurito returned to the skiff.

"We welcome," Zurito announced, though from all that he'd witnessed so far, Jake found this pronouncement difficult to believe.

Hughes went into action. Before leaving the *Tapuya*, he and Brent had loaded two large crates into the front of the skiff. Now he ordered Zurito to take one and the others to bring the second.

Zurito appeared to have no trouble handling his crate alone. Balancing it on one shoulder, he forged up the bank.

When Brent reached for the rifle under the seat, Hughes barked, "Leave it."

Reluctantly, Brent covered it with a corner of a canvas tarp, and stepped forward to help Jake and du Pont with the other crate, which they found awkward to carry.

Cautiously, following the path just left by the *cushma*-clad natives, the men picked their way through the dense underbrush at the river's edge. Within yards, they found themselves inside what seemed like a cool shaded room made entirely of foliage and filled with more forms of life than they could ever have imagined. Jake recognized a mahogany tree, but as far as he could tell, every other tree within sight was different, with not a single species repeating itself.

Pushing on in the wake of the lone native left behind to guide them, the group soon stepped into a clearing, in which a random group of six or seven cane-and-palm-thatched huts stood. From each doorway and the space between several huts dark-skinned women, also attired in *cushmas*, stared at the approaching group.

THE YOUNG NATIVE beckoned Jake and the rest of the GenChrom team into the clearing with a wave of his hand.

"Let Zurito lead," Hughes ordered.

With Zurito directly behind him, the young man led them to a platform made of split palm wood. The men they'd seen on the shore minutes earlier now sat on the platform, cross-legged and stern-faced, in a semicircle.

The eldest stood and addressed himself to Zurito in a native tongue.

Zurito answered by walking to the center of their circle, then lowering himself like the others.

Hughes, Jake and Brent settled on the floor behind Zurito, awkwardly assuming the same cross-legged position. Du Pont stood, leaning against one of four poles that supported the platform.

A heated debate began immediately between Zurito and the natives.

Hughes leaned over Jake and murmured to Brent, "What are they saying?"

"I don't have a clue," Brent answered.

The debate seemed to go on for hours. Zurito's tone alternated between soft and soothing, then threatening. The women had by now lost interest, though Jake noticed them glancing their way occasionally, their expressions more curious than anything.

Hammocks creaked; hens cackled. Muted voices filled the late afternoon air.

Finally, the eldest man in the group on the platform rose and followed Zurito toward the two crates, which sat on the dirt next to the platform.

"He have to see," Zurito told Hughes as he passed the group.

Zurito pulled his hunting knife out of the leather sling on his belt and used its blade to pry the top off the larger of the two crates.

The moment the lid popped off, the village came alive with an air of excitement. All the men hurried over to encircle the crate. Women and children gathered behind them, straining to see.

As if on cue, several of the men—those close enough to see inside the crate—began making clucking noises.

At Zurito's nod, the leader reached inside and began lifting items from the crate, holding them high for the rest to see.

First, a roll of nylon fishing line. Heads nodded enthusiastically. Jake saw the young boy they'd seen fishing eagerly tugging at the *cushma* of one of the older men and whispering in his ear.

Next, a bag of colored beads. This created a great stir among the women, many of whom smiled and hopped back and forth eagerly from one foot to another, as if warming up to dance.

Soon another man, impatient to see the rest, started reaching in and raising items into the air. This clearly annoyed the other elder, who picked up the pace.

Chocolate bars, hand mirrors, cheap hair ornaments, a portable radio. Batteries. A box of tampons.

A bobble-head doll wearing a Mariner's uniform drew cheers.

"Ichiro," Jake murmured to du Pont in amazement. "Do you suppose they actually recognize him?"

"If they do, I'd say this sampling's a bust. My guess is it's just the head thing. And maybe the uniform."

The doll was passed around eagerly.

The assembled group—Jake counted thirty-one in all—had begun chattering among themselves noisily, now almost oblivious to the strangers who had brought the goods.

When Zurito raised a hand in the air and shouted, it brought the festivities to a complete halt.

His voice stern, he turned and addressed the elder leader, who in turn issued an order. One by one, with great reluctance, the villagers put the items taken from the crates back. Zurito made a show of replacing the lid, snapping its clasp.

The two men—Zurito and the leader—returned alone to the platform, where they continued their earlier discussion. Finally, about half an hour later, Zurito walked away from the elder and returned to the crates, upon which Hughes, Brent and Jake now sat.

"They agree you take blood," Zurito said. "But not tonight. Tomorrow."

Hughes looked less than pleased at this news.

"I thought this would be quick," Brent sulked. "In and out."

"So did I," Hughes said. "We'll just have to go back to the *Tapuya* and anchor her till morning."

"*No,*" Zurito said, raising his voice. "Deal is sleep here, keep crates here."

He pointed emphatically to the ground under his feet.

"Here?" Hughes echoed.

"*Here,*" Zurito answered.

OF THE SEVEN HUTS, five were for sleeping, while the two offered to the GenChrom group for the night functioned as combination kitchens/ chicken coops.

The tribe had resumed their normal activities. They offered their visitors the same fare they ate—fish that had been drying on slats outside the kitchen huts, along with rice. The fish had been heavily salted; still Jake would have found it enjoyable had it not been for the layer of insects literally coating it by the time it reached his hands.

After the evening meal, the tribe broke off into several groups, the women tending to babies, the children playing a game in which they tossed pebbles into a turtle shell, while the group of five adult men, plus the young man who'd led Jake's group to the clearing, hovered together in quiet discussion, their voices a low hum.

The men from the *Tapuya* stayed close to the crates of goods, which had apparently worked nicely to gain the natives' cooperation. But just before sunset, Brent sneaked back to the skiff.

He returned only minutes later, a bundle of canvas in his hands. None of the tribe seemed to notice.

"I've got my rifle," he reported under his breath.

Hughes appeared pleased by this news, but Zurito did not comment. Jake didn't know whom he felt more comfortable with having the rifle: Brent or the natives, who appeared peaceful enough to Jake. Du Pont, propped up against one of the four poles that anchored the platform, with eyes closed and face turned to the sinking sun, seemed either not to have heard the announcement or not to care.

As the sun set, two of the oldest women approached the men shyly, eyes downcast, carrying sheepskin rugs. Thanking them, Jake took the filthy skin given him into the kitchen hut and settled on it in a corner. Jake hadn't seen the inside of the sleeping huts, but this hut's simple design—bamboo poles for walls, thatched roof, mud floor and a mud fireplace in one corner—made him wonder why the tribe crowded so many people into the four sleeping huts instead of simply building more.

Throughout the evening, he'd watched the chickens and pigs running about freely, in and out of the opening that served as a door, but when Jake settled on the floor, the two pigs still inside scrambled out. Du Pont nearly tripped over them coming through the door.

"Guess we're bunking together," he said. He carried his pack and a rug similar to Jake's, which he held up to his nose.

"Phew," he said, his face scrunching in disgust at the odor.

Du Pont threw the rug to the ground, then tossed his pack alongside it. Rummaging through the pack, he withdrew a large square of material—it looked to Jake like canvas—which he laid over the sheepskin before lowering himself onto it.

Through the hut's door, Jake noticed Zurito sitting on one of the crates.

From where he lay on the floor, du Pont's eyes had apparently followed Jake's.

"Let's just hope he's really on our side."

Jake looked over at du Pont to see if he was joking. He couldn't tell.

"Zurito?"

Du Pont nodded.

"Tricky business down here," he said. "A man's gotta keep his antenna up at all times."

Jake studied him thoughtfully. Doc du Pont fascinated him. Despite his relaxed exterior, there was an air of danger about him. Jake had met many researchers, but none like du Pont.

"How is it you know Hughes?"

"Never laid eyes on him before yesterday," du Pont answered. "He'd been calling me for a few months. Guess he read something about one of my other discoveries down here. I told 'im I wasn't available. I'd just secured funding from a start-up biotech company out of Los Angeles, for a trip of my own, but then that fell through and when Hughes e-mailed me about the blue-eyed native, this started to look good to me."

Now du Pont turned curious eyes on Jake.

"So why do you s'pose Hughes never told you about those rumors? Why'd he wait till you were already down here?"

"I've been wondering that myself," Jake answered.

"This business's full of paranoia. Some reason he might not trust you with the information?"

"I hold the patent on a technology that Hughes wants to use in research on G32. My guess is he was afraid I'd try to go it alone if I knew too much."

The light had faded, leaving du Pont's face entirely in shadows. Still, Jake thought he saw the corner of the Australian's mouth rise in amusement.

"So that explains it," he muttered. "Bloody looks like I'll be earning my keep on this trip."

Without explaining, he rolled over and instantly dropped off into a deep sleep.

Sleep did not come that easily to Jake.

Caught up in the excitement of the day, he hadn't paid much attention to the wild chorus that constantly assaulted the ears. Parrots,

jungle hens, macaws, toucans, turkeys, hundreds of swinging and gib-
bering monkeys and a continuous buzz of insects had filled the daylight
hours. But as the sun set, silence had slowly replaced the din. And
then, as the moon's beams rippled over the dense canopy surrounding
the clearing, a new concert had begun.

Jake lay there in the dark, listening to du Pont's heavy breathing,
interspersed with fierce growls and bloodcurdling screams of nocturnal
predators. He could hear them crashing through dense undergrowth in
relentless pursuit of prey. A chorus of croaking frogs and toads came
in waves, punctuated by the occasional owl's call.

For a while, there was also the murmur of voices from other huts,
even occasional song. When the Ucayali finally fell silent, Jake turned
to see Zurito's imposing form filling the open doorway.

Zurito lowered himself to the floor, his back propped against the
side of the door, and quickly fell asleep, sitting up. Jake had seen
Hughes take the crewman aside and whisper in his ear earlier in the
evening.

Had Zurito chosen this position to keep an eye on the crates?

Or was it Jake that he guarded?

CHAPTER **TWENTY**

THANK YOU FOR seeing me on such short notice."

Several hours into her American Airlines flight, it dawned on Asahel. The reality that GenChrom had almost a full week's head start on her had been weighing heavily on her heart and mind. Would trying to find them now be a little like the proverbial searching for a needle in a haystack?

She had never felt so alone. Aside from Stan and Sarah Moen, her old college roommate, whom Asahel recruited to help, no one knew her plans. Fearful of the extent to which her father might go to find her, she'd decided to buy as much time as possible at work by having Tammy tell everyone she had the flu. It would take several days for anyone at GenChrom to become suspicious, but if anyone showed up at her apartment looking for her when Stan was there—Caina was strictly forbidden to answer the door—he would tell them Asahel had gone to visit Sarah, who lived in a remote Alaskan village. Sarah, a staunch environmentalist who'd finally dropped out of the movement but still harbored enough anger at the establishment to welcome a chance to screw with it, had cheerfully assured Asahel that she would keep any pursuers at bay a good long while with a wild-goose chase that only the Alaska wilderness could deliver.

Not even Sully knew Asahel was leaving the country. He suspected she was planning something. Asahel felt certain that if her ex found out, he'd do everything in his power to stop her.

Still, as alone and fearful as she felt, as the plane leveled off at 35,000 feet and Asahel stared out the window at a floor of clouds far below, for the first time since Angie's death she realized that she felt at peace with herself—almost like she'd felt before her world was turned upside down. Like during her IPAF days.

And that's when it dawned on her, another memory from her IPAF days.

It had been so long ago that it hadn't even occurred to her until now.

The Lost Tribes Project. Asahel had communicated with its director, Diego Cavallero, on several occasions.

Long before she ever spoke to him, Asahel had heard wild stories about Cavallero, who was legendary amongst indigenous rights groups—both for the success of his efforts and for his bold means of achieving that success. Means that rarely took into account something as trivial as the law.

One story often passed around at international protests described a confrontation between Cavallero and Peruvian loggers who'd invaded protected Indian territory in Brazil. Single-handedly Cavallero had confronted the armed logging crew, demanding that they withdraw from their position at the fork of two rivers, which had long served as the home of the Halo Te Su, a tribe that had dwindled over the latter half of the century to only forty-two members. When the loggers refused, Cavallero flew his single-engine Cessna over their camp at dawn and dropped a hand grenade into it, destroying their equipment and their logging truck, which happened to be their only transportation out of the less than friendly surroundings.

The Brazilian government was tired of outside loggers sneaking onto their lands. It chose not to prosecute, based on "insufficient evidence"—despite the testimony (and documented injuries) of five loggers.

It was said that after that incident several interest groups, including the loggers, put a contract out on Cavallero's life for standing between them and the rich Amazon rain forest lands they coveted.

When she was with IPAF, the two times Asahel had spoken with Cavallero—once during preparation of a paper Asahel was to present to an international conference on globalism, the second time when an activist Asahel had known from her ALC days had been arrested in Brasilia—he'd been more than gracious about offering both his knowledge and assistance.

Perhaps Cavallero would be willing to assist her again.

Only this time she had a much bigger favor to ask of him.

After landing in Manaus, Asahel had hired a cab to take her to the Lost Tribes Project offices. Like most activist headquarters, the IPAF offices were nothing to write home about, but she'd been shocked to see just how substandard Diego Cavallero's offices were.

"Anyone from your organization's welcome here anytime," Cavallero answered now in response to Asahel's apology.

They observed each other through a cloud of smoke. His eyes reminded Asahel of a hawk, a bird of prey.

"Tell me, Ms. Sullivan, how may I help you?"

He ran his hand through a tangle of wiry gray hair, revealing a flashy gold ring on his third finger.

"Actually, I'm no longer with IPAF," Asahel said.

One of Cavallero's bushy eyebrows shot up.

"No?"

"No."

"Then you have come on personal business."

"Not exactly. It's related to my work years ago with IPAF."

"Senorita, you are a very mysterious woman. Would you like to tell me the purpose of your visit?"

Asahel leaned forward. Eyeing the open door to the corridor, she lowered her voice.

"Your agency's in charge of finding new tribes, isn't it?"

"Yes."

"Do you also keep tabs on existing tribes, tribes that have been around for a long time? Do you watch over them, too?"

Cavallero's expression darkened.

"It's unrealistic to think two pilots and a handful of agents can safeguard the thousands of tribes living in the Brazilian rain forests," he replied, clearly curious, but also guarded. "But, of course, we do what we can."

"Certainly you hear rumors, don't you?" Asahel pressed.

"Everyone hears rumors."

"Can you tell me if there have been any reports, *rumors*, of murders being committed in the rain forests of the state of Acre?"

Now it was Cavallero's turn to lean forward, braving his own cloud of smoke to stare Asahel down.

"What are you saying?"

"Mr. Cavallero," Asahel said. "I'm afraid I have some very disturbing news."

"IF IT'S TRUE, I'll kill the sons of bitches."

Diego Cavallero's wrath had erupted like Mount Saint Helens when Asahel told him Caina's story.

"You've never heard anything about this?" Asahel responded. "About a tribe being slaughtered?"

Cavallero was on his feet now, pacing. An inch of ash dropped to the dingy linoleum flooring from the cigarette pinched between yellowed fingers.

"No," he practically shouted. "There have been no such rumors. But you're right about one thing. If she's from the rain forest, she has to be a Naua. The Naua are the only tribe ever known to have blue eyes. We call them an 'invisible tribe.' A tribe that we know is there despite the fact we never have sightings."

Cavallero drew on the cigarette in short, deep drags. It had burned down to his skin, but he did not seem to notice.

"It could happen," he continued, his voice tight and angry. "Someone could slaughter the whole tribe and we'd never know."

Without warning, his fist lashed out and struck the wall. Asahel noticed several other indentations in the wall, shoulder high, no doubt left by his ring.

Cavallero issued a string of words in Portuguese, his wild expression leaving little doubt as to what he was saying.

"I know how you feel," Asahel said. "They *have* to be found and punished. That's why I came to Brazil."

Cavallero's laughter startled Asahel. It echoed from one wall of the small office to another.

"You?" He turned his face to the ceiling and muttered in Portuguese. Then he fixed disbelieving eyes on Asahel. "If what you say is true, you actually think you can fix this? You can make this right?"

"I have a plan. It's not perfect, but it can work. Please, hear me out."

Despite his words, Cavallero listened intently as Asahel revealed her plans to follow GenChrom. She saw Cavallero perk up instantly when she mentioned her plan to write an investigative report revealing their activities.

"But I'm afraid I'll never catch up with the GenChrom team now," Asahel finished. "I need your help, Mr. Cavallero. I've lost valuable time. Can you help me find them?"

"Screw da Luz," Cavallero said.

"Pardon me?"

"Da Luz. He's a congressman from Amazonia who's trying to get all the funding for the Lost Tribes Project pulled. I'm supposed to be focusing all my efforts on public relations right now, making sure da Luz doesn't succeed. But screw da Luz. Screw 'em all. I've done all the ass kissing I'm gonna do."

"Does that mean you'll help me?"

"*I'll* go after them. If they're doing what you say, nothing will stop me from getting the bastards." His gaze zeroed in on Asahel's. "But I'll go alone. The jungle's no place for a woman."

Asahel reached across the desk and grabbed his forearm.

"You have to take me with you."

She could tell her reaction startled him, but she did not let go her grasp on his wiry arm.

"It could take days to find them," Cavallero said, shaking free of her grip. "Maybe even weeks. The jungle, it swallows people. You have no idea what you're asking. And when we do find them, what then? Do you think these scientists will just turn themselves in? Give you an interview? You said it yourself. They might be murderers." As if to punctuate the statement, Cavallero jammed another Marlboro into his mouth. "I'll have my hands full enough without worrying about keeping you out of trouble."

When he reached into his shirt pocket for a match, Asahel's hand shot out and ripped the cigarette from between his lips.

"I will not be left behind. Do you hear?" Her wild-eyed determination matched that of Cavallero. "If I have to rent my own boat and follow them, I will. Tomorrow morning I'm leaving, with or without you."

Cavallero stared at her, appraising her.

"This GenChrom, you really think they could be responsible for killing Caina's tribe?"

"It's a shot in the dark," Asahel answered. "But we know they've been coming down here a lot recently. Either way, I'm convinced that if I follow the GenChrom scientists I'll end up with a story that needs to be told."

For the first time, Cavallero grew thoughtful, temporarily forgetting his cigarette, and his anger.

"A story like that could be very important," he said. "Your scientists are raping our country, destroying our lands and native cultures. I try to get the media to report what goes on, but when it comes from me, hell, they think I'm *un loco*, or, if they're being kind, that it's just my job.

"Except for people like you, nobody in your country gives a damn what happens down here. But a story written by *you*"—the inference was clear: Asahel was beautiful, white and a part of the world's ruling class—"and published in your *americano* papers . . . well, that might actually make a difference."

He reached out, snatched the cigarette back from Asahel and slowly, deliberately, held a match to it.

Asahel stood to go.

"What is it, Mr. Cavallero?" she asked, facing him head-on. "Do I hire my own guide? Rent my own boat? Or do you take me to find them?"

Settling back in his chair, Cavallero leveled his intense gaze on her. Asahel's heart raced with suspense.

"We won't be traveling by boat," he finally said. "And you'd better start calling me Diego."

As A CHILD, Asahel had taken enough trips on her father's company jet that early on she'd overcome any fear of flying in smaller planes; but the takeoff of Cavallero's seaplane on the busy Amazon—dozens, no, hundreds, of small craft either oblivious to the oncoming plane or overly trusting of its pilot—rattled her.

Seated beside her, long, wiry gray curls sticking out from underneath a baseball cap, Cavallero leaned on the plane's horn and swore up a storm at those boats that didn't give him what he considered an adequate runway.

One in particular, the rare motorboat capable of some speed, had so maddened Cavallero that once airborne he banked the plane and returned to buzz it—coming within a dozen feet of the terrified driver, who waved his shirt wildly in the air to ward Cavallero off.

Letting loose with a roar of laughter, Cavallero reached out the window of his plane, flashed a middle finger, then pulled sharply into the wide open sky.

Holding on for dear life, Asahel couldn't help but smile, too.

She had teamed up with a wild man.

CHAPTER **TWENTY-ONE**

I N THE MORNING, the chickens and pigs woke Jake up before the villagers began stirring. Soon he heard a *thwop, thwop, thwop*. Someone chopping wood.

Lying there, staring at the dried gray thatched roof overhead, Jake became aware for the first time of several large spiders moving just above him, one easily the size of his fist. A lizard poked its head through the woven fronds, then disappeared.

When Jake rolled over and looked toward the doorway, Zurito was gone. Du Pont's sheepskin rug lay, expertly rolled, next to his bag. He, too, was nowhere in sight.

Jake stood, stretching, desperately hoping that Amazonian tribes included coffee in their diet.

Through the open door he saw Hughes bent over one of the two crates, whose lid was lying on the dirt next to it. He wore a white lab coat. Doc du Pont stood at his side, also in a white coat. Squinting against the morning sun, Jake approached.

Hughes was finishing the methodical removal of the crate's contents, placing them piece by piece on the platform the men had all sat upon the previous evening: boxes of sterile needles, vacutainer tubes, subzero cryo-vials, latex gloves, rubber tourniquets. Alcohol and cotton balls. Scissors and a Swiss Army knife.

Hughes looked up as Jake approached.

"Put that on," he ordered, nodding toward a white lab coat lying on the platform. "We want to be out of here within the hour."

"Mornin', mate," Doc du Pont said.

Hughes placed each of three boxes—the syringes—approximately two yards apart on the dirt, establishing the workstation for each man.

Zurito and Brent had appeared, in the company of four of the men from the night before, who still wore the same long tan-colored gowns.

"Tell them to line up," Hughes ordered.

Zurito spoke to them in their native tongue.

Hughes pointed. "Behind du Pont, Skully and me. Now let's get going."

With no additional fanfare or preparation, Hughes approached the first man. Grabbing his arm, Hughes twisted it to expose the inner elbow, dabbed the skin with alcohol-dampened cotton and without hesitation inserted the needle.

The man winced, but keenly aware of the eyes of the others, he lifted his chin defiantly and did not alter his expression as first one, then two, tubes filled with dark, lipstick red blood.

"What's holding you?" Hughes barked when he saw that Jake was still watching him. Du Pont had already finished drawing his first sample.

Zurito pushed one of the other men forward, toward Jake. Jake grabbed a syringe from the box on the ground and carefully inserted the needle into the dark skin, drawing ten milliliters of blood. Then, his head held high, Jake's donor proceeded immediately to Brent, who had opened the second crate. With a sweep of his hand, Brent motioned for the three men who'd gone first to make their own choices.

One man chose the radio. The other, the spool of nylon fishing line. Jake's patient chose a mirror framed in a gaudy floral material.

By now, most of the village had assembled. Seeing that it was first-come-first-served when it came to the allocation of the rewards, several men and boys quickly stepped forward to volunteer. A brief scuffle ensued between two of the teens, settled only when one of the elders backhanded them both across the face.

With the used syringe in hand, Jake looked around for a Sharps Disposal. He did not see one but noticed that du Pont was using the lid of the syringe box to dispose of his used syringes and needles. Jake followed suit, then grabbed another new syringe.

Hughes had already drawn another sample when it dawned on Jake.

"Who's labeling these?" he asked.

He nodded toward the rack, into which Brent was depositing the drawn samples.

"Don't worry about it," Hughes replied. "We'll label when we're back on the *Tapuya*."

"We won't be able to keep track of which sample came from which person," Jake said. "Brent, get over here and begin labeling."

Brent smirked in Jake's direction, then turned and took the newest tube full of blood from Hughes.

Now Hughes turned and directed piercing eyes on Jake.

"I told you, don't worry about it."

"If we don't identify the donors, they'll deny our patent," Jake said. "And where are the consents?"

At this question, Hughes jerked the needle out of the next donor's arm so roughly that the man called out angrily at Hughes's back as Hughes stormed over to Jake.

Standing eye to eye with Jake, Hughes glared at him.

"I have a stack of fucking consent forms in my briefcase. Already signed. Now get to work."

He started to turn away, but Jake grabbed him by the arm.

"Wait a minute. When did they sign them? I've never even seen the forms."

Zurito, clearly tuned to the conversation, eyed the two men with interest, as did du Pont, though he did not stop sampling the villagers lined up in front of him.

Hughes lowered his voice, but that did nothing to hide his anger.

"You saw what happened last night. They *gave* us their consent. Hell, we had to sit on that fucking platform for hours while they made their decision. If that's not consent, then I don't know what is."

"You know as well as I do that it has to be in writing. For our protection as much as theirs. And you also know that dangling that box of goodies in front of them might very well negate any consent they've given us anyway."

"I told you," Hughes said, beginning to turn back to his line. "I have signed consent forms. Draw the fucking blood."

Jake grabbed Hughes and jerked him back around. Nose to nose now, he spoke in a low, threatening voice.

"And I told you—"

Immediately du Pont stepped in, grabbing each man by the shoulder.

"Listen, mates, cool it," he said, nodding toward the villagers, who'd uniformly turned nervous eyes on the three men. "Believe me. Get them riled up and there's no telling what they'll do. We're walking a fine line here, gents."

Looking at the faces gathered around them, Jake sensed the truth in this statement.

"He's right," Hughes said. "If we start asking them to sign forms they don't understand, this whole thing will fall apart. They gave their consent last night; you saw that. Now let it be. Get to work."

Unclenching his fists to peel off his disposable gloves, Jake threw the gloves to the ground and walked away without looking back.

DU PONT WATCHED JAKE storm away, in the direction of the river.

It took less than an hour to draw samples from the rest of the men and boys in the village, most of whom eagerly eyed the crate of goods while waiting their turn.

The women came next. Their huge, fearful eyes, as they bravely stepped forward, some with babies hanging, hidden, in the slings over their shoulders, disturbed du Pont.

And then Hughes ordered Zurito to line the children up.

Du Pont hurried over to where Hughes stood.

"Listen, mate," he said. "We've got ourselves plenty of samples. We don't need the kids. Look at 'em. They're bloody scared to death."

Hughes pushed him aside.

"We're doing the kids. The elders agreed to it. It's part of the deal."

"The men agreed. Not the women."

"Line them up," Hughes ordered loudly.

Zurito spoke to the group in their native tongue, but no one responded. The men, trinkets clutched tightly, simply stood staring as the children scampered to hide behind the women who stood in clusters.

Hughes looked at Brent and nodded decisively. At that, the guide strode to the crates, removed the lid from the medical supplies and withdrew his AK-47. Aiming it in the air, he shot off an ear-shattering round. The sky immediately filled with brightly colored birds, fleeing in every direction. With a second blast, a macaw fell to the ground.

The eyes of every Ucayali widened in horror.

"Zurito," Hughes said. "Tell them they made a deal. If they don't cooperate, we'll take back everything."

Zurito relayed the message, which caused a great deal of shouting among the Ucayali. The men had no intention of giving up their trinkets.

Slowly, with their mothers at their sides, the children formed a line.

"We don't need their blood," du Pont repeated. "We already have a strong sampling from this population base. I can assure you, we already have a complete DNA collection."

"I'm not leaving here without samples from the kids," Hughes snapped.

Du Pont sarcastically murmured, "You might see it different if you had children of your own."

Hughes turned on him with a fury.

"How the fuck do you know I don't have kids?"

"Then at the very least," du Pont replied angrily, "do cards on them."

Du Pont braced, ready for Hughes to strike out, but instead Hughes said, "All right. We'll do cards."

Relieved, du Pont hurried to the supply crate and withdrew a dozen of the two-and-a-half-inch-square cards of absorbent white paper that he'd seen when Hughes was unloading supplies that morning. The cards only required a prick of the finger and a few drops of blood instead of the vials they'd drawn from the adults.

With the first child's mother restraining him, du Pont pricked the finger of a small boy, squeezing until several drops of blood fell to the card du Pont held below it. Hughes had already strung a piece of twine between two trees. He grabbed the card from du Pont and clipped it to the twine to dry. Back in Seattle, researchers would use a hole punch to create tiny dots of dried bloods. They would then immerse the blood in chemicals that would suck out the DNA, enabling researchers to examine individual fragments.

As Hughes had predicted, thanks to their breach of sampling protocol it took less than two hours to sample the entire village, minus the infants, whose blood even the elders declared taboo.

Zurito and Brent began repacking the crate of medical supplies as Hughes unclipped the bloodstained cards. Du Pont collected the syringes used by himself and Jake, which both men had carefully placed in the lids of the syringe boxes after they sampled each donor.

Du Pont placed both boxes in a plastic garbage bag. Then he walked to where Hughes had taken his samples. He found only one syringe, lying in the dirt.

"Just leave it," Hughes barked. "We can't travel with those."

Du Pont straightened from his bent-at-the-waist position.

"Where are your others?"

"There were no others," Hughes replied matter-of-factly.

MOVEMENT ABOVE THE SHORELINE drew Jake's attention. He'd been sitting in the skiff, debating his options, when Doc du Pont emerged from the forest with long strides, carrying both his pack and Jake's and wearing an expression that contrasted starkly with the du Pont Jake had thus far known.

"You look like I feel," Jake commented.

"Son of a bitch forced the children to give samples. Then I discovered he'd used one syringe for all his sampling," du Pont answered.

Jake jumped to his feet.

"The same syringe?"

"Aye," du Pont said. "You know what the incidence of AIDS is down here? The whole tribe's probably exposed."

Jake jumped out of the boat, which rocked wildly.

"That's it," he said, landing on the slim strip of sand. "That son of a bitch. I'm heading back home, and when I get there, I'll report him."

"What about your son?"

This question stunned Jake.

"How did you know about Michael?"

"Hughes told me."

"Michael's the reason I'm here, but there have to be other ways. Other research teams that would be interested in finding G32."

"Oh, there're other teams looking for G32 all right," du Pont replied.

"What do you mean?"

"I have it from a reliable source—an industry spy actually—that another American pharmaceutical company is hot on G32's trail. That's the reason I joined Hughes. Time is critical."

Jake found this news extremely disturbing. If another company beat them to G32, it could be years before it became available for Michael's use; whereas if the GenChrom team succeeded in finding it first, Jake planned to include Michael even before they reached the first clinical trial.

Still, how could Jake be part of what du Pont had just described?

"That may be," he said, "but I can't work this way. I can't use my son's condition as an excuse to throw ethics out the window."

"I have to say," du Pont replied, "I've never sampled blood with a machine gun pointed at me and the donors. They were children, just a bunch of little kids . . . scared out of their minds."

"We have to stop him," Jake said. "We have to do something—"

At that moment, Hughes, Zurito and Brent emerged from the forest, carrying the crates, one of which was considerably lighter than it had been on the way into the village.

"Shhhh," du Pont cautioned, throwing his pack into the skiff. "You're not gonna do your son any good if you get yourself shot by that Nazi Hughes brought along."

"Let's talk tonight," Jake said, his voice low. "Back on the boat."

CHAPTER **TWENTY-TWO**

BACK ON THE *Tapuya* that evening, it shocked Jake to find Hughes in a celebratory mood about the success of their blood sampling— so celebratory, in fact, that after downing one shot of tequila, Hughes quickly poured another. And then another.

Jake tried to catch Doc du Pont's eye. Hughes well on his way to becoming drunk and Brent already in the bag might just give Jake and Doc the lucky break they needed—the chance to sneak off and talk, without raising suspicions.

But Doc apparently had a liking for tequila, too. So far he'd matched Hughes, drink for drink. In keeping with his nature, alcohol only seemed to further mellow the already laid-back Aussie.

As for Hughes, alcohol worked to loosen his tongue.

"Way I see it," Hughes pontificated, "the early twentieth century was all about the power that came with discovering and conquering continents.

"Well, the twenty-first century's going to be all about biology. The power will be in the hands of biotech pioneers and explorers. That's what we are, you know. We're explorers. No different than Magellan, or Columbus. Except it's DNA we're searching for, and in the long run, it'll be a hell of a lot more valuable than land ever was."

Hughes clearly liked that analogy. He'd even impressed himself.

"DNA will be the currency of the new millennium," he continued, blowing a long stream of cigar smoke toward the boat's ceiling. "And I'm going to grab my share of it early on. And nobody," he looked Jake's way, "*nobody's* gonna get in my way. You hear?"

Jake's failure to respond infuriated Hughes.

"What the hell were you trying to do back there? Do you know what's at stake here? You could've blown the whole sampling. That blood could be worth a fortune, and you're worried about how we're treating those fucking savages. What's wrong with you?"

"Could've got us killed," Brent added, his speech heavily slurred.

Jake stared Hughes down with a clenched jaw.

"Do you realize how many times you violated international protocol back there?" he said. "No consent, not keeping track of samples. *Forcing* the sampling of children. Any one of those would be enough to invalidate any patent you're granted on those cell lines."

Hughes half rose from his seat, his eyes glassy from alcohol but wide with rage.

"Just who do you suppose would be foolish enough to alert the USPTO?"

Jake's fists clenched on the table in front of him.

"If you think I'll just go along with this, and keep my mouth shut, you'd better think again."

"Oh, you'll go along with it all right," Hughes said.

"Yeah," Brent echoed. He reached over to the empty seat next to him and came up with his rifle. "You'll go along with it."

At the sight of the automatic, du Pont rose from his chair.

"This is going too far. Put that bloody gun down."

Instead of complying, Brent raised its barrel and pointed it directly at Jake. When du Pont lunged across the table at him, Brent stepped back, a wide grin playing across his narrow face.

"Put it down," Hughes ordered.

When Brent did not move fast enough, Hughes pointed to the table and yelled, "Now."

Brent placed the rifle on the far end of the table.

As if suddenly realizing he and Brent had both gone too far, Hughes looked sheepish.

"You'll have to excuse him. Course you can't blame him. There's a lot at stake for all of us on this team. We can't let our differences sabotage the mission, can we?"

"Either you give me your word that the rest of the samplings will be done according to protocol, or I walk."

Du Pont murmured in agreement.

Instead of Hughes blowing up, as Jake had expected, his eyes lit with humor at this pronouncement.

"Really?" he said.

It took all of Jake's resolve not to lunge across the table at the son of a bitch.

"Really," Jake declared. "Now which is it? Do we play by the rules, or do I pack up and get off this boat?"

•   •   •

"THAT'S ENTIRELY UP TO YOU," Hughes answered. "But if you think you're going to dictate protocol on this trip, think again. I'm in charge here and I call the rules."

Jake stood so abruptly that his chair fell backward and clattered noisily to the floor.

"All right then," he said. "I'll be leaving."

He'd crossed half the distance between the table and the door to the corridor that led to the cabins when Hughes's voice behind him stopped him in his tracks.

"Before you do anything too rash, you might want to hear about a call I got today from Leah. It's about your boy."

Jake turned. Slowly, a sinking feeling weakening his knees, he took two steps in Hughes's direction, then stopped.

"Which boy?"

"The blind one," Hughes answered nonchalantly. "Michael, isn't it?"

Jake knew that Hughes knew Michael's name all too well.

"What about Michael?"

"Leah called from Harborview. The emergency room. She said Michael should be fine. Physically, at least."

Jake crossed the rest of the distance separating them in such a flash that Hughes didn't even have time to raise a hand in self-defense.

Grabbing Hughes by the shoulders, Jake literally lifted him from his seat and threw him against the wall.

"Talk to me, you bastard. What? What happened to Michael?"

Brent lunged for the rifle, but du Pont had already grabbed it. He had it aimed at the ceiling, but for the first time since joining the others, the Aussie looked angry enough to use it.

Still, Hughes managed a smirk.

"Your son swallowed a bottle of pills this morning," he said. "Michael tried to commit suicide."

CHAPTER TWENTY-THREE

"ELLO?" JAKE YELLED into the phone's receiver. "Can you hear me?"

The static made it impossible for him to understand Leah Clay's reply.

Before leaving Seattle, Hughes had promised Jake he could stay in touch with Michael and Antony via his satellite phone. That had just turned out to be another lie. The first day on board the *Tapuya*, Jake discovered they'd already left the satellite phone's coverage area. He'd tried to use it several times since. Each time he failed to get through, and with each failure his frustration and worry grew by leaps and bounds.

"Please," Jake repeated. "Can you put Michael on?"

Jake couldn't believe his luck. The phone had worked for Hughes earlier that day, when he'd talked to Leah Clay, but now—when Jake was frantic with worry—he got nothing but static.

He screamed into the phone again.

"I have to talk to Michael."

Suddenly snippets of Leah's voice came through.

". . . hospital . . ." she said. ". . . overnight."

Then nothing.

Jake spotted the flagpole, which, during the day, waved the flags of Brazil and the *Tapuya*. Half-crazy now, he jumped up on the yacht's railing. He'd shimmy up the pole. Maybe if he could climb high enough, the reception would improve. His heart sank when he gripped it and realized immediately it couldn't support his weight.

The second his hand came in contact with the pole, however, Jake heard Leah loud and clear. He'd inadvertently come up with a make-shift antenna.

"They said they'd release him to me tomorrow," Leah was saying. "Thank God we had the foresight to have you sign that medical consent. He's going to be okay, Jake. They pumped his stomach before the aspirin could do any real damage."

Jake swiped at the tear trailing down his cheek with the back of his hand.

"Why, Leah? Why? What happened?"

He heard Leah catch her breath.

"Michael didn't want to go to school," she said haltingly. "I knew that. He said he hates his new school. That he hates it here, in Seattle. I should never have insisted that he go. I'm so sorry, Jake. I'm so sorry."

Jake swallowed.

"It's not your fault, Leah. Listen, I'll head back to Manaus first thing tomorrow and catch the first flight home. Tell Michael that, will you?"

There came no response.

"Leah?"

Had he lost the connection? The static had returned. Desperate, Jake cried out.

"*Leah?*"

When Leah finally replied, he had to strain to hear her.

"Are you sure that's what you want to do?"

"Of course," Jake answered. "I'll go mad if I stay here, if I can't be with him now."

Another pause.

"Jake. You don't understand. Michael told the hospital psychiatrist . . ."

She stopped.

"What? What did Michael tell the psychiatrist?"

"He told him," she said, "that he didn't really believe you could find a cure for him. And that if he never sees again . . . he doesn't want to live."

"No," Jake cried. Yet he knew, had known all along, that that was how his son felt. He'd heard stories of kids adjusting to terrible misfortune—amputated limbs, loss of hearing, loss of sight. But Jake had known from the start that his Michael was not one of those kids.

"Don't you see, Jake?" Leah continued. "It would destroy all his hope to know you'd given up. How do I tell Michael you're coming home?"

THE KNOCK ON THE DOOR came at half past two A.M.

Jake had lain fully clothed on his bed ever since returning from the top deck. Ever since hearing about his son's attempt to take his own life. He'd tried to place another call—to Harborview—but the phone had cut out entirely, leaving Jake with a sense of isolation and helplessness so keen that it threatened his sanity.

At the sound—three soft taps—Jake rose, padded to the door and opened it just a crack.

Doc du Pont stood in the hallway, completely sober.

"You got my note," Jake whispered, quickly opening the door to let du Pont slide inside.

Jake stuck his head into the corridor and looked both ways. Total silence. Hughes and Brent would be in their cabins, sleeping it off.

"You okay, mate?" du Pont asked once Jake had closed the door.

"Yes," Jake answered.

"Did you make contact? Were you able to talk to your son?"

Jake shook his head.

"Not to Michael. They're keeping him in the hospital overnight. I talked to Leah Clay, the woman he was staying with."

"And is he all right?"

"They pumped his stomach. They say he'll be okay."

Du Pont reached out and placed a comforting hand on Jake's arm.

"You'll be leavin' then, back to the States?"

Jake temporarily ignored the question. He needed to know that the empathy in du Pont's eyes was real.

"Do you have children?"

"Two," du Pont replied. "And they're the light of my life."

"No," Jake said. "I won't be going back. Not until I find G32."

"Well, all right then, mate. That's what we'll do."

"But not like this," Jake said. "Not with Hughes."

"What do ya mean?"

Jake met du Pont's questioning gaze.

"Why can't we do it on our own? You know this region as well as Brent. *I've* got the technology. Together we can accomplish everything we both came to accomplish—without trampling over basic human rights along the way. Without dealing with that madman."

Du Pont's eyebrows came up. He shook his head.

"For starters, mate, we don't have the equipment we'd need. Our own boat, supplies, the sampling inventory—"

Jake held a hand up to stop him midsentence.

"We go back to Manaus and get it."

Falling back to sit on the bed's edge, du Pont mulled this over, silently, for several minutes while Jake alternately paced and stared at him.

"It's not a bad idea," du Pont finally said. "But it'd never work. You've seen him. Hughes'd never let us go, especially not together. No tellin' what he'd do to stop us." An involuntary shudder shook his shoulders. "I wouldn't even want to speculate on that."

Jake's hopes thudded back down to earth.

"You're right. He'd do anything to stop us."

He shook his head and dropped to the bed next to du Pont.

"He knows I'm trapped," he muttered, his voice low and pained. "That I'll do whatever it takes to find G32, for Michael's sake. Including putting up with his crooked practices."

"Wait a minute."

Du Pont's forehead furrowed as he worked through the situation.

"You're right about Hughes," he said, stopping to look at Jake. "He does think he has you trapped. But not me. Hell, he didn't even know till the last minute that I could join in. I was just frosting on the cake. A name on the patent app and papers to give credibility. He doesn't really need me. So long as he thinks he still has you and your technology, he won't bat an eye if I leave."

Jake's eyes widened.

"You're leaving?"

"No, mate, it's not what you think. Listen to this. What if I tell Hughes I'm quitting the search for G32? He'll be a mite pissed off, but it won't amount to much more than that. In reality, I'll go back to Manaus and get us equipped for our own expedition. Then I'll meet back up with you. Upriver. We'll be all set to go into the rain forest and find the Naua. He won't be able to stop us then. Whereas if we try to leave together now, we could both end up alligator bait."

Adrenaline kicked Jake's heart rate up a notch.

"Where upriver?"

"There's a small settlement up ahead. Pauhiny. I'll meet you there."

"How's that going to work? You'll be downriver from us. You can't beat us there without passing right by us. And you'd never catch up with us."

"That's right, mate, but I'll be passin' ya from above. In the air. Instead of a boat, I'll charter us a plane. That way I can get back to Manaus, get the supplies we need and be waiting for you at Pauhiny. All you 'ave to do till then is make Hughes believe you're still part of the team. Buy enough time for me to catch up with ya."

"What if you're not there when we get there?"

"I'll be there. You can count on it."

"It's not a bad idea," Jake muttered. "Not a bad idea at all."

They stayed together, quietly making plans, for another two hours, until the first light of dawn, filtered through the forest's canopy outside, skipped like a carefully aimed pebble across the inky water and entered Jake's cabin window.

They had decided that du Pont would announce his departure immediately and ask to be dropped off at the first raft or vehicle heading downriver.

Jake was to stay on, with Hughes and Brent.

TWO HOURS LATER, when Jake stepped into the *Tapuya*'s main cabin, he immediately sensed that something was wrong.

Brent sat alone in the dining room.

"Where's Hughes?" Jake asked. "And du Pont?"

"Hughes is upstairs. Your buddy's gone."

"Gone?"

"Yep."

"Where?"

"Guess he had a change of heart about a few things. He went home. Caught a ride with a rafter."

Jake had to watch his response—too little a reaction could indicate he wasn't surprised, while too strong a response could also raise suspicions.

"I didn't hear anyone out on the river this morning."

Brent looked up from the map he'd been studying when Jake walked in.

"What the hell does that prove? Except maybe that you drank too much last night."

Had Jake actually slept through an encounter between the *Tapuya* and a rafter? In theory, it was at least possible. After Doc sneaked back out of his cabin, Jake had lain down again on the bed, intending only to think things through, but the next thing he knew, he woke to full daylight. A quick glance at the clock told him he'd slept almost two hours.

Two hours during which Doc du Pont had apparently informed Hughes of his departure and hitched a ride back to civilization.

How had Hughes reacted to du Pont's change of heart? Why hadn't Doc come to Jake's cabin to say good-bye? Because he feared arousing suspicions?

Jake could feel Brent's eyes on him, studying him.

Jake hated that he hadn't been there to see Doc off, yet another part of him thought it might be fortuitous. Maybe Doc feared that Hughes would pick up on something between the two of them. They'd already made their plans. Why give the appearance that they were friendly enough that Doc felt compelled to say good-bye?

As if reading his mind, Brent offered, "Current was too fucking strong to tie the raft to the *Tapuya*. Du Pont had to go for it while he could."

"Where'd you say Hughes is?" Jake asked.

Brent pointed toward the stairs that skirted the sweep of dining room windows on the aft side of the boat.

Jake found Hughes sitting on a bench alone, in the shade of the upper deck, pecking away at his laptop.

"Suppose you're next," Hughes said, his voice heavy with sarcasm.

Jake could not see Hughes's eyes, which were hidden behind dark glasses.

"I've decided to stay on," Jake announced simply.

Hughes's jaw tightened as he stared at Jake.

"Then it's my turn now to lay down some rules."

The pure, visceral hatred in Jake's eyes did not cause Hughes a moment's falter.

"The next time you stage a protest, or refuse to assist us in drawing blood," Hughes declared, "we'll leave you on the fucking riverbank. You can find out for yourself just how far your goodwill gets you with these savages. Understand?"

Jake did not argue. All that mattered here was Michael. If temporarily putting up with Hughes was what it took to help his son, so be it. Hughes's suspicions must not be aroused.

"Is that all?" Jake replied sharply.

"No, it's not."

Hughes reached for a brown leather organizer lying on the bench beside him.

"If you want to continue with our team," he said, "there's one more thing."

Jake watched Hughes open the organizer. A stack of papers about half an inch thick had been stuffed into the pocket on the right side. Hughes separated the top document, two pages stapled together, and handed it to Jake.

"You'll also have to sign this," Hughes said.

Jake took it.

Though he couldn't see Hughes's eyes, he could feel the pleasure Hughes derived from watching him as he read the document's title:

Agreement to Transfer Patent Ownership, Patent # 044392888432 (TS 47)

CHAPTER TWENTY-FOUR

THE NEXT DAY, the *Tapuya* reached the mouth of the Purus, a tributary that flowed from the southwest. When the river narrowed—as it frequently did, especially around sharp twists and turns—the forest's canopy closed overhead, forming a tunnel, its roof so thick it completely blocked out the sun's rays, so thick, Jake noticed, that when the rain came, it sometimes took minutes to finally work its way through the layer of vegetation and fall to the river.

Jake spent most of his time on the observation deck, away from Hughes and Brent.

Du Pont had been his lock on sanity. His symbol of reason and hope. Hope that they would ultimately manage to redeem the evil that had poisoned this trip from the start, with a genetic find that would change the lives of people all over the world, including Michael's.

The stakes had never been higher. Jake had believed for some time now that Michael's chances for seeing again depended on his finding G32.

Now he feared Michael's life also depended on it.

And now, more than ever, du Pont symbolized Jake's hope of finding G32—and still being able to live with himself for the acts he would have to commit in the process.

He clung to that hope, to his and Doc's plan. But in this world of the Amazon, where so much was wildly beyond Jake's control, having so very much hinge on that one plan scared the hell out of him. He must not let anything stop him from meeting up with Doc du Pont.

With du Pont gone and the satellite phone useless—leaving him unable to check on Michael—Jake felt an isolation unlike anything he'd ever experienced.

Keenly feeling the need for an ally on board the *Tapuya*, he'd become friendly with Pedro, using his hands to sign greetings and, occasionally, ask questions.

Zurito captained the boat and busied himself with the maintenance of supplies and equipment, which meant he was rarely to be seen. This suited Jake just fine.

The day was coming, all too soon, when they would leave the *Tapuya* and be forced to continue on in the skiff. They would leave Pedro behind, anchored on the *Tapuya*. Jake tried to avoid thinking of the proximity that he would be forced into with the other three when that day came. He tried not to think of the infinite variety of events that could threaten his meeting up with Doc du Pont.

Instead, for hours at a time, Jake stared at the passing shoreline.

A tangle of dense brush lined the river. Fallen trees littered its waters, their branches sometimes spreading fifty feet or more just above or under the surface. The strong currents continually wore away the river's banks, causing entire sections of earth and trees to tumble into the water, creating an unpredictable, hellish quagmire for boaters to negotiate.

For wildlife, the fallen debris offered welcome camouflage.

Jake had been staring at a log when suddenly he saw it slither into the water. At least eight feet long, the caiman stared with its beady eyes at the *Tapuya* from just over the water's surface before it dived, disappearing into the murky brown river.

Suddenly more movement, ahead, on the water, drew Jake's attention. A lone kayaker.

"Ahoy," a male voice called.

Jake hurried down to the lower deck, where Hughes and Brent had also assembled in response to the greeting.

"Mind if I come on board?" the kayaker yelled as he approached. "I could sure use a break."

He paddled adeptly, fighting the river's current as he tried to bring the kayak even with the *Tapuya*. Golden sun-bleached hair, bronzed arms and face—he looked to Jake like he should be on the shores of Mailbu, not paddling solo down a treacherous river, keeping company with alligators and snakes the size of his boat.

Jake saw Hughes and Brent exchange quick glances. He had a momentary panic that they would refuse.

"He might be able to tell us about the portage around the waterfall," Jake suggested.

"He's right," Brent said.

"Throw him a rope," Hughes ordered.

Zurito had appeared. With practiced skill, he tossed the young man a line, landing it just upstream from the kayak. When it swept by, the kayaker grabbed it and, in hand-over-hand fashion, pulled himself alongside the *Tapuya*, which was now idling in neutral.

Grabbing hold of the steel ladder, the young man stepped up on it, simultaneously lifting his kayak from the water with the other hand. Long, sinewy muscles popped out in his arms as he swung the craft onto the *Tapuya's* deck.

On deck, Jake saw provisions stashed in its bow.

"Thank God you're going upstream," the kayaker said good-naturedly, shaking water from soggy Nikes as he stepped over the guard rail.

"Why?" Jake asked. "You were headed downriver."

" 'Cause I can hop on board and get a little break without cheating on my record."

The kayaker's grin gave Jake inexplicable comfort.

"What record's that?"

"The first to kayak from the Peruvian Andes to the Atlantic. I can ride upstream with you a ways, enjoy some good company, and hopefully some equally good food," he winked slyly at this, "then double back. Adds some miles, but after the last couple days I've had, it'll be worth it. My name's Michael." He extended his hand, a wide smile revealing perfect white teeth. "Michael Faulk. From Ennis, Montana."

Jake took his hand enthusiastically.

"Jake Skully."

CHAPTER **TWENTY-FIVE**

I T SOON BECAME clear that Hughes and Brent had made a pact not to allow Jake time alone with Michael Faulk. Despite the fact that there was no love lost between Hughes and Brent, they appeared united on at least one level: their distrust of Jake and determination to keep him in line.

To Jake's great annoyance, Brent followed the friendly kayaker around the *Tapuya* like a trained Doberman. After Jake offered his bathroom to Faulk to shower in, Jake even came across the guide standing in the hall outside Jake's room.

"Give the guy a break," Jake said, scowling.

Hughes invited Faulk to stay for lunch. Over fruit and chicken salad, he and Brent grilled the adventurer about the journey that lay ahead.

"I tell ya," Faulk said. "The river stays wide enough for this baby for several more days, but it's an obstacle course a little farther up there. I was running into logs thick as a freakin' oil barrel. My kayak's pretty resilient; it just bounces off. But there are submerged boles of trees, covered by floating algae, that are impossible to avoid 'cause you can't see them. And some of those babies must weigh more than a ton. This boat hits one of those and you'll end up with a punctured hull."

"So you're saying we may want to transfer to the skiff pretty soon," Hughes observed.

"Hey, man, it's your call ya know, but I'm just warning you. I wouldn't be in too big a hurry to leave this baby, either, but before too long, you're gonna have to."

"Our biggest concern is the waterfall," Hughes said.

"The waterfall. Yeah. It's amazing," Faulk said, stuffing another forkful of chicken salad into his mouth. "Eighty-foot drop. I camped on its lower shores. I've never seen rainbows like that. Mind-blowing. Absolutely phenomenal."

"What about the portage?" Brent said impatiently, clearly not interested in the aesthetics. "How bad is it?"

"For me?" Faulk answered. "Not that bad. My kayak's light. And remember, I was heading downhill. I was able to slide my boat down a lot of it. Biggest problem was the ants and mosquitoes. 'Bout ate me alive." He lifted his shirt and stood, turning to display his back, which was covered in huge, hideous red welts. "Suckers are practically the size of mice."

"You need an antibiotic cream on those," Jake said. "I'll give you some to take with you."

"That'd be sweet," Faulk responded.

"How long'd it take you?" Hughes asked.

"The portage?" Faulk replied. "Maybe seven, eight hours. But you'll be hauling that fifteen-foot launch you showed me. And how much gear?"

"One large crate, food, camping gear," Hughes answered.

"I dunno. That's a completely different story. It'd be a helluva job for three men. Can't you ditch the crate? What's in it?"

"Medical supplies," Hughes replied.

"So you guys are on some kind of mission, huh? Where you headed?"

"Yes," Hughes answered. "We're taking badly needed supplies to the Apurina."

This was the first Jake had heard of the Apurina.

"Cool," Michael Faulk said. "They're good people. Seen a lot of them. They're pretty much scattered all along the Purus, from Rio Branco to Manaus. Nothin' to be scared of with them."

"I understand they're Christian," Hughes replied.

"I don't know anything about that, but they dress like us. Poorer, of course, but shorts, shirts. You know what I mean," Faulk said. "Different story with some natives I ran into along the Tamaraca."

Hughes perked up immediately.

"How so?"

"All decked out, painted faces, G-strings, feathers in their hair. Bastards shot at me from the shore. Felt like I'd traveled back in time. I kayaked all night long to put some distance between me and them. No way I was camping along that stretch of the river."

"The Papavo," Brent murmured, his eyes connecting with Hughes's. "There've been rumors of them, but their existence has never been confirmed. Can't be more than a handful of them."

"A handful?" Hughes parroted, clearly intrigued. "How many?"

"Probably a dozen. At most."

"Exactly where's the Tamaraca?" Hughes asked, turning to Michael Faulk.

"Follow the Purus on down to the River Acre, and it's the first tributary you'll come to," Faulk answered. "Narrow sucker. No way you'd get a boat this size up her, least not any distance."

"Let's take a look at the map," Hughes said. Looking at Brent he added, "Sounds like a detour is in order. I'd like to find this tribe."

"What do you mean, detour?" Jake asked, incredulous. "We're looking for the Naua."

"The Naua?" Faulk echoed. "Never heard of 'em."

Hughes's eyes quickly darted from Faulk to Jake.

"We'll have that discussion later," he said sternly.

"Hell we will," Jake said, rising so abruptly his chair clattered to the wood floor. "Let's get this straight right now. This trip isn't about the Papavo."

Hughes's eyes shone with cold, emotionless determination.

"This trip is about what I decide it's about."

Jake wanted to lunge across the table and kill the son of a bitch, but he could not afford to jeopardize his plan to meet up with Doc du Pont.

"You know I'm not in a position to take any side trips," he said with barely contained rage. "I have to get home to my son."

"Your son is fine. Leah's taking good care of him. Of both of them."

"Leah couldn't stop . . ."

Jake caught himself.

Michael Faulk looked on, clearly torn between curiosity and embarrassment at witnessing the tension between the two men.

"Stop *what?*" Hughes said, a glint of humor creasing his eyes.

Furious, Jake turned and stormed out.

JAKE HATED TO SEE Michael Faulk depart the *Tapuya*, but after eating, the kayaker announced he was eager to resume his voyage. Jake couldn't help but wonder if Faulk hadn't, in fact, sensed that this "mission" he'd stumbled upon was not what it seemed and decided the wisest course would be to part company ASAP.

Hughes's nearness didn't stop Jake, walking the deck back to Faulk's kayak, from asking, "We've heard rumors of a blue-eyed tribe in the state of Acre. Any chance you've run across some of them?"

Faulk ran a bony brown hand across his scruffy blond beard.

"You know," he said, "an old settler who put me up for a night told me he'd seen a blue-eyed native. A woman. He'd chased her away from his garden. I thought the old geezer'd been hittin' the sauce a little too heavy, 'cause blue eyes . . . well, I haven't seen a pair of baby blues since I left Montana."

Despite the look of disapproval Hughes shot at Jake, he couldn't resist probing.

"How long ago did he see her?"

"He didn't say. You know these people. Time means nothing to them."

Jake watched as Faulk retrieved his kayak, lowered it from his perch on the ladder to the water and, with the agility of a gymnast, climbed into its narrow opening.

The expression on Faulk's face as he turned to say good-bye—his eyes lingered on Jake until the current grabbed hold of his kayak and demanded his full attention—conveyed to Jake that the young man grasped that all was not right on board the *Tapuya*.

Battling to keep his kayak abreast of the *Tapuya* for just a moment longer, Faulk lifted his free hand and gave Jake a thumbs-up.

Jake mouthed a "you too" and nodded in response as the young man from Montana drifted away.

BEFORE THE KAYAK had even disappeared from sight, Hughes turned on Jake.

"What the fuck are you thinking, mentioning the Naua in front of him?"

Jake drew back in surprise.

"Why is that a problem? You should be glad I asked. It just confirms the rumors. Now, you explain to me why you'd consider detouring for a handful of hostile natives? This trip is about G32, not the Papavo."

"G32's just one of the reasons for this trip," Hughes replied. "Blood from an isolated tribe like the Papavo could be worth a fortune. If we don't sample them, you know damn well someone else'll come along and do it. If a little detour's all it takes, I'm not going to let that happen."

"You don't even have an indication yet—a therapeutic use for the patent application. That takes time, research. Even if you're the first to sample them, someone with a leg up on research could beat you to the patent on their cell lines. There's no guarantee that won't happen."

"You're walking a thin line here, Skully. Another stunt like that outburst in front of a stranger and you may just find yourself leaving this boat the way your pal du Pont left."

Jake grabbed Hughes by the collar and threw him up against the side of the boat's main cabin.

"What does that mean?"

Hughes looked around for Brent. When he did not see him, his eyes finally reflected something Jake had never before seen in them. Fear.

Jake loosened his grip on Hughes, letting him fall forward, and then slammed him against the wall again.

"What do you mean?" he shouted. "What did you do to Doc?"

"Nothing," Hughes replied. "Nothing. I swear. He quit. He left on some rickety raft. That's all I meant—that that boat he got on just didn't look like it'd make it all the way to Manaus. I just meant the same thing could happen to you."

Jake breathed his anger—spewed it—in Hughes's face.

"Why should I believe that's what happened to Doc?" All his fears and worry and rage mushroomed toward the sky like some miniature H-bomb. "Tell me why. *Tell me.*"

By the time Jake noticed that Hughes's eyes had strayed to the deck behind him, he had only enough time to see him nod.

And then, in a sickening explosion of pain, Jake's world went black.

CHAPTER **TWENTY-SIX**

"DO WE *HAVE* to pull up so fast?" Asahel screamed at Cavallero over the roar of the plane's engine.

"Safer that way," Cavallero yelled back. "Water's too dirty to see what's under the surface. Rough takeoff's a hell of a lot better than running into something."

He'd already explained that to her, the last time they landed, on a small tributary just off the Amazon. He'd ordered her to buckle in tight.

"Ever been upside down in one of these things in the water?" he'd asked.

With most people, Asahel would assume this to be a rhetorical question, but Cavallero seemed to believe other people encountered the same kind of insane dangers he dealt with on a daily basis.

"No," she'd answered, deadpan. "Never have."

He'd then proceeded to give her a short lesson in evacuation of an upside-down seaplane in fast-moving water that, he explained, might well be so thick and brown that vision under its surface would be impossible.

Remembering it now, Asahel cut short her complaint about the takeoff. If she wanted something to worry about, she had plenty of other options that were far more important to her than Cavallero's abrupt takeoffs.

She'd been to the Amazon once before, had trekked through it visiting tribes. But now that she'd returned, now that she'd seen the endless forest again firsthand, so dense and brutal and unforgiving—Cavallero delighted in pointing out the anacondas and caimans and piranhas inhabiting its waters—she couldn't imagine actually finding someone in it. The enormity of her mission, its sheer impossibility, sank deeper into her soul with each passing hour, and the guilt and grief she felt about everything—Toby, Caina, Angie, her own decisions—almost paralyzed her at times.

Cavallero didn't even know which tributary Hughes's party had taken. There were two, the Purus and the Juruá, that Cavallero seemed focused upon.

Cavallero. If there was just one thing giving Asahel any sense of hope—the same thing that terrified and infuriated her daily—it was Diego Cavallero.

"What's next?" Asahel yelled to Cavallero. She'd waited for the plane to level off. They flew low, close enough to see the smallest craft on the waters. Close enough to see children playing along its banks. Cavallero liked to hang his head out the window. It reminded Asahel of a dog on a car ride with its ears flapping happily away. But Cavallero wasn't exactly that happy right now.

"We'll find the motherfuckers," he called back. "We'll start down the Purus since it's closest. Someone will have seen them."

They'd stopped twice now to question fishermen. One swore that he'd seen the *Tapuya* go up a small tributary off the Amazon's north shore. Even though that made no sense to Cavallero—it took the *Tapuya* off-course from their destination in Acre—he'd followed the tributary for hours, finally stopping at the home of a settler he knew, who proclaimed proudly that nobody traveled by his place unnoticed.

"I heard rumors of some gringo doctors taking blood from Indians downriver," the settler explained. He spoke with an English accent, was all skin and bone and looked to be in his late fifties. Asahel wondered if he were a fugitive of some sort. "Not the first time it's happened. Them natives are happy to trade blood for just about any piece of crap a white man brings in here."

"That's them," Cavallero had cried. "Where? What village?"

"There're a couple of little villages just before the big river," the settler replied. "It was one of them. Not sure which. But I can tell you, they never made it up here. I'd have seen them. Must've turned round and got back on the Mother River."

Cavallero had thrown his cigarette to the ground, stamping it out with a ferocity that made him look quite ridiculous, then grabbed Asahel by the arm.

"Let's go."

Now, airborne again, the simple fact of hanging his head out the window, flying over the land and people he'd designated himself to protect, seemed to abate his anger somewhat.

They'd flown for several hours when Cavallero's voice broke through the constant, near deafening drone of the plane.

"Look," he yelled.

Beneath them, along the shores of the great Amazon, almost a mile wide at this point, skimmed a slim lone craft.

"A kayaker."

THOUGH STILL THE SIZE of a newborn's fist, the knot on the back of Jake's head only throbbed now when he lay on his back.

Once he'd come to from his surprise encounter with the butt of Brent's rifle, Jake had gone over and over Hughes's explanation about Doc du Pont's departure from the *Tapuya*. He'd finally come to the conclusion—a conclusion undeniably fortified by the fact that there were no other viable options that would enable him to make his rendezvous with Doc—that he had no choice but to operate on the assumption Hughes was telling the truth.

Doc and Jake had, after all, agreed that Doc would depart the *Tapuya* as soon as possible. The only real surprise had been how quickly that had happened—and the fact that Jake had slept through it. But knowing Doc as Jake did, it made some kind of sense. Doc probably wanted to avoid giving Hughes any opportunity to observe the two of them together, any reason to suspect there might be something going on between him and Jake.

Of course, Hughes had to be harboring some suspicions about Jake and Doc now, based on Jake's reaction to Hughes's comment about Doc. But at this point, both men knew that Jake was, effectively, Hughes's captive on this trip. They were only together out of necessity—Jake's to cure Michael, Hughes's to get his hands on TS 47. Both knew the other man would just as soon slit the other's throat as he would trust him.

Now that Hughes had made the decision to detour to the Tamaraca, in search of the tribe that Brent believed to be Papavo, the waterfall ceased to be an issue.

The *Tapuya* maintained its course on the Purus, stopping frequently whenever one of the men on board sighted clusters of huts. They had developed an efficient routine. Zurito would grab a handful of trinkets from the treasure chest, motor over to the shore in the skiff, where, in keeping with Michael Faulk's prediction, he usually received some form of welcome.

A conversation would ensue. As it turned out, Zurito was fluent in Portuguese, Spanish, several Indian dialects and Lingoa Geral, the river language common to communities along the vast network of Amazonian rivers. He also proved to be a man of persuasion. More often than not, he would return with word that the tribe had agreed to sampling.

At that point, Jake and Hughes would motor back, along with Zurito, quickly draw samples, dole out the goods and depart.

Jake had given up fighting Hughes on these sampling side trips, telling himself that maybe, just maybe, they'd find G32 in one of the gene pools. He'd also given up the consent form battle, but back in the boat he would label samples with whatever name Zurito had been able to draw from his introductory conversations. Sometimes just a first name—in the Amazon, Jake learned, everyone went by first names only. Usually when he inscribed a label Jake ended up writing a tribe's name, followed by a number. Apurina, #4, female, EA (estimated age) 25; or Baniwa, #2, male, EA 40.

After a fair amount of cajoling, Hughes had even taken Pedro's blood. But Zurito resolutely refused.

After most stops, Jake noticed Brent consulting a file he frequently carried along with him.

One hot, muggy morning Zurito spotted two fishermen up ahead. When the *Tapuya* reached where they'd been, they'd disappeared, but Zurito gamely set off in the skiff after them, pulling it up on a rare stretch of white sandy beach and disappearing into the forest in pursuit. Perhaps an hour later, he returned, reporting that the two belonged to a tribe known as the Katukina. They refused to cooperate, even threatening Zurito with a raised bow and arrow. Excitedly Brent paged through his file.

"Here," he said, reading, "just what I thought. They think there are less than two hundred Katukina. They're found in both Amazonas and Acre. Their dialect is Marubo."

Hughes had turned to Zurito.

"How far away is their village?"

"I think not far," Zurito answered.

"Are we going in after them?" Brent asked.

Hughes stayed silent for a good long while.

"We can't take on two hundred. If that's the reception Zurito got, we'd be wasting our time. Besides, with two fragments of the tribe—one in Amazonas and another in Acre—chances are someone else has already gotten to them. Or will in the near future. Let's keep moving."

There was no longer any question in Jake's mind that Brent was not your run-of-the-mill Amazon guide. To start with, he had to rely on Zurito tremendously. Zurito's navigational skills, knowledge of plants and insects, familiarity with the river and its peoples all greatly exceeded those of Brent. Yet Hughes clearly put great stock in Brent's knowledge of tribes, which seemed to be especially keen in the case of tribes whose existence was in question or who were believed to be nearly extinct.

Jake wanted to get ahold of Brent's file. Maybe it would explain Hughes and Brent's strange coalition.

But he would have to wait for the right opportunity. Hughes and Brent continued to keep a close eye on him.

Did they suspect his plan to meet up with Doc du Pont? Jake could only remind himself that with each stop they made, each vial of blood drawn, he was that much closer to finding a cure for Michael.

Calmed by this thought and relieved at the news they would not be trekking into the forest after bow-and-arrow-armed natives, Jake went back to studying the shoreline for wildlife. And swatting at the constant veil of flies and mosquitoes.

CHAPTER **TWENTY-SEVEN**

J AKE NODDED AT Pedro, who raised a hand in the air from the bow of the *Tapuya*, as the skiff motored away.

"Hasta luego, Pedro."

He watched until first Pedro and then the *Tapuya* shrank from view, a gloom descending upon him.

In their final hours on the Purus, its waters had narrowed, causing the *Tapuya* to get caught up on a newly formed island that had broken off the riverbank upstream. Still, once they'd freed her, the *Tapuya* had been able to navigate all the way down the Purus to the River Acre.

But the Acre had given the *Tapuya* trouble right from the start. Its narrower width made avoiding debris nearly impossible. Yesterday had been pure hell. The final straw.

"Zurito say everybody on deck."

Jake, Hughes and Brent had been eating lunch when a thud that sent them tumbling, coupled with Pedro's alarm, caused all three to bolt for the door.

Outside they immediately saw the problem.

The *Tapuya* had become sandwiched in the branches of a downed tree, caught like a fly in a spider's web. The tree itself still clung to the shore by a handful of thick roots. The wild, fast River Acre buffeted the *Tapuya* into the V formed by the two main branches of the tree, each of which was at least four feet in diameter. As the yacht was drawn into the V, hundreds of smaller branches had closed behind it, sealing the *Tapuya* in its trap.

Zurito had made his way out on to the largest limb, carrying a chain saw, which he brandished like a conductor's wand, swiping at this branch, then that, balancing barefoot as he disentangled the *Tapuya* from the tentacles.

Suddenly, unable to withstand the strain any longer, the roots gave way. *Pop-pop-popping* like a downed electric line as one after another snapped at its base.

The river's enormous power swung the uprooted tree around, twirling it wildly, 270 degrees, taking the *Tapuya*, and Zurito, clinging to the branches, along for the ride.

Caught in a giant whirlpool, the *Tapuya* was blocked by the network of branches. But at just the right moment, when the section he'd cleared lined up with the river's flow, Zurito hopped back on board and threw the motor into reverse. As the network of branches closed back in on them, the *Tapuya* shot free of the web.

Once they'd regained control, Jake heard the words he'd been dreading.

"That's it," said Hughes. "Tomorrow we board the skiff."

Even the fastest of rivers in the Amazonian network had stretches where the waters widened and grew more quiet. They'd waited for just such a stretch, then anchored the *Tapuya* next to shore as they lowered the sixteen-foot skiff into the water. Zurito had climbed in and seen to its loading—an important job, for they had a great deal of gear, plus the four men.

"Got to make sure balance," Zurito said. "Rough water ahead. Not load right, we end up swim with piranhas. And eels."

Jake swore Zurito smiled then, at the look on Brent's face.

As the *Tapuya*, with Pedro on board, faded in the distance, Jake now contemplated his misery. If Michael Faulk's estimates were correct, it would take two days to reach Papavo territory.

Two days of traveling the murky, muddy waters, sweltering under a merciless sun while futilely swatting away insects, of sitting, cramped, side by side with Hughes, who shared the middle seat of the skiff with Jake, while Brent took the bow and Zurito steered the fifty-horsepower motor from behind.

Two days of riding out rapids and whirlpools, dodging debris, knowing all the while that the only thing separating him from the stingrays capable of incapacitating a man for days, the electric eels that could knock him senseless, and the minuscule, spiny *carnero* that enter a person's smallest orifices, open their spines and have to be cut out was Zurito's skill as a navigator and boat packer. And half an inch of aluminum.

Most important, for Jake, two days wasted—days that only served to threaten Jake's rendezvous with du Pont.

Jake had asked Zurito if their search for the Papavo meant they'd bypass Pauhiny. He hadn't dared ask Hughes or Brent, fearing it would cause a deliberate avoidance of the town where Jake was to meet up with du Pont. Jake felt certain Zurito understood the question, but Zurito had shrugged his shoulders and said, "No comprendo."

And so the two days also meant growing anxiety over his chances of ever seeing Doc du Pont again.

The only redemption Jake found in those two days came in the form of the wonder and beauty everywhere he looked. They helped put his situation in perspective. The Amazonian world—sometimes brutally, sometimes beautifully, but always dramatically—constantly reminded its visitors of the vast power and wonder of nature, and the insignificance of a single human being. A single human being's problems.

Pierid butterflies, the color of gold and the size of a hand, floated everywhere on the breeze. Water lily pads, large enough to nap on, danced on the waters. The serene beauty of the occasional lagoon stunned the eyes.

Still, most of the journey they were walled in by trees, imprisoned within a veritable aviary of shrieking, singing and jabbering birds and monkeys.

That first day, they didn't see another soul on the river.

In late afternoon, Zurito announced it was time to stop and make camp. They pulled over to the riverbank. Relieved to be able to stretch his legs and distance himself from the others, Jake helped hoist the heavily loaded skiff half out of the water, tying it to a thick *sumauma* tree. By now Jake had seen so many trees its size—almost 150 feet— that had been downed by the swift undercurrent that he couldn't help but wonder whether it, the tree, with the skiff attached, would still be standing when they returned in the morning.

Penetrating the thick growth bordering the riverbank involved brutal work. Large iguanas disturbed by their passage glided slowly out of the way looking like cartoonish prehistoric monsters, the kind Antony liked to watch on television. Swarms of ticks and caterpillars six and seven inches long, of vibrant colors—some hairy, some smooth—hung from leaves that blew in the breeze. Jake walked through a silky web that clung to his face and arms tenaciously, hugging him close, like a second skin that he could not shake free, or even peel off.

Zurito had packed two machetes. He put Jake and Brent to work clearing a site to camp for the night. Rivers of sweat poured down Jake's forehead, back and arms, but he found it impossible to cut through the thick stalks of undergrowth.

"Like this," Zurito said, grabbing the long blade from him. He demonstrated an easy sharp-angled slash that sliced through everything in its path.

Zurito and Hughes hauled gear from the boat, then dragged several fallen logs into the clearing and arranged them like spokes of a bicycle wheel. At their center, Zurito squatted and constructed a grill made of green branches. He gave Hughes the job of peeling the bark off pieces of firewood.

Jake had built many campfires. He saw that all the wood being used was waterlogged, still damp from the rainy season, during which waters from the rivers rose for miles, literally turning the forest floor into an endless lake spiked with trees. He watched Zurito's attempt to light the whittled pile made by Hughes with equal parts dread and humor—amusement at the idea that the omniscient Zurito could be so foolish, dread at their fate should Zurito's jungle skills prove a farce.

But Zurito's eyes quickly moved from his failed attempt to the trees lining the clearing. They came to rest on a trunk pocked with clumps of sap.

Zurito walked to the tree, pulled off wads of the sticky brown material, which oozed from every crevice. Returning to the grill, he grabbed a short stick and used it to push the molasseslike goop into the middle of the kindling.

When he dropped another match into the pile, it instantly exploded in a smooth *whoosh*.

All three men stared in amazement.

"Kerosene tree," Zurito muttered.

Dinner consisted of a meal from a pouch bought at REI, dried meats and pasta dumped into boiling water. Zurito did not have to go far to supplement it with Brazil nuts and several fruits. *Acaí, graviola* and *cupuacu*, which Hughes promptly spit on the ground. Jake enjoyed them.

Zurito warned that when they abandoned the skiff for their expedition inland to find the Naua, the luxury of hauling water and cooking utensils would be left behind.

"We mebbe walk for days," he said. "Carry only what we gotta have."

As the other three ate, Zurito set about constructing an open-sided hut. He hacked down several small trees, which became the framework. He used strands of the *tamshi* vine to lash it together and to tie down palm fronds on its roof. Finally, he threw palm fronds on the floor.

When the light started to fade, Hughes and Brent began setting up their pup tents, one on each side of the hut.

"Big enough," Zurito said, motioning toward the hut. "Hot in tents. No air."

Hughes and Brent declined, but Jake took Zurito up on his offer, stringing up his mosquito net next to Zurito's.

Jake's previous night in the jungle, with the Ucalayi, hadn't prepared him for this one. The clamor of alarming, bizarre sounds surrounded the tent. Screams. (Were they human? Cats? The last mournful cry of dying prey?) Thuds, crackling, crashing. As soon as one sound died down, another—with equal capacity to stand the hair on the back of his neck on end—rose to replace it. When something scurried across his face, Jake reflexively swatted it away. In the moonlight, he turned to eye a tarantula. Only inches away, it seemed to stare back at him.

Fruits, nuts and branches broken in the wake of acrobatic monkeys dropped constantly from the canopy overhead, clattering all the way down as they bounced from one branch to another before hitting ground.

Jake swore he could hear the forest vegetating around him. Feel it. Smell it.

He strained to make out Zurito's form in the parallel planes of moonlight filtering through the palm fronds and realized that it was the first time he'd seen Zurito sleep. He marveled at how peaceful Zurito appeared, in stark contrast to the wildness surrounding them and his usual expression.

Not even the blasphemous epithets being hurled from the pup tent on either side of their hut disturbed Zurito this night.

WHEN THEY AWOKE the next day, the sight of fresh footprints around their campfire and tents—there were three sets, all noticeably wider than any Jake had ever seen—didn't exactly give Jake the warm and fuzzies, but it noticeably unnerved both Brent and Hughes.

Zurito offered little reaction, as though he'd expected visitors.

The four men ate more of the backpacking fare from REI, then made their way back to the river, where the boat was tied. Their visitors had not disturbed its contents.

Jake climbed in, anxious to get going. He had no choice now but to accept Hughes's decision to find and sample the Papavo. The sooner they got it over with, the better.

He'd had a dream the night before. As their visitors padded barefoot around the hut, he'd dreamed about the envelope.

He'd dreamed there was a letter in it when the police found it in the bathroom wastebasket. A letter from Ana. Sergeant de Santos had waved it in front of Jake's face, refusing to let Jake see it first, in private. He'd read what Ana wrote—in words that sounded just like they came from Ana's mouth. But Ana would never do such a thing.

In the letter, Ana told Jake she'd decided to take her own life. That she couldn't live with a man she didn't trust and she also knew she couldn't live without Jake. Which left her little choice.

In the dream, Jake sat, sobbing, his head in his hands, while de Santos cruelly recited Ana's words. But then he'd heard a sound at the door and looked up. There stood Michael. He'd heard it all.

Maybe that's why the discovery that they'd had visitors at their campsite the night before did not faze Jake. He was still shaken from that dream. From the look on his son's face.

As the morning passed, the river grew wider. The maze of gnarled and snaking branches from submerged fallen trees that lined both shores left them no choice but to travel down the Acre's center, which offered no shade from a relentlessly glaring sun.

After they'd motored up the river for almost eight hours, Zurito suddenly pointed toward the shore.

"There."

A simple bamboo lean-to, abandoned.

"Someone fish there, use for shade," Zurito explained.

The first day they'd left the *Tapuya* and boarded the skiff, Jake saw Zurito place a conch shell on the floor, under the bench seat that ran across the back of the skiff. The native reached for it now and blew the first of several long mournful blasts, which echoed down the tunnel of river.

"What are you doing?" Hughes snapped, turning to snatch the shell from him.

Zurito pushed Hughes's hand away.

"In jungle, only enemies not announce they coming," he said. "We close now." He pointed to a ribbon of smoke rising from the jungle. "Maybe Papavo."

"You idiot. We wanted to sneak up on them," Brent said, clearly angry.

Zurito gave him a disdainful look.

"No find Papavo if Papavo no want be found. Good we on river; we mebbe escape if they—"

The first arrow split the sky in front of the boat before Zurito could finish his sentence. All heads turned toward the eastern shores of the river, where, as if on cue, an apparition stepped out from the dense forest lining its banks.

Completely nude, save for a small feather shield over his loins, he was painted with bright yellow lines on one side of his chest, black stripes on the other. He wore a headdress of black and yellow feathers and carried a powerful-looking bow and several long arrows decorated with feathers that matched his head dress.

"Holy shit," Brent cried out when similarly painted figures emerged from the forest to stand on either side of him.

Zurito had pushed the motor's throttle to full speed before the first arrow even landed—luckily short of the boat.

"Down," he yelled.

Within seconds, a wall of arrows—some trailing colorful feathers behind—floated toward the skiff, almost as if in slow motion, from the east bank of the river. Jake grabbed his laptop from under the seat. Holding it over his head for protection, he heard the *piiiing* and felt the vibration of an arrow deflected off it. Hunkered down, he could hear other arrows hitting the aluminum boat, while still others sliced, hissing, into the water.

The attack seemed to go on forever. The boat was loaded to its maximum capacity, and slow.

Suddenly Jake fell sideways. The boat had swerved violently. A sharp cry from the back of the skiff caused him to risk looking.

Doubled over, Zurito clawed frantically over his right shoulder, at his back.

An arrow with a yellow feather in its quill protruded from just below his shoulder.

The boat was almost out of range of the arrows now. Jake threw his laptop down and climbed over Hughes, who remained huddled on the floor, his head still hidden under the metal bench. The only part of Brent visible in the front of the boat was the seat of his khaki shorts.

Grabbing the throttle handle from Zurito, who'd miraculously managed to maintain enough presence of mind to keep a hold on it, Jake steered the skiff back on-course. One last arrow sang by Jake's ear before disappearing into the murky water.

When the wildly painted war party had shrunk to mere dots of color moving along the shore, their shrieks and cries echoing like a jaguar's across the water, Jake yelled for Brent.

"Get back here and steer."

Moving low, his eyes scanning the shorelines, Brent crawled over the bench seats and took the throttle from Jake.

"Throw me my bag," Jake ordered Hughes.

Hughes, who had finally pulled his head out from under the bench, threw the black medical bag in Jake's direction. He eyed several arrows that had landed in the skiff.

Zurito sat, silent but with a dazed look that indicated shock. He remained quiet while Jake used scissors to cut his T-shirt off. The arrow had penetrated several inches.

"Can you move your shoulder and arm?"

Silently Zurito lifted both shoulders in an exaggerated shrug. He issued just one short yelp when Jake rotated the affected arm.

"It's embedded in your muscle, and it's gonna hurt like hell to take it out, but I don't think anything's broken."

He turned to Brent.

"Pull over. We need to get on land."

"Are you crazy?" Brent replied. "I'm not pulling over yet."

"Keep going," Hughes shouted, looking over his shoulder.

Blood oozed down the dark skin on Zurito's back. Jake had no choice but to remove the arrow right then and there. If its point severed a blood vessel, Zurito could bleed to death.

When Jake held up a syringe of lidocaine, Zurito pushed his hand away.

"So you won't feel the pain," Jake explained.

"No," Zurito answered fiercely. "Pain okay."

He reached for the shirt Jake cut off him, which Jake had thrown to the floor. Soaked with blood, and the water pooling at the boat's bottom, Zurito felt for a dry spot and stuffed a corner of the shirt into his mouth, clamping down on it with his starkly white teeth.

As the scalpel pierced the skin on his back, Zurito issued a single high-pitched cry, muted by the cloth. He held completely still while Jake first probed for the severed vessel that was causing the bleeding, then tied both ends off. Throughout the rest of the procedure, he remained silent. Even when Jake sewed the gaping hole left by the arrow with a dozen crude stitches.

Jake had spent two years in a Nogales ER and never had he seen a man endure pain with more stoicism.

After Jake washed his hands in the river's water, he retrieved the bloody arrow from the floor of the boat and held it in the air for all to see.

"You're lucky this didn't kill you."

Jake could not resist admiring its beauty. Each component crafted by hand, its feather the color of a setting sun.

Zurito rested, dazed, against the side of the boat, his face and chest drenched with sweat.

"Mebbe kill Zurito," he murmured, his voice low and even.

"It'd take a helluva lot more than a shoulder wound to do in a man like you," Jake replied.

"Mebbe," Zurito replied. "Mebbe not. We know soon."

"What are you saying?" he asked.

Zurito stared straight ahead, expressionless.

"Soon," he said. "We know soon."

"Know *what*?"

"If arrow had poison."

"WHAT KIND OF POISON?" Jake asked.

It had never occurred to him that the arrows might have delivered deadly toxins to their victims.

Zurito shook his head.

"Many kind," he said, his voice low and weak. "Spiders. Scorpion. Or mebbe plants, like *barbasco*. Different tribes, different poison."

"This is great," Hughes muttered. "Just great."

Jake rummaged through his bag and withdrew a small glass vial, holding it up in the fading afternoon light and rolling it between thumb and forefinger.

"Antitoxin for snake venom," he said, locking eyes with Hughes.

"That's a shot in the dark, and you know it," Hughes replied. "How many doses did you bring?"

"One."

"Why the hell would you only bring one? You heard him," Hughes said. "We don't even know if the arrow's poisoned, much less whether they used snake venom. We can't waste the only dose you brought."

"If that arrow was coated with snake venom, you know as well as I do that time is critical," Jake replied angrily. "If we wait until he shows symptoms, it'll be too late."

Hughes reached out and snatched the vial from Jake's hand.

"Give that back," Jake shouted, lunging at him.

As the two struggled, the boat rocked violently, threatening to capsize. Hughes stretched a long arm out toward Brent. A ray of sun glinted off the vial's glass in his hand.

"Take it," he ordered Brent.

Brent reached for the vial, but as he did so, the boat suddenly shuddered violently. They had sideswiped a submerged log. As he lost his balance, Brent's arm flew up and struck Hughes's outstretched hand. It launched the vial airborne.

As all four men watched, the vial sailed through the air, beyond the reach of Jake's hand, which shot up to catch it.

Then, like a lone drop of rain, it fell into the muddy waters and disappeared.

CHAPTER **TWENTY-EIGHT**

THEY'D MOTORED ON another two hours in absolute silence, the mood on board the skiff so foul that every person on board intuitively realized that any further decay of civility had the potential to spell disaster for all.

Still swelteringly hot, the sun had begun dropping in the sky when they saw a patch of white sand. Brent aimed the skiff at it. Jumping out, he and Jake pulled the skiff up on the beach. Hughes wandered down the shoreline while the two men, maintaining the tense silence, began to make camp.

With Zurito drifting in and out of consciousness, the lean-tos that they managed to construct were pathetic, but Jake simply wanted shelter from the sun for Zurito.

Hughes returned. Breaking into the crate of exchange goods for some line and hooks, Hughes and Brent decided to fish for dinner from the shore.

Jake hovered over Zurito.

He had developed a fever. Back on the river, Jake had given Zurito a massive dose of penicillin. Now he had a hard time deciding whether to attribute Zurito's temperature to the heat—still over one hundred degrees—or an exotic poison.

"He's coming to," Jake called when Zurito's eyes finally fluttered open.

Over Zurito's shoulder, Jake saw Hughes approaching.

"Let's go," Hughes ordered.

"What do you mean?" Jake replied. "He can't travel now. Look at him."

Hughes barely glanced the native's way.

"I've had enough. We wasted days for the Papavo for nothing. Not a single sample. It's time to get what we came for and get the hell out of this fucking jungle."

He crouched and put his face in Zurito's.

"How far are we now?" he asked. "You've seen Brent's map. How much longer is it going to take us to reach the Naua?"

Zurito had to fight to keep his eyes open.

"One, one and half more day on the river," Zurito replied slowly. "Then one, maybe two days walking inland, to terra firma."

"What about Pauhiny?" Jake blurted out without thinking.

"What about Pauhiny?" Hughes replied.

"We need to get Zurito there. Get him off the river."

"Pauhiny's not on this route," Brent said. "We're approaching Acre from the southwest now. We'd have to backtrack to the last tributary to get to Pauhiny."

"Then that's what we have to do," Jake said.

"Wrong," Hughes replied. "No way we're doing any backtracking. Zurito's gonna either make it through this or die on us. And if he dies, he'd be gone before we even reached Pauhiny. Look at him."

Beads of sweat dripped from Zurito's chin as his eyes slowly rolled back in their sockets. Jake knew that Hughes's words rang true, but he had to get to Pauhiny.

"The only place we're taking Zurito is to Pauhiny," he said. "We can't let him die."

The metallic *swoosh* stood out among the jungle sounds. Jake looked up from where he crouched beside Zurito to see Hughes standing over him with a machete.

There was no ambiguity in the message.

"Wrong," Hughes declared. "We're taking the shortest route to the Naua. We'll travel all night. So get him back on the boat."

CAVALLERO HAD FOLLOWED the Amazon for nearly two hundred miles, then veered off at a large tributary coming in sharply from the southwest. The Purus. Not more than ten minutes later, Cavallero began a steep bank of the plane.

"We're going down," he called to Asahel.

Asahel checked her seat belt, then strained to see directly beneath the plane. Something had caught Cavallero's eye. Something he felt warranted a stop. Her heart racing at the possibility that he'd spotted the *Tapuya*, she scanned the waters below.

Along the shore, a balsa wood raft carried four men and one woman.

The landing was smoother than most—this close to the Amazon, the Purus was nearly half a mile wide, which helped ease Cavallero's mind about debris. Most of it would be along either shore. He brought the plane to a near standstill about one hundred yards from the raft, then opened his door and climbed out, onto a pontoon, waiting for the flimsy handmade craft to drift by. When it came within yards he lifted his hand in the air and called out in a tongue Asahel did not recognize.

The natives seemed to recognize him. Several waved back.

Cavallero tossed them a coil of rope as they approached, and for several minutes the two vessels floated side by side, while Cavallero fired a series of questions at them. Asahel could not understand what he said, but she heard him mention the *Tapuya* several times. The group clearly did not feel threatened by Cavallero or his plane. Asahel suspected they'd seen him before.

When he bid them farewell, released the rope binding them together and climbed back inside the cockpit, Cavallero wore a determined expression.

"What?" Asahel asked. "What did they tell you?"

"They've seen the *Tapuya*. It's been stopping along the river, drawing blood from the Apurina."

Asahel's heart quickened at this news.

"How long ago?" she said. They were close, very close now.

"Two or three days, which means by now they've already reached a dozen forks. No way to know which they took. We could spend days searching each of them, and by then, they could be on foot, hiking into the jungle. We might never find them."

"I thought once we knew which tributary they took," Asahel said, "either the Purus or the Juruá, we'd be able to find them."

Cavallero snorted a laugh.

"Nothing's that simple in this part of the world," he said. "I was hoping they'd taken the Juruá. It doesn't have so many tributaries or a tenth of the *igarapes* the Purus has."

"*Igarapes?*"

"Streams that go deep into the rain forest. Problem with the Purus is it branches into so fucking many rivers you can hardly keep track of them. The Pauhiny, the Yaco, the Acre, the Puncaya, the Ituxy. All of 'em could eventually get them where they're headed, if we're right about that. Hell, we could even have *that* wrong, couldn't we?" He hesitated, then reached for the key to restart the plane. "Which is why we're turning around."

Asahel reached out and grabbed the plane's steering wheel.

"No," she cried. "You can't give up now."

CHAPTER **TWENTY-NINE**

WHEN HUGHES ANNOUNCED there'd be no more nonsense in their quest to find the Naua, he meant it.

The Amazon and its tributaries presented enough danger during daytime, but in the dark the risks multiplied.

"We're not stopping, period," Hughes declared. "I'm not spending one more night in that fucking jungle than I have to."

With Zurito sleeping fitfully in a makeshift bed on the skiff's floor, Brent took over as captain. He'd cut the boat's speed almost in half. Jake kept watch from the bow with a powerful flashlight, which he swept back and forth continuously along the water's surface.

During the day it was difficult to gauge the distance and direction from which the jungle noises came. The moonless night made it nearly impossible.

Suddenly Jake's light caught something.

A snake's head, raised high out of the water, moved toward the skiff, its coal black body undulating through the currents like an elongated letter *s*. When Jake leaned forward for a closer look, Zurito's voice from behind startled him.

"*Get back*. Jararaca. Muy peligroso."

This small exertion sapped what little energy Zurito had left. Almost immediately he fell back to sleep.

At a point where the river narrowed and began a series of switchbacks, Jake noticed a new phenomenon. Glowing coals along the water's surface, just ahead of the light's sweeping arch.

It took him a moment to realize that they all came in pairs.

Eyes, reflecting the lamp's light. Jake raised its beam.

Caimans. Their long snouts just breaking the surface, they stared, unblinking, back at Jake.

Minutes later, up ahead, something else drew Jake's attention. A log—the length of an 18-wheeler and width of a fifty-five-gallon drum—headed their way.

"On the left," Jake shouted to Brent, training the beam on it.

Brent adeptly maneuvered the boat out of the way.

What if they had hit it?

With a dozen pair of eyes still staring back at him, Jake couldn't fight back a shiver at the thought.

"LOOK," ZURITO SAID, pointing to the sky, which had just begun to lighten with day.

When Jake had to take over the throttle, Brent fell asleep almost as soon as they'd switched places. By that time, Hughes had already been asleep for hours.

Jake didn't hear Zurito's voice over the boat's motor, but he saw his hand and followed it with his eyes.

Smoke. A thin plume, rising above the forest in the distance.

Jake kicked at Hughes, who'd fallen asleep in the fetal position on the middle bench of the skiff.

"Look."

Hughes backhanded his puffy eyes, squinting. Then he bolted upright.

"Brent, wake up."

"What . . . what is it?" Brent muttered.

"Get your map out. See if that could be the Naua."

A consultation over the map resulted in a consensus that they were indeed in the general vicinity of the Naua.

When Zurito spoke again, Jake strained to hear him over the motor.

"We close," he said. "Only day, two days."

"Take her in," Hughes ordered.

They pulled the skiff to shore, then hauled supplies inland two hundred yards and made camp.

For the next two days, Zurito continued to worsen.

"When's he going to be ready to go farther inland?" Hughes asked several times each day.

"The antibiotics haven't touched his fever," Jake answered. "And he's got constant abdominal cramps. He's bordering on severe dehydration."

They were standing by the fire, staring into the lean-to Jake had moved Zurito to during the day.

Hughes didn't respond.

"And that wound is mean-looking. It's festered. The antibiotics aren't even helping that."

"That's because he was poisoned," Hughes finally replied. "Nothing's gonna help him. We're just wasting our fucking time here."

"I can at least keep him cool. And hydrated."

Hughes shot him a look of contempt.

"What, so it takes longer for him to die?"

HUGHES AND BRENT SPENT their time venturing into the forest, in the direction of the plume they'd seen, and fishing. They had returned with several fish that no one recognized, except Zurito, who, in a feverish state, simply shook his head yes when asked if they were edible.

He did little but sleep now, sweating profusely and moaning frequently. Often from a dead sleep he would bolt into a sitting position, roll on to his knees and vomit violently. The diarrhea of the first day on land had lessened. Zurito took in no food, only water, which Jake had to force him to drink.

Hughes and Brent were in foul moods, arguing over every decision and the simplest chores. They managed to keep a fire going, over which they cooked the fish. In light of the pathetic lean-tos and two snakes and a scorpion that Brent had spotted, Brent and Hughes had chosen to sleep under their mosquito nets in the skiff, while Jake slept—or tried to—sitting up, under the lean-to with Zurito.

On the morning of the third day, an iron grip on his shoulder awakened Jake.

"We're leaving."

Jake held his hand up to shield his eyes. Hughes and Brent stood over him. Both men wore backpacks.

Jake jerked his head round to look at Zurito. He appeared as he had for days now, sound asleep, gaunt. But his chest rose and fell. Still breathing.

"He can't go anywhere," Jake said, nodding at the form lying next to him.

"We're going without him."

"Are you crazy?" Jake asked. "He'll die if we leave him."

Hughes snorted a half laugh of disgust.

"He's going to die anyway," he said. "You heard what he said. We're only a day away now. Maybe two. There's no point in waiting for him to get better. We're going to find the Naua."

Wide awake now, Jake felt Zurito stir next to him.

Rising, he motioned for all of them to move away, out of the sick man's earshot.

"You can't do this," he said when he and Hughes turned to face each other.

"We're going," Hughes replied. "Now pack your things."

"No."

"What do you mean," Hughes said, *"no?"*

"I'm not leaving him here to die alone."

Hughes's eyes shifted to Brent.

"Looks like it's just the two of us," he said.

"Fine with me," Brent responded.

Jake watched as the men gathered up everything they could carry, leaving Jake and Zurito only two gallons of drinkable water. Before the two men strode out of the camp, Hughes turned to Jake.

"You're not only risking your life, you know," he said. "What about your son?"

Jake had gone over and over his options for two days now. He might be able to hijack the skiff and head back to Pauhiny. But that plan had several problems with it. To start with, he had no idea how to find Pauhiny.

Second, to do so would strand the other three men and surely doom them to die. Zurito appeared close to death already. And as much as he loathed Hughes and Brent, was he capable of killing them?

Finally, even if he was able to escape and find du Pont, Hughes and Brent would surely beat them to the Naua village. If they managed to be rescued, they could end up patenting G32 first.

All things considered, at this point Jake's best shot of helping Michael was to continue as part of Hughes's team.

Still, he could not abandon Zurito to die.

"I'll catch up with you."

Hughes appeared on the brink of smiling. He looked over at Zurito, long and hard.

"He'll be dead within twenty-four hours," he said matter-of-factly. "When we get to the Naua, we'll build a fire. It will help you find us."

Jake watched them disappear into the green curtain.

"If you get to them," he muttered to himself.

CHAPTER THIRTY

WE CAN'T TURN around now," Asahel cried, tightening her grip on the plane's steering wheel. "I won't let you."

Cavallero grabbed her by the wrist.

"Calm down, girl," he said. "We're just going back down the river a little ways. To have a chat with someone who might know where these scientists of yours are heading."

"Who?"

"Remember that kayaker we flew over a while ago?"

"Yes."

"Well, according to the Apurina I just talked to, he spent time on board the *Tapuya*. Maybe they told him where they're going. He might be able to help us find them."

Asahel let out a shout of excitement.

"What are we waiting for?" she yelled over the sound of the plane's propellers. "Let's find him."

"THE TAMARACA?" Cavallero scratched his head, confused.

"What's down there?"

"I ran into some real savages down that way," Michael Faulk replied.

It had only taken a few hours to locate the kayak again, and its occupant, a handsome beach boy type, had been all too happy to tie up with the seaplane and swap stories.

"War paint, bows and arrows, the whole nine yards," Faulk said excitedly as he reached for another can of the cola Asahel had offered him.

"Sounds like Papavo to me," Cavallero said.

"Yeah, Papavo," Faulk said. "That's what their guide thought they were. I warned those guys on the *Tapuya* that they were pretty scary dudes, but the head guy, he really got all fired up about the Papavo. Wanted to go find them."

"Why?" Asahel asked.

"I dunno. They were on some kind of a medical mission. I guess he wanted to help them out."

Asahel held back the cynical reply that first came to mind. Medical mission.

"How many men were on board the *Tapuya*?" she asked instead. Adrenaline coursed through her veins at the realization that Michael Faulk had actually spent time with the GenChrom team. She and Cavallero were on the right trail.

"Besides the natives?" Faulk asked. "Three. Two scientists and a guide."

Cavallero broke in.

"What can you tell us about them?"

Faulk reached for a handful of trail mix.

"They were pretty serious dudes," he said, throwing some into his mouth. "At first I thought one thing was kind of weird."

"What?" Asahel asked.

"That they brought an American guide with them. But turns out the guy knew a helluva lot about the tribes down here."

Cavallero's face contracted into a scowl of puzzlement.

"If this guy's been down here awhile, I'd know him. What's he look like?"

"Sandy hair. Fit. Maybe thirty," Faulk replied. "Cocky son of a bitch."

"What'd you say?"

Cavallero's eyes had narrowed to angry slits.

"Just that he's cocky," Faulk answered, "the guide."

Asahel had been staring at Cavallero. His entire demeanor grew suddenly more agitated.

"Are you okay?"

All that Asahel recognized from his response—which was delivered in a torrent of wild gestures and inflamed Portuguese—were the words *"fucking American."*

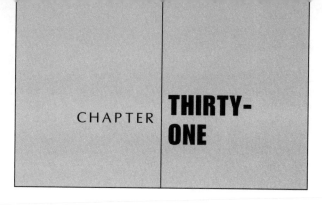

CHAPTER **THIRTY-ONE**

HERE," JAKE SAID. "Drink this."

Jake lifted Zurito's head to help him sip from the water he'd poured from their last jug of water.

Zurito did not respond.

"You have to drink," Jake said, his voice sharp.

Hughes was right. Zurito would die today.

The snake antivenom might have saved Zurito's life, but instead it now lay at the bottom of a river.

Jake had also practically exhausted his supply of antibiotics, to no avail. Zurito's fever had never abated. Without an IV setup, keeping him hydrated in one hundred degree–plus temperatures had been a daunting job.

At least, until now, Zurito had cooperated by drinking regularly, but now it was clear. Zurito, too, knew that death was imminent.

And he'd apparently decided there was no reason to delay it any longer.

"Zurito," Jake shouted. "Drink. You'll die if you don't."

He knew Zurito heard him, but he lay still.

Jake had come to love and hate the rain forest at the same time. All around them, life vibrated so raucously, and with such force, while Zurito lay dying. It was a violent place, a place so rich with life, yet so eager to take it.

Perhaps, left alone, Jake would be next.

Who would take care of his boys?

Or would it only be Antony left behind?

Drink, dammit.

Jake took the native by the shoulders and shook him until Zurito's eyes opened. They were angry, resentful. But his voice came out a whisper.

"Let . . . Zurito . . . die."

Jake loosened his grip, but he did not let go. He held on, forcing Zurito to face him.

"You must fight," he said. "I will not *allow* you to die. Do you hear?"

The faintest of smiles drifted across Zurito's eyes.

"You . . . no . . . have . . . choice."

Zurito was right. *Jake had no choice in the matter, did he?*

Jake held on, staring into those dull eyes, as if by holding Zurito's gaze he could stop his life from ebbing away.

And at that moment it came to him.

Zurito's lids had dropped, but Jake squeezed his shoulders, shook him again. The eyes opened wearily.

"I *do* have a choice," Jake said. "So do you. *Look.*"

Lowering Zurito against a tree trunk, Jake lifted his shirt. Despite everything, a glint of curiosity ignited Zurito's eyes.

Underneath the shirt, still secured to the belt around Jake's waist, hung the snakeskin pouch given him by the old lady at the market.

Jake slid it off his belt and withdrew a small clay pot from it.

Holding it up, he met Zurito's gaze.

And then he uncorked it.

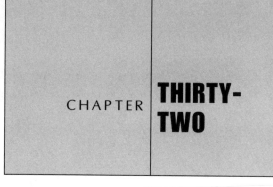

CHAPTER **THIRTY-TWO**

CAVALLERO HAD NEVER explained his outburst over hearing Michael Faulk's description of the American guide accompanying the GenChrom team, but Asahel sensed it had a lot to do with the mean mood he'd fallen into.

They'd slept on board the seaplane the first two nights. Asahel was thrilled when Cavallero announced they'd be spending tonight in a hotel.

Her expectations took a nosedive, however, when the plane taxied up to an old half-submerged wooden dock. A single-story dilapidated building with a sign announcing *Pension Purus* sat just off the riverbank.

They'd rented both rooms—the pension housed only two—from a grizzled, toothless white man with whom Cavallero clearly shared a history. The two sat in the hotel's "lobby" drinking *cachaza*—native spirits made from cane sugar—while Asahel strung the hammock given her by the owner up on two hooks in a room devoid of furniture, save for a single chair.

Cavallero explained to her that beds were never used in the Amazon.

"The mattresses become infested with bugs and lice," he'd said. "By morning they'd have set up house in that red hair of yours."

With that thought in mind, Asahel had tightly braided her hair before climbing into the hammock, then pinned each braid to her head in a coil. The mosquito net they'd used on board the plane offered some protection from the gigantic moths and flying cockroaches. Asahel found herself wishing that Cavallero had strung his own hammock in her room.

She slept fitfully, waking when she heard Cavallero stumble into his room next door sometime during the night.

In the morning, she awoke to the sound of the plane's propellers kicking into gear.

Jumping out of the hammock, she grabbed the bag she'd left on the chair and wandered sleepy-eyed out into the bright morning sun.

Cavallero greeted her with his first smile in a long while.

"This is the day," he said. "They came by here three days ago. This is the day we finally catch up with the fuckers."

ASAHEL SAW IT FIRST.

"There," she cried, pointing east, a short distance up one of dozens of small *igarapes* they'd already passed since veering off the Purus, along the River Acre, ten miles earlier.

Cavallero was flying higher than usual, to give them as expansive a view of the *igarapes* as possible. Now he banked the plane and took it low, leaving Asahel's stomach in her throat.

A motor yacht, anchored in a spot where the stream widened enough that the water grew still, so still that the plane's reflection in the water was nearly perfect. A lone figure slept on the top deck. When Cavallero buzzed the boat, he jumped to his feet, clearly startled.

Two words, painted in bold script on the boat's side, came into view.

"It's her," Asahel cried.

The *Tapuya*.

CHAPTER THIRTY-THREE

THE SINGLE CREWMAN on board the *Tapuya*, who introduced himself as Pedro, had visibly struggled with whether or not to give Cavallero and Asahel the information they wanted. But, in the end, Cavallero had convinced Pedro that Asahel was part of Torrell Hughes's team, that Hughes would, in fact, be delighted to learn she'd followed him to Brazil.

Pedro had informed them that Hughes, another scientist by the name of Jake Skully, a man who fit a description Cavallero supplied of the American guide—a description, Asahel could not help but note, far more detailed than that supplied by Michael Faulk—and someone named Zurito had left the *Tapuya* and boarded a motorized skiff three days earlier. Their destination: terra firma in Acre, but first, as Faulk had already revealed, they planned to try to find the Papavo. Pedro explained that he had never been involved in the meetings of the others, but when he looked at the map produced by Cavallero he traced a course along the network of rivers and *igarapes* that he believed he'd seen the American kayaker trace earlier, on board the *Tapuya*.

"Terra firma, in Acre," Cavallero repeated. "That would be Naua territory."

Asahel suddenly realized that she might just accomplish two of her missions—investigating what GenChrom was up to and visiting the site of the massacre witnessed by Caina—at once. Still, nothing fit.

"Why would they return there?" she asked, thinking aloud. She paused. "Maybe they found something. Something so valuable they're returning to the area to look for more."

Cavallero only shook his head. Whether it was in acknowledgment or an expression of confusion Asahel could not tell.

Their nearness to the GenChrom team had ignited a smoldering fire within Cavallero. As they refueled the plane from the huge canister Cavallero loaded on board in Manaus, Asahel heard him mutter, "I'm gonna nail the son of a bitch."

"Who?" Asahel asked. There was something personal, very personal, in Cavallero's determination. "Do you mean the American guide? Do you know him?"

He'd refused to discuss this matter with Asahel when she'd brought it up earlier, right after their meeting with Michael Faulk.

But now Cavallero answered, simply, *"Quizás."* Perhaps.

"Who is it?"

Cavallero did not look at her.

"We have to hurry," he said.

They flew low, along the course set out for them by Pedro. Their target was now a fraction the size of what they'd been looking for before. A small motorized boat. Cavallero produced a pair of binoculars for Asahel.

"If they're still on the water, we'll see them," he'd yelled over the plane's engine. "But if they've gone inland already, then we're looking for a boat pulled up onshore. That's not gonna be as easy to spot."

Against Cavallero's wishes, Asahel unbuckled her seat belt, in order to have complete freedom to move around and scan first one shore, then the other.

Nothing. Mile after mile, hour after hour, without any sign of them.

Early on, they flew through a small storm, during which she'd had to rebuckle her seat belt, but within minutes they exited the squall's other side and Asahel immediately unfastened again and went back to hanging out the window, scrutinizing the shorelines below.

After several hours, her eyes ached with the strain, but she could not afford to miss anything. Not a single thing . . .

"There," she shouted. "There, along the shore."

She'd jumped up in such a state of excitement that she knocked her forehead into the plane's ceiling.

"See it?" she cried. *"Do you see it?"*

Cavallero had indeed seen it. The back end of an aluminum boat that had been pulled up out of the river and onto the shore. He'd already begun banking the plane, the look of a demon in his already wild eyes.

"Fasten your seat belt," he yelled.

He was taking it in at a steep angle. Asahel looked ahead and saw why. Branches from a gigantic tree spread across the water and protruded a dozen feet into the air about fifty yards upriver. Asahel had already logged enough experience to know the landing would be rough, but she also knew that Cavallero could handle it.

She grabbed hold of a bar on the door on her right, and the edge of her seat on the left.

They were both so focused on the debris ahead that they did not see it—a loose log, floating mostly submerged, its surface covered with a thick green moss that made it blend in with the muddy water—until too late. They'd already touched down and were racing toward it at top speed.

"Look, ahead," Asahel screamed.

"Cover your face," Cavallero yelled back.

In the next instant, the plane's left pontoon skimmed over the log.

The plane lifted on its left side and, for what seemed an eternity, teetered in midair. Asahel had a fleeting belief that it would plunk back down in the water again, but instead, a second later, all hell broke lose.

The world began spinning wildly, bags and supplies flying through the air in the cabin as the plane cartwheeled crazily up the river. Completely disoriented, Asahel held one hand over her face; the other gripped her seat's edge. She could hear Cavallero swearing up a storm beside her and took comfort, at least, in knowing he was conscious.

The plane flipped over, on its roof.

When it finally came to rest, Asahel and Cavallero hung from the ceiling, restrained only by their seat belts. Water had already begun seeping through the windows and the cracks along the door openings.

Cavallero released his seat belt and dropped to the plane's ceiling, then, with lightning quick reflexes, reached up and released Asahel's. He caught her as she dropped beside him into the pooling water.

"Stay calm," he told her. "Do you remember what I told you before?"

Asahel could not find her voice. She shook her head. *Yes.*

"You must swim to the shore quickly. Do not wait for me. Do you hear? Do not hesitate even a moment. Just swim, like your life depended on it."

Because it does.

Asahel knew that, knew what was on Cavallero's mind. She was grateful that he did not come out and say it.

Cavallero reached up and unzipped a pouch attached to the door on his side. An object dropped into the water with a splash. He reached into the water and grabbed for it.

A knife. He slid the sheathed blade into the waist of his pants.

The water had already risen to their chests.

"I'm gonna kick the window out now," Cavallero yelled. "The water will rush in, but I'll be behind you, pushing you through. Try not to get cut, do you hear? The edges of the window will be jagged."

He doesn't want me bleeding in the water.

Asahel nodded again.

"When I say *now*," Cavallero continued, "take a deep breath; fill your lungs. Don't worry; you'll rise to the surface. Just get to shore."

His eyes had been scanning the windows, searching the waters outside the plane, as he spoke. But now they came to rest on Asahel.

"Once you get on land, hike due west. Do you hear? That's the direction they're headed."

"Why are you telling me that?"

"Because," he answered. "Just in case. And one more thing. Let's promise each other something."

"Yes," Asahel said, "anything."

The expression on Caballero's face frightened Asahel.

"That if one of us doesn't make it, the other will get the sons of bitches."

Asahel wanted to argue with him, to tell him that he shouldn't be thinking that way. They would both make it.

But there was no time.

"I promise," she said.

"NOW."

Her head held high, in the few inches of space remaining between the rising water and the floor of the plane, Asahel sucked air into her lungs, then dropped into the water alongside Cavallero. With him at her back, pushing her against the enormous force of the water rushing into the plane, she maneuvered her way, mostly blind, through the window's opening.

Don't cut yourself; don't cut yourself.

The murkiness of the water made it impossible to see more than four or five inches ahead, but as Cavallero had assured her, her full lungs brought her to the surface quickly. She found herself about fifteen yards from the shore. Ignoring Cavallero's orders, she turned to look for him.

His head popped up almost immediately, just feet away.

"Swim," he yelled.

Asahel put her head down and swam with all her strength, the smooth crawl that had won her blue ribbons as a child, each stroke bringing her that much closer to shore. Out of the corner of her eye, she saw the splashes made by Cavallero's choppy stroke, and took great comfort.

They would make it. Just a few more yards now. They were almost there.

Suddenly a wild, horrific shriek filled the air.

Asahel stopped, treading water and turned.

Where was Cavallero?

The water churned several yards behind her. Seconds later, a prehistoric-looking scaled tail rose from a set of ever-widening concentric waves, slapping the water powerfully. Immediately after, two hideous snouts broke the surface.

Not one caiman, but two, their loathsome bodies squirming in a joyous frenzy.

"Diego," Asahel screamed.

Cavallero's head popped up suddenly, in the midst of all the bubbles and splashing.

Asahel saw him gasp for air. Saw the absolute terror in his eyes.

And then he was gone.

CHAPTER **THIRTY-FOUR**

JAKE HAD CHECKED Zurito frequently throughout the day. Still warm to the touch, Zurito slept the sleep of the drugged. Or dying.

The magic potion had turned out to be a cruel joke—a brief glimmer of false hope. How foolish could he be, to think that a foul-smelling milky liquid sold him by an old woman in a market could save a man's life when the most advanced of antibiotics could not?

Jake had gone without sleep for two nights now. That, combined with the growing recognition of the hopelessness of his mission to reunite with Doc du Pont, had him bordering on despair. He'd finally closed his eyes, hoping for at least a brief reprieve.

Perhaps, like Zurito, it would be better to simply not open them again. . . .

At first he was certain he was dreaming. He'd dozed off and slept for hours now, throughout the night. A new day had broken.

The voice that awakened him was clear, and strong.

And it belonged to Zurito.

"Time to go."

Jake's eyes popped open.

Holding a hand up as a shield against the morning light, Jake squinted and blinked—once, twice, three times. He had to be dreaming.

Zurito sat on his haunches, his face just inches away. He shook Jake's shoulder.

"Time to go," Zurito repeated, and for the first time since Jake had met him, he saw a smile spread slowly across those dark features.

"This can't be. You were poisoned."

"Sí," Zurito replied. "Poison."

"Then how . . . ?"

Zurito pointed at the small clay pot, lying on its side on a log next to the fire pit.

Jake shook his head, still trying to clear it. Could the bottle given him by the old woman actually have worked such a miracle?

"How can that be?" Jake asked. "What was in it?"

Zurito's expression told Jake he thought the question foolish, but he answered nonetheless.

"Magic," he said, quietly. "The magic of my forest."

JAKE INSISTED THAT THEY stay put one more day.

Zurito's recovery astounded him. It defied every medical truth Jake had ever known. Zurito's color, his balance, even his strength seemed to have returned.

Zurito urged Jake to break camp immediately and head toward the Naua village.

But Jake refused.

The man had gone without food and hovered near death for days. As eager as Jake was to follow Hughes, his professional judgment warned him it would be foolhardy to do so yet. Instead, with Zurito's instructions, Jake spent the day gathering a food supply. Mostly grubs—which Zurito ate raw, while Jake grilled them over the fire— and nuts and grains. Jake also replenished the half-empty jug of water with liquid from coconut-sized *chambira* nuts and a thick, woody vine that Zurito taught him to identify.

It was late in the afternoon when they first heard it. The distant drone of an airplane.

Jake's heart began to race. Could it be du Pont? Had he discovered somehow the detour they'd taken and realized that the original plan to meet in Pauhiny would no longer work?

The sound grew as the plane continued flying in their direction.

As Jake rushed toward the river, with Zurito close behind, he heard the hum of the plane's engine drop in pitch. The plane was losing altitude, preparing to land.

Doc du Pont.

And then came an unmistakable, sickeningly wrenching sound. An incredible *thwooooosh* that seemed to go on forever, as if the river had slowly opened up and swallowed something large, and alive. It was followed by the sound of metal crumbling—like some giant fist closing around a thousand beer cans at once.

"*It crashed,*" Jake cried, branches whipping his face as he ran through the dense growth. They still had at least an eighth of a mile to go before reaching water.

The moment they broke through the foliage, they spotted the plane. Upside down, one pontoon bobbing in the air, the other merely a fragment. Branches overhanging the shoreline had entangled it, but the hold was precarious and the plane appeared ready to break loose at any moment.

Rushing toward it, dodging and leaping over vegetation along the river's shoreline like a running back over downed linemen, Jake saw immediately that the front window of the cockpit had shattered. The cockpit itself looked fully submerged. But maybe there was a chance, just the slightest chance, that a pocket of air existed inside. Perhaps he could still save du Pont.

Suddenly blocked by denser growth, Zurito handed Jake the machete he always carried and Jake began swiping a path ahead of them.

But then Jake felt a tug at the back of his shirt.

"There."

Jake turned to look in the direction Zurito's long finger pointed, down the shoreline some twenty yards.

Across the river, draped over a log. A body.

That of a woman, her hair, long and red, trailing down the back of her white shirt, her blue jeans torn the length of one leg.

She did not move.

"Hello," Jake called.

And then Jake became aware of another presence. In the water. Caimans. Several of them.

It took a few seconds to realize that what at first appeared to be a branch clutched in the jaws of one was really a human limb. Three or four monstrous snouts snarled and snapped at one another, making eerie high-pitched sounds, as they tore at the shreds of flesh still hanging from it.

"The boat," Jake yelled. "Take the boat."

Zurito had already begun running downriver toward it.

By now, one of the beady-eyed creatures had spotted the woman on the log.

Almost simultaneously, she lifted her head.

"Caiman," Jake shouted. "Get up."

The woman, who was obviously seriously injured from the plane crash, sat up, then pulled herself to her knees. She moved as if she was in a daze. Her motion drew the attention of the other caimans, one of which turned away from the feeding frenzy and began heading instead in her direction.

Zurito had already pulled the boat free of the shore. He jumped in and, without waiting for Jake, started the motor.

"Go," Jake yelled to him. *"Go."*

Trying to divert the hideous beast's attention, Jake waded into the water and began splashing. But it had fixated now on this other prey, across the river.

"Hurry," Jake shouted to both the woman and Zurito. "Hurry."

The woman had finally risen to her feet. She stood staring blankly toward Jake, one arm hanging limply from her side. Jake could see it had been broken, a clean break. He could tell, even from a distance, that she was in shock.

With a shudder, he realized she was incapable of reacting, much less climbing a tree with one good arm.

The caiman streamed across the river toward her.

Jake dived toward deeper water, calling out to get the caiman's attention. He began swimming.

In the skiff, Zurito had now drawn even with the creature. Reaching for a paddle from the boat's floor, he batted its head, screaming wildly.

This worked to distract the beast from the woman. Suddenly the caiman turned, drawn now to Jake's calls and his splashing.

When he saw two nostrils streaming toward him, Jake turned back toward shore.

He'd succeeded in turning the caiman's attention away from the woman.

But now could he outswim it?

CHAPTER THIRTY-FIVE

ZURITO LIFTED THE woman into the boat. One of her arms hung, lifeless, misshapen, over his shoulder as he half dropped her on the boat's floor. There was no time to tend to her now.

She stared blankly and did not speak.

Within thirty seconds, he'd pushed back off, turning the skiff up-river, toward Jake, whom Zurito could see, literally swimming for his life, a caiman closing on in him as he approached the shore. Two others followed, a short distance behind.

Zurito gunned the motor, steering directly toward the bumpy snout in the lead.

Jake was ten feet from shore with the caiman practically in reach of his frantically kicking feet. Sensing victory, the beast lifted its head.

It had just opened its enormously powerful jaws when Zurito plowed into its midsection. The motor sputtered briefly as the boat skimmed over the creature, its propeller slicing through bone and tissue, instantly turning the muddy river a wine red.

Zurito watched Jake reach safety; then he circled the boat back around to join him.

The other caimans immediately abandoned their interest in Jake to ravage the bloodied body that still twitched occasionally with life.

JAKE STOOD ONSHORE, hand outstretched to catch the rope. Once, as he waited for Zurito to throw it, his eyes strayed to the sickening frenzy taking place in the water. They did not linger.

When the rope flew his way, Jake nabbed it, then, leaning against it, began backing up, using all his weight to haul the boat in against the strong current.

As he pulled the skiff closer to shore, Jake could see the woman's features twisted with pain.

Zurito lifted her out of the skiff. Jake had already made his diagnosis, based on the way her arm dangled. A clean break of the humerus.

"Is there anyone else in the plane?" Jake asked as Zurito lowered her to the ground.

Her eyes fluttered open.

"No," she answered. "He's dead. The alligators got him."

The limb he'd seen in the caiman's mouth must have belonged to Doc du Pont.

Jake had to fight back the revulsion, the utter horror, that gripped him at the news that his friend—and greatest hope for helping Michael—had died in such a brutal fashion. He couldn't afford to give in to his feelings now, not when he had a patient to tend to, one in critical need of medical attention. He stripped off his shirt and wrapped the broken arm tightly against her body for the short trek to the camp.

Once there, Zurito again lowered her to a sitting position, with her back against a fallen tree.

Jake gently unwrapped the shirt and straightened the broken arm. She moaned in pain.

Jake ran his hand softly down her arm, stopping to palpate. He felt three distinct pieces in the humerus.

"What's your name?"

"Asahel Sullivan."

"I'm going to give you a shot, Asahel. For pain."

She did not respond, didn't flinch when he gave her the shot.

Within minutes, her face began to relax, and Jake was struck by its beauty. Gently he lifted her arm again to examine it more closely.

The clarity of her voice surprised him.

"Shouldn't you set it?"

Jake looked up, met her gaze.

"I'll do what I can, but I'm afraid setting it won't be enough. It's a clean break. You need surgery. The good news is that it's not an open fracture."

"Oh, that's good news all right," Asahel Sullivan said.

Jake studied her face. She'd squeezed her eyes shut. The pain had to be almost unbearable.

"Are you the pilot?" he asked, eager to learn as much as possible before the morphine fully took effect. Before departing the *Tapuya*, Doc had said he'd charter a plane.

She shook her head.

"No." Her chin quivered. "He's dead. They got him. . . ."

Visions of the snarling caimans fighting over the limb slipped back into Jake's head.

"Doc was flying the plane?" Jake asked.

Her brow creased in confusion.

"Doc?"

"Doc du Pont. Did he hire you to come along?"

"I don't know what you're talking about. I came here with Diego Cavallero. He was the pilot."

"It wasn't Doc in the water? With the caiman...."

"No. I don't know anything about anyone named Doc."

A surge of relief—joy, actually—ripped through Jake. He knew it was wrong. Someone had just died an unimaginably horrible death. A friend of this poor woman. This Asahel Sullivan. But all Jake could feel was relief.

He took the hand of her uninjured arm and held it firmly, until the full force of the morphine finally kicked in.

Just before she slipped into a deep slumber, she muttered, "Thank you. You saved my life."

Not yet, was what came to Jake's mind, but he said, "You're a lucky lady."

Throughout all this, Zurito had hovered nearby, watching nervously.

"What we do with her?" he asked when Asahel Sullivan had drifted off.

Jake, still sitting on his haunches at her side, studied her arm.

"We have to get her out of here. She needs surgery." He raised his eyes to Zurito. "How long would it take? To get her back to the *Tapuya?*"

"Going back, all downstream," Zurito said. "Not long. Day and a half, if we don't stop."

"Are you up to it?"

Zurito nodded.

"No problem," he said. And then, hesitantly, he added, "But what about your son?"

"You know about my son?" Jake asked, startled.

Zurito had always appeared entirely aloof from the conversations that took place among Jake, Hughes and Brent. Jake had assumed that he either did not understand much of what was said or he simply did not care enough to listen. But in the native's expression now, Jake saw deep concern.

"We find blood, make your son see."

Jake swallowed against the lump in his throat and nodded toward Asahel.

"But if she doesn't receive proper treatment, she could lose use of that arm," Jake replied. "Maybe even die."

"*I* take her back to *Tapuya*. You go. You find Naua."

Slack-jawed, Jake stared at Zurito.

"You save my life," Zurito said. "We brothers now. I take care lady. You take care son."

ASAHEL SULLIVAN HAD SLEPT the entire time that Jake and Zurito went over their plans.

Zurito had insisted that he was well enough to ferry Asahel back to the *Tapuya*, where Pedro could radio for a seaplane. He had convinced Jake that Jake wasn't necessary for Asahel Sullivan's well-being, that Zurito could even administer more medication, if needed. If they kept her doped up enough, she would sleep most of the way.

Zurito's bigger concern had been coaching Jake on the dangers of pursuing Hughes without him.

"You listen and nothing bad happen you," he'd told Jake before proceeding with instructions on everything from finding food and water to what plants, animals and tribes to avoid.

Jake did not like parting company with Zurito, but he felt an enormous sense of relief to know he could resume his mission to find G32.

"If we are truly brothers, maybe you'll help me with something very important," he told Zurito. "When you get back to the *Tapuya*, I have a very important favor to ask of you. I want you to contact Doc du Pont."

Jake reached into his pocket and withdrew a folded sheet of paper.

"Here's a number where you can leave him a message. Tell him where we are. Tell him to come quickly. That I've gone into terra firma with Hughes, to find the Naua. Tell him I'll delay them as long as I can, until he can get here."

Zurito's eyes met the urgency in Jake's gaze.

"I leave message, but your friend no get," he said.

"What do you mean?"

"Your friend dead."

Jake grabbed Zurito by the shoulders.

"That can't be. Both Hughes and Brent told me he'd hitched a ride on a raft."

Zurito shook his head.

"No. No raft on river that day. I see your friend in water. He float-ing, on him chest." He pounded his chest to illustrate.

A sick feeling swallowed Jake at that moment. A feeling that all was doomed. That any last remnant of hope had just died.

"His face in water," Zurito continued. "I try get him, but Hughes, he say to leave. I go down below, where Hughes no see. I get hook, pull him to boat. That when I see."

"What?" Jake asked, his grip on Zurito's shoulders tightening. "What did you see?"

Zurito turned around and placed his hands behind his back, crossed at the wrist.

"I see rope tied round Doc du Pont hands," Zurito said. "Like this."

JAKE'S SHOCK AND DESPAIR so numbed him that he didn't notice that Asahel Sullivan had come to.

Her voice startled him.

"You're with Torrell Hughes? You're one of the GenChrom scien-tists?"

He turned toward her.

How would this woman know anything about GenChrom?

"Yes," he answered dully.

Her face drained of color. Jake reached for her wrist to take her pulse.

Asahel pushed his hand away; then she actually slapped at him, missing.

"Who are you?" Jake asked. "What brought you here?"

Asahel began struggling to her feet. When Jake reached out for her arm, she hit him.

"Don't touch me!"

Jake watched her wobble, nearly teeter over, as she finally managed to make it to her feet.

"I'm here to find out what your company is up to," she said, grop-ing with her good hand for one of the lean-to's poles for support.

Jake let her stand there, light-headed, swaying from one side to the other like a drunken boatman. The dizziness, however, didn't reach her eyes. They glared at Jake with a hatred that could not have been more clear.

"Why would what we're doing down here be of interest to you?"

"Because you're all murderers," she answered. "And you know what? I'm not going to let you get away with it. I'm going to expose you."

Jake drew back

"Me? You can't be serious."

Asahel Sullivan looked him square in the eye and announced the mission of her voyage. The reason she'd come to the Amazon.

"Serious?" she said. "How's this for serious?"

Looking at her, her eyes black with anger, her jaw tight and defiant, Jake could only wonder how he'd found her beautiful.

"I came here to destroy you," Asahel Sullivan declared.

ALMOST INSTANTLY THE realization hit Jake, that if Asahel returned to Manaus telling wild stories about GenChrom's activities in the Amazon, authorities there were likely to apprehend them once they returned—and prevent them from taking G32 out of the country.

Jake could not allow that to happen.

"I don't know what you're talking about," he replied fiercely. "You've got your facts backward, lady. GenChrom is a research team, down here to look for drugs that *save* lives, not take them. I suggest you get your information straight before you start throwing around false accusations—especially accusations concerning the people in whose hands you've placed your life."

"Is that a threat?"

Jake did not respond. All of his plans to restore Michael's sight were spinning out of control.

One thing he knew with total certainty. Asahel Sullivan was bad news. The sooner he got her out of the way, the better.

Her last words to him were spoken as the skiff pushed off from shore, as Zurito skillfully avoided debris from the plane that Jake had hoped carried Doc du Pont.

"Don't think your heroics with me change anything," Asahel Sullivan called. "You'll pay for what you've done. I'll make sure of it."

CHAPTER **THIRTY-SIX**

BY THE SECOND day of hiking through the rain forest, Jake felt the thick green canopy that had shut out the sun ever since he parted ways with Zurito and Asahel Sullivan closing in on him. The intense heat, coupled with the smell of rotting leaves and fruit, nauseated him; and the farther inland he trudged, the stronger the odor became.

In the hours before they parted, Zurito had scratched a map for Jake in the rich dirt beside their campfire. So far, it had been accurate right down to the *igarape* that Jake ran into. As Zurito instructed, Jake had followed it for half a day, until he reached a narrowing that allowed him to wade across, in chest-high murky water. Zurito had warned him about the eels. Their sting could paralyze, and they were especially common in still water, like this.

Fortunately, on his crossing, Jake only encountered a mildly curious turtle.

The first day he'd forged slowly but steadily through the *varzea*—that part of the rain forest that flooded during the rainy season. The flooding made the undergrowth less dense and easier to move through. But on the second day, after fording the *igarape*, true to Zurito's prediction, Jake began climbing.

"Terra firma," Zurito had called it. "Higher, above flooding."

As appealing as that at first sounded, Jake soon discovered that terra firma also meant denser growth and even slower progress. He had run out of water and now depended on the thick, woody vine that Zurito taught him to identify. Whenever he saw it, he slashed it down with his machete. He drank the precious liquid that bubbled from its core greedily, each time fearing that he'd never find the vine again.

He made slow but steady progress. When he finally reached a clearing, he would go to its center and rotate full circle, searching the sky in every direction for the signal fire Hughes had promised. But all he saw was interminable blue heavens blanketing a sea of green canopy. The endlessness of it gave him a feeling of hopelessness.

Then, late afternoon of the second day, Jake discovered a narrow trail. It had seen little wear, but his heart quickened when he saw that the foliage had been macheted down quite recently.

The trail had to have been made by Hughes and Brent.

Jake followed the trail, picking up his pace. It led just where he wanted it to—in the direction scratched by Zurito in the dirt.

The Naua village had to be near. G32, the mythical, miraculous gene that would enable his son to see again—it was practically within his reach. Soon he would help Hughes draw the precious blood. Perhaps even that evening.

The fact that he hadn't run into Hughes as he returned to the river meant the other GenChrom scientist had stayed at the village longer than anyone planned. Jake wanted to believe that was a good sign. A sign Hughes had come across a much bigger find than they'd anticipated. Perhaps he was lingering, taking data, absorbing as much information from the Naua—their history, herbs used medicinally—as possible. Propelled forward by such thoughts, the weight that had slowed his legs magically lifted.

Then, just before the sun set, just when he'd gone so far without seeing other hopeful signs that he'd begun to have doubts about the trail, Jake heard voices.

Zurito had told him that the natives would always hear and see him coming but that Jake would never, ever see or hear them unless they wanted him to. Word would travel throughout the forest of his presence, and he would be watched all along his way, by first one tribe and then the next. If Jake minded his own business and the tribes determined he did not present a danger to them, he would probably be allowed passage without any interference.

At several points during the past two days, Jake suspected he was being watched, but just as Zurito predicted, he never saw or heard another soul.

Which meant the voices he heard now had to belong to the Naua or to Hughes and Brent.

Jake began to run. The time had finally come. His plan with Doc du Pont had failed, but he was within reach of G32 now. Hughes didn't matter at that moment. Only Michael.

Panting, sweating in bullets that completely drenched both his shirt and pants, Jake broke into the clearing, then came to a dead stop.

A dozen or so crude huts filled the sun-drenched center. The village was surprisingly quiet. Confused, Jake stood there, his eyes roaming everywhere. And then he heard them again. The voices.

Jake recognized them. Hughes and Brent.

At the same time, another sound also wafted his way. A sound that Jake recognized from the many times he'd heard it as a child, on his grandfather's farm.

Jake hurriedly rounded the nearest hut.

Immediately he saw them. Hughes and Brent.

Their backs were to him. Standing beside a mound of dirt and rocks, Brent held a makeshift shovel. The pile was long and wide, at its peak, almost two feet tall. Brent bent and rhythmically plunged the tool into the mound, removing a shovelful of dirt and tossing it to the side.

Jake's eyes widened when he saw that both men wore masks.

They grew even wider as he stared at Hughes. The GenChrom CEO knelt on all fours, sifting through the loose dirt at the mound's edge, with gloved hands. Behind him, partly obscured by Hughes's body, lay a stack of kindling.

What the hell were they up to?

And then suddenly something struck Jake.

The village. Half a dozen huts and everywhere Jake looked—from the fire pit at the center of the clearing, to handmade tools lying on the ground and against the back of huts, to the wooden grates used for drying fish—plenty of signs of its inhabitants.

Yet when Jake's eyes swept the clearing, he saw just two figures moving about.

Hughes and Brent.

There was not a single sign of another human being's presence.

No movement, no sound. Nothing.

Where were the Naua?

BRENT TURNED, FREEZING midswing of the shovel when he saw Jake.

Hughes looked up, first at Brent, then in Jake's direction.

Neither man said a thing.

"What's going on?" Jake called, walking quickly toward them. "Where is everybody?"

Sweat dripped from Hughes's brow. He reached up and, with the back of a dirt-coated hand, wiped it away, leaving dark streaks.

Suddenly Jake saw that he'd been wrong about the kindling.

The pile behind Hughes, the one he'd been stacking, did not consist of sticks of woods. They were bones.

His pulse throbbing in his temples, Jake walked to the pile and picked one up.

A femur. A *human* femur.

Stunned, his eyes swept the ground. The dirt surrounding Hughes contained dozens, no more, perhaps hundreds, of smaller pieces. Fingers, toes, a small jaw.

The truth hit him in thunderous waves.

"Tell me these aren't the Naua," Jake said, dropping to his knees, staring in horror at the pile.

Hughes's blank expression finally cracked. His chin appeared to quiver.

"It's them all right," he answered. "They're dead. All of them. Fucking dead. This is what we found."

Jake stared at the mound. Thick green vines had begun snaking their way up and over it, through its surface.

"This doesn't make sense. This grave was dug just recently." He picked up a bone. "Yet there's nothing on these."

He would have expected decaying flesh. The smell alone should have overpowered them.

"Follow me," Hughes said, his voice again flat, his face once again void of all emotion.

He rose, one hand holding his back as he straightened slowly. He'd aged a decade in the two days since Jake last saw him.

Jake followed, numb, not able to think—not wanting to—as Hughes strode to the far edge of the clearing. He stopped at the edge of a large irregular ring made of rocks. There were numerous markings on the ground and on the rocks.

At closer look, Jake realized they were drawings. Spiritual drawings, depicting death and the afterlife—in the form of winged stick figures rising from a pile of burning bodies.

The ground within the circle was charred black and void of growth—too hostile even for the hardy plants of the rain forest.

"They burned the bodies here," Hughes said. "Then buried the bones."

Jake stood staring at the drawings.

"An epidemic?"

But he knew, even before Hughes responded, that no disease had caused this tragedy.

"They all died together."

"Who would do such a thing?" Jake asked. "Who would slaughter so many people? A whole tribe? *Why?*"

Hughes's face sparked back to life.

"Who? Why?" he parroted, his voice rising. "I'll tell you who. Someone who knew the value of the Naua blood. Someone who wanted to make sure nobody else got their hands on it."

"The Naua were killed for blood?" Jake asked, incredulous. "That's ridiculous. There must have been a war, some kind of tribal war. No one would kill an entire tribe for its blood."

"Are you really that naive?" Hughes asked. "Then how do you explain *that?*"

Jake's eyes followed the direction in which he pointed.

The day's last light reflected off an object on the ground. Jake walked to it, bent and picked it up.

A glass vial. The same kind Jake and Hughes had used to collect blood from the Apurina and Ucalayi.

Stunned, holding it in front of him like an altar boy with a chalice, he walked back to Hughes.

"Why?" he murmured. "Why?"

"Don't you see?" Hughes practically shouted. "If the Naua blood contains G32, the patent on it is worth a fortune."

"That's insane," Jake said. "You're saying someone killed these people in order to patent their blood."

"No shit, Sherlock," Brent replied.

Hughes simply stared back at Jake.

"And you're exhuming the bodies now hoping to be able to mine G32 from the bones, their marrow."

"You're goddam right I am. We'll at least be able to confirm whether G32's part of the Naua's genetic makeup. Of course, these will be worthless in terms of getting our hands on viable G32, but we'll know, once and for all, if it even exists."

As the realization that his mission to find G32 had failed, Jake dropped down to one of the stones circling the Naua cremation pit.

"It's so sick, so senseless," he muttered. "All of them, dead. And Michael's chance to see again . . . gone."

A rustling sound drew Jake's attention.

"Maybe not," Hughes said. He unfolded a sheet of paper and pushed it under Jake's nose.

An article. From some kind of newsletter.

As Jake read it, he realized why Hughes had stuck it in his back pocket and kept it there throughout their trip. What, indeed, had driven Hughes to come to Acre in the first place.

"Look at the date," Hughes said. "Only five weeks ago. That grave is fairly new all right, but I'd bet anything it's more than five weeks old. What if that blue-eyed native was seen *after* that grave was dug? That kayaker said a settler had seen her—recently."

Jake looked up at Hughes. For the first time in a very long time, his eyes held something akin to admiration.

"That would mean a Naua survived the massacre."

"Exactly."

"And just think about it," Jake added. "If the Naua were *all* murdered, who buried them? Who went to the trouble of burning their bodies, then burying them? Of honoring them with those drawings?"

Only Brent seemed less than thrilled by this line of thinking.

"Another tribe probably buried them," he said. "They're all so fucking superstitious about death."

Hughes turned on him.

"What makes you so sure the Naua are all dead?"

Brent shrugged and turned away.

Jake, however, stood and faced Hughes.

"For once, Torrell," he said, "I'm with you. It all adds up to one thing. A Naua has to be out there."

Hughes nodded.

"Now, all we have to do is find her."

WITH NIGHT FAST approaching, they'd decided to get some sleep. They would leave for Manaus at dawn.

Jake could not bring himself to bed down on the same crude wood floor where Naua women and children had recently lain, no doubt secure in the knowledge they were safe. Instead, he unrolled his sleeping pad beside the fire they'd built (more to ward off the eerie chill of recent death than for its warmth, which the ninety-degree night made entirely unnecessary). But neither Hughes nor Brent suffered from the same reservations. They bedded down in the largest hut.

Their silence indicated they'd had no trouble falling asleep; but Jake had lain, staring into the embers of the fire. Finally, hours after Hughes and Brent disappeared into the hut, he drifted off.

When he awoke some time later, only a few embers glowed from the pit.

The jungle's night sounds never ceased. Still, Jake had learned their pattern. They rose in crescendo, then fell, coming at him in waves. During one of the troughs, he heard the murmur of voices.

Rising slowly, Jake crept toward the back of the hut where the other men slept.

Jake had watched Zurito steal like a cat through the forest, and now, without any conscious effort, his own moves mimicked Zurito's.

The voices were so soft that Jake could not make out their words until he cupped his hand around his ear and pressed it to the hut's back wall.

He recognized Brent's voice first. It lacked the sleepy quality Jake would have expected had the guide just awakened. Could the two men had been awake all this time, just waiting for Jake to doze off?

"I tell you," Jake heard Brent say, "this is crazy. There are no Naua left."

"And I've told you, this blue-eyed woman means a Naua survived."

For several minutes, the voices fell silent. But then Brent spoke again.

"Okay, I can understand your wanting to check out the rumors. But there's no reason for you to stay here. No one's in a better position to find her than me."

"I can't leave," Hughes said. "Every day we waste is a day they could file on G32 before we do."

"Wait a minute," Brent said. "Think about it. If they think they've killed all the Naua, what would be their hurry to file for patent protection?"

"You're right," Hughes replied. "If they realized someone survived, they'd still be out here looking for her."

"Exactly. Since they think they've eliminated any chance of someone else trying to patent the Naua blood, they'll feel safe doing preliminary research, before they file. The way I see it, the smart thing for you to do would be to go home and make sure you get GenChrom's application ready to go while I track down this woman."

"You might be right," Hughes said. "Gina still hasn't filed on all the blood I brought back last time. That's what I should do. Go back to Seattle, get the patent claim in order and leave finding her to you."

"That makes the most sense. But just do me one favor."

"What's that?"

"Get rid of that fucking Skully."

"My guess is he won't agree to go back to Seattle with me. Not without G32."

"That's not what I mean. Listen, if we'd found the Naua alive, we were gonna get rid of the son of a bitch. We both knew he would never stand by while we wiped them out. He's already signed over TS 47 to you. Why take a chance that he could fuck things up for us?"

Hughes paused, thinking.

"You might be right. Even after he signed TS 47 over, I kept him around 'cause I figured he could be useful to us once we got here. But what good is he to us now?"

"There you go," Brent answered.

BY DAYBREAK, JAKE had covered as much ground as possible.

Hughes and Brent had taken the team's only lantern into the hut with them. With no light to guide him, Jake had to pick his way carefully, for the trail forged by Hughes and Brent, and then again yesterday by Jake, already had new growth over it.

Zurito had promised to get Asahel Sullivan back to the *Tapuya*, then double back up the river system to pick up Jake, Hughes and Brent.

Had Hughes and Brent discovered his absence yet? Were they closing the distance between them right now, with the use of the lantern?

All Jake had to do was beat them back to the river. He'd make his way downriver. As long as he stayed ahead of the others, he'd run into Zurito first. They'd turn right around, head for Manaus. They'd leave Hughes and Brent behind.

Would that amount to murder? Without a boat, without any form of communication, the odds of their surviving, of their making it back, were slim.

So be it.

Nothing shocked Jake anymore. Not the news about du Pont, not the deaths of the Naua, not his own actions. He could no longer afford to be shocked.

Instead, he must remain focused on his mission.

G32 was still out there. He just had to find Zurito before Hughes and Brent did.

As he trotted down the trail, tripping frequently over roots and branches, even now that the sun had come up, Jake thought about the little Blue Heeler his grandfather used to own when Jake was a kid. According to his grandpa, that Heeler was "the best goddam cattle dog this side of the Rockies." Jake had never forgotten that little dog. He'd watched him run himself into the ground herding Jake's grandfather's cattle, day after day, always trained on one thing and one thing alone.

Well, right about now, Jake felt just like that little Heeler.

He had never felt such single-mindedness. He would find G32.

And as he'd forged his way, half-blind, through the forest, heading for the river where, God willing, he'd run into Zurito, Jake had realized who could help him do just that.

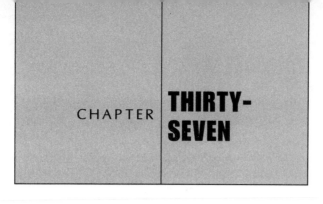
WHAT'S IT FOR ?"

Asahel had to raise her voice to be heard over the rhythmical *clank-clank-clank* of the worn-out ceiling fan rotating above her hospital bed.

In addition to offering respite from the suffocating heat, the fan provided another form of welcome relief. It drowned out the cries and groans of the ward's other occupants.

Pretending not to understand, the nurse obstinately pushed her hand forward again, under Asahel's nose. It held a small paper cup, which, in turn, held two capsules.

"Para que es?" Asahel repeated more loudly, this time in Spanish.

"Dolor," the nurse answered. Pain.

"No," Asahel said, pushing the cup away. "No quiero."

Suddenly a voice sounded from over Asahel's shoulder.

"It might be a good idea to take at least one of them."

So welcome was the crisp English that Asahel barely noticed the bolt of pain that seared through her arm as she turned, eager to see its source—eager, that is, until she saw Jake Skully standing at the head of her bed.

"What are you doing here?"

"Checking on you," he answered.

Skully held the chart that had been hanging from her bed.

"I saw your X rays," he said. "You're lucky. You had a good surgeon. The repair turned out to be more complicated than I'd hoped, but your arm should heal nicely."

"Who gave you the right to snoop into my medical records?" Asahel asked. "Put that down."

Skully's eyes fell to the clipboard in his hand.

"You must have a high tolerance for pain," he said. "Only one day on Percocet, then down to acetaminophen with codeine."

"Give me that," Asahel hissed, reaching for the chart.

This time the pain caused her to cry out and grab her injured arm with her good hand.

"Nurse," Skully called to the dark-haired beauty who had moved on to the other side of the ward.

The same nurse who'd never so much as cracked a smile at Asahel now turned and grinned coyly at Jake. Carrying a tray filled with paper cups, like the one she'd offered Asahel, she approached, her hips swaying rhythmically.

"Da me," Jake said, nodding toward the tray. "La medicina para la señorita."

Sweetly she handed the cup to Jake, but not before she gave Asahel the evil eye.

"Gracias," Skully said.

"De nada," she replied, lifting her chest for effect.

Skully seemed not to notice. He turned to Asahel with the cup.

"Here. Take both of these. This place is bad enough without your lying there in pain. If it's addiction you're worried about, don't. You haven't taken nearly enough. And I can already tell, you don't have the personality of an addict."

"You don't know a damn thing about me," Asahel said, but when Skully followed the pills up with a glass of water, she quickly swallowed them. Anything to dull the pulsating pain.

Skully had moved to the foot of the bed.

Asahel glared at him.

"What do you want? Why are you here?"

"I'm here because I think you can help me."

Asahel let out a caustic laugh.

"Help you? Didn't you hear me back there, on the river? I'm going to destroy you. You *and* GenChrom."

Skully's intense gaze unsettled her.

"What are you?" he asked. "A reporter?"

"That's a scary proposition, isn't it? A reporter following you to the Amazon. Reporting what you do?"

Skully's jaw tightened.

"If it makes any difference to you," he said after several seconds' silence, "I'm not proud of what we've done. But back there, on the river, you called me a murderer. I'm not what you seem to think. I'm no saint, but I'm also no murderer."

To spite him, Asahel reached for a small tarnished bell sitting on the bedside table. Holding it in the air, she shook it wildly. The other patients and several visitors turned to stare.

Jake reached out and cupped his hand around the bell, silencing it.

"What?" he said, his eyes flashing with anger. "Do you plan to have me arrested? On what charges—saving your life? 'Cause that's all I've done and you better start getting used to the idea."

"No," Asahel replied. "I'm going to get you kicked out of here. The arrest will come later—when I get out of this place and get the evidence I need to prove what you did to the Naua."

Jake froze, eyes wide and fixed intently on Asahel.

"There's only one way you could know about what happened to the Naua."

"What are you talking about?"

"Only one person, besides the murderers, could possibly know what happened to the Naua. The only way you could have found out is from *her*. From the sole survivor of the massacre."

Asahel gasped involuntarily.

Suddenly a uniformed officer appeared in the doorway. Asahel waved him over. The stout Brazilian strode purposefully toward them.

"Get him out of here," she ordered.

She began searching her memory, hoping to come up with any of these words in Spanish, but she drew a blank. The officer surprised her by grabbing Skully's elbow.

"Fuera," he said.

"I'm a doctor," Skully protested. "*Un* doctor."

When the officer hesitated, Asahel said, "He's not my doctor. No es mi doctor. I want him out."

"Out," the officer repeated, this time in English as he led Jake to the door.

"I'VE GOT IT."

Asahel had just dozed off when she felt her bed tremble.

She opened her eyes.

Jake Skully sat on the mattress next to her, the bell in his hand. He held it up.

"The bell," he explained.

"Get the hell out of here," Asahel said, reflexively pulling the sheet that had slid down to her lap up over her thin hospital gown.

She spotted the same nurse who'd made such a transparent display for Skully the day before.

"Nurse," Asahel called to her. "I don't want him here. No quiero. *Out.*"

The nurse simply lifted her shoulders in a shrug and went back to changing an IV bag. Asahel turned back to Skully.

"What do you want with me? Why won't you leave me alone?"

Skully leaned toward her and put his hand on her knee.

It was an intimate gesture, but Asahel sensed no intimacy on Skully's part. Only urgency.

"I saw the aftermath of the Naua slaughter." He waited, watching Asahel's reaction. "But whoever did it didn't finish the job. There was a survivor. A woman with blue eyes. I believe that somehow you've been in contact with her. I want you to help me find her."

Asahel struggled to hide her surprise at Skully's revelation. How would he have found out about Caina?

"I don't know what you're talking about," she said.

"Then why did you call me a murderer back there on the river? At the time, I didn't know what the hell you were talking about, but then I saw it myself. The Naua village."

"Of course you saw it. You were there. You were one of them."

"*No.*" Jake's hand clamped down hard on her knee. "I wasn't there. Are you crazy? Do you honestly think I could take part in that? In the slaughter of innocent people? Women? Children?"

"You medical gods think you can justify anything in the name of science, don't you?"

"For the love of God. I'm a doctor. It's my job to save lives, not take them."

Either Jake Skully was the best damn actor Asahel had ever seen or he was telling the truth.

"When did it happen?" Skully pressed. "Can you at least tell me that? When were the Naua slaughtered?"

"A month or two ago," Asahel answered. "Maybe longer."

"So you *do* know about the Naua," Skully said.

Angry for allowing herself to be tricked into an admission, Asahel stared at Jake icily.

"Well, if that's true," Jake went on, "I can prove my innocence. I've only been working for GenChrom a month. If you want proof, I'll get it for you. If it would make a difference."

"That doesn't mean GenChrom didn't do it. And now you're working with them. Why would I trust you?"

"GenChrom had nothing to do with what happened to that poor tribe. Nothing."

A teenage boy pushing a cart loaded with pitchers of lukewarm water stopped and placed one on Asahel's bedside tray. Shyly he eyed Asahel.

"If you weren't working for them when it happened," Asahel said, "what makes you so sure? They've been bioprospecting down there. I have it from a reliable source. GenChrom's scientists have been down in that part of the Amazon several times recently."

Jake studied her.

"Who are you? An investigator of some kind? Who do you work for?"

"I work for Mercy Pharmaceuticals," Asahel replied. "But that has nothing to do with my coming down here."

Jake shook his head.

"You are one confusing lady. You show up out of nowhere on a dangerous river, breathing fire about pharmaceutical companies bioprospecting in the Amazon, and it turns out you work in the industry. What are you? Some kind of pharmaceutical spy?"

Asahel snorted a contemptuous laugh.

"What's so funny? Why else would you be down here, snooping into GenChrom's business?"

"Tell me what you saw," Asahel said in response.

"You mean the Naua village?"

"Yes."

"You were headed there, weren't you?"

"I may have been," Asha replied.

"Of course you were. That's what this is all about. Why you threatened me, called me a murderer. Why you said you'd destroy me. You have some connection with the Naua. What is it?"

Asahel turned away. Jake reached for her chin, forcing her to look at him.

"You're obviously in no shape to go there now," he said. "What if I help you? What if I tell you what I saw, give you the information you came for?"

He leaned toward her, his face so close she could feel his breath.

"*Then* will you help me?"

ASAHEL WAS NOT about to admit to knowing Caina, much less give Jake Skully the information he wanted. However, at the same time, she'd come to the realization that Skully might prove to be valuable to her. Her gut instinct told her Skully had information that could help in her mission to find out who had killed the Naua.

She just had to play this right.

"What do you want from me?"

"I need to find the woman who survived the massacre."

"Why is she so important to you?"

"Because her blood contains a very valuable gene. A gene that we believe will cure a serious condition."

"You son of a bitch," she said. "You're no different than the rest of them. Anything to make the god almighty dollar. Well, I can tell you this: I wouldn't help you if my life depended on it."

Asahel rose and began rummaging frantically through the small cupboard next to her bed, looking for her clothes.

When she couldn't find them, she ripped the sheet from the bed, wrapped it around her and headed for the door. She'd put as much distance as she could between her and Skully.

"This isn't about money," he called after her. "It's about my son."

Her back still to Skully, Asahel hesitated. The anguish she heard in his voice seemed genuine. Still, she could not risk letting him manipulate her.

Skully's next words froze Asahel in her tracks.

"He's blind."

Slowly, stunned by this revelation, Asahel turned back around to face him.

"Your son is blind?"

"Michael. He's thirteen now. He lost his sight about a year ago."

"And you're trying to find a cure for him?"

"Yes."

This was unreal. Asahel's mind began racing, trying to assess this new information. How did it fit into the big picture? There was a tie somewhere. There had to be.

And then the link came to her. A terrible realization. She could only hope she was wrong.

Warily Asahel approached Skully, who still stood alongside her hospital bed.

"Why should I believe you?"

Skully reached out and lightly cupped Asahel's chin in her hand, forcing her to meet his gaze.

"What's made you so incredibly cynical that you have trouble believing a father would go to any lengths to help his blind son see again?"

Asahel turned her head to escape his touch.

"Plenty," she said bitterly. "Believe me."

Jake studied her for several seconds.

"Please, can we just put down our artillery and talk?"

Asahel's eyes returned to the man standing before her. He looked every bit as exhausted as she felt, every bit as disillusioned.

"Yes," she said. "We can talk."

CHAPTER **THIRTY-EIGHT**

CAME DOWN here to stop just this type of thing. Do you actually think I'd help you exploit Caina?"

Caina. The Naua woman had a name now. Jake tried to hide the excitement, the spark of hope, that simple fact fanned in him.

He'd entered some kind of game with Asahel Sullivan. A cat and mouse thing. He felt like he was picking his way across a deep pond covered by the thinnest layer of ice. Each step required cunning, skill. And simple luck.

He still regarded Asahel as the enemy. In part, because he knew she was playing the same game with him. Asahel wanted to use him in some way, while keeping her own risks to a minimum. She'd never actually come out and told him about the lone Naua survivor—he had no idea how Asahel knew about her or why, and he knew better than to press for too much information right now—but at least his original hunch had turned out to be correct.

"How is it you know so much about this?" he asked. "About bio-piracy?"

"In my old life, it's something I cared deeply about."

"Your old life?"

He watched Asahel weigh the pros and cons of answering, knowing that if she did provide an answer, it was only because she believed it might further whatever mission had brought her this far.

"I was an activist," she finally said. "I worked for a group called IPAF. The Indigenous Peoples—"

"Advancement Foundation," Skully finished with her.

"You know about IPAF?"

"I've been a member for years. My wife got me involved."

"How does she feel about what you're doing?" The disdain in Asahel's voice made it clear what she thought Jake's response should be. "About you working for a company like GenChrom?"

Jake flashed back to the argument he'd had with Ana about whether to accept Hughes's offer to come work for him. Jake had recently read about G32 and Hughes's active search for it and thought taking the job was a good idea, but Ana was dead set against it. She believed that moving Michael when he was already depressed could push him over the edge.

"How can you possibly know that?" Jake had argued.

"I'm his mother. I know."

As much respect as Jake had developed for Ana's instincts as a mother, he hadn't been willing to accept this as an answer.

"I won't just sit by any longer, Ana. We've taken him to what— half a dozen specialists?—and ended up with nothing. No answers. No explanations. I can't stand this . . . this feeling of helplessness. I have to *do* something."

He'd turned away from her, not accustomed to feeling such anger with her, not knowing what to do with it.

Ana grabbed his arm, spinning him back around.

"We *will* do something."

He'd seen it in her eyes then. The fact that she had a plan—a plan she'd been contemplating for some time.

She'd stepped closer to him, placed a gentle hand on either side of Jake's face, and, as she'd always been able to do, in an instant Ana had sucked him in with her passion, and those huge, dark eyes.

"We're both doctors," she said. "We both did research early in our careers. And you hold the patent to a technology that may be the key to succeeding with *any* genetic treatments for Michael's problem. *You and I* can do it, Jake. We'll find the cure. Together."

The idea—the sheer preposterousness of it—had stunned Jake. Yet he'd lain awake all that night thinking about it.

He knew that many biotech companies had started with just one researcher, just one idea. A simple lab.

Why not?

The next morning he'd found Ana in the kitchen, washing dishes, her back to him.

"Let's do it," he'd said.

She'd turned slowly, biting her lower lip.

"You mean it?"

"Yes," Jake had answered. "We'll get through this—we'll find an answer—together."

Of course, that had turned out to be a lie. For while Ana had taken on the responsibilities for two medical practices, Jake spent long, lonely hours in a lab conducting research. And then he'd turned to Francesca for comfort.

"My wife's dead," Jake said now, pushing those memories out of his mind.

For the first time, Asahel seemed to miss at least half a beat.

"What makes you think the Naua have this gene you're looking for?" she asked quietly.

"It's a very rare gene," Jake replied. "So far, researchers have only been able to isolate a canine equivalent of it, from a mixed breed of dog. Dogs that, by all previous rules of genetic makeup, should have brown eyes. But instead they have remarkably blue eyes. Researchers have been searching for the equivalent gene in humans for years."

Asahel absorbed each word thoughtfully.

"And the Naua," she said. "They're dark-skinned people with blue eyes, the genes for which, you can bet—because of the tribe's isolation—were not introduced from outside. So you think they carry the gene."

"Exactly. The Naua are the only tribe in the Amazon with brilliantly blue eyes. If the gene we're looking for exists in humans, that's where we'll find it. Tell me, is that how you'd describe Caina's eyes—as brilliantly blue?"

Asahel did not respond, did not admit that she had used those exact words to describe Caina to Toby.

"I'm only asking you to introduce me to Caina so that I can explain to her what I want and why. I give you my word, if she doesn't want to be a donor, it will all end right there."

Asahel crossed her arms over her chest.

"I can't do it," she said.

"Didn't you come down here to help her?" Jake pressed. "To find out what happened to her people?"

"Of course."

"You just said yourself you want to stop biopiracy. Well, I'm offering to help you. I can give you information that will make people's hair stand on end." A glimmer of interest suddenly appeared in Asahel's eyes. Jake had hit upon something. "I can provide testimony about the slaughter, from what I saw there at the Naua village. I'll tell the authorities, the FBI, whoever you want me to talk to."

"That would be too easy for you to make up. If you want to prove you're innocent, take me there."

"Where?"

"To the Naua village."

Jake sighed.

"There's no time. I have to find Caina now, before Hughes does."

He paused, desperate for ways to get Asahel's help. "There's another way I can help you."

"How?"

"By telling you exactly what I witnessed during the time I was with GenChrom, the sampling that took place before we reached the Naua village. By giving you the story you came down here for."

"Names? Dates?"

"If it gets you to lead me to Caina, yes. I'll tell you everything."

Asahel studied him.

"You don't let anything get in your way, do you?"

"Not when it comes to my son."

"Let me think about it," she said. "I won't make any decision without first talking to Caina."

"Fair enough."

THE INSTANT JAKE STEPPED inside the ward the next morning, he could see something was terribly wrong.

"She's gone," Asahel cried when she saw him approaching. "Caina disappeared."

"Disappeared from where?"

"Seattle. I left her there, at my apartment. A friend of mine was staying with her. He came home from work and found the apartment ransacked, and Caina gone."

Jake groaned.

"We need to get up there right away. I'll go, too, to help you look for her."

Asahel shook her head.

"She's been gone two weeks. Stan's been looking for her all that time. He's been trying to get ahold of me, but of course there was no way to reach me. I've got my ex-husband looking now, too. He's FBI."

That explained one piece of the puzzle. Asahel Sullivan's ex-husband must have been the source of her information about Gen-Chrom's trips to the Amazon.

"I'll talk to your doctor," Jake said. "He'll let you leave for Seattle if I'm traveling with you."

"No," Asahel said adamantly. "I can't leave Brazil. I have this terrible feeling . . . We can't leave now."

"Why?"

"Because I have a hunch."

"What is it?"

"That Caina would try to return here."

"To Brazil?"

Asahel's eyes locked with his as she nodded her head.

"To her village."

"That's assuming she left of her own free will. The fact that your apartment was ransacked—"

Asahel cut him off.

"Don't say that," she ordered, her slender fingers balling into tight fists. "Don't even think it. We have to assume Caina got away."

"One thing we can assume," Jake said, "is that if whoever killed the rest of her tribe knows Caina survived, they'll be looking for her. For one purpose only. To get rid of her.

"And then there's Hughes. He knows she survived. You can be sure he's after her, too. He'll leave no stone unturned."

"To get her blood?"

"Yes," Jake replied. "And then murder her. I overheard him the last night we were together. He was planning to do the same thing the other researchers did. Kill the Naua. He just didn't get there first."

Asahel's knuckles had turned white.

"We have to find Caina before anyone else does."

"Maybe you're right about Caina. Can your ex be trusted to let you know the minute he finds her?"

"Yes. I trust Michael. And I made him promise he wouldn't get the Bureau involved until I get back."

"Maybe you're right," Jake repeated slowly, thoughtfully. "Maybe she decided to come home. Since your ex has Seattle covered, it could make more sense for us to go to the Naua village and look for her."

"Since when is it *us*?" Asahel said.

"You know you can't go alone," Jake said. "You need someone with you, someone you can trust. You're just out of surgery. I can get you discharged right away and make sure you don't have any complications. You need me, Asahel. You must realize that."

He could practically see the wheels turning in that stubborn head. Only one thing would convince Asahel to accept Jake as a partner in this undertaking, and that was her belief that he served a purpose.

Still, he could see it wasn't an easy sale.

"Okay," she finally said. "Let's go."

CHAPTER **THIRTY-NINE**

DESPITE CAINA'S STATE of exhaustion, the jungle's night chorus gave her the first glimmer of comfort and peace she'd experienced since it all began.

Perhaps she would even be able to sleep for a while, rest up for the final push. She had survived a trip to hell and back, and now it was almost over. Nothing could ever cause her more pain than she'd already endured. What more was there to fear? She had survived it all, even managed to escape her demon pursuer—the ghostly pale monster of a man whom she'd glimpsed through the glass door in the foyer of Asahel's building. She'd watched as he headed around the building, then disappeared up the side stairs. She'd barely had time to run back up the inside stairwell to Asahel's apartment and grab her pouch before she heard him playing with the lock on the kitchen door.

She gave thanks to the gods for that—the fact that she'd been able to retrieve the pouch.

Her recent exposure to spoken English, along with Asahel's clothing (which she'd been wearing at the time), had helped immensely on her return trip. But, of course, she'd still be wandering the underbelly of Seattle if it weren't for the diamonds. If only she'd had time to leave one for her friends, Asahel and Stan, but when she heard the doorknob turn she knew that even a moment's hesitation could cost her her life.

Yes, she had survived the worst that she could possibly endure, and now she was back in her beloved rain forest. For the first time, she felt safe again. Safe enough to doze.

Sleep, sweet sleep. So welcome. So needed.

But then, as she began to drift off, images from the last time she'd ventured through these forests alone wrestled their evil way into her subconsciousness.

The nearness to her village had brought it all back to her again. Her tribesmen's spirits must have sensed her presence. She dared not sleep, dared not let the thoughts and images come alive again.

She hugged her knees to her chest, leaning against one of the mahogany tree's giant roots, which encompassed her like the gnarly legs of a spider. She would just rest her head here on the root for a few seconds.

Just a precious few seconds . . .

HER BANISHMENT WAS over now, and her heart soared with joy at the prospect of returning home. There, just ahead, she could see it—the clearing.

She paused, savoring the hot, moist air she drew into her nostrils, deep into her lungs. Then she smelled it. The evening meal. Her mouth watered at the familiar scent of wild pig, roasted in a pit until its meat fell away from the bone into the eager hands of the skilled Naua hunters who'd speared it, then hauled it, sometimes for days, back to camp.

The past three weeks had been the worst of her life. Tribal banishment. The Naua way of punishing those who violated sacred tribal precepts. A way of teaching the wayward young.

She had lived in extraordinary fear of its threat for most of her twenty-two years, had seen her older brother banished for showing disrespect to the tribe's shaman, who'd treated their father's yellow fever by draining so much blood from his body that within two hours he lay dead. She had wished then, fervently and passionately, that it had been the shaman banished. Instead her beloved brother was sent away.

His banishment was to last a full two moons. But the two moons passed and then three. He never did return. Many moons later Naua hunters came across a skeleton picked clean by flesh-eating insects.

A necklace made of bones and feathers was the only means of identifying it as her brother. Caina had made him that necklace as a child, and so it had been returned to her.

For six years now, ever since her brother walked bravely into the jungle, without looking back, the necklace had symbolized Caina's own fear of banishment. Yet it had not, in the end, served its purpose.

For she had done the unthinkable. She had broken a sacred tribal law, and, rightfully, she had been punished for it.

Deep in the terra firma rain forest of Brazil, in the state of Acre, the small Naua tribe had lived in relative isolation for centuries. The Naua were not a hostile warrior tribe, as were many of their neighbors. Most of the world was not even aware of their existence, which is just how the Naua liked it. Other tribes living in the deep, hard-to-penetrate reaches of the Amazon, tribes who had not protected their isolation as the Naua did, had been decimated by disease and violence, both compliments of the white man.

But the Naua kept to themselves, kept a low profile, which they believed helped ensure their survival.

Keeping a low profile required them to keep their numbers low. This goal, in fact, had long been a primary focus of tribal life. It was the source of the young woman's trouble that had led to her banishment.

The Naua practiced rigid population control. For generations, the Naua had enforced a system of birth control that allowed only those chosen by the elders to procreate.

Caina was not one so chosen, yet she had allowed herself to become pregnant. Banishment had been inevitable, but not until the herbal brew concocted and fed her daily by the tribe's shaman had worked its magic. Once she'd miscarried her forbidden child, she'd been banished. Like her brother.

But unlike her brother, Caina had survived.

And now her heart soared.

Triumphant, repentant, she was finally home! Back to her people, her nieces and nephews, her role as a caretaker to them. All the things that made up her life and gave her comfort.

Unable to wait a moment longer, she began to run toward the clearing. She no longer worried about the reception she would get, the shunning that always followed banishment. She could stand anything, just so long as she was reunited with her tribe, just so long . . .

The first sign that something was wrong—horribly, horribly wrong—hit her before she actually saw the blood.

Silence.

The rain forest was a place of joyous noise, crazy, riotous chaos that was as natural to her people as the sun coming up each morning or the rain pouring like a waterfall from the sky.

But as she neared the clearing, the noise began to dim. And then, it stopped altogether.

Howler monkeys no longer shrieked in the forest canopy above. The parrots, macaws, owls . . . all silent overhead. Deathly silent.

And then she saw it. The pool of blood. And lying in it something small, grotesque.

Caina's gasp echoed across the clearing.

A hand. A child's hand, its fingers curled into a ball.

Recoiling in horror, she fell back, and in that moment something in the corner of her eye caused her to turn, then shrink into the shelter of the trees.

She bit the flesh of her right hand to keep from screaming.

On the opposite side of the clearing, her entire tribe knelt in a pack. A good thirty yards separated her from them, but she had always had the eyes of an owl. She could see the expression on her mother's face, the sheer, absolute terror, as a group of six men with ghostly light skin, armed with rifles and machetes, circled the group, moving erratically, shouting to one another in a tongue Caina could not understand.

Her cousin, a young mother of two, wailed loudly, holding the form of her dead child, his right hand now only a bloody stub. Instantly one of the men raised his rifle and pulled the trigger, putting a bullet into her forehead. She slumped forward, her child still cradled protectively in her arms.

In a state of shock, hidden by the dense underbrush, Caina looked on, helpless to do anything. The joyful homecoming she'd been anticipating had now turned into a nightmare too hideous, too evil, for her mind to even process.

The pain and anger and fear seared through her like a finely chiseled arrow. Still, she could not turn away. She watched, trancelike. Not one of her tribesmen offered resistance, yet one by one every single Naua, young and old, male and female, was murdered—either slashed to death or shot—with ruthless precision.

Right before her eyes.

Eyes the color of a summer sky.

CAINA AWOKE WITH a start. The dream. It had seemed every bit as real as when it actually happened.

She knew what caused it. As she drew near, her brothers and sisters had sensed her presence, and they were calling her now. Perhaps they did not understand why she had deserted the sacred ground upon which they were buried, upon which their spirits now danced. Perhaps they were angry with her for leaving.

Didn't they realize that the only reason she'd made her long journey to that wicked other world was so that she could try to bring them back in the flesh and blood? Her uncle, who played dead until the white men left, had survived one day. He had explained to Caina about the magic the white men had told her people of. A magic that could convert her people's blood into real-live beings again. Her tribe. Her family.

She'd thought if anyone had the power to make that happen, it would be Asahel Sullivan.

She had never forgotten Asahel from her visit years earlier. Asahel had been the only light-skinned person Caina ever saw—until that terrible day.

That, together with her promises, made Caina believe Asahel held magical powers.

But it turned out that Asahel had no such power. Asahel could not bring the Naua back to life. All she could do was promise to find who was responsible for their deaths.

Caina had decided she could not bear to be away from her people, her village, any longer.

Her tribesmen's spirits knew she was near.

She'd finally returned home.

CHAPTER FORTY

"CAN'T WE GO faster?" Asahel yelled across the noise and the spray of water.

They were roaring up the same rivers they'd each recently traveled down on their way to Manaus, retracing their course, but this time they traveled in a high-powered twenty-four-foot speedboat.

"It's not safe," Jake yelled back. "We're already going faster than we should."

"You said yourself, we might not be the only ones thinking that Caina will return to her village."

The moment Jake stood, a moth the size of a sparrow slapped noisily into his forehead. He wiped the sticky mess it left with his hand; then, crouching low against the wind, he moved to the front of the boat.

Zurito, his neck periscoped up over a windshield so clouded with smashed insects that he could no longer see through it, seemed impervious to the near constant sting of small bodies smacking his bare skin. Jake's reunion with Zurito along the shores of the River Acre had been a joyous event.

Now Jake tapped Zurito on the shoulder.

"Zurito, faster."

Zurito lifted an eyebrow, then responded by shoving the throttle forward. Jake stumbled backward, half his body landing on Asahel's lap.

Asahel pushed and slithered her way out from under him so quickly Jake couldn't help but grin.

"What's so funny?" Asahel asked, glowering at him from the bucket seat she'd moved to.

"You can't think I did that on purpose."

"Oh, can't I?"

Jake shook his head in amusement.

"That's right. I managed to get you to ask me to have Zurito speed up, just so I could go flying into your lap. How transparent of me."

"It doesn't matter to me whether or not it was deliberate."

"I see," Jake answered, studying her.

The message was clear. Asahel's opinion of Jake had not changed. They'd formed a partnership, but it was tenuous, and based solely on their mission.

Finding Caina.

"And quit looking at me all the time," Asahel added. "Do you think I don't notice?"

"Don't flatter yourself. All I'm doing is monitoring your condition. You come down with an infection and we're all screwed."

Jake was not about to admit that he also enjoyed watching her.

"Is that why you went through my bag? To monitor my health?"

So she'd seen him. Over the past three days, as they traveled to Acre, Jake noticed that Asahel had clearly overcome her earlier reluctance to take the codeine her doctor prescribed. Yesterday, when she dozed midday—a rare occurrence—Jake slid his hand into her duffel bag, removed the tinted prescription bottle and counted the pills.

"I was worried you were taking too much codeine. I'm sorry. It was wrong of me to go into your bag without your permission."

Asahel had opened her mouth to reply when the boat swerved sharply. Jake braced himself to avoid another scene with her.

The river had taken a sudden sharp turn. As they rounded its bend, the skiff came within several feet of colliding with a native piloting his balsa raft with a long bamboo pole.

"Let's talk to him, Zurito," Jake shouted. "Maybe he's seen Hughes."

Zurito swung the boat in a wide circle, pulling even with the raft.

A bone-thin rafter, clad only in a dirty white cloth tied around his waist, waved and greeted them with a broad smile.

Asahel and Jake looked on as Zurito jabbered to the native in riverspeak. The rafter's wide eyes, their whites shockingly bright in the canvas of his dark skin, alternately drifted between the sleek boat and Asahel as he spoke.

Zurito translated for Jake and Asahel's benefit.

"He say white man like Hughes pay one of his tribe big money to take him downstream to settlement."

"When was that?" Jake asked.

"Four or five days. Mebbe six."

"Was he alone?"

"That's what he say."

Jake fell silent. What had happened to Brent?

"Didn't you say Hughes had an American guide with him?" Asahel asked.

"Yes. But that night I left them behind, at the Naua village, I heard them discussing the possibility of the guide staying to look for Caina. That must be what happened. Hughes must have returned to the States alone."

They parted ways with the rafter and resumed their course. If all went as planned, by nightfall they would reach the site of Asahel and Diego Cavallero's deadly plane crash.

ONCE THEY REACHED what remained of the plane's debris, Jake and Zurito teamed up—Jake offering his earlier experience and Zurito his jungle skills—to speed the way inland, toward the Naua village.

The first night of camping, Zurito and Jake built lean-tos while Asahel gathered firewood. Food presented no problem. They'd stocked up on dried goods before leaving Manaus. While Jake and Asahel nursed the fire into flames to boil water for rice, Zurito set out for postre. Dessert.

Dusk had fallen. Gradually, the screams and chatter of the macaws and monkeys had given way to the buzz of insects, pierced by the occasional shriek of the owl or wildcat.

The day's heat had not abated. The air, stagnant and thick with moisture, clung like a net to their skin, making the simplest of acts—even breathing—a chore.

Jake had grown so accustomed to the silence between them that Asahel's voice startled him.

"Was Ana your wife?"

His head snapped around. Looking at Asahel—staring into the flames—Jake wondered if he'd imagined it.

"Why?"

Now she turned and met his gaze.

"The first night, when you were sleeping. You called her name."

Jake looked away.

"Yes."

"When did she die?"

"Six months ago."

"I'm sorry."

Jake simply nodded.

"May I ask . . . ?"

Now Jake turned to meet her gaze.

"I'm not supposed to even look at you, much less accidentally touch you, but you feel free to dig into my private life? Tell me, what rules are we playing by here, Asahel?"

Asahel did not shy away from his piercing eyes.

"I'd say we abandoned most of the rules when we climbed on board that boat together."

"Except the ones that protect you?"

Asahel looked away, in the direction Zurito had disappeared, and they returned to their silence.

"They say it was suicide," Jake finally said, gazing into the fire. "They say my wife killed herself when she found out I was having an affair."

Jake didn't hear Asahel's quiet gasp. The screech of an owl drowned it out.

THE FIRST BULLET SOUNDED like a laser as it zapped by their ears.

Dropping to the ground, Zurito screamed out a warning to Jake and Asahel in his native tongue. It wasn't necessary. They had already hit the dirt.

The second bullet ricocheted off a branch overhead. In the next instant, the forest all around them began exploding, one section at a time, under a barrage of rapid fire.

Waving for Jake and Asahel to follow him, Zuritio wiggled out of his backpack and shoved it into the dense growth lining the trail until it disappeared completely from sight. Then, machete still stuck in his belt, he began burrowing on his belly, headfirst, into the vegetation. Asahel and Jake followed suit. More bullets sang by above as Asahel entered the gap left behind by Zurito.

Like a worm breaking its way clumsily through clotted earth, Zurito pushed slowly forward for what seemed an eternity. Immediately behind him, Asahel felt the world closing in on her. The heat in the dense, low brush became quickly unbearable, so stifling that Asahel had to stop every few seconds to suck air deep into her lungs. The vegetation was so dense and the tunnel forged by Zurito so narrow that Asahel couldn't even raise her one good hand to protect her face from the branches that raked it as she inched forward, frequently kicking Jake Skully, who followed directly behind her. Terror and terror alone kept Asahel from feeling the pain that ratcheted through the arm fixed close to her body by a sling.

Soon panic began to set in. When Asahel tried to draw air into her lungs, it no longer seemed to exist. Convinced she was suffocating, Asahel felt her heart begin to race. She was trapped! Zurito blocked her way ahead and Skully from the rear, and she could not communicate with either. Closing her eyes and willing herself to continue inching forward, Asahel felt herself simply fading, passing out, when suddenly the soles of Zurito's shoes disappeared. A wave of fresh air washed over her face.

They'd broken through into a pocket—a small cave in the forest's undergrowth. It measured less than a meter in every direction, so cramped that as each of the three emerged from the tunnel, finding room for their arms and legs was like working a jigsaw puzzle.

But at least they could rise to a sitting position. And breathe.

For several seconds, Asahel simply sat, eyes closed, hugging her knees with her good arm and sucking air into her lungs to clear her head.

"Are you okay?"

Asahel opened her eyes. The concern on Jake's face—just inches from her own—appeared genuine.

She nodded.

"I just needed some air."

Jake turned to tend to Zurito, whose hands and face had been scraped raw. But Zurito pushed him away.

"Who is it?" Asahel asked, her eyes traveling from Zurito to Jake. "What tribes have guns?"

"No tribe have gun like that," Zurito replied.

"Like what?"

"That was an automatic that fired on us," Skully answered. "An AK-47."

"How would you know that—that it's an AK-47?"

Asahel saw Jake and Zurito exchange glances.

"I've been around one before," Jake replied. "That's how."

"We close now," Zurito said suddenly. "Close to Naua."

His attempt to divert Asahel's attention from the subject of the gun worked.

"How close?" she asked.

"Trail wide. Very close."

"I agree," Jake said. "It's the same trail I took. We're almost there. Zurito, can we approach the village from another direction? Circle around from behind?"

Zurito appeared to have been thinking the same thing.

"Yes," he said. "Just take longer."

"That's what we'll do then," Jake said.

He turned to Asahel.

"You're not in any condition to go with us now. We need to see what we're up against. We'll come back for you."

Asahel opened her mouth to protest, then changed her mind.

"Maybe you're right. I'd just slow you down. But give me your word you'll come back for me before you actually enter the village."

"I can't give you my word," Jake replied testily. "It'll depend on what we find."

Asahel grabbed him by the arm.

"*Promise me.* If Caina sees you first, if I'm not with you, she'll run. You may never find her. I have to be there. Give me your word. Otherwise I'll follow you right now. Whether you like it or not."

The corners of Jake's eyes hinted of a smirk.

"You mean my word actually means something to you?"

Asahel did not flinch.

"Just promise me, dammit."

"All right," Jake answered. "You've got my word. We'll come back for you first."

As soon as they were out of earshot of Asahel, Jake tapped Zurito on the shoulder. They were far enough now from the trail where they'd been ambushed that they felt safe standing.

Zurito swung his machete expertly, slicing a path through the tangle of vines, chest-high grass and gnarly shrubs, many of which sported thorns and branches several inches thick.

"Are you thinking the same thing I am?" Jake asked.

"Sí," Zurito replied, pausing from the backbreaking work to swipe away the sweat on his brow. "Brent. Him have automatic."

"That's right," Jake said. "An AK-47. Maybe that explains why the native you talked to on the river hadn't seen him. Maybe he's still here. Maybe he's waiting for Caina to return."

Zurito's eyes slowly scanned the forest surrounding them.

"Or mebbe waiting for us."

It felt like they'd set Asahel's legs on fire.

Ants—if these inch-long creatures qualified for so modest a name— had managed to work their way into her pants in spite of the fact that she'd tucked her long khakis into the tops of her hiking socks, and now her skin served as dinner to the armies that had swarmed over her as she sat, helpless to stop them, on the rain forest's floor.

Trying to unzip her pants and remove the offenders would only give more of them access. Asahel could only slap at them through her pants as she suffered their fiery bites, up and down both legs.

Ironically, less than half an hour before they'd been ambushed, Zurito had had Asahel rub crushed brown tree termites over her hands and face. But her sweat, which rushed from every pore, had made short life of the termites' insect-repelling properties. To make matters worse, the air had now come alive with loudly buzzing mosquitoes and flies the size of moths, all eager to feast on every patch of Asahel's skin not already covered with ants.

Misery, thought Asahel, *thy name is Amazon.*

Still, Asahel's physical torment paled in comparison to the mental anguish.

What made her think she could trust Jake to keep his promise to return to get her before entering the Naua village? And even if Jake could be trusted, with a sniper out there gunning for them, anything could happen now. She might never see Jake and Zurito again.

She could literally be eaten alive if she waited.

She had come too far to allow anything to stop her now. She simply had to witness, firsthand, what had happened to Caina's tribe. She had to bring home evidence to prove the truth of Caina's story.

Evidence.

Asahel bolted upright. She needed her camera to document what had happened. But she'd left it in her backpack, which she'd hidden alongside the trail.

Before he and Zurito left, she'd told Jake that she'd wait for him right there.

But sometimes promises became impossible to keep.

Asahel took several large gulps of air and then, dropping onto her one good hand and both knees, in a lopsided slither she disappeared.

CHAPTER **FORTY-ONE**

THEY WERE RACING against time. Only a few precious hours of daylight remained, during which they had to reach the Naua village, then return for Asahel—for both Jake and Zurito knew it would be impossible to find her once night fell. And to leave her there alone overnight was unthinkable.

Driven by these fears, Zurito and Jake called upon every ounce of remaining strength to hack their way through the thick growth, taking turns at the lead, until finally, two and a half hours after leaving Asahel behind, Jake turned to Zurito and, over a sweat-drenched shoulder, pointed.

"That's it."

Just ahead, the tops of the huts where he'd last seen Hughes and Brent punctuated the powdery blue sky above the clearing.

The trail they'd recently deserted, the one they'd been on when they were ambushed, opened onto the clearing, approximately forty-five degrees from where they stood. Crouching for cover, they could see no activity in the village. Their sniper might still be out on that trail, searching for them, or waiting somewhere along it, hoping to ambush them again.

But it was also possible he'd returned to the village and that at that very moment his automatic rifle was trained at the mouth of the clearing, waiting to pick them off as they approached.

Not a very welcome thought.

Still, the likelihood that the village was completely empty disturbed Jake most. Thoughts of Asahel, alone and unarmed, crept into his mind.

What if their sniper discovered the crude tunnel they'd forged?

"We'd better get back to Asahel," he said.

Zurito seemed to feel it, too.

"Sí," he replied. "We must hurry."

• • •

ASAHEL MADE THE TRIP back to the main trail in a fraction of the time it had taken them to forge their way to the small safe haven where Zurito and Jake left her.

Her plan was simple. To find the backpack and retrieve her camera, then return to wait for Jake and Zurito, as she'd promised.

But when she found the pack she'd stuffed into the shrubs bordering the trail, something came over Asahel. Her eyes strayed ahead. The trail beckoned, wide and clear. Then she glanced back, to the pathetic hole in the undergrowth, which required her to slide forward painfully on one hand and knees.

What if Jake and Zurito didn't keep their promise to get her before entering the Naua village? If Caina saw them, they could ruin everything she'd come so far to accomplish.

Crouched low, Asahel waited, listening, her eyes scanning every direction, and then—it wasn't even so much a conscious decision; it simply seemed her only alternative—when she saw no hint of their sniper, she slipped her one good arm into the strap of her backpack and set off down the trail.

In the direction of the Naua village.

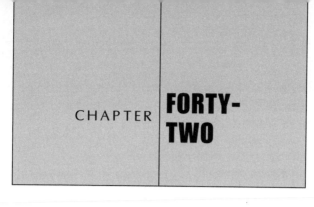

CHAPTER **FORTY-TWO**

SHE'S GONE."

Panic twisted Jake's gut as he shimmied on his belly into the shelter where they'd left Asahel.

They'd made the ultimate mistake: leaving her behind, alone and unprotected.

Seconds later, Zurito appeared in the opening behind Jake, his eyes quickly scanning for Asahel, then mirroring the concern in Jake's eyes.

"Maybe she decide not wait."

"Maybe," Jake replied. "But wouldn't it have made more sense for her to follow us than to go back to the main trail, where someone just tried to kill us?"

"That girl not always make sense," Zurito said, though his tone was filled more with concern than disapproval.

"You're right about that. Maybe she's at the village now," Jake said. "Maybe we just missed her."

"We go. Hurry."

Zurito disappeared into the tunnel that led to the trail. Both men cut themselves raw in their hurry to make it back to where they'd stashed their bags and made their getaway from their ambusher.

Once back on the trail, they knew, from the route they'd just finished carving, that they couldn't be more than half an hour or so from the village. The curtain of vegetation closed in on them, darkening with the setting sun, as they ran at full speed.

Jake struggled to keep up with Zurito, tripping several times.

Zurito suddenly stopped, a troubled expression spreading across his face.

"What is it?" Jake asked.

They could both feel their nearness to the village.

Zurito held a finger to his lips.

"Shhhh," he cautioned, turning back toward the clearing, which lay just ahead.

Suddenly an ungodly sound pierced the air. A sound that neither man had ever before heard—not even Zurito, who'd spent a lifetime in the rain forests.

A scream of utter terror and grief.

ZURITO TRIED TO hold Jake back before they reached the clearing.

"Mebbe ambush," Zurito warned.

But Jake would not listen. He shook free of Zurito's restraint and sprinted the last few yards, breaking into the clearing.

The sound of sobbing, wafting toward him from one of the huts, guided Jake.

A hide hung over the hut's doorway. Jake threw it aside and stepped inside. Despite the shadows, immediately, in the center of the floor, he recognized Asahel. Her back to him, she was huddled over a still form—from the legs and hair Jake could see it belonged to a woman—wailing and rocking as she clutched the body to her chest. Dried blood, the consistency of setting glue, surrounded the two like a melted snowman.

Jake approached quietly and placed a hand on Asahel's shoulder.

"We have to get out of here," he said. He heard Zurito's footsteps fall in behind him. "It's not safe here."

Asahel drew back to look at him, her face streaked with a mixture of dirt, blood and tears. The sight that met his eyes would stay with him the rest of his life.

Jake did not know whether the involuntary moan that filled the air belonged to him or to Zurito.

The corpse's face—what remained of it—had been grossly mutilated.

"It's Caina," Asahel sobbed. "It's Caina. Look what they've done to her."

Jake suddenly realized why the lifeless expression held such horror.

Like a jack-o'-lantern, Caina's eyes had been carved from their sockets.

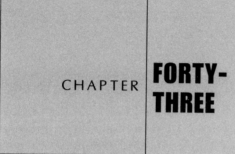

CHAPTER **FORTY-THREE**

I T WAS CAINA'S murderer who fired on us back on the trail."

Jake looked first to Asahel, who did not respond, then Zurito, who nodded in agreement.

"We assumed that he was on his way here," Jake continued, "but at the time we ran into him, he must have been leaving. He'd already accomplished his mission. He was heading back to the river."

The buzz of insects filled the air. Night had fallen. Light of a half-moon fell softly across the clearing, but Jake, Zurito and Asahel crouched close to a hut. They had not built a fire, for fear it would draw the murderer back to the Naua village.

Asahel had not said a word since they'd buried her friend—alongside the mound containing the remains of her tribesmen and family.

Finally, she broke her silence.

"Let's go after him."

Jake turned and studied her.

The hut's dark shadows made her eyes appear dull, lifeless. Or perhaps, thought Jake, it had little to do with the lighting. Though Asahel had maintained an outward calm ever since he'd pried Caina's mutilated body from her almost superhuman grasp, he suspected that something had broken—no, snapped—inside her.

"We will," Jake replied. "At first light."

"By morning he'll be on the move again. He won't expect us at night."

"I've made that trip once before at night," Jake said. "It's hard enough under the best conditions, but in the dark, with your injury—"

"Can you do it, Zurito?" Asahel asked, dismissing Jake and his objections. "Can you find him at night?"

Zurito nodded.

"Zurito find. No problem."

"Then let's go."

•　　•　　•

HE'D HAD AT LEAST a four-hour start on them. And the benefit of traveling in daylight. But with a single flashlight to lead them, Zurito made amazingly good time.

Zurito had strung a braided rope from the back of his belt to Asahel's and then on to Jake's. To avoid being detected, Zurito used the flashlight sparingly. With it off and the canopy overhead shutting out the moon's light, only Zurito seemed able to make out anything at all in the blackness.

Even with the flashlight on, Asahel was having trouble seeing. When Zurito suddenly stopped short, Asahel stumbled into him and then Jake into her.

"What is it?" Jake asked.

"Shhh," Zurito said. He turned off his flashlight.

Their world went black.

Jake heard Zurito sniff the air. Jake, too, lifted his nose in the air, inhaling deeply, but he did not detect anything other than the pungent smells that assaulted his nostrils day and night since he entered the rain forest.

Zurito whispered, "Fire."

The fire surprised Jake. He hadn't thought that Caina's murderer would dare light one tonight.

Since they were unarmed, they decided to split up and approach from two different directions. At best, this would confuse their ambusher and, they hoped, allow at least one of them to disarm him. At worst, he might only be able to target one, instead of all of them.

Asahel did not respond when Jake told her she'd have to stay put. They would signal for her when it was safe.

As they inched closer, they made out a form slumped near the fire.

What luck! Their ambusher was sleeping. Or perhaps, thought Jake, remembering another evening weeks earlier, on board the *Tapuya*, he'd passed out—welcome news indeed when you're trying to sneak up on a man armed with an AK-47.

The automatic was nowhere in sight.

Jake noticed Asahel staring at the sleeping form, totally fixated upon it. It wasn't difficult to imagine the hatred she held for this man, who had butchered Caina.

"Listen to me, Asahel," he said. "You'd better not pull another stunt like you did last time. You gave me your word you'd wait for us to come back for you."

"I didn't think you would."

"But we did, didn't we? We kept our word. Now I'm asking you to keep yours. Stay out of sight until we signal for you. Do you hear?"

"I hear," Asahel said, her eyes never leaving the man beside the fire.

Jake gave her one last nervous glance, then turned to Zurito. They had to focus on one thing: Disarming their ambusher and confiscating his precious cargo. Caina's blood.

Jake and Zurito spent several minutes whispering a hastily formed plan. Once Zurito was in place on the other side of the campsite, he would signal Jake with a catlike shriek. Simultaneously they'd rush the campsite.

They stood face-to-face now, both glistening with sweat, their foreheads, noses and cheeks streaked with dirt, both knowing full well what they were up against.

Jake reached out and placed his hands on the shoulders of the man who had become his friend—perhaps, he realized suddenly, the best friend he'd ever had.

"Don't try to be a hero," he said. "You hear?"

Zurito smiled good-naturedly.

"Jungle Zurito's home. Safe for Zurito," he said. He pointed at Jake's chest. "You be safe."

With that, Zurito turned and disappeared silently into the foliage.

As he waited for the signal, Jake's entire body felt like a coiled spring.

When it came—the shriek—Jake took one quick look back at Asahel. And then he charged.

Jake's worst nightmare was realized when he saw that Zurito's call had also set the slumbering form in motion.

With the heart-wrenching realization that he'd allowed Zurito to make himself a target, Jake saw the glint of flames reflecting off the barrel of the gun.

"Zurito, *look out*," Jake screamed.

A sickening crackle filled the air, and as he lunged for the gunman Jake watched Zurito's body convulse and dance under the barrage of bullets.

"You bastard," Jake screamed.

As Jake landed at the gunman's feet, he briefly caught sight of Zurito's body, lying lifeless and twisted on the dirt.

And then the steely butt of the gun came crashing down on his skull and Jake, too, went limp.

•   •   •

HE REGAINED CONSCIOUSNESS and found himself looking up, into the barrel of the gun.

Hughes's guide stood over him, sweat pouring from his face, his eyes wide and, for a man clearly in charge, looking strangely panicked.

And then Jake heard the strangest thing of all. From the blackness surrounding them.

"Don't do it, Brent."

Gun still trained on Jake, Brent turned, slowly, toward the voice.

"You," he cried, falling back, as Asahel stepped into the fire's light.

Slowly, a twisted smile crept over his face.

"Well, well, well," he said. "Look who's here.

"My baby sister."

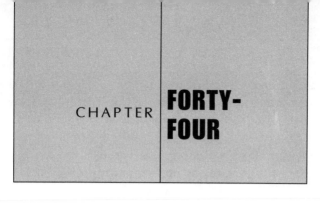

CHAPTER **FORTY-FOUR**

JAKE STARED, EYES jolted wide in disbelief, as Asahel approached Brent.

She looked like a woman possessed by demons—eyes on fire, chin jutting out. Slowly, in total disregard of the gun Brent waved between them, she advanced.

Rage made her voice unrecognizable.

"You killed Caina."

Brent's grin spread.

"She had a name?"

As Asahel drew nearer, Brent lifted a heavy booted foot. It came down on Jake's abdomen, pinning him to the ground. Brent raised the gun, pointing it directly at Asahel's chest.

"Don't come any closer."

"Asahel, stop," Jake warned.

Asahel continued forward.

When Jake saw Brent's grip on the gun tighten, he grabbed the booted ankle, throwing Brent to the ground. The two men rolled, fists flying, while Jake tried to wrestle the gun out of Brent's hands.

Suddenly a *rat-tat-tat* split the air.

Asahel let out a scream of pain and crumpled to the ground.

Reflexively Jake let go to rush to Asahel.

Free of Jake's hold, Brent stood, then backed away, holding the gun on both of them.

"Get away from her," he ordered.

Jake ignored him.

Blood seeped through the thigh of Asahel's khaki pants. Ripping the pant leg open, Jake breathed a sigh of relief when he saw the wound. A bullet had nicked her skin, leaving a deep gouge two inches long. Painful but not dangerous. However, in this instance it had succeeded in endangering both Asahel and Jake. For now, with his rifle held above their heads, Brent had regained control of the situation.

"You heard me," he yelled. "Get away from her."

Jake had removed his shirt and wrapped it around Asahel's thigh. Now both of them sat, side by side on the ground, staring up at the rifle and a man who, strangely enough, looked like *he'd* been the one shot.

Studying him, Jake suddenly realized why. And why Brent had risked starting a fire that might draw them to him.

"You're sick," Jake said. "Aren't you? Malaria."

Brent had begun shaking.

"Fucking Hughes left me without any of those pills. This started a couple days ago. When I realized I was being followed, I was hoping it was you. Where's your black bag? What do you have to treat me?"

Next to Jake, a twistedly vicious laugh issued from Asahel.

"Shut up," Brent said, shoving the gun's barrel directly in her face. Asahel did not flinch.

"You never could stand to be sick," she said. "You were always a coward. I've seen people die of malaria." She smiled, a slow, merry smile. "It's a terrible way to die."

Brent's mouth tightened in anger.

"It's not me who's gonna die now, Ash. Say good-bye to your pal here. I'm gonna keep him around for a few more days, just till I'm sure I'll make it out of this hellhole. But you, I've never had any use for you. Just like Dad never did. This will be an early Christmas present for him."

"You don't have the guts to do it," Asahel said.

Brent cocked the gun.

Jake quickly jumped up, shielding Asahel.

"You hurt her," he said, glaring at Brent, "and you die, too. I won't lift a hand to save you."

Brent shoved the barrel of the gun into Jake's shoulder.

"In that case, all I need is your bag. Now get it."

"You find it," Jake replied. "But even if you do, there's nothing in there that can help you."

He sensed the truth in Asahel's taunt—about Brent's cowardice—and decided to play upon it.

"I've treated malaria before. Asahel's right. It's a hideous disease. Before you make it back to civilization, you'll get so sick you'll need fluids, so sick you won't be able to walk. Or even handle a boat. You need me to stay alive. And the only way I'll help you is if you let her live. Do you understand?"

Brent and Asahel stared each other down silently. Jake had never seen such hatred.

"Besides that," Jake pressed, "Hughes wouldn't want you to kill me. He needs me. He needs TS 47. So you see, you can't kill me, and I won't let you kill her."

"Don't bullshit me," Brent said, finally breaking gaze with his sister. "You already signed TS 47 over to Hughes."

"The version of TS 47 Hughes had me sign over to him was the first version. Why do you think I went along with him without even putting up a fight? It'll be useless with G32. It's the newer version Hughes wants. The version my father and I developed right before his death. Hughes still needs me."

Asahel finally broke her silence.

"It's not Hughes he's working for."

Jake turned and stared at her.

"That's crazy. I was with them. He's Hughes's guide."

Asahel's eyes never left her brother.

"I don't know what the hell he was doing with Hughes, but believe me, he was working for my father."

Brent's chuckle could only be interpreted one way. As a confirmation.

"You've always been the smart one, haven't you?" he said to Asahel. "Too smart for your own good."

He turned to Jake now.

"She's right. Hughes thought I was working for him, but I was there for my father. To keep an eyes on Hughes, and make sure he didn't get his hands on G32."

"None of this makes sense."

Asahel's next statement left Jake slack-jawed.

"Oh, it make sense all right. You see, our mother is blind."

"YOUR MOTHER?" JAKE REPLIED. "She has something to do with all of this?"

"Something?" Brent's laugh came out as a snort. "Try *everything*."

"Mother lost her sight a long time ago," Asahel added. "For years Dad obsessed about finding the cure." She paused. "But I thought he'd given up."

"Hardly," Brent said. "Remember when you came back from Brazil and told Angie and me about the tribe with blue eyes?"

Asahel felt her gut tighten. She did not want to hear this. She dared not make the connection, for she knew that it carried the potential to shatter her.

"Yes," she said, sounding suddenly tentative.

"Well, Dad almost lost it when I told him," Brent said. "Even back then, he knew the Naua's blue eyes had value. It's all he talked about. He assigned a special team to look into it. Then researchers at USC discovered G32. That's when Dad got me on the Lost Tribes Project. So that I could locate the Naua for him, and direct his researchers to other remote tribes."

"You worked on the Lost Tribes Project?" Asahel asked, her voice rising shrilly. "For Diego Cavallero? *You* were the American?"

Brent's chest rose visibly with the pride he felt.

"Yeah, I worked for that holier-than-thou son of a bitch. It was the perfect fit. I directed Dad's scientists to the Naua and a bunch of tribes. A fucking gold mine of DNA."

Asahel's mind spun with the horror of what she was hearing. The braggadocio in Brent momentarily allowed him to forget his illness. He couldn't get the words out fast enough.

"Then the plane carrying the Naua blood crashed on its way out of here. Dad was furious. He'd lost G32.

"But I kept hearing rumors down here, from the natives, about a lone blue-eyed woman wandering the *varzea*. And Dad heard that Torrell Hughes was heading down here to look for G32, so he came up with a brilliant plan: for me to contact Hughes and volunteer my services, as a guide."

Jake's mind whirred with the implications of Brent's story.

"What if Hughes had found Caina?" he asked. "What if we'd been successful in getting our hands on G32?"

Brent smirked.

"That's what I was there for," he said. "Just in case Hughes happened to succeed. If he had, he'd never have made it out of here. Neither would you. You see, Dr. Skully, my father's a brilliant man, and a man still deeply in love with his wife. Nothing—not you, not Hughes—would stand in the way of Project Greta. Nothing will stop him from finding a cure for my mother."

"Project Greta?" Asahel gasped. Suddenly Toby's last words to the EMT made sense. That's what Toby had come to tell her that day. About Philip Esser's efforts to find G32.

Asahel fell to her knees and buried her head in her hands.

All the anger, the grief, the speculation . . . only to find that she was to blame for all of it. The Naua slaughter, Toby's death and now Caina's and Zurito's.

It had all started when she came back from Brazil and reported seeing a blue-eyed tribe.

"See what I mean, little sis," Brent said. "You've always been too smart for your own good." He snickered, then looked over at Jake and said, "I wouldn't get too close to her if I were you. Likely to end up a corpse if you do."

Asahel let out a grief-filled sob.

"Shut the hell up," Jake told Brent. "Leave her alone."

When she felt Jake's hand on her shoulder, she lifted her head.

"He's right." She turned to glare at Brent. "Go ahead. What's stopping you? Why don't you tell him about Angie, too?"

Brent only smiled cruelly. Bullets of sweat dripped down his face. Jake could see that delirium was not far away.

With Brent holding a gun on them the entire time, Jake and Asahel silently buried Zurito in the dark. Asahel sat watching Jake pray over the mound, the flickering firelight picking up the tears that dropped from his chin to his folded hands. Finally, she went over to him and pulled him gently away.

For once, in their grief, they were united.

By now Brent had dropped to the ground, leaning against a tree stump with his AK-47 in his lap. He may have given in on the matter of letting Asahel live—though both Jake and Asahel knew that decision would last no longer than until they neared civilization—but he had no intention of relinquishing the AK-47.

But for now, the fever had taken over and he slept fitfully, clutching the automatic. Their odds of disarming him had improved, but before dozing off, Brent informed them that, in anticipation of their finding him, he'd taken steps to ensure they did not try.

"I hid her blood. You won't find it without me," he'd said, his eyelids thick with the sickness.

As they sat side by side, across the campfire from Asahel's own flesh and blood, her *brother*, Asahel felt Jake studying her.

"How could your father hate you?"

Asahel turned to meet Jake's questioning eyes.

From the start, she had been determined to hate him. But the past few hours had radically altered her perception of him, had revealed him to be a man of courage, integrity and humanity. And a man quite capable of suffering, and understanding suffering.

She drew in a deep breath of air and began her story.

•   •   •

"HE DIDN'T ALWAYS," she said. "Hate me, that is. He never loved me; I knew that. But I wouldn't describe what I felt from him growing up as hatred. Resentment, maybe, especially after I moved out and got involved with IPAF. He always said I was just doing it to hurt him. To get back at him."

"Get back at him for what?" Jake asked.

"He never said just what. But I knew. It was for his loving Angie more than me." Jake noticed that Asahel could not look at him. She stared into the fire, as if she were drawing strength from its flames.

"Who's Angie?"

"She was my little sister. Me, he had no time for. Angie, well, that was another thing entirely. For my father, the sun rose and set in Angie."

"And Brent? What about him?"

"Brent's the oldest. My father's not his biological father. My mom had been married once before. Brent always idolized my dad. He wanted his love and approval so damn much. He'd do anything for him."

"Did Brent resent the way your father felt about Angie?"

"I don't think so. And the truth is, while I resented my father, I never resented Angie. It would've been impossible to resent her. I loved her more than anyone in the world. Angie was . . . well, Angie was just about the best thing that ever happened to me. She was just one of those people who see the world through rose-colored glasses. Who want to believe only in the good. I always thought she was naïve, but at the same time, the world always seemed a better place when I was with her. I soaked up being in her presence, like an old dried-up sponge."

It was hard for Jake to understand this young beautiful woman thinking of herself in such terms.

"So what changed things?" Jake asked. "You said your dad didn't always hate you. What made him start?"

Asahel closed her eyes for several seconds. For a moment, Jake thought that she would not go on.

"It happened thirteen months ago," she said. "Almost to the day. It was right after an Ecko gas line explosion in Nigeria that killed five hundred villagers—literally burned them to death while they slept. The oil companies aren't usually a big focus for organizations like IPAF, but Ecko's caused so much suffering for so long. They go into these third world countries and exploit the people, destroy the environment.

They reap billions, yet they won't use a penny of it to help the natives whose lands they're raping. After the Nigerian explosion, IPAF decided it had to do something. The Ecko protest was my idea. My brainchild.

"Ecko's headquarters and biggest plant is located just outside Xalapa. President Bush was down there, in Mexico City, meeting with President Fox. We figured it was the perfect time to draw attention to what had happened in Nigeria, which the U.S. press had hardly picked up.

"The plan was to shut down the plant. We had about fifty demonstrators. Most of them blockaded the entrance and climbed onto the roof of the building and several oil tankers that were sitting outside.

"Four of our group from Seattle prevented tankers from going in and out of the plant by chaining themselves inside two shipping containers we'd bolted to the road. Another group climbed fifty-foot light pylons inside the property and chained themselves to them. They all kept the police and media busy while my group went to work.

"I was on a team of three whose job was to punch holes in the pipeline that runs from the plant to the Gulf. Back in Seattle, before we left, there'd been a lot of discussion about blowing the pipeline up. It was the only way to affect distribution, really hit them where it hurt. But I was set against it. Punching the holes was my idea—a compromise to assuage the more radical elements going down there, without endangering anyone. Or so I thought."

She paused now, clearly tortured by the mental road she'd started down. Jake sat, silent. He knew the leap of faith Asahel had already shown by confiding in him. He would not pressure her to continue.

She surprised him when she did.

"We'd taken a Jeep into the backcountry, the hills behind the plant. We could hear helicopters—the media had been alerted in advance—so we had to work fast. We split up.

"Angie was supposed to be back in Seattle. I'd been trying to talk her into getting involved with IPAF. I thought maybe coming to Mexico, seeing things firsthand, might make an impression on her. But she'd turned me down. She knew IPAF's position on the pharmaceutical industry and she wasn't willing to upset Dad. I never even dreamed she'd changed her mind. That she'd follow me . . .

"We had these two-way radios with us. I was calling the shots. The sun was beating down; the helicopters sounded closer and closer. I'd sent one of my colleagues, Alain Wooley, up ahead, in the Jeep. He was supposed to punch the last hole in the line, then get back to where

I was cutting mine and pick me up. We'd been warned not to use the two-ways around the gas leaks, but I could hear the helicopters getting closer and closer. I started panicking. I radioed Alain to come and get me. The next thing I knew there was this unbelievable explosion. It threw me back; then it rippled down the line like a derailed freight train.

"Alain showed up right away and picked me up. We were both okay. But as we approached the plant, we could see sirens, and lights. Someone had been hurt, walking alongside the line. It wasn't until we got right up there that I saw her.

"It was Angie. She died instantly. She'd been coming out to find me. She'd asked several of the demonstrators where I was, and someone who recognized her as my sister finally told her where I'd gone."

"So you see, I killed my own sister," Asahel said, finally turning to face him. "That's why my father hates me."

Jake closed his eyes momentarily and took several deep breaths. He didn't even realize the words had left his mouth.

"Like Michael hates me."

"Your son?"

"Yes. He blames me for Ana's death."

Asahel studied him.

"Maybe we're not so different after all."

Jake met her gaze.

"Maybe not." He paused. "But this isn't about me. Tell me, why would your father hire you if he hates you? Why would he want you to work for him?"

Asahel's expressionless face finally cracked, with the bitter hint of a smile.

"To keep an eye on me. Now I realize why it was so important for him to get me out of IPAF. He apparently had plans to come into the Amazon, the very region in which IPAF was most active. He always said I was too much like him—that if anyone could bring him down it was me. And he hated the publicity factor: the activist daughter out to destroy her father. He knew the media would pounce on it."

"But why would you do it?" Jake asked. "Why would you go to work for him, in light of how you feel about the pharmaceutical industry?"

Asahel's face returned to its blank, emotionless stare.

"Because he blackmailed me."

The pause lasted so long that Jake felt certain this time Asahel would not take the story back up again.

But she did.

"That day, the day of the explosion, I was thrown in jail. The Mexican police wanted to charge me with Angie's murder. I was in shock, brokenhearted over Angie and incapacitated with guilt. I didn't think things could get any worse. And then they did.

"They put me in a cell by myself. That night, four guards took turns raping me. It went on for hours."

Jake cringed at the image these words conjured.

"The next day my father showed up. He'd already had an investigator following me around, back in Seattle. They had tapes of conversations I'd been involved in about blowing up the pipeline, punching holes in it. They'd edited them, edited out any indication I'd been opposed to blowing it up. From the tapes my father brought with him, it looked like I'd planned the whole thing. Planned the explosion. If the Mexican authorities got hold of them, I'd have spent the rest of my life in prison.

"My father offered me an out that day. He told me he could get me off. It's easy to pay off those small town Mexican cops. He told me he'd withhold the tape. On one condition. That I give up my activism. Once and for all. And that I go to work for him.

"I said yes. I would have done anything at that moment to get out of that prison. Away from those guards. But I had no intention of going to work for him. No, I planned on coming home and ending it. Committing suicide."

"No!" Jake cried.

Asahel did not even seem to hear.

"But then, after I got home, I realized that my killing myself would accomplish nothing besides letting my father off the hook. He would've won. And I wasn't going to let that happen.

"So you see, I killed the only person whom I really loved in this world. The only person who really loved me. I killed Angie."

Jake placed his hand on Asahel's.

It surprised him when she did not pull her own out from under it.

Neither he nor Asahel had been aware that Brent's eyes had rolled open until his voice, derisive and shaded with humor, shattered their silence.

"Actually, that's not exactly how it all happened."

Asahel jerked her hand free of Jake's and turned hateful eyes on her brother.

"What do you mean?"

"You didn't kill Angie," Brent said. "In a way, Dad did. He planned the explosion. He'd had you followed, knew you were planning to punch holes in the pipeline. But he thought an explosion would get you in enough trouble that you'd finally decide to get out of that activism shit once and for all. Last thing he ever expected was for Angie to be there, for Angie to get hurt. That about killed the old man. But Angie'd found out about his plan. She was going down there that day to warn you."

Like a bull taunted by a waving red flag, Asahel was on her feet and charging Brent so quickly that he didn't even have time to lift his rifle in defense.

Flailing at him, she screamed, "You bastard. You knew all along? You knew that it wasn't my fault, and you let me live with thinking I'd killed Angie?"

Brent pushed her away roughly, sending her flying backward.

"You did kill her. If it weren't for all your goddamn activist bullshit, Angie'd still be alive. I wish Dad had never bailed you out of that Mexican jail. I wish those guards were still gang-banging you."

Jake jumped up and grabbed Brent by the shoulders.

"That's enough," he yelled, shaking him.

Brent lifted the AK-47, smashing it into Jake's crotch. With a groan, Jake fell to the ground.

"This is between me and my sister," Brent railed. "You hear?"

Asahel had not moved from where she half lay, half sat on the ground. Her eyes bored into Brent, demanding the entire truth.

"Why didn't he just leave me there?"

"You know what happens to activists that end up in jail. They become fucking heroes. Celebrities. It would have drawn too much attention to Dad and to Mercy, and what he was doing down here, in the Amazon. He figured the best way to shut you up was to have the guards scare the living shit out of you, so you'd do just anything to get out of there and stay out. Even work for him."

For the first time, the fire left Asahel's voice. It came out weak, defeated.

"Dad had the guards rape me?"

Brent chuckled.

"He paid them good money," he said, and then added, "though from what we heard later, he wouldn't've had to."

CHAPTER **FORTY-FIVE**

JAKE ROLLED TO his knees, crippling pain still shooting through his gut.

"No more," he said, rising to his feet, then stumbling toward Brent. "She's heard enough."

Brent turned the raised gun in Jake's direction, but his eyes stayed fixed on Asahel.

Her brother's depraved story had managed to do what a plane crash and broken arm hadn't—reduce Asahel to a shaking, broken-spirited shadow of her usual self.

She sat on the ground, knees hugged tight to her chest, arms covering her head.

A torrent of sick laughter pealed from Brent at the sight.

When he heard that—the laughter—Jake lost it. He charged, swinging, indifferent to the gun, and landed a right hook squarely on Brent's jaw.

"I told you to shut up."

Holding one hand to his jaw, Brent lifted the gun with the other and glared at Jake.

"Don't think I won't kill you."

"You won't."

Jake took a step toward Brent, his hand extended.

"Give it to me."

Brent looked panicked, but then a sudden sick glint lit his eyes. Instinctively, even before Brent pivoted, Jake saw it coming.

He dived for Brent's legs, knocking him off-balance, just as Brent turned the gun on Asahel. It went off.

The volley of bullets sang over Asahel's head, missing her by inches.

As they fought for the gun, Jake could feel that the malaria and their earlier struggle had sapped Brent's strength. It didn't take much to wrestle the rifle free.

Once he did, Jake stood over Brent, who lay on the ground.

"Any piece of shit who could kill his own sister isn't worth saving," Jake said.

He lifted the gun. Pointed it at Brent's forehead.

"Jake, don't," Asahel screamed from behind.

"I'm sorry. I know he's your flesh and blood, but he's left me no choice."

"Don't you think I want him dead?" Asahel's voice drew nearer, until finally she spoke into his ear. "Don't you think I'd like to pull the trigger myself? But no matter how worthless he is, you'll never be able to live with yourself if you kill him."

"I won't be able to live with myself if this scumbag gets loose. If he hurts you, or anyone else."

The force of Asahel's grip on Jake's shoulders surprised him.

"Then let *me* do it," she said calmly. "Give me the gun."

Ignoring her, Jake kicked at Brent. He'd made up his mind. There was no talking him out of it now.

"Get up. I want to look into your eyes when I kill you. Did *you*? Did you look Caina in the eyes when you slit her throat? Or had you already carved them out?"

He kicked Brent's back again, harder this time.

"Answer me."

A low, animal-like moan rose from the dirt.

"You can't kill me," Brent moaned. "You need me."

"Need you? How could anybody need scum like you?"

"I can testify against Hughes."

"I don't need your testimony. I saw it all. Everything you saw."

"No, I don't mean on the trip." Brent lifted his head and trained terrified bleary eyes on Jake. "I can testify about your wife."

The words hung in the air, expanded, until they filled every crevice and cranny and barren branch in the forest. And then they filled the sky.

Slowly, Jake handed the gun to Asahel, then reached down and jerked a pathetically limp Brent up by the shirt collar.

Holding Brent's face within inches of his own, Jake tightened his grip with each word.

"What . . . do . . . you . . . know . . . about . . . my . . . wife?"

Brent shook his head weakly.

"If I tell you now," he said hoarsely, "you won't have any reason to keep me alive."

Jake's hands closed around Brent's neck.

"Tell me, you son of a bitch. Tell me or die."

Brent's eyes flickered, rolling back in his head as his brain searched for oxygen.

"Keep me alive," he whispered to Jake. "Get me to a hospital. . . . Then I'll tell you."

FOR THE NEXT TWO days, the trio made frustratingly slow progress through the forest, with Brent complaining that he felt too ill to hike more than a couple hours at a time and Asahel, limping from her leg wound and still reeling from her brother's revelations, mostly silent.

On the third day, the day they reached the river, Brent developed shaking chills and an intense headache. His fever climbed to 105 degrees.

As Jake loaded their minimal supplies and precious cargo—Caina's blood samples and her carefully preserved eyes—into the boat, Asahel stared at her brother, who lay on the shore, oblivious to the army of ants that swarmed over his pant legs.

Without expression, she asked, "Will he die?"

Jake brushed the ants off Brent and in one sweeping motion hoisted Brent over his shoulder.

"It depends on a lot of factors, including what strain he has. I'm watching for delirium. Only two kinds of malaria cause it, and they can both be fatal."

Asahel helped Jake settle Brent in the prow of the boat, where the breeze would cool him. Jake rigged a small tent of mosquito netting around him.

Brent never fully woke.

By late that afternoon, he began ranting incoherently, then falling into fitful sleep.

Delirium had set in.

Whether prompted by the realization that her brother hovered near death or out of consideration for Jake, who had his hands full tending to a critically ill patient while navigating the river, Asahel began helping more with Brent's care.

At one point, his thrashing pushed aside the mosquito netting.

Asahel knelt over him to straighten it, and Brent's eyes popped open.

"Angie?"

Asahel physically recoiled, withdrawing her hand.

"No," she said, her voice barely containing her rage. "Remember? I killed Angie."

"Oh," Brent mumbled in a moment of clarity. "It's you."

Asahel pushed herself away.

"You son of a bitch. I should just let you die."

JAKE DIDN'T TRUST HIMSELF to navigate the treacherous waters at night. When the sun set, they pulled the skiff up on a patch of white sand and made camp.

Leaving Asahel by the fire, Jake went to check on Brent, in the lean-to they'd built several yards away. He found Brent semialert.

"Am I gonna die?" Brent murmured as Jake crouched beside him, checking his vitals.

His temperature had come down to 102. But sweat still poured from Brent's cheeks and the eyes looked unfocused. His color had not improved.

Malaria attacks came and went. Despite the drop in temperature, Brent hovered near death.

Jake's silence unnerved Brent.

"Am I dying?" he repeated, his voice cracking.

Jake's hatred for this man made it difficult to even look at him.

"What do you know about my wife?"

Brent turned his head away, pressing his lips and eyes closed tightly.

"I want answers," Jake said through a clenched jaw. "Now."

Brent did not respond.

Jake stared at the bag of fluid lying next to Brent. Brent needed the bag. Without it, tomorrow's heat could send him into organ failure.

Jake stood.

Brent's eyes fluttered open.

"You're going to give me those fluids, aren't you?"

Jake glanced back, over his shoulder, at Asahel.

"I won't make another move to help you until you answer a question for me."

The tremor in Brent's voice betrayed his nervousness. But he'd found the only way to force Jake's cooperation and he knew better than to give it up.

"And I won't tell you what I know about your wife until we make it back to Manaus."

"It's not about Ana," Jake replied.

Brent eyed him warily.

"What?"

"What happened to Doc du Pont?"

A look of panic crossed Brent's glazed eyes.

"Hughes did it. You gotta believe me. He saw du Pont come to your room that night. He was sure you were up to something. He knocked him unconscious and threw him overboard."

Jake stood and turned his back to Brent, both fists clenched.

"You have to save me," Brent cried. "Don't let me die. Not here. Not this way."

Slowly, Jake turned back to face him.

"You're right. I have to save you."

He reached for the fluids. As he inserted the IV in Brent's arm, Brent grew silent, absorbing the reality of what lay ahead if he did live.

He wasn't through negotiating yet.

"If you turn me in when we get back, the authorities will take the samples. Have you thought about that? You'll go home without G32. You'd better think about that."

Jake had already considered this. If Jake turned Brent in, Brazilian authorities would never let Jake leave the country with the samples.

That meant there were only two ways that Jake could take G32 home. If he didn't turn Brent in to the authorities once they got back to Manaus. Or if Brent died.

And there was apparently only one way that Brent would tell Jake what he knew about Ana. And that was if Jake kept him alive.

Brent had figured this out, too.

"It's a nasty situation," he said, his voice lightening. "Isn't it?"

"Listen, you piece of shit, I'm done playing your games. Do you actually think I'd let a cold-blooded murderer like you go free?"

Brent reached out and grabbed Jake's bare forearm.

"Don't be such a fool. If Hughes found her first, he was planning to do the same thing. Why do you think he had me buy the AK-47?"

Physically repulsed by Brent's touch, Jake ripped his arm loose.

"You expect me to believe these scientists are all so ruthless they're willing to murder entire populations in order to keep their competitors from beating them to a patent?"

Brent managed a chuckle.

"This isn't about two pharmaceutical companies trying to get an edge on each other. Dad and Hughes aren't just business competitors."

"What is it about, then, Brent?" Jake turned to see Asahel standing directly behind him. "What are Dad and Hughes?"

"You really don't know, do you?" A sneer crossed Brent's face.

"Course, you were just a kid. But it went on for years. Hell, sometimes I think it's still goin' on."

"What?" Asahel asked. "What went on?"

"Their affair."

Asahel rocked back on her feet.

"Whose affair?"

As sick as he was, Brent did not let it rob him of the pleasure of the moment. His smile split his face as he fixed his gaze on his sister.

"Our beloved mother," he answered. "And Torrell Hughes."

JAKE AWOKE TO ASAHEL shaking his shoulders.

"What? What is it?"

"Shhhh," she whispered, eyeing her brother, who had fallen back into a stupor. "Follow me."

They slipped out of the lean-to.

Grabbing Jake by the hand, Asahel led him to the water's edge. The moon's light danced on its waves, allowing Jake to see that in her other hand Asahel carried his medical bag.

She placed the bag on the sand and bent over it, rummaging inside.

"What are you doing?"

When Asahel stood, she held a short length of rubber tubing that Jake used to take blood samples.

"Put it on me," Asahel ordered, extending her arm with the inside of her elbow facing Jake.

"I don't understand."

"Take my blood."

Jake felt a momentary panic. He reached out and placed his hand flat on Asahel's forehead.

"Are you okay?" he asked.

Asahel pushed the hand away and bent to look inside the bag again.

When she found a needle and syringe, she thrust them in Jake's hand.

"Sample my blood," she ordered. "Quick, before he wakes up."

"Why would I want your blood?"

"To substitute it for Caina's."

Suddenly Jake understood.

This warrior woman who'd come all the way to the Amazon to avenge the death of two friends, to destroy researchers like Jake, who sampled the blood of indigenous people, was now offering to become his accomplice.

"You mean . . . ?"

"Yes," Asahel replied, for once not shying away from Jake's intense scrutiny.

"So that you can take Caina's blood back to the States with you. So you can use it to help your son see again."

BRENT'S CONDITION DECLINED markedly the next morning. As they raced downriver, toward Manaus, he had few lucid intervals over the next two days.

"You have to talk to Michael Sullivan for me, Ash," he said during one.

Asahel ignored him.

"You have to get him to cut me a deal. I can give him all the proof he needs about what Hughes and the others were up to, so long as they let me off easy."

"What about Dad?" Asahel asked, toying with him. "Will you tell them everything about Dad, too?"

"Dad, too," Brent replied eagerly. "I'll tell them everything they want to know. Will you do that, Ash? Will you help me?"

"Please, Ash," Brent sobbed, when she did not respond. "I'm your brother. It was all Dad's idea, not mine. Angie would want you to help me."

Sobbing, he'd slipped back into a semiconscious state.

They entered Manaus that night.

As they drifted toward the public docks, Jake gave the wheel to Asahel and went to where Brent dozed at the front of the boat. He grabbed his shoulders, shaking him.

"What . . ." Brent mumbled, only half-conscious.

"I got you here," Jake said. "You made it. Now tell me. What do you know about my wife?"

Brent's eyes squinted as he tried to orient himself. They strayed to the lights, several hundred yards ahead. Manaus.

"Will you let me go if I tell you?"

Jake winced. He'd known this would come.

"That wasn't the deal. The deal was I get you here alive. To Manaus."

Suddenly Jake felt Asahel's hand on his shoulder. She'd left the boat idling. She leaned over Jake, bringing her face close to her brother's.

"Tell him, Brent," she said. "Tell him and we'll let you go."

Jake looked up at her, his eyes having trouble focusing.

"Asahel . . ." Jake said. What was she doing? They couldn't just let Brent go.

She squeezed his shoulder, silencing him.

As Brent's head cleared of its fog, a smile spread slowly across his washed-out face.

"You really expect me to believe you?" he said, a sick smile swallowing the rest of his features. "That you two do-gooders would let me go?"

Ready to explode, Jake shook him again.

"Tell me, dammit."

Brent's eyes rolled shut. He moaned and fell back to the floor of the boat.

"Fuck you."

Jake stood, staring at Brent. Then, slowly, he turned and returned to the captain's chair.

Gunning the boat's motor, he roared up to the deserted floating market, jumped out of the boat and bounded up the steps in search of a public phone.

As SHE SAT IN the boat waiting for Jake to return, Asahel's heart pounded ferociously against her ribs.

Could they pull this off?

Before reaching Manaus, with Brent unconscious at the front of the boat, they'd removed two vials of Caina's blood from the cryo-cooler and replaced them with the two vials Jake had drawn from Asahel.

Jake watched as Asahel slid one vial between her breasts and the other inside the front of her panties.

She'd come to the Amazon determined to destroy Jake Skully.

Now that Caina was dead, now that she had all the answers she'd come for, Asahel's greatest fear was that Jake would go back to Seattle without G32.

She rationalized that her feelings came from her need to see something positive come out of all the evil and suffering she'd witnessed.

She was not yet ready to face the fact that her feelings for Jake played any role.

As she watched Jake descend the stairs, Asahel became aware of sirens in the distance. They grew louder as they approached the market. Soon flashing red lights lit the night and the water, which reflected them.

Manaus police.

Asahel looked at Brent, who awoke with a start and cowered at the front of the boat.

"Who'd you call?" he screamed at Jake. "What's going to happen to me?"

A team of six uniformed men, guns drawn, ran down the steps in SWAT team style as Jake headed to meet them.

"There are four vials of blood in there," Brent cried, pointing to the cooler. "And her eyes. They did it. And now they're trying to frame me."

The officer in charge visibly startled at the disclosure, then looked from Brent, to Asahel, to Jake, trying to make sense of the scene. His eyes came back to rest on Brent.

"Take him to the station."

Two armed officers had to literally pull Brent out of the boat and onto the dock, where they read him his rights. He was being charged with murder.

"Ash, don't let them take me," Brent cried as they led him away. "You know what they say about prisons in countries like this. You can't let them take me."

Keenly aware of the two hidden vials pressed against her clammy flesh, Asahel watched the two hefty men carry her brother up the stairs.

The officer in charge now turned to Asahel and Jake.

"I'm afraid you two must also accompany us to the station."

"What for?" Asahel asked. "We've done nothing wrong. I'm an investigative reporter. I accompanied Dr. Skully down here to write about biopiracy. To tell the world about researchers who prey on your people."

The officer eyed her suspiciously.

"In that case," he replied, "we would be most interested in your information."

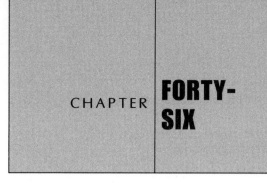

CHAPTER **FORTY-SIX**

AT 3:00 A.M., only a skeletal force staffed the Manaus police department. The officers who'd dragged Brent up the stairs had gone out on another call, leaving only the chief and one other man to deal with their three new American interests.

The chief allowed Asahel and Jake to place a single call while he handled Brent's booking.

Asahel stared numbly through the plate glass at her brother, who alternately sobbed, then turned to mouth—first angry, then pleading—words at her, which, thankfully, she could not hear.

Ever since they arrived at the station, Jake had been digging in the pockets of his shirt and pants. Finally, he produced a business card.

When Randall Oates strolled into the station just ten minutes later, he appeared amazingly good-natured about being awakened in the middle of the night.

"Good to see you, mate," he said, laying a big hand on Jake's shoulder. He quickly took in Asahel, then turned to the chief, who had just reentered the room after sending Brent back to a cell.

"Jefe Urbina," he said. "It's good to see you again. These people, they are your country's friends. They put their own lives in danger to expose their fellow countrymen. I can vouch for them."

Chief Urbina's demeanor softened with Oates's arrival. Still, he eyed Jake with suspicion and Asahel with curiosity.

"We will need to take their statements," he said. "As well as any other evidence they might have to back up this story they tell about the Naua."

Urbina could not keep his eyes off Asahel.

Jake knew at that moment that he'd made a terrible mistake allowing Asahel to risk being arrested by letting her conceal the vials. He could see the absolute terror in her eyes. He recoiled to think of the memories that had to be running through her mind at that moment.

"Randall," Jake said, motioning the huge Australian aside. "Just get her out of here," he whispered, nodding toward Asahel. "I'll stay. I'll answer any questions. Just get her out."

"Hang tight a moment, mate," Randall replied. He patted his pockets, which Jake suddenly noticed bulged softly. "I came prepared."

"Jefe Urbina." Oates returned to where the officer stood. "May I have a word with you in private?"

The two men disappeared into a cluttered office, closing the door behind them.

Jake lowered himself onto the bench next to Asahel and took her hand, clasping it tightly to stop its shaking.

"I won't let them separate us. If they try, I want you to run. Do you hear? I'll keep them distracted. Don't look back. Don't wait for me. Just go. Find your way to the Australian embassy."

Asahel closed her eyes and nodded.

"I DON'T KNOW HOW to thank you."

Randall Oates towered over them in the light of the street lamp.

"No need, mate. That's what friends are for. But I'd suggest you stay somewhere out of the way tonight, then hop the first flight out of the country. Just in case our buddy, Chief Urbina, has a change of heart."

Asahel's eyes glistened as she silently stepped forward and embraced Oates.

"Hop in," the gentle giant said, motioning toward a black Ford Taurus. "I'll give you a lift to a motel."

He dropped them at a small hostel downtown, near the opera house.

When the clerk asked how many rooms they wanted, Jake replied, "Two."

But Asahel grabbed his arm.

"Please," she said. "I don't want to be alone."

The clerk, a leathery-skinned woman who was clearly indifferent as to their decision, simply stared expectantly, waiting for an answer.

"Make that *one*," Jake said.

THEY CLIMBED ON THE bed, fully clothed, too exhausted to shower. Too drained to speak.

Asahel slid under the sheet. Jake did not.

He watched her as she lay there, her back to him, her shoulders rising with each breath. When they fell into a soft, steady rhythm, he reached across her shoulder to turn off the lamp on the bedside table. As he did so, Asahel's hand reached for his, pulling it to her chest, where she hugged it tightly.

Jake wondered briefly if she might still be asleep.

He hugged her back, drawing his body up close, molding it to hers.

They fell asleep like that, Jake's arm around her, Asahel still clutching his hand to her chest.

Sometime during the night, Jake woke.

He lifted himself up on his elbow. In the stripes of light falling across the bed from the window blinds, he studied Ashael's face.

The strain had left it. The pain and grief and anger. He imagined this was how she'd looked before her world turned so cruel and ugly.

Gently he freed his hand from hers and, with the back of it, stroked her cheek.

Asahel's eyes opened at his touch. She turned to gaze up at him. Jake couldn't read her emotions. When she placed a hand on each side of his face, he bent to kiss her.

At the touch of his lips, she stiffened. Jake pulled back.

"I'm sorry," she said. "I haven't been with anyone since—"

"We don't have to," Jake whispered.

She looked at him with an expression of longing that stirred him, reawakened parts of him he thought had died with Ana.

"*I* do," she replied.

There was no more discussion, no more thinking. Perhaps because they knew that to do either might alter the next few hours before sunrise—perhaps even the rest of their lives.

Jake led Asahel to the shower, where they undressed each other. Gently he washed the dirt and pain and fear from her skin. He kissed the ugly black bruises still remaining from the plane crash she'd finally described to him as they floated down the Purus.

She had held back the tears when discussing Diego Cavallero, but Jake could see the effort it took. He had marveled at the courage and determination of this young woman. At her willingness to risk her life in order to fulfill a promise she'd made to a woman who showed up, uninvited, on her doorstep.

And now he marveled at her physical beauty. Her hair cascaded in ringlets all the way down to her small, perfectly formed breasts. Her skin—where it hadn't burned and freckled—was cream-colored and had the feel of silk.

Jake pulled her to him and took her face in his hands. She'd had her head thrown back in pleasure and her eyes closed, but now she opened them.

"You are so lovely," he said.

She turned away and began to cry, but Jake would not allow it. He kissed the tears, then her neck, then down her flat abdomen. He made her forget the pain.

Was it wrong to make love in the face of so much evil, so much suffering? When your beloved wife and soul mate had been dead less than a year?

Before this moment, Jake would have answered yes.

But he'd learned something, an important lesson, that he doubted would ever leave him. A lesson taught to him by the Amazon.

On the surface, there appeared to be only one rule in the Amazon, a premium on only one thing. Survival. Life did not come in a neat package; it had no set order, appeared to bear no mandates other than the instinct to survive.

But those living in the Amazon had demonstrated to Jake one important lesson that the rest of the civilized world apparently had never learned, or else had forgotten.

Survival, in the truest sense of the word, required a loyalty to family and community. It required respect for all forms of life. It required large amounts of heart, and passion. And courage.

Those who lived in the Amazon were always looking over their shoulders, always aware of the fragility of their very existence. A fragility that caused them to cherish their very existence, and every moment of it.

And so, in making love to Asahel, Jake honored those lessons—though none of these thoughts occupied his mind during the few hours in that cramped, musty hotel room. The experience was purely visceral, and spiritual, and immensely pleasurable.

The experience transformed his life.

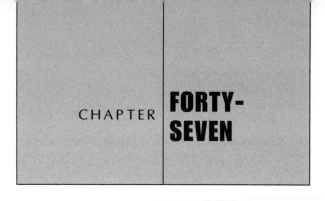

CHAPTER **FORTY-SEVEN**

YOU NEVER HAD any reason to suspect?" Jake asked. "That your mother was having an affair with Torrell Hughes?"

Asahel turned away from the window, where she'd watched the city of Manaus disappear as the plane rose through the layer of high, thin clouds.

"No. Never. I always thought my parents' relationship was odd, but it never occurred to me that there was someone else involved."

"Tell me about your mother," Jake said. "What kind of woman inspires such incredible love that two men will go to such extremes to cure her blindness?"

Asahel grew thoughtful.

"She was incredibly beautiful. She still is. And frail. People always wanted to protect her. Even as a child, I can remember feeling that way, even before she went blind.

"Of course, part of that was because of Mother's asthma. We never knew what would trigger an attack. I remember as a little girl watching her struggle for air and crying my eyes out because I was sure she was dying. It scared me so much, I never wanted to leave her side."

Her words caused Jake to draw in his breath sharply.

No one had to tell him about the terror of a child who fears the loss of a parent. For four days he'd seen that terror in his sons' eyes as the police searched for Ana.

And then the fears became reality, and the terror was replaced by despair.

Jake felt Asahel's hand close over his.

"I'm so sorry," she said. "I wasn't thinking. Are you okay?"

"Yes," Jake replied, but the reminder of those first days, of what Michael and Antony had been through, caused a sudden acute sense of his own despair to descend upon him. Would his two boys ever be the same? Would they ever feel safe, truly happy?

What if G32 failed to cure Michael?

"I think I'll stretch my legs," Jake said, unable to stand the thoughts, the moment.

"Want some company?"

When Jake hesitated, Asahel's lips lifted in a kind smile.

"I understand," she said. "You go ahead. I think I'll try to take a short nap."

Jake leaned over and pecked her on the cheek.

"Thanks."

"YOUR MOTHER HAD ASTHMA?"

Asahel's eyes popped open.

She had no idea how long she'd been sleeping. She'd only used the nap as a way to let Jake off the hook, to give him some space. She could see how upset her comments had made him and she felt terrible about it. She hadn't really expected to doze, but now that the adrenaline that kept her going the past few weeks had dropped to its normal level, she felt exhausted.

"Yes," she answered, shaking her head to clear it. "Why?"

Jake stared at her intensely.

"So does Michael."

Asahel's brow furrowed.

"I don't understand. Why does that matter?"

"Think about it," he replied. "Both Michael and your mother have asthma; then they both lose their sight."

Asahel felt a growing sense of concern about Jake.

"What are you suggesting?"

"Did your mother use an inhaler?"

"Yes. It's the only thing that controlled it." She studied Jake as he stared at the back of the seat in front of him. "What is it? What are you thinking?"

Suddenly Jake slammed his fist down on the armrest between them.

"That's it!"

"You're saying Mother's and Michael's blindness are related?"

"It's too big a coincidence: they both have asthma, then they both lose their sight."

"I agree it's a big coincidence, but one that's easier to swallow than the idea that their blindness is somehow connected. That makes no sense at all. They've never even met. And they went blind more than ten years apart."

"None of that matters," Jake replied. "They never had to meet. There was one common factor, one person who ties it all together."

"Who?"

"Torrell Hughes."

Asahel's mouth dropped open.

"You're right. But how? How could Hughes do it?"

"He had the perfect tool. An inhaler. He'd spent decades learning about genetic damage caused by pollution—air pollution, water pollution. For a man like him, it would be child's play to aerosolize a mutagen." Jake paused. "That's what he was doing with those dogs!"

Asahel shook her head. Things just kept getting crazier.

"*What* dogs?"

"Hughes had these dogs, puppies, that he used to bring to the office. At first they were fine, perfectly healthy. But then they began stumbling into furniture. He was blinding them! Just like he'd blinded your mother, and then Michael."

Jake grabbed hold of Asahel's arm, unaware of how tightly he squeezed it.

"You see," he continued, "before he started GenChrom, Torrell Hughes was a leading expert on environmental mutagens. On the damage they're capable of inflicting on human DNA. Both your mother's and Michael's blindness were caused by damage to their DNA."

"Do we know that for sure?"

"I know it from firsthand research on Michael's DNA. And why else would your father and Hughes be searching for G32? They had to know that your mother's blindness was the result of genetic damage, too."

"But why? Why would he do it? Blind my mother? And then Michael?"

"Your mother, I can only speculate. Maybe because she refused to leave your father for him."

Asahel drew her breath in sharply.

"And maybe now he thinks she will leave him," she said. "If he's the one to find a cure for her."

"Exactly."

"But why Michael?"

"That's easy. Because he needed TS 47 and when I refused to go to work for him he decided to change my mind for me."

Unwelcome as it was, the thought just came to her, entered her mind spontaneously. Instinctively Asahel's hand flew up to cover her mouth.

"What?" Jake asked, his brow furrowed. "Are you all right?"

Asahel had no choice but to answer.

"I asked you once what your wife thought about you going to work for GenChrom. You never answered."

"Ana wouldn't let me accept the job Hughes offered me. She refused to move Michael to Seattle." His scowl deepened. "Why would you ask that now?"

Asahel swallowed.

"Is it possible . . . ?"

The thought was so hideous, she couldn't bring herself to voice it. She did not need to.

Insane rage crept into Jake's eyes, transforming them into spheres of hellish torment. His grip on Asahel's arm came close to crushing it.

"Hughes! He killed Ana. To force me to come to work for him."

"It would fit with what Brent said, what he hinted at."

Within seconds of Jake punching the empty seat in front of him, two flight attendants and three burly passengers descended upon him.

Only after they wrestled him to the ground, only after Asahel explained that he was a medical doctor and that he'd just received shocking news, would they let him return to his seat—with an armed air marshal watching closely from across the aisle.

They made the rest of the trip home in silence.

JAKE KNEW THE MOMENT he pulled into Leah Clay's driveway that something was wrong. Terribly wrong.

No lights. The drapes closed. And a pile of rolled newspapers, wrapped in plastic bags to protect against the rain, lay on the front porch.

With his heart pulsating in his ears, Jake pounded on the door.

"Michael?" he called. "Antony!"

Jake circled the house. At the back of the house, he grabbed a fist-sized rock used as part of a border for the garden. He strode to the back door, the top half of which was glass, shattered the window with the rock and reached inside to unlock it, his hands shaking.

His plan, his entire plan . . .

Once he realized the evil Hughes was capable of, Jake knew that he couldn't afford to do anything until he got Michael and Antony back. Then, he would go after Hughes. If what he suspected was true, if Hughes had killed Ana, only Jake's love and concern for his boys would keep him from killing him.

He'd make sure Hughes paid. He wouldn't rest until the man roasted in hell.

However, there was one thing that troubled Jake. That didn't fit the picture. The letter Ana had written him. A letter apparently so disturbing she'd destroyed it rather than deliver it.

Over the past few weeks, Jake had finally, slowly, come to wonder whether his steadfast denial about Ana committing suicide was based more on rational facts or on his inability to handle the truth. For there was one truth he could not deny: he'd destroyed the most precious thing in the world to both him and Ana—their relationship. As impossible as it would be for Jake to accept, as frightened as it made him for Michael (studies had, after all, shown that suicide sometimes ran in families), perhaps Ana had indeed decided she could never forgive him.

He still couldn't bring himself to believe it, but perhaps Ana had committed suicide.

But Jake knew one thing—he could not afford to get to the truth about Ana's death until he had Michael and Antony back, safe and sound.

As he entered Leah's house and walked from one empty room to another, panic gripped him. Where were his boys?

The first door he opened off the hallway led to a bedroom that clearly belonged to Leah.

He walked down the hall and opened the next door.

Two beds. Both unmade. Lying on one, Michael's portable CD player.

Antony's school bag lay on the floor next to the other bed.

Jake entered the room and bent to pick up the bag.

"So you're back."

Jake jerked around at the sound of a voice.

Torrell Hughes stood in the doorway.

"Where are they?"

Jake started toward Hughes. Then he saw the pistol.

"You just keep fucking up my plans," Hughes said, shaking his head like he was scolding a child. "Don't you? You were never supposed to make it back from the Amazon. By now, I was supposed to have G32, your patent and a nice story about how one of my most valued researchers—that's you, by the way—got eaten by alligators in the godforsaken jungle. It's a dangerous place. Happens all the time. Nobody would've blinked an eye at the story. But you keep screwing everything up."

"Where are my sons?"

"It was a measure I was forced to take," Hughes explained. "When I realized you couldn't be trusted. You knew that version of TS 47 you signed over to me was worthless. Consider this payback. If you cooperate, you'll see your kids again."

"I'll kill you if anything happens to them."

"Sounds like you may have spent a little too much time among those savages."

"How do I get my boys back?"

"Well, for starters, you sign over the most recent version of TS 47. But you won't see either of your kids until you hand over the blood, too."

So Hughes already knew. Brent must have contacted him from Manaus and told him about Caina. But something didn't add up. Brent had no way to know that the blood Brazilian authorities confiscated belonged not to Caina but to his own sister.

"When?" Jake replied. "Where?"

Hughes's eyes lit up. He chuckled in delight.

"You actually have the blood?" he said. "I was just shooting blind. That's fabulous. Fucking fabulous."

"I have it, and I'll turn it over to you, but not until I see that Michael and Antony are okay. Not until I actually have them back."

"To some extent," Hughes said, his eyes still bright with pleasure, "we'll both just have to trust the other, won't we? Leah will be in touch with you."

He turned to leave.

"Hughes," Jake called after him.

He had told himself not to go there, but he couldn't stop himself.

Hughes turned, eyebrow raised.

"You killed my wife, didn't you?"

The smile spread slowly. As if the subject didn't merit his undivided attention, Hughes reached into his pant pocket and withdrew the automatic opener to the Range Rover that sat in Leah's driveway.

"Me?" he said, pressing the button to unlock his vehicle. "Of course not. You should know better than anyone. There's never any need to get your hands dirty down there. Not when Mexican labor's such a good deal."

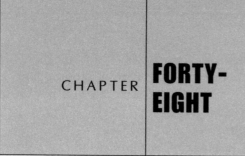

CHAPTER **FORTY-EIGHT**

NOT THIS TIME," Asahel said.

"I told you, you have to stay in the car."

They were on the last ferry from Seattle to Bainbridge Island. The wind swept rain horizontally across Jake's windshield as he sat in his Explorer in the ferry's lower, open section, talking on his cell phone to Asahel, whom he could see two cars behind.

Afraid to trust the authorities, Jake had allowed Asahel to convince him that two sets of eyes and two cars added a measure of security to this mission, but now he regretted allowing her to come along.

"Asahel, you stay in that car. I can't afford for anything—anything—to scare Hughes off. Do you hear?"

Jake hung up and looked at his watch.

Eleven P.M. Hughes had given him explicit instructions to wait until 11:20 (twenty minutes into the thirty-minute ferry ride), then go to the upper deck, where he would be waiting with Antony and Michael.

At 11:17, Jake climbed out of his car and headed up the stairs, briefcase in hand. He did not make eye contact with Asahel when he passed her car.

A third of the ferry's booths in the main floor were filled, mostly with couples returning home from a Saturday night date in the city. Jake strolled briskly to the doors at the rear end and stepped outside.

A gust of rain and wind met him.

Heading up the exterior stairs to the top deck, he passed a steward who looked at him with curiosity.

"Pretty nasty up there."

"Just need some fresh air," Jake replied.

At the top of the stairs, he stopped. Sheets of rain whipped the deck's surface. Not a soul could be seen.

Jake proceeded forward, toward the shielded passenger section. Hughes, Michael and Antony must be waiting there, out of the rain.

He began to run, slipping and falling to his knees.

The rain and lack of illumination—only one light—made vision difficult. Still, as he approached the seating section, Jake could not see anyone through the glass partitions that allowed passengers a view of the Seattle skyline.

Had Hughes double-crossed him?

He rounded the partition, a sense of panic overtaking him.

And then he saw it.

A lone figure, clothed in a parka, hood up over the head.

The figure turned.

"*Leah.*"

Leah Clay rose and strode toward him, her face, to Jake's surprise, a mirror of his own terror.

"Where are the boys?"

"He wants me to bring him the briefcase. He'll release the boys once he verifies that it's really G32."

"No," Jake cried. "You know he'll never do that, Leah. Those boys are his only assurance I won't go to the authorities."

Frantic, he grabbed Leah by the shoulders.

"How could you let this happen?" he said, shaking her.

Leah did not resist.

"Jake," she answered. "Don't mess with him. He's a desperate man. Do what he asks. I'll try to keep the boys safe."

"Yeah, like you kept Michael safe?"

"Jake, that never happened. Michael didn't try to commit suicide. Torrell just used that as a way to pressure you. To make sure you stayed in line."

Jake wanted to strike out at Leah for allowing him to go through the hell of believing Michael had tried to take his life. But right now, she was the sole thread between Michael and Antony and him.

"I can't give you this, Leah. It's all I have to negotiate with him."

Leah Clay looked him in the eye.

"If I return without this briefcase, you'll never see either of your sons again."

Jake knew—intuitively, unequivocally—that she was telling the truth.

He extended his hand with the briefcase.

"What's that?" he asked.

A deep blast from the ferry rumbled through the vessel. Jake looked up to see the lights of the city of Winslow piercing the night's fog. They were almost there.

"Handcuffs," Leah answered. "You have to let me cuff you, to the chairs."

ASAHEL WAITED JUST THIRTY seconds, then followed Jake up the stairs. When she saw him disappear out the main passenger section to the deck, she seated herself in an empty booth, facing the door.

Less than five minutes later, a woman—soaked to the skin and carrying Jake's briefcase—entered the cabin through the door Jake had exited. As she strode past Asahel, she spoke into her cellular phone.

Asahel got up and followed her as she blended into the line of street passengers—those who had not driven onto the ferry.

Asahel fell in line behind Leah Clay, fearing that she stood out too much. All the other foot passengers either wore hooded parkas like Leah's or carried umbrellas.

The ramp for disembarking passengers ended in a parking lot. The passengers dispersed in every direction, most heading to the parked cars, but Leah stood, her eyes scanning the lot.

Asahel distanced herself from Leah and pretended to also be looking for her ride.

A four-door Mercedes pulled slowly into the parking lot, its lights sweeping both Leah's and Asahel's faces. It inched forward cautiously.

Seeing it, Leah stepped off the curb and reached for its door handle.

When she opened the door and the car's lights went on, Asahel gasped.

Two dark-haired boys sat in the backseat.

"Excuse me," Asahel called, stepping up to the woman and grabbing her door, preventing her from closing it behind her.

"Do you think I could bum a ride into town? My boyfriend must have forgotten about picking me up."

Leah looked over to the driver. It had to be Torrell Hughes.

Asahel noticed that the back doors were locked.

When Hughes shook his head no Asahel reached down and pressed the automatic unlock button on the passenger door.

"*Michael, Antony, run,*" she screamed.

Hughes accelerated, dragging Asahel, still clinging to the passenger door, along. Almost immediately the Mercedes rammed into the back of a VW bus stalled at the lot's entrance.

Asahel heard one of the back doors of the Mercedes open.

APRIL CHRISTOFFERSON

"Run, Antony," Michael called. "Don't wait for me."

Antony had jumped out his door and run around to open Michael's.

Asahel jumped free of the car and grabbed Michael, yanking at him in the backseat as Hughes and Leah both tugged on whatever part of him they could get ahold of to keep him inside the car.

"Help," Leah screamed. "She's kidnapping our boys."

Her plea went unheard. The VW screeched out of the lot, which had emptied.

Holding Michael by one hand and Antony by the other, Asahel ran, dragging them back up the now deserted ramp, onto the ferry. They threaded their way through the short line of cars still waiting to disembark until they entered the next level, now completely empty.

Asahel heard footsteps from behind, echoing on the pavement.

"Run, boys," she cried.

A bullet rang out just as they reached the end of the second level of parking. They were trapped.

A second shot rang out, ricocheting off one of the steel beams supporting the upper floor.

"Can you both swim?" Asahel screamed.

Wide-eyed, both Michael and Antony nodded.

"Then jump. Push off, away from the boat. Then swim toward shore. Antony, you go first; then help Michael."

Antony looked behind him in terror, then climbed over the waist-high railing and with one last glance at Michael disappeared into the night.

Asahel helped Michael climb over the railing. Then, with a gentle shove, his form also disappeared.

IT HAD TAKEN several minutes for Jake to get the steward's attention, then a maddening few minutes or so for the boat's mechanic to pry the seat loose from the floor and free Jake.

Suddenly screams filled the air. They were followed closely by gunshots.

The steward, hanging over the top deck's railing, straining to see what was going on, yelled, "Holy shit."

Jake sprinted to the boat's railing just in time to see both his boys disappear into the black waters below.

He kicked off his shoes.

"Sir, you can't do that," the steward yelled. "*Sir.* Get down from the railing."

CHAPTER FORTY-NINE

HUGHES'S HAND PULLED her back from the railing, throwing her violently to the parking deck's floor.

Asahel looked up, right into the barrel of a small revolver and the face of Torrell Hughes.

"Who are you?" Hughes demanded. "What business of yours is this?"

Scooting backward, away from him, Asahel stopped when she came up against the cement half wall. She had nowhere left to go.

"I'm Philip's Esser's daughter," she answered. "Or should I say Greta's?"

Hughes drew back with such force that Asahel thought for a moment he'd been shot.

"You're Asahel?"

Frowning, Asahel nodded.

"Yes."

Hughes's face twisted with rage as he advanced on her.

"You're the one who killed my baby. My Angie."

"*Your* Angie. What are you talking about?"

He grabbed Asahel by her shirt collar and yanked her to her feet. Then he shoved the gun in her face, pressing it against Asahel's forehead.

"Angie was my child. Mine and your mother's. And you killed her."

Stunned, Asahel's eyes widened in horror.

"Brent was right. You and Mother had an affair. You blinded her, didn't you?"

"Since you won't live to tell anyone, I'll answer that. Yes, when she wouldn't leave your father, I blinded her."

"And you're still in love with her."

"In love with her?" Hughes's laugh was so big, so spontaneous, that he momentarily lowered the gun. "I despise the wretched creature. She allowed the only thing in my life that still mattered to be taken from me. She knew what your father was planning that day, and she allowed Angie to go to you, to try to save you."

"But you never even knew Angie."

Hughes looked Asahel in the eye, lifted the gun and pulled back the hammer.

"In my heart I did."

Suddenly another shot rang out, and in the next instant Hughes crumpled to the ground.

He lay on the wet cement, both eyes open, as two police officers ran up to him. One kicked the gun out of his hand. It spun like a top across the pavement.

Wrapping an arm around her shoulders, the other cop tried to guide Asahel away, but she pushed away.

"Two children just jumped in the water," she cried. "I've got to help them."

Grabbing hold of her arm to prevent her from escaping, the officer immediately held a radio to his mouth.

"Two children overboard," he called into it.

The first officer climbed over the railing and, without hesitation, jumped.

Asahel shrugged loose of the officer's grip and fell to her knees at Hughes's side, kneeling over him.

"Don't you die on me," she screamed over the wail of approaching sirens.

"Not before you tell me. If you're not still in love with my mother, why have you been so desperate to find a cure for her?"

A weak smile spread across Hughes's face as all color drained from it onto the parking deck's floor.

"So that I could patent it," he answered softly, his words coming with each exhale. "Then keep it from her . . .

"I did it to make sure she'd suffer . . . for the rest of her life."

CHAPTER **FIFTY**

THE NIGHT HAD come alive with lights and sirens. Asahel raced to the ferry's lowest level and leaned over the railing. Searchlights from several boats skimmed back and forth across the surface of the murky water.

Ambulances waited along the shoreline, their lights blinking out of sync with each other like a poorly timed Christmas display.

Out of the blackness, beyond all the commotion, a voice suddenly called out. A voice Asahel recognized.

"Over here."

The lights played frantically across the water's surface, sweeping in every direction.

"Jake," Asahel screamed.

Fifty yards out, she saw them: Jake swimming, raising one boy's head above the water with one arm, while the other boy followed behind, holding on to his father's shoulder.

The boats went into immediate action.

Asahel watched from the ferry until they'd pulled all three out of the water; then she ran up the stairs to the ferry's belly and raced down the passenger ramp.

By the time she reached them, they'd already loaded both Michael and Antony into the ambulances.

Jake was about to climb in behind them.

Asahel ran to him, grabbing him by the arm.

"Are they all right?"

He turned, and for the first time since that day in the hospital, a broad smile split Jake's face. He grabbed Asahel and pulled her to him.

"They're fine," he told her, stroking her hair. "I have my boys back."

CHAPTER **FIFTY-ONE**

CHARGES SHOULD BE filed later this week," Michael Sullivan announced, slapping shut the thick manila file with the word *Gen-Chrom* printed in bold type on the file's label.

Asahel looked around the office—a small but tidy affair with a row of windows looking down on Elliott Bay. Now that the FBI had become fully involved with the *Biopiracy Scandal*, as the national media had gleefully labeled it, she'd finally agreed to meet Sully on his turf.

It didn't surprise Asahel that Sully's office lacked any hint of his personal life, though there was a framed photograph sitting on his desk, its back to Asahel.

"I read just this morning that Asahel's brother cut himself a deal," Stan Yasavich said. "That he'll walk free. Please tell me that's not true."

A momentary look of disappointment had crossed Sully's face when Stan followed Asahel into his office a short while earlier. The night before, when Asahel and Jake met Stan for dinner, she'd invited him to come along to today's meeting. She hoped that being kept privy to the legal developments in the situation might give Stan some measure of closure.

When she introduced Stan as Toby's partner and, briefly, Caina's caretaker, Asahel was pleased to see Sully clasp Stan's hand warmly.

"I'm sorry about your loss," he'd said. "Please, have a seat."

Now, as he responded to Stan's comment, Sully's eyes traveled back and forth between Asahel and Stan.

"That's partly true," he said. "Brent cut himself a pretty sweet deal. He's given Brazilian and U.S. prosecutors enough details of your father's and Hughes's activities that even when the Brazilians are through with him and he's extradited back home Brent could be a free man in five, maybe seven years."

"But he killed Caina," Asahel cried. "Mutilated her, for God's sake. Five years would be outrage."

Sullivan nodded, his thumb thumping rhythmically on the government issue desk.

"That's true. But he's the best witness to the slaughter of the Naua, and that's what the Brazilian government wants to focus on. There's a lot of discord down there about the constitutional protection given the Indians. Pro-native leaders want to rub what happened to the Naua in the faces of Marco da Luz and all the others who are trying to revoke that protection. Brent can name names, provide details, that only someone who was there would know. The story he'll tell should make the hair of the hardest nosed Brazilians stand on edge. In the long run, more people will pay, more goodwill will come of this this way than if prosecutors throw the book at Brent and he refuses to cooperate."

Asahel reached for Stan's hand and gave it a tight squeeze, knowing the news that her brother had weaseled leniency for his horrific crimes would upset Stan almost as much as it did her.

"What about Hughes?" Asahel asked.

"We're talking to Mexican authorities about Ana de Zedillo's death. It's a touchy situation because it looks like several members of the Nogales police force—Sergeant de Santos in particular—were involved. Hopefully we'll be able to get murder charges to stick. We have no doubt Hughes orchestrated it and paid for them to kill her, then make it look like suicide.

"We're confident about the kidnapping charges for the two Skully boys. And felony assault and battery, based on Hughes's role in causing your mother and Michael Skully's blindness. Those'll be tough charges to prove, but Leah Clay's caved; she's singing like a canary. So has GenChrom's attorney, Gina Castle. Seems Hughes broke her heart and she's ready to do everything in her power to get back at him, including implicating herself in some fraudulent patent applications. They apparently committed so many violations of international protocol in their DNA sampling down in the Amazon that it's taken a whole team of lawyers to sort out the charges there. We should be able to put Hughes away for at least a decade."

Asahel took a deep breath.

"And my father?"

Sullivan's eyes took on a hard edge.

"We've got him, Ash. The information we got off Toby's computer should be enough to send him up for the rest of his life. It's amazing how these big companies think their firewalls are actually impenetrable. But Toby managed to download top secret files that should make it pretty easy for the prosecutor to piece together your old man's plan."

"Which was to sample indigenous populations, looking for G32," Asahel broke in, "then wipe out the ones no one would miss."

"Exactly, so nobody else stood to come along afterward and beat them to a drug based on that tribe's DNA. All of which Brent was able to monitor in his work for the Lost Tribes Project. It's a pretty ingenious plan, if it weren't so sick."

Stan had fallen quiet.

As he leaned forward and directed penetrating eyes at Sullivan, his grasp on Asahel's hand tightened.

"And who pays for Toby's death?"

Sully met his gaze.

"Esser," he said. "And the investigator he hired, the one who discovered Toby was breaking into Mercy's most guarded files. When he heard about that, Esser ordered Toby's death. The investigator followed Toby to Asahel's apartment that night. Best we can figure, Toby was going there to tell Asahel what he'd found when he finally broke through Mercy's firewall."

"Project Greta," Asahel said.

"Yep. Project Greta. Naturally, your father was too high up to ever actually get his own hands dirty, but with the files Toby downloaded, we can make sure he's held accountable for the slaughter of those people—as responsible as if he'd been there, as if he'd been the one pulling the trigger, swinging the blade. He masterminded it; then he picked people he could trust to do the job for him.

"They'll all go down, but your father will be the kingpin. He'll never see the light of day again. In fact, his attorney's talking like your father may admit to a lot of the charges, if we agree not to send him down to Brazil. He knows he'll never be a free man again. Last thing he wants is to die in a prison down there. Things that go on in those places, they're hell, pure—"

A look of horror crossed Sullivan's eyes as they fell on Asahel.

He stood, quickly rounded the desk and dropped on one knee in front of her. He placed both hands on her knees.

"God, Ash, I'm sorry."

Asahel shook her head.

"No, Sully, please, don't be. There's nothing for you to be sorry about. I'm so grateful for all you've done. You'll never know."

Stan leaned back in his chair, trying not to intrude on this intimate moment between two people who obviously still cared for each other.

"You sure you're okay?" Sully asked.

"Yes."

Asahel felt a surge of affection for Sullivan. She reached out and touched the side of his face.

For a moment, she thought he might cry.

Still on one knee, he cleared his throat and began speaking slowly, thoughtfully, the crisp professionalism, for once, gone.

"You know, Ash, I always had a hard time with your activism. I mean, I was born into a patriotic family, real red, white and blue. All I ever wanted was to serve my country, wave the flag, enforce its laws. I may have fallen head over heels in love with you, but the last thing I wanted was to buy into that radical shit you were always talking.

"I never stopped to think that what you do can't exactly be fun. People like you sacrifice a lot. Nobody gets rich, that's for sure. And if you're not thrown in jail for trying to change things, at the very least you're made to look like criminals. You end up on a list in some file like those." He nodded toward a stack of thick files sitting in his in-box. "In the office of somebody like me.

"I always bought into that thinking that being an activist is unpatriotic," he continued. "But I see things in a different light now. I've changed.

"Don't get me wrong, I love my country more than ever, especially after September eleventh, but I see now that loving it doesn't mean you can't criticize it. Turning a blind eye, that's what will hurt this country the most in the end."

Asahel's lower lip began to tremble. She bit down on it.

Her activism had cost her dearly—her family and her marriage. But the worst part had been the isolation. The sense that none of the people she loved most had an inkling—even the tiniest glimmer of understanding—of why she did what she did. Of what made such great loss worth risking.

"Thank you," she said. It came out barely more than a whisper.

"You okay?" Sullivan asked, reaching to wipe a tear that zigzagged its way down her cheek.

Asahel nodded.

She looked over at Stan. He'd pulled a plaid handkerchief out of his jacket pocket. He dabbed quickly at the corner of each eye, then handed the handkerchief to Asahel.

Asahel took it; then she laughed.

"Yes," she said. "I'm definitely okay."

EPILOGUE

ASAHEL."

At Asahel's knock, the door had opened slowly, cautiously.

"How did you know?" Asahel asked.

"I'm your mother," Greta Esser answered. "I may be blind, but I could still pick you out of a crowd."

Asahel did not respond. She stood there, wanting to run. No—despite her anger, despite her mother's long-standing affair, despite learning that her mother had known about but had not stopped her father's plan to sabotage Asahel's protest in Mexico—what Asahel really wanted was to wrap her arms around the mother she hadn't seen since her baby sister's funeral.

As she always had, she wanted to protect her.

"Will you come in?"

Asahel stepped inside, then followed her mother.

Dressed in a white linen shirt and slim black pants, Greta led Asahel into the living room. Her strawberry blond hair, once much like Asahel's, had now turned white, but with it swept up on top of her head Greta still looked like she'd stepped out of the pages of a lifestyles magazine.

The waters of Lake Union glimmered below the immense wall of living room windows like a field of shattered glass, the city's skyline silhouetted against a perfect blue sky.

Greta seated herself in a Queen Anne chair, her back to the windows. Asahel took the chair opposite her.

"How are you, dear?" Greta asked graciously, as though Asahel were a fellow parishioner come to call.

"I'm fine, Mother. I came to see how you're doing." She hesitated. "With Dad gone."

With her back to the bright sun, shadows hid most of Greta's face, but Asahel swore she saw the corners of her mother's mouth lift.

"I'm fine, Asahel. It's quiet here alone. But Patty takes excellent care of me. I'm fine."

Asahel hadn't planned to ask—she'd, in fact, told herself that she would not—but the words simply came, seemingly of their own free will.

"How is Dad?"

"I don't know, dear. I haven't communicated with him."

Asahel paused. Had she heard correctly?

"You haven't been to see him? Or talked to him?"

"No. He's written, but I haven't had Patty read any of his letters to me."

"Do you mind if I ask why?"

Now it was unmistakable, the smile on Greta's face.

She even laughed then.

"What's left to hide?" she answered.

She paused, composing herself.

"I realized something when your father went to prison," Greta said slowly. "That he had cost me everything I hold dear in my life. First Angie. Then you. Now Brent. I blame him for losing all of my children."

Asahel stared at her mother. At the slight quiver of her proud chin.

"And then Torrell."

Asahel drew back.

"*Torrell Hughes?* You're angry with Dad for what happened to Torrell Hughes?"

Greta answered clearly and immediately.

"I still loved him."

"Even after what he did to you?"

"I understood. But of course, that was before the trials. Before I learned what else he'd done, to all those poor people down there. I could never love *that* person. But I still love the Torrell Hughes I fell in love with. I think I always will."

They sat in silence for several minutes. Greta, the proud, grieving mother; Asahel, the angry, confused daughter.

When Greta finally broke the silence, her voice trembled with emotion.

"I don't know how it's even possible to apologize for all that's happened. I brought it all on. It's a terrible burden, but one that I must live with."

She reached out her hand then, reached for Asahel. It hung in midair, Asahel simply staring at it.

And then, slowly, Asahel took it. She clasped it in both of her hands.

"I love you dearly, Asahel," her mother said.

Asahel could not speak.

"I've always had such admiration for you. But you frightened me. I realized long ago that it was because you were the most like me. So strong-willed. So fiery, unwilling to compromise.

"But your compassion, your sense of right and wrong, they exceeded anything I was capable of. You were the only one of us who dared stand up to your father. Silently, I always applauded you for that."

"If only I'd known," Asahel said, her voice bitter and sad at the same time.

"Yes," Greta replied. "If only I'd told you."

Asahel dropped Greta's hand. She stood and walked to the window, arm braced on its frame. She pressed her forehead against its cool glass.

"Are you leaving?" Greta asked.

Asahel turned.

"I came here to tell you something, Mother. Something wonderful."

Greta turned sideways in her chair, as if looking at Asahel.

"What is it, Asahel?"

"I want you to join a clinical trial. My friend, Jake Skully, is conducting it. His son was blind, too. He's already regained some of his sight. It's nothing short of a miracle, Mother."

Greta turned back, away from the window.

"It's G32," she said, her voice dull. "Isn't it?"

"Yes. G32. It's all they hoped it would be."

"No, dear," Greta said. "But thank you for asking me."

Asahel went to her mother. She knelt at her feet and placed her hands on Greta's frail knees.

"Mother, there are no guarantees, but Michael's recovery means you should have the same results. You'll be able to see again."

Greta Esser shook her head slowly.

"This is my world now, Asahel. I choose to live in it." She paused and then added, without a hint of self-pity, "This is my punishment."

She reached up and placed a cool hand on either side of Asahel's face, then leaned forward and kissed her forehead.

"You have no idea how good it is to see you."

JAKE SQUINTED AGAINST the fall sun, eyes glued to the soccer field.

Antony's game had ended half an hour earlier. When Jake started for the car, Michael's "What's the hurry?" had stopped him cold. He was scheduled to pick Asahel up before long, but he did not mention that fact.

They'd waited until all Antony's teammates and their families loaded into their SUVs and BMWs, and left the city park. And then Michael had turned to Antony and said, "Wanna kick the ball around a little?"

Jake's heart had leapt into his throat.

"Sure," Antony replied.

Michael missed the first, second and third kicks by a long shot, but his attempts meant he'd seen the ball coming. When he finally landed a solid foot on it, Michael turned, a huge grin taking over his usually somber face, to where Jake sat on the sidelines.

But when he saw Jake's expression, the grin disappeared and he ran to him.

"Don't cry, Dad."

Jake pulled Michael to him, crushed him, really, and said nothing.

"I'm sorry, Dad."

Jake pulled away, to look his son in the eye—eyes that still had some of the dullness that had once blinded them but that now also had a hint of the joy they used to hold.

"Don't ever be sorry, Michael. For anything. Do you hear? I'm the one who should apologize."

Without warning, Michael's chin dropped to his chest. He reached into a back pocket of his jeans, then raised his eyes back to Jake's. They were filled with tears.

He extended his hand. It was shaking.

"Here," he said in a small voice, the voice he'd had as a little boy. "I've been wanting to give this to you, but I was scared. Scared you'd never forgive me. Scared you'd stop loving me."

It was a folded piece of paper.

Jake took it and slowly unfolded it. He recognized the writing right away. Ana's.

He looked back up at Michael.

"I don't understand."

Michael took a deep breath.

"I found it the first night she disappeared," he said. "Under your pillow. I took it. I didn't want you to see it."

The empty envelope with Jake's name written on it. Ana had indeed written Jake a letter.

"Michael, why?"

"Because Mama told me what it said. She was in her room, crying, that day she was leaving for Tucson with her friends. I heard her and went in. She was writing this. I'm sorry, Dad. I hated you for hurting her. I wanted to punish you. I didn't *want* her to forgive you."

Michael suddenly crumpled, crying, in Jake's arms.

"I wanted it to be your fault that she died," he sobbed. " 'Cause I was afraid it was really my fault. I thought Mama couldn't stand taking care of me anymore and that that's why she went away that day. I thought maybe she knew she was never coming back, and I was so mad at you for hurting her and making her cry that I wanted it to be your fault. Not mine. I wanted it to be your fault that she died."

"Shhh, it's okay," Jake murmured, stroking Michael's back. "We know now that it was Hughes who caused your mother's death. It didn't have anything to do with you. Or me."

Michael raised his tearstained face to Jake's.

"Will you forgive me, Dad? Please?"

Jake took Michael's chin in his hand and locked eyes with him.

"There's nothing to forgive you for, Michael. I just hope you know how much I loved your mother. I made a terrible mistake, but I never stopped loving her. Never. And I could never, ever stop loving you. Do you understand?"

Tears dripped from Michael's chin as he nodded.

"Now go play with your brother," Jake said, gently pushing him away.

Michael turned and took two steps toward the soccer field, where Antony waited. Then, he turned back to Jake.

"Thank you, Dad. I love you."

"I love you, too, Michael."

As Michael ran back to Antony, Jake raised the letter that Ana had written him that day—the one missing from the envelope that the police found in his bathroom—and, his own hands shaking now, he began to read.

> *My dearest husband,*
>
> *It is good that I am going away for a few days. I am brokenhearted and angry. I feel betrayed by the one person I have always counted on to protect me. But I've had time now to see that I was not without fault for what happened.*
>
> *When Michael lost his sight, I felt my life had lost all joy. I pushed you away. I see that now. You were hurting inside as much as I was, but in your usual way, you did not tell me.*

*You did not ask me for support. Instead, you just tried to do
everything in your power to help both Michael and me. I
didn't see that at the time. I was too angry and frightened. All
I could think about was Michael's pain, and my pain. I see
now that you needed help, too. You needed someone to hold
you, someone to tell you everything would be okay. And I
wasn't there for you. It wasn't me who comforted you.*

   *What you did was wrong, but I guess I'm just saying that
I am beginning to understand.*

   *I see the fear, the guilt, in your eyes every time you look at
me. I have loved you too long and too much to let that go on.
In my head, I forgive you, my husband, for what you have
done. And when I come home, after spending some time away
from you, I hope to forgive you in my heart also.*

   *I love you, Jake. We'll get through this, together, as we
have everything else.*

Forever yours,
Ana

Jake folded the letter and placed it in his shirt pocket.

Ana had forgiven him before she died.

A shout from the field drew his gaze up.

Tears now dried, Michael had kicked the ball past his little brother, into the goal's net. He and Antony jumped up in the air, both arms raised to the sky.

Michael turned to look for his father's reaction.

Jake threw both arms into the air.

WHEN SHE STEPPED outside the building's lobby and saw the Explorer round the corner, Asahel began to run toward it.

Jake pulled up to the curb, leaned across the front seat and opened the door for her.

She slid in.

"How'd it go?" he asked.

"Fine," Asahel nodded. "Fine."

She turned to look in the backseat.

"Where are the boys?"

"They wanted me to drop them off at your apartment. They tell me your computer has better games than ours. I hope that's okay."

"Of course it is," Asahel replied. "I'm glad they're comfortable there."

She turned to study Jake.

"Everything okay?"

"Yes," he said. He reached out and placed a hand on the side of her face. It looked to Asahel as if he'd been crying. But his smile seemed genuine.

She reached up and took his hand in hers.

"I've made a decision," she said. "I'm going to accept my old job at IPAF."

Jake studied her face, searching for clues, for signs of what she was feeling. He did that often.

"Was it something your mother said?"

"In a way, yes."

He lifted her hand to his lips and kissed it.

"Good for you."

Asahel smiled.

Something was different about Jake. Something had changed.

Maybe he would explain. When he felt ready.

"Let's go see the boys," she said.